HEARTLESS
A CROSSBREED NOVEL

USA TODAY BESTSELLING AUTHOR
DANNIKA DARK

All Rights Reserved
Copyright © 2020 Dannika Dark
First Edition: 2020

First Print Edition
ISBN-13: 979-864-8390-13-3

Formatting: Streetlight Graphics

No part of this book may be reproduced, distributed, or transmitted in any form or by any means, or stored in a database retrieval system, without the prior written permission of the author. You must not circulate this book in any format. Thank you for respecting the rights of the author.

This is a work of fiction. Any resemblance of characters to actual persons, living or dead, is purely coincidental.

Edited by Victory Editing and Red Adept.
Cover design by Dannika Dark. All stock purchased.

www.dannikadark.net
Fan page located on Facebook

Also By Dannika Dark:

THE MAGERI SERIES
Sterling
Twist
Impulse
Gravity
Shine
The Gift (Novella)

MAGERI WORLD
Risk

NOVELLAS
Closer

THE SEVEN SERIES
Seven Years
Six Months
Five Weeks
Four Days
Three Hours
Two Minutes
One Second
Winter Moon (Novella)

SEVEN WORLD
Charming

THE CROSSBREED SERIES
Keystone
Ravenheart
Deathtrap
Gaslight
Blackout
Nevermore
Moonstruck
Spellbound
Heartless

We often give our enemies the means of our own destruction.

— *Aesop*

Chapter 1

Ruby's Diner was one of those old-fashioned joints that stood frozen in time, and tonight it was lit up like a pinball machine. I parked my blue pickup truck on the side of the building near the row of windows. Beyond the booth seating were small tables and a long counter, but I didn't see any sign of my father. He might have been sitting at the front of the diner, thinking I'd come in through that door, but I always took the side entrance. Aside from the food and hospitality, I liked Ruby's because it was open twenty-four hours a day and mostly served humans. I glanced up at the sign on the window advertising today's special: homemade chili.

I hopped out and took in a deep lungful of the warm evening breeze, which smelled like charred hamburgers. *God, is it June already?* I'd been with Keystone for a year now.

Halfway to the door, I spun on my heel and glared at my truck. "Are you coming?" I asked quietly.

Christian's dark shadow remained on the passenger side for a beat before his door swung open and he got out with a long-suffering sigh. He looked *smoking* hot, and if I were a girl who easily swooned, I might have blushed when our eyes met. I'd selected his outfit, and he despised me for it. Not because Christian had anything against tank tops, but he didn't wear them in public. Tonight was special. I wanted him to show off the raven tattoo on his right pec. The fabric covered most of it, but not the wing that stretched across his shoulder and arm as it reached for his back.

The tips of the black feathers were dipped in blood, the right eye just as pale blue as mine.

"I don't see why you dragged me along," he grumbled. "You know I don't eat."

"Who says you have to eat?"

"Your da will have a go at me if I don't."

I hooked my arm in his and coaxed him to the side door. "Crush doesn't bite. Besides, he doesn't think you really care about me."

"Is that so? And what have you been telling him?"

"I don't have to tell him anything." I reached for the handle. "Your absence speaks volumes. You've always got an excuse whenever I go to see him. Look, just be yourself. Wait. Scratch that. Just be respectful."

Christian snorted. "And is your da going to share the same courtesy?"

I bit my lip and opened the door. "Grab a seat. I'll be right back."

Christian sat down in my regular booth while I headed to the front of the diner. Elton John was singing "I'm Still Standing" at a low volume, and one of the waitresses was shaking her hips behind the counter as she refilled the coffee machine. The real noise was up front where they were handling take-out orders. I spotted Crush in a red vinyl booth near the door. His eyes were fixed on the window, and when he caught my reflection in the glass, he turned to me with one of his closed-lipped smiles.

Crush scooted out of his seat. "Hey, Cookie." His strong arms and the scent of cheap cologne wrapped around me.

"Hey, Daddy. I'm glad you pried your ass off the recliner to eat in public."

He drew back and narrowed his blue eyes. "Don't give me that sass."

I reached up and pulled the rubber band out of his grey goatee. He winced. "What did you do that for?"

After brushing out his goatee with my fingers, I flicked the rubber band into the trash. "Because you look like a wrestler with that thing on."

Crush straightened his skull T-shirt. "Since when do you care what I look like?"

I glanced at the myriad of tattoos on his arms and the silver tooth that flashed at me when he grinned. I honestly didn't give a damn what he looked like. He was perfect. But I knew if Christian and Crush got into verbal warfare, which was inevitable, that rubber band would be one less thing for Christian to poke fun at.

"I hope you brought your appetite," I said, eager to give him the tour. "This is my absolute favorite place. I figured you'd like the retro look. *And* they've got amazing Angus burgers."

"Extra cheese?"

"How's your cholesterol these days?"

He clenched his jaw. "If you wanted me to eat rabbit food, you should have invited me to that salad bar down the street."

"I'm kidding. Come on. Let's sit."

As we rounded the corner, I heard Crush mutter a curse under his breath. I had conveniently forgotten to tell him that Christian would be joining us. He slid me an *I should have known you were up to something* look but kept his mouth zipped. I braced myself as he put on his war face.

Crush knew Christian and I were serious, but I had always accepted that no man would have an easy task in courting me. A Vampire just made it a hundred times worse.

Three glasses of water and a stack of menus were on the table.

"Mr. Graves." Christian greeted my father with a dark twinkle in his black eyes. "I was just telling Raven how much I missed her da."

"Cut the shit." Crush slid into the opposite bench by the window.

Suddenly the two men were looking at me—waiting with bated breath to see which one I'd sit beside. I bit my lip. On one hand, sitting by my father would give him reassurance, but I needed him to acknowledge that there was another man in my life.

Just as I sat next to Christian, I glimpsed a pear-shaped waitress with bright orange hair approaching.

Christian lifted his glass in a victory toast and held it to his lips.

Betty sidled up to the table and gave me a soft squeeze on the shoulder. "Good to see you, honey." She turned her gaze to my father. "And who is this handsome wildcat you brought with you?"

Christian choked on his water and quickly grabbed a napkin to clean the mess.

Crush hadn't heard anything Betty said because he was too busy staring at Christian's tattoo.

"This is Crush, my dad. Crush, this is Betty." I kicked him under the table and dipped my chin to give him a scolding glance. Manners had never been his strong suit.

He dragged his gaze up to the seasoned woman in a waitress uniform. "Nice to meet you."

"Do you need a minute to look over the menu?"

"That's okay," I said. "I'll have my usual, and my father will have a number two."

Christian chortled.

I collected the menus and handed them to her. "Do you have any orange soda?"

"Is Crush okay?"

I cracked a smile. "Perfect."

Betty tucked her notepad in her apron. "You betcha. And for you, sir?"

Christian never ordered food when we came here, and Betty probably knew that. Still, she remained cordial even though she didn't much care for Christian.

Christian glared at Crush, his fingers lightly drumming the table. With a look of defeat, he made an unexpected move. "I'll just be having a bowl of soup."

"Chili it is." She spun on her heel before Christian could retort.

I tried to contain my laughter and looked in the opposite direction. Christian would never forgive me for making him eat a bowl of chili. Ruby's made theirs with beans, beef, and a whole lot of hellfire.

Crush didn't pussyfoot around. He leaned forward. "Is that ink real?"

"Aye."

I watched with interest as Crush licked his thumb and reached across the table. When he rubbed at the ink, Christian reeled back his arm.

"For feck's sake. Are you afflicted in some way?"

"Let me see it. All of it."

Christian lifted up his tank top so Crush could see the details.

"That's quality ink." Crush groomed his grey goatee. "You do that for fun? I hear it wears off an immortal in a week."

Christian rolled down his tank top. "It's sealed with liquid fire."

Crush rubbed his mouth with his large hands, skull rings on his fingers and motor oil staining his cuticles. I wasn't sure what he was thinking exactly, but I knew that Christian's permanent tattoo would convey the message more than words. A raven was one thing, but a raven with a blue eye was undeniably specific.

Crush shot me a look before sliding across the bench to sit in front of me instead. "You got any ink?"

"Nope."

He eased back with a sly grin. "That's my girl."

"She doesn't need any," Christian replied coolly. "She has a million-dollar necklace around her neck."

"I didn't ask you, peckerhead."

"You don't think my face would look good on her arse?"

I slammed my hand on the table. "Will you two shut the hell up so we can have a nice dinner?"

Christian's lips twitched.

And so did my father's.

I gripped Crush's hand. "Go easy, you old bulldog. I know Christian isn't what you had in mind for me, but he's saved my ass more than once. He loves me as much as you do."

Crush shook his head adamantly. "I'll never leave you. Can he say that? He obviously left Ireland. Or did they kick him out?"

Not even attempting to hide his apathetic look, Christian folded his arms on the table.

Betty hustled back with our drinks. "A milkshake for the lady and an orange Crush for the handsome father." She gave him a wink before making herself scarce.

Crush peered over his shoulder at her. "Older women have always had a thing for me."

"She's not that much older," Christian quipped.

Crush gave him an indignant look as he pulled the straw out of his glass. "I'm fifty-eight."

My father had lived a hard life, and he looked all of his fifty-eight years and then some. I had forgotten his exact age until that moment. I thought about how many of those years he'd wasted alone. But he was so hard-core devoted to my deceased mother that he'd never settle for anyone else.

Before they really got into it, I decided to bring up something else that had been on my mind. "This wasn't just an ambush. I also wanted to invite you here to thank you for everything you did."

Crush furrowed his brow. "I don't follow."

"The whole mess with guarding the mansion and Hunter."

Crush laced his fingers together. "That's what good fathers do."

"Switch shouldn't have called you. And you definitely shouldn't have been on the front lines storming into that Mage's apartment. You could have gotten yourself killed."

He grinned like a foolhardy boy. "Took me back to my days in the service. Made me feel young again."

I sipped my vanilla shake and grimaced when my throat froze. "You're supposed to be retired from all that."

"A good Marine never retires. You'll figure that out one day, little girl." After another drink, he leaned in tight. "You wouldn't happen to know anything about a wolf hanging out on my property, now would you?"

I thought back to the deal I'd made with his friend, Wizard. It hadn't felt right leaving Crush completely alone, so Wizard volunteered to place a wolf on his property to keep an eye on him. After the loan shark fiasco ended, I'd just assumed Wizard had pulled back his men. Apparently not.

I drank more of my shake.

"I don't need a damn watchdog."

I shoved my glass toward Christian. "What if something happens and you can't get to a phone? You live by yourself and don't have neighbors within earshot. I can't call you every day, especially if I'm on a mission. What if you slip in the tub?"

"I'm not dying in the damn bathtub."

Christian extracted the straw from my glass. "Imagine the mortifying shame of it. Ass up, lying in a puddle of your own filth. The fire department would have to use the Jaws of Life to get you out of there."

Just as he put the end of the straw into his mouth to lick off the thick milkshake, I kicked him under the table.

Crush played with an ice cube in his glass. "You know what we did to peckerheads like you in the Marines?"

"Fecking hell. I'm starting to regret all those premium steaks I bought you that time when I set you up in that fancy trailer to keep your arse safe."

Crush's shoulders sagged and he sat back. "I'm not denying you've done a lot for me and mine, but you have a mouth on you. What happened to respecting your elders?"

"Now you're starting to talk some sense." Christian put his arm around me. "Did I ever tell you that I was born in the nineteenth century?"

I chuckled. "He's got you there."

"Dammit, Cookie. You're supposed to be on *my* side."

"I'm on *both* your sides," I assured him. "Maybe I should buy a shelf from Ikea and have you two assemble it."

"For what reason?" Christian asked.

"You boys need a special project to work on together. Maybe that'll help you figure out a way to communicate."

Crush cackled. "Maybe *you're* our project."

Betty returned with our plates balanced on her arms like some kind of magic act. She set down the big one first, and Crush's eyes rounded at the double-patty Angus burger with cheese oozing from the sides. When he reached for the saltshaker, I snatched it away.

Then she set down a white plate in front of Christian. A bowl of steaming chili was in the center, surrounded by saltine crackers.

"Do you think you'll have room for pie?" Betty sounded more chipper than usual, but she also seemed enamored by my father.

My mouth watered when I looked down at my burger and onion rings. "Not today. Thanks, Betty. You're a lifesaver."

"That's what they'll put on my tombstone," she said while striding away. "Here lies Betty McGuire. She rescued burgers from the kitchen fire."

We all chuckled.

"I like her," Crush remarked.

Christian lifted a cracker from his plate and studied it. "Shall I retrieve her number for you?"

Crush pounded the bottom of the ketchup bottle until his fries were drowning in sauce. "I think she's more your speed. You seem to like younger women."

"So… how's the shop going?" I jumped in, trying to salvage this dinner.

Crush had just taken a sloppy bite of his burger, and ketchup dribbled down his goatee. "Fine," he said with a mouthful of food.

"Thinking about retirement yet?"

With my help, he had recouped his losses after draining his account on bounty hunters and loan sharks.

Crush grabbed a paper napkin and wiped his mouth. "A man needs a purpose in life. I like fixing bikes and cars. You want me to sit around watching court TV all day?"

"No, but what about traveling?"

"Been there. Done that."

"Oh?" I chomped into an onion ring. "When is the last time you've been to a country where you didn't have a gun strapped to your side and were shooting people?"

He wiped his goatee. "That's a regular Saturday night in my book."

I watched Christian stir his chili. "You should try something new."

Crush ate some of his fries and wiped his greasy fingers across his T-shirt. "You talkin' to me or the Vamp?"

Christian sharpened his gaze. "I'll thank you kindly to refrain from the derogatory remarks, *human*. Why don't you stuff your gob with more artery-clogging meat?"

"Now you're starting to sound like Raven. Why can't a man just enjoy a good meal without someone harping on him?"

Christian lifted his spoon and studied it. "I ask myself the same question every day. Why can't a Vampire just have an empty plate? But Raven enjoys her petty little torments."

Crush gave a hint of a smile before eating a few fries. "I thought she was a handful when she was fifteen, but that was nothing compared to now."

Suddenly, Crush and Christian had found common ground. Me.

"I liked you two better when you were enemies," I grumbled.

Crush pinched another cluster of fries. "One time when Raven was seventeen, she tried to give me a makeover for Father's Day. She went to the thrift store and bought a white button-up, slacks, and a pair of shiny-ass shoes that were two sizes too small—just like the shirt."

"*Jaysus.*"

"Couldn't just stay home. No. She wanted to go out to a fancy restaurant."

Christian tasted the chili and didn't look repulsed. "Is that so?"

"She knew I'd never spend that kind of money on food, so she told me she'd saved up and wanted to take me out. What could I say to that?" Crush lifted his glass and pinned me with an icy stare. "Found out later that she sold some of my tools to pay for dinner."

"Oh, come on," I argued. "Why does anyone need five power drills? Besides, it was worth it to see you all dressed up."

"Don't you mean undressed? I lost three buttons by the time dessert came." He wiped his mouth again. "Women look at us like a pet project. Always trying to fix us and not taking care of themselves."

"No matter what you do, it's never enough," Christian added. "You spend years trying to be the man they want until you've forgotten who the feck you are. Then they treat you like rubbish and cast you aside."

Suddenly I realized that Christian wasn't talking about me.

Crush folded his arms on the edge of the table and locked eyes with Christian. "How did a romantic like you wind up putting a tattoo like that on your arm?"

There was sarcasm in his tone. Christian wasn't one to wax poetic, and his negative remarks on relationships and women clearly alarmed my father.

"I'm not trying to change anyone," I pointed out. "That's why what we have works. Christian doesn't make any demands, and neither do I. All I want is honesty."

Crush shook his head.

I met eyes with Christian. "Look, I'm sorry I made you wear that tonight. I'm not trying to change you. I just wanted my father to see that beautiful tattoo without a strip show." I turned my attention back to my father. "And I'm not trying to control your life either. If I take away the salt, it's because I want more years with you. If I'm asking about retirement, it's because you've worked your ass off your whole life and if anyone deserves a vacation, it's you. Maybe it's not what you want, but it's just my way of looking out for you. I've got a suitcase full of my own issues, so I'm hardly in a position to tell anyone what they should do with their life."

When I leaned back, Christian reached under the table and held my hand.

"I'll be regretting the chili later," he said. "But you were right. It's not half bad."

Crush pushed the salt away. "I don't need that stuff anyhow. They already salt it before it gets to the table."

When Christian squeezed my hand again, I cautiously looked into his insightful eyes. He studied me for a beat, and by his perplexed gaze, he couldn't read me. Perhaps my furrowed brow and slowing heart rate signaled something was amiss, or maybe it was when I averted my eyes.

Had I pressured him into this too quickly? Even my own father hadn't been ready for the love of his life despite his tattoo and even my mom's pregnancy. They'd had an amicable relationship, but it wasn't what it should have been. Crush had demons he wasn't able to shake.

What worried me most was that Christian and I had a few of our own.

Chapter 2

AFTER PARKING MY PICKUP TRUCK in our underground garage, Christian and I strolled up the driveway. "That went well," I said, reflecting on our evening with Crush.

"You mean the part where he pointed a steak knife at me when I suggested that Ducatis are superior to Harleys?"

"He didn't stab you with it, did he? Like I said, it went well."

"Your da is a real piece of work."

"It's not personal. I don't think he'd give anyone a fair shot of winning him over. He's not just doing it because he's hardheaded." I stopped to face Christian, and a lightning bug flashed between us. "He's got doubts because of his own past. The only woman he's ever been completely devoted to is me. He gave up alcohol so he wouldn't lose me. He couldn't even do that for my mother."

Christian swept a lock of my hair aside and gingerly held my necklace between his fingers. "He's afraid if I take you, he'll have to let go."

"It's not one or the other."

"Aye. But that's not how a father sees it."

"And how would you know what a father sees, Mr. Poe?"

"Because long ago I was human, and I imagined a family life." He released the ruby from his grasp. "The foolish dreams of a young lad."

It was hard to imagine Christian as anything but a Vampire. He offered me glimpses of his past—a dashing young man with blue eyes and a pocketful of dreams. But connecting that image with the man in front of me proved impossible. It was as if they were different people. Christian had chosen a life where children weren't an option, and now neither of us was fit to raise a child even if we wanted to.

When we reached the front door, Christian fell back a step.

I glanced over my shoulder, wondering if he'd left something in the truck. "Are you coming?"

Christian moved swiftly past me and opened the door. "My lady," he said, holding it open like a gentleman.

"Why are you acting strange?" I kept my eyes locked on his as I moved inside the house.

Christian closed the door and held his reply. He could be moody sometimes, so I shrugged it off.

Damn, he looked good. The tank top wasn't a typical sleeveless but had narrow straps and a U-shaped neckline that showed off his pecs and defined muscles. I wanted to lick his clavicles. I flashed him a wicked smile.

"What's on your mind, lass?"

"I just might have room for dessert after all."

He headed toward the dining room, and I didn't mind following. Christian had a commanding walk—squared shoulders, straight back, and an aura about him as if he were about to destroy a city.

"Where are you going?"

Christian didn't look back. "We have guests."

It wasn't unusual for Viktor to invite guests over for a drink, but we didn't crash those parties. Not unless he summoned us. I pulled my phone out of my back pocket to check my messages, but I didn't see anything from Viktor.

I strutted into the dining room, my black boot heels knocking against the stone floor. The gathering room beyond the open archways was dark and empty. Viktor normally invited people for a drink by the fire, but to my surprise, he and his guest were sitting at the dining table to our left. A ring of candles on the iron chandelier cast a warm glow in the room, as did the lanterns on the walls. But those weren't the only old flames in the room. Lenore Parrish set down her wineglass to greet us with a smile.

It was easy to see why Christian had once obsessed over the woman. Her feminine features, blond hair, and lithe body were beguiling. She stood three inches taller than me and never slouched.

Lenore rose from Wyatt's usual seat and approached me. Her long white dress floated behind her, and the empire waist brought attention to her small breasts, which looked like two dinner rolls that someone had pushed together.

To my surprise, she greeted me first with a kiss to the cheek. "Darling, so good to see you."

Her radiant, flawless skin was almost unnatural. A few wisps of blond hair had fallen loose from her clip, but nothing ever seemed unkempt about her. She centered her black eyes on mine and gently held my chin, turning my head from side to side. "I see a summer glow on your skin, but it's fading. I remember a time when only the lower class had brown skin. That was how you could tell them apart from the aristocrats. Well, that and their fingernails. So many people tried to infiltrate good society by stealing a few nice clothes, but a fraud is easily seen when you know what to look for." She gave me a quick once-over before turning her attention to my partner.

"Miss Parrish," he bit out.

"No need to be so formal." When she leaned in to kiss his cheek, he tensed up. She flicked a glance to his tattoo and gave him an impassive look. "You've changed since I last saw you."

"Aye, I have."

"You two make a darling couple. Can I say that?" She looked back at Viktor. "Or is this another secret?"

"Join us," Viktor said, waving us over.

Christian and I took our usual spots while Lenore returned to her seat across from me.

She pinched the sleeve of Viktor's grey cardigan. He often wore something similar at night when the house got cool.

Viktor scooted his chair back and collected two wineglasses from the table behind him. "Miss Parrish was just entertaining me with stories about ancient Greece."

She lifted her crystal glass and smiled. "Your leader is a charming host. He indulges me with his patience. My stories can be quite dull."

Viktor filled our glasses and sat down. "On the contrary, you have a most captivating background."

She swirled her drink. "All ancients have stories. The retelling diminishes my enthusiasm, but I am delighted that you are entertained." Lenore initiated a toast by raising her glass. "To interesting stories."

Everyone's glasses touched and made melodic chimes that filled the open room. I gulped my wine and then wiped my upper lip with the back of my hand.

"And what brings you all the way out here?" Christian asked, his tone flat but courteous.

"I was in the neighborhood, visiting an old acquaintance. Despite my first formal event, I find it difficult to form any new relationships. So much has changed. Mr. Kazan has been a gracious friend."

"Spasibo. You are welcome here anytime, Miss Parrish."

She touched his arm and gave it a light squeeze. "So generous of you to open your home to me."

Blue coasted in with an empty glass in her hand. She froze when she noticed Lenore. "Sorry I barged in. I didn't know you had a guest."

"Nonsense," Viktor said. "Join us. There is plenty of wine."

"I love those earrings." Lenore tapped her chin. "So very… What is the word they use these days? Earthy."

Blue reached up with her free hand and touched her earring hesitantly. The feathers belonged to her falcon, souvenirs left behind after a shift. "Thanks."

Lenore drank her wine, and it got uncomfortably quiet.

"I'll just put this in the dishwasher." Blue hurried into the kitchen, and not three seconds later she made a fast exit.

Lenore squeezed Viktor's wrist, which she'd been holding. "Such a beautiful creature, that one. I used to have blue eyes."

Lenore touched her chin and looked up. "Or were they green? Sometimes I can't remember. It's not as if I have a picture to go by."

Christian continued turning his glass by the stem.

"You have an interesting dynamic in this house." Lenore folded her arms on the table and held my gaze. "I met Switch. Wasn't he your companion at my party? I had no idea that he lived with you. Such a handsome man."

"Perhaps you should ask him out," Christian suggested.

Viktor cleared his throat. "I think you should treat Miss Parrish with more respect."

"My apologies."

Lenore tilted her head and gave Christian a loaded glance. "Perhaps Christian's right about widening my dating pool—I've spent far too much time in the shallow end. It's no wonder I haven't found a worthy companion."

I jumped when Christian scooted back and the chair's feet scraped against the floor.

"If you'll excuse me, I have work to do." Christian gave everyone a polite nod before making himself scarce.

Viktor frowned at the empty doorway. "I apologize. I forget you are old acquaintances. Perhaps I should have left you two alone to catch up."

"Nonsense." Lenore gave Viktor a gentle smile. "I think I've outstayed my welcome. Your team must have important work that I'm keeping them from, and I did come by unannounced."

"You are welcome here anytime. Do not worry about such formalities. It is an honor to have such a prestigious figure as yourself as our guest."

She glanced at the delicate gold watch on her wrist. "Where does the time go? My driver should be back soon. Mr. Kazan, it was generous of you to offer me your vintage wine. I hope we can do this again so you can tell me all about your early memories of Russia." Lenore stood and offered him her hand.

Viktor kissed her dainty little knuckles. "The pleasure was all mine."

I chuckled under my breath. Watching immortals was like

watching a period piece. Viktor was a gentleman at heart, but he treated us differently than he did those outside the house.

Lenore reached for her white clutch. "Would you mind if Raven escorts me out?"

There was no getting out of this one. Maybe I could escort her right out the door and into a shallow grave.

"Raven will see you to your car. I will be sure to look for that wine you recommended."

She touched his shoulder as he rose from his chair. "If you have any trouble with the merchant, give me a call."

We both rounded the table and quietly headed through the doorway. Lenore pulled a small pocket fan out of her clutch and snapped it open.

"You should open the windows in here. A house can get stuffy and acquire a certain odor."

I opened the front door to let her out. "So can a person."

She breezed outside, her sparkly heels making her a tad overdressed for a casual visit. "Don't you adore Viktor? He's not only a shrewd businessman, but he knows how to make a person feel important and valuable. That's why so many people in this city respect him."

I shut the door behind me. "Who do you know on this side of town?"

"An old friend." She clutched my arm. "Let's walk. It's a beautiful night, isn't it? So quiet. I should buy a house in the country. I hadn't realized how much quieter it is than where I live now."

I tried to pull away, but Lenore held on as if she might trip in her shoes. "You obviously haven't been out here when the cicadas start up."

"What a dreary existence they live. Can you just imagine living in a dark hole for seventeen years, only coming out once to mate and die?"

"Isn't that what you do?"

She chuckled and pulled me close. "I like you, Raven Black. Believe it or not."

I wrenched my arm free. "Sorry to say the feeling isn't mutual."

"After all the help I've given? Dear, oh dear. Just to put your mind at ease, the money I made from the auction went to good use."

"Filling your wardrobe?"

Halfway to the gate, she came to a stop. "Filling the pockets of abused women."

I studied her face, waiting for the punch line.

"Did you really think I'd keep it? Viktor enjoys donating to children, but so often adults are neglected. There are organizations that help abused women and men escape frightening situations like those wretched slave auctions or fighting rings. Some have no pack or family and wind up destitute. Where will the downtrodden turn if they're rejected by society? We have a duty to look after them." She fanned her face and stared off in the distance. "We women have to stick together."

"Do you ask for favors in return?"

"You really don't trust me, do you?" Lenore sighed and folded up her fan. "A few sanctuaries exist around the country that secretly harbor these women and keep them safe. But like everything else, they rely on donations. Humans have taxes to keep such places operational, but we do not. And if you think the wealthy are eager to part with their money, you are mistaken. Most people blame victims. They think they chose their circumstance, so they're less likely to be generous. Everyone needs a purpose, and mine is to empower women. What's yours?"

I suddenly felt as small as the beetle traveling by my shoe. "We pool our money with Viktor's."

"Ah. I suppose that's convenient. But if you want some advice, you should find a passion and use your influence or money to aid in that cause. There is no greater duty you have in this world as an immortal." Lenore stepped closer and tucked a lock of hair behind my ear as she looked deep into my eyes. "What are you passionate about, Raven? What's your cause to fight for in life?"

I felt a fire stirring within me. "Killing evil men."

"What kind of evil men?"

"Men who prey on the weak."

Lenore broke eye contact and admired my necklace. "Working for Keystone isn't about money, is it? Not for you."

"Viktor pays us well."

"But the money isn't what's holding you here. It's not what drew you in."

"I don't think any of us are here for the money."

"Don't count on that." With her clutch in both hands, she resumed strolling toward the gate. "People join an outfit like yours for two reasons: money or protection. Once they've secured their protection, they start thinking about their future. And you can't think about a future without money. An immortal's never-ending quest is to build a fortune. If you haven't learned this by now, you will soon enough. There is nothing more tragic than a destitute Vampire. Or Mage, in your case. You and I are going to live for a very long time, and there's no sense in making your eternity a miserable one. Plus… one can use that money to help others. Like I did with you. I saw a fighter in you, and you're someone I'd like to mentor."

"You called me weak."

"When did I say that?"

I tucked my hands in my pockets. "At the auction."

Her eyes searched the stars. "Oh yes. I forget how personal the young ones take everything. You interpreted that conversation as an insult, but you missed the warning."

"That your talons are still wrapped around him? Think again."

"No, foolish girl. My warning about Christian. Once an addict, always an addict. How many times have you fed him your blood since we last spoke?"

I kept a straight face but felt my cheeks heat.

"Don't let an inferior man lead you." She glanced back at the mansion. "Your friend Switch has quite the tattoo. What is it with men and tattoos? The novelty I get. The permanence of using liquid fire I don't."

I thought about my father and how each of his many tattoos

meant something personal to him. "Because forever is the best way to honor what matters."

"Death is the only permanent thing in this world." Lenore's disposition became calmer and quieter. "Whatever he told you, just remember there are always two sides to every story. Christian was devoted to a fault, and it terrified me. A rejected man can't be trusted. But… people can change. After all, I'm not the same woman I once was. Life shapes us, and we shed our skin like snakes when that change comes."

"You just said a minute ago that once an addict, always an addict."

"Addictions never go away. We only learn to suppress them."

Headlights beamed on us as a car buzzed through the gate.

She stopped to look at me. "Maybe you *are* doing this job for the noblest cause. Charity donations go toward fixing the broken. But killing—now that's a solution. You understand the value of stopping the problem before it escalates out of control. That takes gumption. I admire you, Raven. You're not obsequious, and so many in your line of work are. You have far more power than you realize for a woman your age."

From there, Lenore and I parted ways. She got inside her car, and I strolled back to the house. What a strange conversation. It almost felt cordial, and yet I hated the woman for what she'd done to Christian.

Once inside, I returned to the dining room, but Viktor was gone. The smell from the snuffed-out candles on the chandelier was strong, some of the sinuous trails of smoke still rising to the ceiling.

"Viktor gave Kira the rest of the night off," Blue said while clearing the table. "Figured I'd clean up before we attract rats."

"Do you need help?"

After setting the empty glasses on the cheese tray, she looked around. "No. I just need to scrape wax off the table and wash the dishes. How's your dad?"

"One step closer to a quadruple bypass, but we had a good time."

She slowed her pace when she reached me. "He's human. When you only have limited time, you want to do the things that make you happy."

"Even if it means cutting your life short?"

She snorted. "We're hardly ones to talk, Raven."

"Good point. Christian might not make it through the night after that bowl of chili."

Her eyebrows drew down in a slant. "I thought he didn't like to eat."

"I think he was trying to impress me."

"Serves him right."

We branched apart, and I headed out. Sometimes I liked to take a stroll and admire the grandeur of it all. Keystone didn't have opulent chandeliers or garish décor. It was designed like a river— the hallways flowing into each other, the steps cascading down the winding staircases in an architectural waterfall. Archways framed the hallways and entrances to rooms, and most of the doors were hand carved. Well, except for the soundproof ones made of steel. We used three main stairways, each located in a different section of the mansion. I went up the central one, and when I reached the third floor, I headed toward the interior balcony. We used to keep the doors unlocked, but after Gem's recent abduction, Viktor was still keeping them locked at night.

"What are you doing out here? I thought you had work to do."

Christian didn't move from the stone railing, which overlooked the front property. We had a clear view of the road that led to the circular driveway. But mainly the balcony provided a stunning view of the surrounding meadows and distant trees. Foggy mornings were especially breathtaking.

"What were you two talking about down there?"

I hopped onto the flat railing and leaned against the archway, my right leg higher than my left. "Girl talk."

He flashed me a look of reproach.

"If you heard everything, why should I repeat it?"

"Maybe I wasn't listening."

I bit back a laugh. "Oh really?"

When he looked at me, his eyes got all serious and a crease appeared between his eyebrows. "You told me more than once that you didn't care for my eavesdropping on your private conversations. I never made you that promise, but I'm trying, Raven. I'm trying real hard to be the man you deserve."

I found it hard to believe he'd resisted that kind of temptation. Especially when it came to Lenore the—

"Can you not tell me? I'm only making conversation."

I sighed and searched the darkness. "She talked about charity and finding a passion. I brought up her calling me weak and all the shitty things she said to me at that auction."

"*Jaysus*. You shouldn't make an enemy of that woman. Did you tell her you know about her past?"

"Do I look like an idiot? Besides, you haven't really told me anything she's done. Not specifically. Just all the things *you've* done."

"Better that way."

I reclined my head against the wall and closed my eyes. Christian eased between my legs and put his hands on my hips.

"I'll not have her get between us," he said, placing a hungry kiss on my neck.

"I don't think it's us you have to worry about anymore."

He leaned back and studied me for a beat.

I dipped my chin and threw him a skeptical look. "You didn't notice the way she was all over Viktor?"

"He's not her type."

"Viktor's charming. He's a silver fox with a big heart, connections, and lots of money. He's everyone's type."

"And Lenore is a Vampire."

"Yes, but that aside, she's stunning. Maybe a little small on top, but men prefer blondes."

"Not this man." Christian's mouth dragged below my jaw and was getting a rise out of me.

"Funny. I seem to recall you seducing a blonde around the time Viktor hired me."

"That didn't turn out well, did it?" His kisses moved up to my cheek and then the other, intentionally passing over my lips and making me yearn for that connection.

Christian seduced me like no other, drawing out my lust in a game we often played to see who would beg first.

I lifted up his tank top and pitched it over the ledge. Then I kissed his tattoo all the way down to his nipple. When I circled my tongue around the hardened peak, he sucked in a sharp breath.

Christian's fangs punched out, and a wild look stirred in his eyes. I knew exactly which vein he wanted to sink those teeth into, and it wasn't the one in my neck. Sexual energy buzzed at my fingertips, but it melted away when I touched his shoulders. Mage energy had no impact on a Vampire, so at least I never had to worry about shocking him to death.

I arched my back when he slid his hand up my shirt. With a quick pinch, he ripped my bra open and dragged his palm over my breast.

I moaned. Christian's touch was so easy and left me wanting. I raised my shirt and pressed myself against him. When our heat collided, our lips found each other. The feather-soft kiss grew desperate and deepened into something passionate and primal.

My fingernails scored his back as I nibbled on his bottom lip. "I want a hot bath."

"Aye. What else?"

"Lots of soap. Get myself all slick."

His head dipped down, and he took my nipple into his mouth.

I tunneled my fingers through his hair and felt myself close to actually climaxing right there on the ledge of the balcony with my pants still on. "Then I'm going to rub oil all over my body. My breasts, my hips, my ass—everywhere." I sucked in a sharp breath when his tongue flicked my nipple.

"And then what?"

I slid off the ledge and wrapped my arms around his neck. "Then I'm going to crawl onto the bed and lie on my back… with my knees bent."

Christian liked the sex talk, but I was unraveling in his arms. When his fangs pierced my neck, mine punched out.

"What else?" he growled.

"I'm going to touch myself, and you're going to tell me how to do it."

The button and zipper on my jeans broke away as Christian wedged his hand into my panties. "Like this? Do you want more, lass?"

"*Yes.*"

His touch was gentle, lightly stroking until I was wet and needy. "Where am I?"

"You're sitting in a chair at the foot of the bed."

His beard brushed against my skin as he kissed my throat, my clavicle, my shoulder, and down to my other breast. How did he know exactly how much pressure to apply and when to speed up or slow down?

"And when do I join you?" he inquired.

My cheeks burned and my arms quivered as he stroked me faster. When a finger slipped inside, I gasped.

Christian kept a firm hold. "Answer me," he said, his mouth between my breasts.

"You don't join. You just watch me."

His dark eyes rose to meet mine as if I'd said the magic words that awakened the beast in him. He straightened up, clutched me with one arm, and stroked me to the edge of release.

"I can't do this out here," I gasped.

"Aye, you can."

"No, stop."

Christian not only stopped, but he pulled his hand free and stepped back. When I felt the absence of pleasure, I decided it didn't matter who the hell heard us.

I yanked him close. "Don't stop."

"Then tell me what you want."

Our lips touched. "Put your hand inside my panties."

He released a shaky breath and obeyed my command. But his hand was still, and I knew where this game was going.

"Touch me."

And he did, but with a look of mischief on his face. "Like this?"

"No. *Harder.* Stroke me harder like before."

Christian obediently ran his fingers over my clitoris as if waiting for more instruction.

"I can't think, Christian. Just fucking *touch me*. Make me come. *Hurry*. I need it."

"Open your legs wider, Precious. Are you ready? It's taken me decades to learn this little trick." He gave me a sardonic smile as he skillfully touched, stroked, and revered me.

Christian did something with his fingers that I couldn't describe, nor did I have time to process exactly what had happened. My release came suddenly, and my entire body locked as every muscle tightened. Hungry eyes watched mine possessively, and I cried out. He made no attempt to silence me. Instead of drawing out my pleasure and letting me ride those final pulses, he abruptly pulled down my shirt and swept me off my feet.

"Where are we going?" I asked, out of breath.

"Quiet, lass." Once inside, he locked the door and carried me all the way to my room.

I felt like I'd just had a taste of the most heavenly cake, and I wanted the whole damn thing.

"Do you want me to just skip the bath?" I suggested. "Light a fire, and I'll get you a chair."

After setting me on my bed, he struck a match and lit a candle. "No need."

"Right to the sex, huh? Mr. Romantic."

He set the candle on the bedside table. "As much as I'd like you to show me your fanny, this is where we part ways."

I eased up on my elbows. "Huh?"

Christian circled his hand over his stomach. "I'm afraid your all-American chili has given me a case of indigestion."

I fell back. "I'll get you back for this."

"You already did."

"I hate you."

Christian swaggered through the door and then peered back, a twinkle in his eyes. "Not as much as I hate you."

Chapter 3

Gem gripped the long rope that hung from the gym ceiling and ran until her feet lifted off the ground like Tarzan swinging on a vine. Her purple hair had a silver sheen to it. Claude had uniquely layered the colors, and the gym lights were really drawing my attention to it. Sprawled on the floor mat, I stared at the ceiling, wishing that Christian had brought me a second thermos of coffee this morning. I'd stayed awake much of the night, hoping that maybe he had been teasing about the chili and would sneak in and rekindle some of that passion.

No such luck.

But at least he remembered my coffee.

Shepherd's muscles looked like boulders as he continued doing his reps on the pull-up bar. He'd done about sixty. Shep always worked out in either track pants or sweats, but he never wore a shirt. His scars and tattoos blended right in with his gruff demeanor and stony look. His buzz cut made his square jaw and stern brow stand out even more. He was the kind of man who made people cross over to the other side of the street. Rough around the edges didn't begin to describe Shepherd Moon.

We had an awesome gym. All the workout equipment was on the right side of the room, and the floor mat in the center. There were kettlebells, pull-up bars, jump ropes, and the climbing rope. Since the gymnasium was big enough, we used it like a track, making sure that nothing obstructed the path along the walls. Sure, the property outside was large enough to run, but nobody liked jogging on uneven terrain. Especially in the rain. Unlike your typical gymnasium, ours had weapons and target boards mounted on the walls. It kept things fun and allowed us to sharpen our skills.

Christian took a seat on the weight bench on the far side of the room. The rest of us were clustered together. Blue and Claude continued their game of rock, paper, scissors from their seat on the floor near Shepherd.

The door slammed as Wyatt made a dramatic entrance. Clutching a shirt in one hand, he hitched up his sweatpants. Judging by his messy hair and unshaven face, he obviously hadn't been awake when Viktor had sent everyone a text to meet in the gym. Punctuality wasn't his strong suit. "What the immortal hell is so important that I have to get out of bed this early? I didn't even get to brush my teeth." He yawned wide and sat next to me. "Is this all your fault?"

I threw my arm over my eyes, shielding them from the bright overhead lights. "Maybe this has to do with your cannabis farm that you think nobody knows about."

"Don't let us interrupt your workout, Rocky Balboa," Wyatt said, ignoring me.

I heard Shepherd's feet hit the ground. "This isn't a workout. I'm warming up."

Shepherd liked to work out alone. He also meditated in his room alone. He used to spend more time with Christian than anyone, but Hunter had been bringing him out of his shell.

"Someone should have brought food down," Blue remarked.

"Mmm, blueberry pancakes and maple syrup," Gem drawled.

I pushed myself to a sitting position. "Bacon and french toast with powdered sugar."

Wyatt rested his arms over his knees and locked fingers. "Buttermilk biscuits and homemade gravy—but only the way my granny made them. You know, I'm still not sure to this day what kind of meat she really used to season it."

Claude crossed his feet at the ankles. "Beignets and hot chocolate."

Shepherd gripped the bar over his head and wiped his sweaty

forehead against his bicep. "A big plate of sausages and coffee. Not those flat patties but the real ones."

Niko crossed the floor and leaned against the wall by Shepherd. "Natto, rice with eggs, and hot tea."

"A breakfast burrito," Blue joined in, licking her lips. "I can still remember the first one I ever ate."

"Was that before or after your first kill?" Wyatt quipped.

I glanced over my shoulder. "What about you, Christian?"

He gave me a frosty look. "Pepto-Bismol."

Viktor entered the room in dark slacks, loafers, and a pressed grey shirt.

"What about you, Viktor?" Blue fumbled with a pocket on her black cargo pants. "What's your breakfast of choice?"

He sat down on a weight bench, and we shifted to face him. "Your scrambled eggs."

"Nothing from your homeland?" While she was pressing him for an honest answer, his compliment lit up her eyes.

"Breakfast was vodka in my boyhood," Wyatt answered in an exaggerated Russian accent that made Gem cringe.

Everyone else chuckled. Everyone except Viktor, whose mind was clearly elsewhere.

He ran a hand over his short beard. "I have accepted an important assignment."

Shepherd took a seat on the floor beside me. "What about the shit we're working on now?"

Viktor always had us working on smaller projects. Gem and Wyatt handled a large bulk of that work, so they stayed busy day and night. The rest of us fought like jackals over whatever we could get between big assignments. Sometimes it was investigating crime scenes, other times it was tracking criminals. I preferred the latter. But we also looked into extortion, fraud, and once a case of stolen identity. A Mage had murdered his Creator, who just so happened to be his twin brother.

"Gem will continue with her special project," Viktor said.

Gem held the rope with one hand. "Do you still want me to translate that recent book I found?"

"Nyet. That will be next. My contact is still waiting on the first two books. Many important details are in them."

"I'm solving a murder case that's eight hundred years old," she boasted to the room.

"Based on a book?" I asked. "What if the author lied?"

Wyatt chortled. "They made a false accusation against someone in a book, hoping it would be discovered almost a thousand years later? Talk about a patient man."

"No, silly." Gem let go of the rope and sat cross-legged in front of me. "We usually have at *least* two sources to corroborate facts, and when names are mentioned, the higher authority can open an official investigation and charm witnesses. I love solving cold cases."

"If you say so, Agatha Christie. I've seen you in action at crime scenes."

She wrinkled her nose. "I don't want to actually *see* dead bodies. There are other methods to solve a crime. After eight hundred years, there's no body left to look at anyhow."

"Why did you call us in here instead of the dining room?" Blue didn't waste time getting to the point, especially since we had a tendency to drift off topic when we were all put in the same room.

Viktor wrung his hands. "I did not want to risk the boy overhearing this discussion. Or Switch. This is a very sensitive topic to Shifters in particular. Because of our living situation, I must be more careful about where and when we hold our important meetings."

With his hands in his pockets, Christian strode over and stood near the wall.

Viktor scratched his ear. "My contact has reason to believe there is a fighting ring in the Breed district. Not the Bricks, but right in the middle of good society."

Blue's eyebrows popped up. "Someone has a lot of gall to do that in city limits."

I'd heard of cage fights, pit fights, and illegal rings where Shifters were forced to fight against each other. Some watched for entertainment, while others engaged in gambling.

"These fights are illegal and immoral. The higher authority punishes offenders to the fullest extent of the law, and that is why most are held outside city limits. Those are difficult to track."

I sat cross-legged. "If the higher authority thinks there's fighting going on, why haven't they sent in Regulators to bust everyone?"

Viktor clasped his hands. "It is more complicated than that. We cannot make arrests based on assumptions. Slander is against the law, so we need to gather hard evidence on who is behind the operation. A smart criminal will go to great lengths to hide their identity. Regulators might break up a fight, but what good will that do if they have no evidence of who is in charge? If you want to kill bees, you cannot smash the hive. You must capture the queen."

Wyatt put on his faded green shirt. "You shouldn't go around killing bees. I read that if bees ever go extinct, so will everything else. Plants and trees won't get pollinated, and people will"—he snapped his fingers—"disappear off the face of the earth."

"What are the clues we have to go on?" Christian asked, ignoring Wyatt's remarks. We'd grown used to him injecting random facts or wild speculation into a conversation.

"We have linked three bodies," Viktor said. "They were dumped in human alleyways where juicers hang out, but none of these women lived or worked in the area where their bodies were found. It is possible they went there for other reasons, but when we discovered the second victim worked at the same club as the first, we suspected something more than a random attack."

"How do you know they worked at a club?" Blue asked.

"They had a tattoo that linked them to the establishment. We can't always tell someone's Breed right away, but all three had a Creator's mark."

"Juicers might have done it," Claude pointed out. "Remember that Creator we recently caught who was giving every random Joe Blow his first spark? Who knows how many he made, and unclaimed Learners are targeted by juicers more than anyone else. They're weak, and it's possible to kill a young Mage if you take too much light. I don't see how a few bodies connect to a fighting ring."

"None of these women were Learners," Viktor stated. "Two were ancients."

I shook my head. "Then how did they die? You can't juice an ancient to death, can you?"

"The first victim had blood on her but no marks. That investigation was handled poorly, and they cremated her body. When a second girl with the same tattoo showed up dead, they called me, and I sent Shepherd to examine the body."

"Ah. So *that's* the case we're talking about." Shepherd bent his knee and draped his arm over it before filling us in. "The first girl I looked at died scared and fighting. It was a long battle, and it didn't take place in that alley. The residual emotions on bodies fade, so the fresher they are, the more I can read. Pride was a big one, and that particular rush I've only felt when someone accomplished something in front of a cheering crowd. She had a few significant injuries. Same on the third girl, except not as much fear. Mostly exhaustion, so she must have fought for a long time. The full sensory experience is long gone after a person dies, but sometimes what's left is enough for me to put two and two together."

"We found no weapons at the scene," Viktor added. "The higher authority sent Regulators to the club after hours to speak to the manager who overlooks the staff."

"Oversees," Gem said, correcting him.

"Spasibo. She told them that just before two of the victims went missing, they mentioned quitting the club because of a side job. She thought it was unusual since the club pays well and customers tip very high. People in those positions will work multiple jobs and rarely quit one for another. She said they weren't the only ones who had mentioned quitting and were secretive about the second job. Shortly after this meeting, the higher authority decided it would be prudent not to send in Vampires for questioning."

I jerked my head back. "Why not?"

"The Regulators' presence in the club got out, and it spooked a few of the girls. They disappeared."

"Disappeared?" I parroted. "Suspiciously?"

"Aren't all disappearances suspicious?" Wyatt asked.

"No. If you pack all your stuff and leave town, that's not as suspicious as vanishing in the night and leaving your cat behind."

"Guess how long cats can live without food?"

"Longer than you."

Viktor cleared his throat. "We think they were involved."

Blue shook her head. "Why run? They could have cooperated and helped take down the ring. People only give a shit about themselves."

Viktor nodded. "*Tak-tochno.*"

Gem smiled. "In English."

"Never mind," he said with a wave of his hand. "Admitting the truth would implicate themselves. The higher authority does not show leniency, especially if they were paid and participated of their own free will. A crime is a crime."

"They were fighting each other?" Christian dipped his chin.

"I do not know. This would be the first I've heard of Mage fights. All the women appeared strong and capable, so the person hiring them is looking for fighters who can hold the attention of a crowd. You cannot just scoop people off the streets and expect that to be good enough for wealthy customers. They want something special. Where do you think one finds such a woman?"

Wyatt bit his fingernail. "Not the library."

"A bondage club," Viktor replied.

Was he for real? "What would a dominatrix know about fighting?"

Christian chuckled darkly. "Sweetheart, this isn't the same world as the one you grew up in. I think Viktor is referring to an adult entertainment club. It's not just BDSM. The women there have to deal with some real wankers who don't know how to control themselves. They're tough women, to be sure."

I tilted my head up at him. "And you know this *how*?"

His gaze drifted off. "A friend of a friend."

"You don't have any friends."

Now I was curious what in the world had attracted Christian to a club like that. Did he participate? Did he watch? Did he take his dates there? Maybe he paid one of the workers to flog him with her leather panties. Suddenly I was feeling like a woefully inadequate lover. He had a century's worth of practice on me.

"Christian is right," Viktor said, snapping me out of my fantasies. "Women who work in these clubs are required to know how to protect themselves. Owners prefer hiring Mage for that reason."

"Why not hire Vampires?"

Christian strode toward the wall next to Niko and leaned against it. "A female Vampire in a fantasy club? That'll be the day."

Blue stood up and brushed off the seat of her pants. "I bet Mage women like the empowerment of being in charge. A lot of the older ones came into immortality as sex slaves or worse."

Claude frowned. "What's worse?"

Without hesitation, I answered. "Having your Creator juice all your light or bind with you against your will."

That put a stake in the discussion.

I swung my attention back to Viktor. "What's our job exactly?"

Viktor sat up straight and planted his palms on the bench. "The owner is cooperating and dealing strictly with my contact. He does not want his club shut down; it would set a precedent for similar clubs, and he feels they are a fundamental right. Those were his words, not mine, but I have to agree. Immortals get bored easily and need an outlay."

"Outlet," Gem said.

He muttered something to her in Russian, and the only word I picked up was *coffee*.

"You want us to visit the club and have a look around?" Christian asked.

I leaned back on my hands. "Don't look so excited."

"Nyet. I need Raven as bait."

I shook my head. "I thought you said some of the employees disappeared? Why not just send in a Vampire to question everyone?"

"Someone is getting their women from this club. Why would we want to tip them off?"

"Don't you think the person running this ring will get their women elsewhere? They might have heard about the raid."

"It was not a raid. The Regulators were discreet," Viktor assured me. "After they questioned the manager, they scrubbed her memory of the conversation. The owner does not want to jeopardize his business with a formal investigation. His workers would leave, his customers would quit coming in, and he might seek compensation from the higher authority for slandering his business."

"Some of those girls who took off might have told the ringleader."

"No one knows why the Regulators were there. They went after hours, but someone must have seen them coming or going from the building. It would be enough to make the employees gossip but nothing more. The owner has pacified his people with a fake story about his lease or some such nonsense. Only guilty people run, and those girls probably left the city. Would you stay here for an illegal job if you knew there was a bounty on your head?"

"I'd be long gone," Shepherd agreed.

Viktor stood up. "We have no reason to believe the person soliciting these women to fight knows about our investigation. In the meantime, the club needs replacement workers, and Raven is perfect for this job."

Christian glowered and stepped forward. "Over my rotting corpse."

"What I decide is my choice." Viktor met eyes with him. "The position is for bartender."

"He or she might approach the other girls instead," I said. "What then?"

Viktor paced the floor. "We have considered different scenarios." Viktor regarded me for a moment. "None of the victims had similar traits, so this is not about a physical preference. You must stand out. I want you to watch the other women in the bar. I'm told that the three victims were strong-willed and… What is the word I seek? Butch."

Wyatt snickered. "You picked the right man for the job."

"What about me?" Gem gave Viktor her best puppy dog eyes. "I'm a Mage."

Viktor shook his head. "This is why I hired Raven and Christian. You are not what these people desire, and I need you working on books."

Realizing there was no way out of working in a sex club, I sat forward and muttered, "This wasn't in the brochure."

"Claude will also be working undercover. He can provide backup if something goes wrong. It is better to work in teams."

Christian cleared his throat to draw attention to the obvious fact that he was my partner.

Viktor shrugged at him. "They have a *no Vampires* policy. What can I do? Vampires are known to cause trouble in such clubs by charming the workers to do their bidding."

"Apparently they're not banned in *all* clubs," I said, smiling at Christian. "Isn't that right, honeybun?"

Viktor put his hands on his hips. "It is very important that you do not show anyone your Vampire side. They are looking for a Mage, so keep your fangs out of sight."

"Got it."

"Do whatever it takes to stand out and show your strength," he continued. "Wyatt, I want you to put a device on Raven that follows her every move. She's prohibited from going anywhere but the hotel and club unless she is invited. If she travels through the human district, monitor any security cameras and document vehicles, plates, and faces. Any place she goes, research who owns those properties. This will require twenty-four-hour surveillance on your part."

"I can just call and let him know if I'm going out for a bite," I suggested.

"Nyet. Your phone stays here. I cannot risk the wrong person accessing your contact list or overhearing your call. We will do this right. Claude will relay any messages. And do not go wandering. It will make Wyatt's job difficult if he is researching property records when you are only going out for ice cream."

"So if someone approaches me with an offer, I relay that to Claude and then you guys bust him?"

Viktor shook his head. "Suspicion or names are not enough

for such a prestigious case. We must go deep enough to get into the fights."

My jaw slackened. "You want me to fight?"

"I do not want you involved in actual fighting, but we need to know who is running the operation. You must be certain of that, because the person who approaches you might not be who we want. I want locations. I want names. I want the identity of everyone involved, including customers. You must get close enough to see the fights. We cannot rely on hearsay. If we have insufficient evidence, they go free and we lose our chance. To fail would mean losing the confidence of the higher authority. We have just enough evidence to build a solid case, so it is up to us to uncover this crime ring."

I waited for Christian's rebuttal, but he quietly listened with everyone else.

"Shepherd, I want you in the club as a customer, but not every night. It is important that we do not reveal our cover."

"Blow our cover," Gem said. She was never rude about correcting Viktor, and he seemed to appreciate it since she had helped him fine-tune his English over the years.

"Talk to bystanders," he went on. "Express interest in watching a girl fight. Portray yourself as a wealthy man, but do not wear a suit. This would make you stand out. You can use your gifts to read people and find suspects."

Shepherd stood up, his arms hanging at his sides like dead limbs. "You want me to go into a sex club with my gloves off? Fuck that."

"Who else can sense a liar except for Claude? He will be doing his own undercover work by talking to customers to see what their fantasies are."

Claude shuddered.

"Touch their glasses," Viktor instructed him. "Or the table. Whatever it is you do. We must narrow down suspects. Anyone you find curious, find out their name. Wyatt will search for a criminal record. We must be cautious. If too many of us are together in one place, someone might make a connection. We go as a group to bars."

"Not lately," Wyatt complained. "Seems like forever since we had a good time."

"Niko is still recovering." Viktor rubbed his neck as if he'd slept on it wrong. "I want him on a mandatory vacation for at least three more weeks."

"I can help," Niko insisted. "I can read light."

"You only just woke up from a long coma." Viktor walked back to the weight bench but remained standing. "It will take time for you to fully recover. Your body is still weak."

"I don't need muscles to read light," he countered. "I've been working in the gym every day and eating twice my calories. It won't be long."

"That is rule," Viktor said, putting his foot down. "I have been fair to each of you when you have had trauma. Raven, Blue, and even Gem. You will accept the time I give you. Raven will be without weapons, so I want you to work with her today."

"Wait a second." I got up, flustered by the idea of going in without my push daggers. "You want me unarmed?"

"That is the club policy. The owner fires anyone carrying, so if you are caught and shown preferential treatment, it will—how you say—*blow* our cover."

Gem smiled approvingly.

Viktor sighed and rubbed his eyes. He must have been up all night working out the details. "Use your Mage skills to protect yourself. No bloodsucking."

I snorted. "That takes the fun out of it. So what do you think happened to the victims?"

"It is possible they made mistakes or tried to quit. Fighters never leave, not unless it is in a body bag. A headless or charred body would draw attention from insiders working for the police, so the person behind this is very crafty indeed. Perhaps a Chitah delivered a fatal dose of venom and sealed the wounds. I think what is more likely is that a Mage killed them. There are a number of those with rare but deadly gifts. You're a Stealer, and your kind were once executioners. Stealing someone's light and then their life is not as messy."

"You said the first girl had blood on her. That sounds pretty messy."

"Da. But no injuries from what they told us. We believe after she was strangled, the culprit dumped her body in the human district in hopes that she would be misidentified as human. We can only speculate what is happening. That is why we need you to go in and gather as much information as you can."

Blue gripped the rope with one hand. "And me? Don't keep me home, Viktor. I've taken enough time off. I'm ready to work."

Viktor gave her a reluctant smile. I'd never met a stronger woman than Blue, and she wanted to get back into the thick of things—perhaps too quickly. Since returning from our last mission in West Virginia, Blue hadn't acknowledged the attack that left her scarred. I felt a kinship to her for that, because I had a tendency to bottle up my rage and pain. I couldn't imagine how the hell she was dealing with those scars, ones I hadn't seen since that fateful night. All I knew was that they covered her torso, and her days of wearing sexy low-cut tank tops had ended—not unless she was wearing a button-up over it. Now most of her shirts had high collars like the flannel shirt she wore today.

"If Raven leaves club with anyone, I want you to follow," Viktor said, giving Blue a respectable role. "We cannot rely on a tracking device that might malfunction."

"My equipment never malfunctions," Wyatt grumbled.

Shepherd snickered. "That's not what your last date said."

"That's it?" Blue cocked her head. "Or am I also working inside?"

"You will wear a small phone around your neck. Wyatt will design something that will not be a danger to your animal." Viktor blushed and averted his eyes. "The club has a provocative dress code that I do not think you can adhere to. That is why I chose Claude."

Blue's lips thinned, and she stormed out of the room. We felt the weight of her fury as the door slammed.

Viktor clasped his hands behind his back and paced toward the door as if he might go after her, but he didn't. "Raven and Claude will stay in separate hotels. Only Shepherd and Blue are permitted to return home. Claude will work as Raven's partner inside the club, and Blue will follow her every move on the outside. These roles are vital to Raven's safety. I must be updated on any new developments."

"And what'll you have me doing? Helping Kira with the dishes?" Christian argued.

Viktor spun on his heel. "I want you to create Raven's alias. Make it believable and something she can remember. You know what men like this might ask her, and I need her to be prepared and consistent with her answers. I will give you what we know about the victims, and you can search for similarities."

Christian seemed satisfied with that answer.

"Any questions?" Viktor asked.

I sprang to my feet. "When do we start?"

"Soon. Everyone except you and Niko can join me for breakfast. I need you sharp, and Niko will work with you. Break only as needed—we have no time to waste." He turned his attention to Niko. "Teach her what she does not know. Without weapons, Raven must learn to control every situation."

Niko bowed.

Holding a hand over my rumbling stomach, I asked, "Can I at least have a bowl of cereal?"

"Food will make you slow and lazy. You must know how to defend yourself in a club without killing anyone or using your Vampire skills. But I also cannot see into the future. It is not my desire for you to fight in a cage match, but if that happens, I want you prepared."

Everyone got up and shuffled toward the door.

Claude yawned noisily. "I need to call my salon and rearrange my appointments. Any idea how long this will last?"

Viktor fell into step beside him. "That may not be necessary. You will spend nights at the club. If you have any important clients, you might be able to work them in during the daytime or reassign to someone else on your staff. I do not want you jeopardizing your relationships with important clientele. We rely on them for inside information. But do not drive your Porsche while on assignment. It's too flashy and will not match your job."

I pulled off my socks and tossed them aside. "Well, Niko. Guess it's just you and me."

"And me." Christian closed the door behind Viktor and joined us.

I stretched my arms over my head to loosen the muscles. "No Vamps allowed."

"Don't be daft. Niko can't rile you up like I can."

"And why would I need someone to piss me off while training?"

"Vampires tend to show their fangs when angry, and the only way to suppress natural instinct is to control your emotions. We need to make sure you can keep your wee little fangs where they belong." He sat down on the weight bench. "Just take a gander at those hideous sweatpants you're always wearing. You'll never pull this off dressed like a panhandler. Do you also plan on packing your enormous knickers? I'm sure *that'll* have the lads wagging their tongues."

"You don't push my buttons, Poe. That's one thing you've never been able to do."

"Aye." He splayed the fingers on his left hand and looked at his ring. "Too bad your da can't say the same. Isn't that one a pathetic excuse for a human? That morose bastard is wasting his life away in a dingy chair, hobbling around like a lame horse. Someone should put him out of his misery."

My fangs punched out.

Christian gave me a sardonic smile. "Ah. There they are." Then he looked over at Niko, who had just removed his shirt. "Looks like we have a lot of work to do."

Chapter 4

I'd never been in Blue's bedroom. Even before Kira came along, when we rotated laundry duties, everyone left their hampers or dirty clothes outside the bedroom door. There hadn't been as many rules in the early days—before my arrival—but now most of us valued our privacy. So showing up uninvited left me with mixed feelings. We didn't have a close relationship, but I wanted to make sure she was okay about guarding me on this assignment.

When I tapped a glass of lemonade on the door, it sloshed on my arm. "Bad idea," I muttered, but I was barefoot and my other hand was full.

"Who's there?" Blue called out.

"It's Raven. I brought lunch."

"Just leave it outside the door."

Viktor had ordered me to take short breaks, but this detour wasn't about feeding Blue. The peace offering was a way inside her room. Blue's door had a lever instead of a knob, so I pushed down on it with my wrist and let the door swing open.

The first thing I saw was Blue's reflection in a full-length floor mirror to my left. Her fingers traced the deep scars through her unbuttoned blue flannel shirt.

When she saw the door moving, she whirled around. "I said to leave it outside."

I thought she might try to cover herself up, but Blue kept her arms stiffly at her sides and closed the distance between us.

My throat felt as dry as the Sahara. Maintaining eye contact,

I pretended not to notice her scars. It was as if a giant monster had raked its claws over her body in a downward, diagonal slant. Because the lion had mauled her falcon, the marks were large and spread apart. One long gash traveled from her left shoulder to her right breast, but because of her bra, I couldn't see the full extent of what I already knew. Another started between her breasts, and a third cut across her belly. From what I remembered, she also had one even lower than I could see.

I stood there like an idiot, holding a plate and glass.

Blue heaved a sigh and took her lunch. "Go ahead and look. There's no point pretending they don't exist."

Ignoring the obvious was futile, so I broke eye contact and slid my gaze down to the grotesque trails that navigated over the valleys and mountainous terrain of her body. "They look better," I said truthfully. The last time I'd seen them, they were open and bleeding.

Blue gave me a curt look and marched over to a table in the right-hand corner. She had a small desk similar to mine. In fact, all her furniture was nearly identical—just a different layout. Located on the second floor, her square room sat on the west side of the mansion, giving her two windows on the northwest adjoining walls. Opposite the door was a black armoire, and her bed was located in the northeast corner, a dreamcatcher pinned above the headboard. The fireplace on the east wall got plenty of use judging by the soot sprinkled about the hearth. But it seemed strange that she didn't have her bed closer to it or at least a chair. Watching the flames could be therapeutic, but maybe her therapy was flying around the property.

With her shirt still unbuttoned, she took a seat in the desk chair and ate her grilled cheese. It was the same sandwich I'd often made for my father—a little mayonnaise on both sides, a pinch of sugar, and Texas toast.

"I've been in the gym all morning," I began. "When I went upstairs to get a drink around noon, Wyatt said you didn't show up for breakfast or lunch." I shut the door behind me and leaned against it. "I feel shitty about the whole thing. You should be the one working inside the club, not Claude."

"It's not your fault," she said matter-of-factly. "I just need to get over it."

"Anyhow, I thought I'd bring a peace offering. My dad used to love 'em."

Blue held out half her sandwich. "Do you want some?"

I fanned my shirt, still cooling down from the fight maneuvers I'd been practicing all morning. "I can't eat. Viktor thinks it'll slow me down."

After another bite, she set down her sandwich and angled her chair toward me. "Hunger motivates a person. Viktor's always right."

Silence blanketed the room. My gaze again fell to her scars through her open shirt.

"It really doesn't look as bad as it did before," I heard myself say. I cringed inwardly and chose to elaborate. "The ointment Shepherd used must have helped. At least the skin closed up."

Blue touched her grey feather earring and stared at the wall. "I'm a monster. Had this never happened, Viktor would have put me in the club. Claude will have your back, but he's not a woman. I would have been able to get workers and customers to confide in me. No matter how you slice it, these scars are a hindrance."

"Don't take it personally. We all have physical traits that eliminate us from certain jobs. Christian can't even go into the club."

Blue played with a small pocket on her right thigh. "I guess."

"Why do you like pants with so many pockets?" I asked, attempting to lighten the mood.

Daytime Blue had a particular style that was different from nighttime Blue. She loved knee-high boots with dark jeans but also wore cargo pants and combat-style boots. Not the heavy ones with chunky soles, but the ones that were feminine and ideal for running.

She opened one of the pockets and pulled out a thin wallet. "Who needs a purse to lug around when I've got these? Hands-free. If I'm chasing someone with an axe, I don't have time to worry about who's going to hold my purse."

I chuckled softly. "That's pretty smart. Maybe I should rethink my wardrobe."

Blue didn't seem especially hungry, but she finished her sandwich.

I drifted over and leaned against the edge of her desk. "I know what you're going through right now."

Blue swallowed her bite and dusted off her fingers. "I doubt that."

"Remember when I was sold to my Creator? That really messed with my head. I didn't want to take any time off or show my emotions to anyone. I was afraid Viktor might think I wasn't cut out for this job anymore." I folded my arms and stared at the bright windows. "Viktor's not trying to shield you from getting your feelings hurt. Put yourself in his shoes. He needs a Mage, and he also needs a second person who won't stand out or distract customers—for *any* reason."

She hooked one arm over the back of her chair. "We're trying to bait someone who runs cage fights. Wouldn't a scarred woman be a sign of a warrior?"

"There's a stigma, and you know it."

"Thank the fates I don't care about stigma. Don't you find it infuriating? Scarred men are warriors. Scarred women are victims."

"Smart people know the truth."

"It doesn't matter. It's always going to hold me back."

I lowered my head. Even though I wanted to make her feel better, there was no denying that her altered appearance would change everything. "I'm sorry."

My external scars were miniscule in comparison. I had marks from an old Chitah bite on my hip, but my Keystone tattoo covered the ugliest part of it. While Blue expressed concern that her scars would ruin her career, it ran deeper than that. She was still a knockout, but her life hadn't gone back to normal, even around the house. Wyatt didn't ogle her body like he used to. At least, not for the same reasons. The world would treat her differently. Men would treat her differently. She'd never liked the attention, but now she had to deal with a different kind of attention.

Blue stood and crossed the room. Her button-up dropped to the floor, and she reached inside the armoire and chose a sleeveless black shirt with a high neck. It was formfitting and accentuated her full breasts, yet it cloaked her scars. Then she turned around and put her hands on her hips, making the point that she could have rocked a sexy look on this mission. The scar on her shoulder was visible, but she easily covered that with her long brown hair.

I heaved a sigh. "If what you're wearing is considered too much for a club like this, what the hell am *I* going to be wearing?"

"Shy?"

I snuck a bite of her sandwich. "You've seen my wardrobe. A short black dress is about as sexy as I get. And how am I supposed to put up with lewd remarks and people leering at me without getting pissed off and showing my fangs?"

Blue returned to her seat and sipped her lemonade. "Christian didn't have any advice? He always keeps his cool."

I gave her a mirthless smile. "He spent all morning teaching me how to control my anger."

"And?"

I pushed off the desk and headed toward the door. "If you find a stake in his chest tomorrow morning, it wasn't me."

Christian propped his elbows on the booth table and watched Niko eat his ham sandwich. On the heels of a new assignment, everyone else must have cut their lunch short to get back to their duties. When he, Raven, and Niko had emerged from the gym for their afternoon break, Wyatt was the only person left in the dining room. He'd briefly chatted with them before heading upstairs with an energy drink in his hand. Niko made himself a plate while Kira cleared the table. What a strange lass. Always consumed with work, her hair pinned up or tied with a kerchief. Servants were common in the world of mortals, but times weren't as hard as they used to be. Christian had once been a servant, and he'd never choose that life again. It was a humbling position, one that required silence, loyalty, and obedience.

Raven whooshed out of the kitchen with a plate and glass in hand. "Be right back. I'm taking this up to Blue."

Christian noticed a guilty look on her face. According to Wyatt, Blue hadn't come down all day. She was vexed about the assignment, but Viktor's options were limited. He couldn't send Blue into the fire like that. It wouldn't be fair to Keystone's mission, and it might traumatize the poor lass if some wanker made crass remarks. Only customers wore latex suits to those clubs. Employees were scantily clad, and there was no way Blue could hide her scars.

Christian lifted his glass of whiskey and took another sip. This was their first break and chance to eat. Not that Christian ever ate at the table, but he enjoyed a glass of alcohol. Right now he needed it.

"You shouldn't feel guilty," Niko said as he finished his sandwich. "Taunting Raven had to be done. She isn't like every other Mage, and she *must* learn to control her Vampire nature. You're the only one who can mentor her. She didn't receive that guidance from her maker, so you and I have a role to play."

"Aye." The whiskey slid down Christian's throat and warmed his belly like fire. "We like to have a go at each other every now and then, but that was torturous."

"But necessary." Niko moved his hand across the table until he found his napkin. "She's intelligent enough not to take it to heart. Raven isn't impulsive, but she's reactive. I've watched her light, and most things don't bother her the way they would others. But everyone has a weak spot, and you need to root that out of her."

Christian stared into his glass. He'd certainly learned Raven's faults. While she brushed off insults left and right, she was fiercely protective of her father. She also didn't like anyone treating her differently because of her gender, so Christian had used those weaknesses to push her buttons. He could have gone deeper by bringing up Fletcher and attacking her mother's memory, which would have been unequivocal trigger points, but he couldn't bring himself to stoop that low.

While a Vampire could keep their fangs from punching out, it sometimes happened involuntarily for a number of reasons. Sexual stimulation, anger, excitement—it was unique to each individual. Raven had a tendency to show her fangs whenever she felt like she was losing the upper hand in a fight. She'd spent the morning learning new moves and brushing up on old ones, but they also subjected her to a different level of training. Raven needed to fight like a Mage and ignore her Vampire nature, something Christian had always discouraged. But now that lack of control could—at the very least—put the mission in jeopardy. Worst-case scenario, it might cost Raven her life.

The timing couldn't have been worse. Raven had not only endured Lenore's recent visit, but the next morning she got berated by the man who loved her. It was a wonder she hadn't gone on a killing spree by now.

"I can't sense your energy," Niko said, "but I can see it. Your emotions light up the darkness at times. Something has been troubling you this morning, even before the meeting."

"Just old ghosts who need to stay in the fecking graveyard."

"I know the burden of secrets. Can you discuss it with Viktor?"

"Afraid not." Christian sighed and sat back. This whole situation felt like a blister on his soul. "Just someone I'd rather forget, but I can't."

"An old flame?" Niko quipped. But then he did that thing where he looked at Christian's skull as if flames were shooting out.

Christian grabbed his drink. "I'll thank you kindly to quit peeping at my light."

"I can't help it any more than you can help noticing facial expressions." Niko bound his nape, using a leather tie from his pocket. "I don't know who this is about, but your emotional energy reveals a lot. I can relate to the struggle of moving on."

"And how's that?"

"My Creator wronged me, but I wound up in an even worse situation after I escaped with Cyrus. Believe it or not, I spent years wondering if I'd made the right decision. Had my Creator been so unfair? A few centuries of slavery and I could have become a strong ally in his army. I could have been someone at the expense of my dignity. I hated him and I loved him. He made me." Niko folded his arms and shifted his gaze toward Christian's chest. "You can still have residual feelings for someone even if they've wronged you. It's hard to let go of the life you imagined with them. It's irrational, and I think it illustrates the complicated dynamic between Raven and her Vampire maker."

Christian couldn't argue. Raven's relationship with Houdini vexed him. But he had to be careful about how often he brought up the subject as it would only drive a wedge between them. She had to learn for herself how toxic a man like that really was, and though Houdini professed to have her best interest at heart, a manipulative person had the gift of convincing others that they could do no wrong.

Niko reached for his water and savored a long drink until the glass was empty. "But your situation is different than mine, isn't it? Old flames are hard to put out because they've burned the longest. I've seen it destroy men, and that is love's most dangerous side effect."

"Who said anything about love?"

Niko impassively touched his lower lip but didn't reply.

Christian shifted his gaze into the gathering room. Despite everything, Christian *had* once loved Lenore. She'd used him, controlled him with her ancient blood, and discarded him like trash. He'd spent decades feeling resentful and angry while devoting his life to protecting others, as if that could somehow wash away his sins. After a while, he'd buried his pain, and life was tolerable again. But Lenore's unexpected return had resurfaced those old feelings—only now his bitterness had turned into betrayal and hurt. Did that mean he had never stopped loving her? Did it mean Lenore still had influence over him? Or did it mean he simply hadn't put the past behind him as she clearly had?

And then there was Raven. Exquisite, confident, capable—everything he desired. Yet she was so young. So very young. What if she one day decided that he wasn't enough, just as Lenore had? Christian didn't exactly have a good track record in the love department. If anything, he'd learned that feelings weren't always reciprocated in the same way.

"If you have feelings for anyone else," Niko said, lowering his voice, "you shouldn't bury them."

"I'd like to."

"I don't mean the person. You have to face your innermost desires and fears and conquer them. It's the only way you'll be able to move forward."

"Been doing a little conquering yourself, have you?" Christian knocked back the rest of his drink.

"Of course not."

"Don't be tellin' me fibs. You've got a woman out there, haven't you? Bet she's still pining over you."

Niko didn't display any physical signs of lying like blushing or sweating. But his capillaries widened just enough that a Vampire would notice, and Christian heard a fluctuation in his heart rhythm. The man had secrets.

Remembering he had a job to do, Christian scooted out of the bench seat. "If Raven comes back, tell her I'm busy. I need to get started on creating her new identity."

Niko felt around the table and collected the dishes before standing up. "I wish I could contribute."

"Enjoy your time off. It's not often we get any. Besides, Wyatt can't do everything, now can he? You might be able to help him make a few calls and reserve a nice hotel for Raven. If it's left up to him, he'll choose the cheapest dump that money can buy."

Niko inclined his head. "I'll work with him tonight, after I'm finished with Raven. She'll need a hotel within walking distance, and Viktor doesn't want her straying far. That will limit our choices."

"Why walking distance?"

"She shouldn't drive her vehicle. Someone might run a check on it, and Wyatt won't have time to change those records to match her fake identity."

Christian nodded. "Good thinking. I'd rather you stay here and help Wyatt. We can't afford to make any careless mistakes."

"Raven will also need proper attire. Wyatt mentioned that Shepherd plans to scope out the club tonight. I assume when he returns, he'll be able to provide information on the employee dress code. Raven will need to go shopping tomorrow."

Christian scratched his head. "Raven isn't the only one who'll need new threads. Claude can't work in a place like that without the right look. I know a thing or two about male workers in adult clubs. Viktor just needs to tell me what his position will be." Christian clasped his hands behind his back and looked at his shoes. "Raven will need contact lenses, and I suspect Wyatt'll need to pick up a few things to make Blue's phone necklace. Might as well make it a team outing."

"We were almost arrested on our last shopping trip."

Christian clapped Niko on the shoulder. "Aye. That's what makes it interesting. Do me a favor: don't tell Raven we had this conversation."

Niko tilted his head to the side. "What conversation?"

Chapter 5

ONE INTERESTING ASPECT OF LIVING with Keystone was watching how the others interacted with humans. My teammates didn't spend time around them, and aside from Christian and Niko, who had once been human, the rest had likely grown up around their own kind. When you isolate yourself in the Breed world, the rules—or lack thereof—rub off on you.

So Shepherd lighting up a cigarette inside a shoe store was a normal affair for him, but the salesman looked like he was on the verge of a conniption.

"Sir, please don't make me call security." The slender man adjusted his wire-rimmed glasses, a vain attempt at signaling who had the authority in this situation.

Shepherd rested his arm over a shelf after putting out the match and dropping it on the floor. "If it's all the same to you, I'll finish my smoke. Cigarettes aren't cheap anymore."

Shepherd didn't do things to be deliberately rude, he just didn't respond to anyone rebuking him for what he perceived as a given right.

As I approached the man, I flicked a glance at his name tag and lowered my voice to make it seem like we were on the same team. "I'll take care of it, Roger."

His beady eyes darted between Shepherd and me before he flounced off.

I took the cigarette from Shepherd's hand and stubbed it out on a Brannock Device used for measuring someone's shoe size.

There wasn't a trash can or empty cup anywhere around, so I had to improvise. "I'll buy you a new pack. You need to follow the rules."

He blew out the smoke he'd been holding in his lungs. "Too many damn rules in these places. A man needs to kick back and relax. Who gives a fuck if I smoke in a shoe store? It smells like cheap rubber in here anyhow."

"Secondhand smoke causes cancer."

"To humans."

"We're in a mall."

Shepherd squinted at me. "You think that salesman was human? Think again."

"Why are you even in here? I thought you guys were in the toy store."

"*Shh.*" Shepherd glanced over his shoulder at Hunter, who was sitting on the floor, attempting to lace up a pair of shoes. "I let him run around in there and show me what he liked. Then Viktor stayed behind to buy all that shit with my money. They're gonna be his birthday presents."

I furrowed my brow. "I thought Breed didn't do birthdays?"

"Some do, most don't. My kid's never had a party, and he still doesn't have any toys in his room. A few plastic cars and finger paint isn't enough. I want him to pick out his own toys. He doesn't realize you can actually buy this shit and take it home. Patrick never bought him a damn thing."

"Are the sneakers part of the surprise?"

Shepherd ran his hand over his short brown hair. "Nah. He's outgrowing his shoes, and I wanted him to pick them out. He's been trying them on for a half hour, but he's never had a choice before, so I guess he's trying to figure out what he likes." A smile crept up his face. "What did you buy?"

I lifted the two bags in my hands. "You don't wanna know."

He chuckled darkly. "Work clothes, huh? Better you than me."

I noticed Shepherd had on his Sensor gloves. They were a thin, breathable fabric—the same as what Hunter was also wearing. Both pairs black.

"Where is everyone?" I asked.

Shepherd gestured toward the front window. "Wyatt's in the arcade on the other side. I don't know about the others."

I strolled to the open doorway. We were on the second floor, and customers down below were shuffling into a popular clothing store for a half-off sale, lured by the signs in the windows. The arcade across the hall was dark, but I could make out Wyatt's back. He was standing in front of a machine called Asteroids.

Shepherd whistled with his fingers, and it gave me a start.

Wyatt gave him the finger behind his back.

Shepherd stalked to the door and yelled, "Get your ass over here before I drop you off in a hospital morgue!"

Wyatt scowled at him for a moment before adjusting his slouchy beanie and swaggering out. Half his shirt was tucked in, revealing a belt with a skull buckle. I rarely saw him in anything but those beat-up black cowboy boots he wore beneath his jeans, and today was no different. "Top score!" he cheered.

These men had no sense of social conduct.

Wyatt crossed one of the bridges and then appeared in the entryway. "What's the scoop?"

"We should start rounding everyone up," I said, eager to get back home. "Did you get what you needed for Blue?"

"Yup." He patted a bag stuffed in his back pocket and grinned handsomely. "Buying some sexy shoes, Mistress Black? You won't find any in this dump."

I gave him a light smack with my bag. "I'm done picking out my wardrobe. Too bad Christian stayed home. I'm sure he would have liked seeing me try them all on. You guys are gonna die when you see what Claude got."

Wyatt scratched his head. "You let him pick out his stuff?"

"No. Christian gave us a shopping list based on Shepherd's feedback, and we weren't allowed to deviate from it. Claude's pissed, but he's going along with it."

Wyatt wagged his finger at me. "Don't you even *think* about leaving the house without putting on a fashion show. So… why are we growing roots in the shoe store?"

Shepherd jerked his thumb over his shoulder. "Waiting for the kid to decide."

Wyatt tried on a pair of mirrored sunglasses from a standing rack. "I think he decided."

We both turned.

Hunter balled up his fists and smiled from ear to ear. His shoes were neon pink with sparkly butterflies on the sides. His heels weren't tucked all the way into the shoes, which were clearly too small for a boy his age.

The salesman noticed us looking and came to investigate. "Those are for girls. Are you a girl? Of course not. If you go over to the little-boys' section, you'll see the blue and green sneakers. Let's put these back in the box before you get them dirty."

Shepherd's entire body went rigid. He stepped up to the salesman and squared his shoulders. "Box up those sneakers in his size or I'll put *you* in a box."

"Sir, those don't come in a larger size."

"What other colors you got in his size of that shoe?"

Roger huffed and scanned the shelves. "White, purple, and… No, that's it. Just white or purple."

"Butterflies?"

"Yes. But they're little-girl—"

"Get them. Now."

Roger snapped his mouth shut when he caught the volatile look on Shepherd's face.

On the verge of tears, Hunter stepped out of the shoes and hung his head.

After the salesman left to run his errand, Shepherd sat down on a bench next to Hunter. "You wear whatever you want, little man. Stupid rules are for stupid people."

Wyatt tucked his sunglasses inside a sneaker on display. "I once went through a phase of wearing an earring in my right ear. I had so many guys hitting on me. Maybe the penny loafers didn't help, but I was in fashion." He shrugged at me. "It was the eighties."

When the salesman approached Hunter with the shoeboxes, Shepherd got up. "What's your point?"

"It doesn't mean he's gay."

Shepherd swaggered up to Wyatt, his voice low and dangerous. "So what if he was? Think I care?"

"I'm just saying you can be straight and play with dolls."

"Or maybe you can be gay. Like I said, he's my kid. He can wear whatever the hell he wants and grow up to kiss whoever the hell he wants."

I rocked with laughter. "You say that now, but just wait until he brings home a Vampire."

"Or a shoe salesman," Wyatt added.

"Or a dominatrix," I said, raising my bag.

Shepherd sighed. "You two knuckleheads wait outside while I pay." He turned on his heel and barked at the salesman, "We'll take both. And get him the blinking ones he was wearing earlier."

Hunter's eyes lit up when he realized he was going home with the shoes. As Roger gathered up all the boxes and tissue paper, Hunter ran to Shepherd and wrapped his arms around his middle. Shepherd's gloved hand rumpled the little boy's black hair.

As soon as Wyatt and I reached the balcony outside, I set down my bags and rested my arms on the metal rail. Weekdays weren't very crowded, but I still enjoyed watching people going about their normal lives.

Wyatt tucked in the rest of his vintage green T-shirt with a Centipede game logo on the front. "Malls used to be hot spots, but that was before your time."

"I'm surprised this one is still around since most of them are closing."

"Not in Cognito. Immortals are the only ones keeping these places alive. We're nostalgic and like to hold on to relics from our past. One day when you're older, you'll understand."

"Whatever you say, grandpa."

Wyatt watched a man trying on a hat down below. "Immortals do a lot of shopping here, and a few of them own some of the little stores. Like that arcade I was in. The owner's a Shifter who was once a pinball champion. I guess you've never heard of pinball."

I turned my gaze at a tall blond man walking jauntily toward the food court on our right. Did he have golden eyes? A Vampire smiled up at me from the jewelry shop on the first floor.

"Quit eavesdropping," I muttered. "Mind your own damn business."

He feigned a look of surprise before steering his black eyes away.

"Immortals, huh? No wonder everyone looks like zombies," I said.

"I'm just bummed they shut down the cookie shop. Everyone's trying to be healthy," Wyatt said, making air quotes with his fingers.

"I think I just saw Niko by the glass elevator." I picked up my bags and headed left.

Wyatt caught up. "Excited about your mission?"

"Sure, but why does it seem like I'm always the bait?"

"Blue was bait at Patrick's party. Before you came along, that was her job. Viktor likes her fighting skills, but she's a better tracker. When we started following rumors about the Shadow," he said, making air quotes again, "and learned more about you, Viktor decided we needed some hard-core people on the team. It used to be Shep and Christian, but Viktor didn't want Shep doing dangerous stuff all the time. Much to his dismay."

"No doubt. He's got an arsenal in his bedroom."

"Yeah. So now Viktor puts him on jobs that require Sensor skills. Like touching dead bodies and murder weapons. But he also helps me out with research."

"I think we found Claude."

We both stopped dead in our tracks and stared at the leather chairs by one of the crossover points. Claude had his legs tucked inside slots on the footrest of the recliner, his eyes closed. A woman eating ice cream on a nearby bench was licking her plastic spoon and gawking at him as if *he* were the dessert.

Wyatt folded his arms. "Hey, Valentine. You practicing for your new job?"

Claude opened his luminous eyes and wet his lips, a blissful expression on his face. "What do you mean?"

Wyatt gestured toward Claude's massive erection.

When Claude looked down, he behaved as if he had no clue how that thing got inside his fitted grey sweatpants. He yanked his bag off the chair next to him and held it over his lap.

"That's one of those massaging chairs, isn't it?" Wyatt cackled. "That's a therapy session I ain't got time for."

Claude blushed all the way down to his neck. "I forgot where I was." When he lurched out of the chair, we glimpsed his erection again.

"I'll say." Wyatt reached for one of his bags. "What's in there?"

Claude jerked the bag away to cover himself, and I threw back my head and laughed.

Wyatt patted him on the arm. "I've heard that thinking of your mother helps."

"The chair has little knobs that go deep. It's like hands rubbing all over your body," Claude said, trying to explain his physical condition. Perhaps the hysterical part was that he couldn't seem to get it back under control. It had a mind of its own, and it wanted more of that chair.

I reached in my bag and showed him a leather bra with silver spikes. "Look what I got."

His eyes rounded before he looked away. "That doesn't help."

"Maybe today wasn't a good idea to wear tight sweats."

Wyatt chortled. "I don't think *any* day is a good day for a man to wear tight sweats."

Meanwhile, the lady on the bench was in a fantasy world that centered on a tall, handsome Adonis named Claude Valentine. Once she realized that he was six and a half feet tall, she drank him in, ignoring all social rules of conduct, sucking on her plastic spoon with wanton abandon.

Claude tunneled his fingers through his golden locks, and it seemed like every gesture made him look like a male model. "Are we leaving?"

"Not yet," I informed him. "Do you know where I can buy contact lenses? Viktor doesn't want me to stand out, so I need a brown contact lens for my blue eye."

"I wager there's one around here. Did you buy a mask?"

"For what?"

A smile touched his lips. "You weren't paying attention in the van."

"I was sending Christian messages on my phone."

"And ignoring Viktor's shopping rules. It wasn't on Christian's list, but he wants us to wear a mask. Just the ones that cover the eyes. Shepherd noticed a lot of workers wearing them, and it'll help us to better hide our identity."

Not a bad idea. We didn't get out much, but there was always a chance someone might recognize us—especially if they happened to be one of the aristocratic bastards we mingled with at charity functions. It was one of many reasons why I didn't mingle. Only a few of the higher authority members knew we worked for Keystone since we didn't go around advertising it, but some might find it odd that a person invited to an exclusive party was working in a fantasy club.

Then again, we lived in an unconventional world.

I walked past Claude. "Any concerns about the mission?"

He fell into step beside me. "I'm worried I might run into one of my clients in the club."

I waggled my eyebrows at him. "That might work in your favor for extra bookings."

He turned toward the elevators. "That's what I'm afraid of."

We stepped inside the glass elevator. Claude smiled sexily at the lady on the bench ahead of us. "Have a pleasant afternoon, female."

As the doors closed, the woman dropped her cup of melted ice cream all over the floor.

"Maybe we should hitch a ride home with Shepherd," Claude suggested as he looked out the glass wall behind us. "Viktor's probably lost."

"No, he just sent a message to wait near the entrance where we came in." Wyatt tucked his phone back in his pocket. "He's buying a watch. You know, watches will become obsolete one day. Phones do everything. I still remember my first pocket watch. It was a dandy. That was before batteries came along. You had to wind them up."

The elevator doors opened, and I stepped out. "What happened to it?"

"My horse ate it."

I turned to see if he was joking.

Wyatt's boot heels knocked against the shiny floor. "Billy was a nuisance."

"You had a horse named Billy?"

He stopped by a palm tree. "He'd eat everything in sight... like a billy goat."

Claude turned in a circle and scoped the long hall. "What happened to Billy?"

Wyatt stood on top of a bench. "Billy dropped dead at a hitching rail. Cause of death unknown."

"I guess his time was up. Maybe it was your pocket watch." I set my bags down when a thought came to mind. "Do you see animal ghosts?"

He shook his head. "Who do I look like? Doctor Dolittle?"

"You sure do little to share your snacks with friends," Claude quipped.

Wyatt jumped off the bench and gave a winsome smile to a short-haired brunette. "Hey, buttercup. May I have the pleasure of escorting you to your destination?" Without asking, he followed her.

Hunter and Shepherd were taking a quick trip down the escalator. Hunter nervously held on to the side as he peered over the edge.

Claude's nostrils flared as he pulled in my emotional scent. "You're nervous."

"I'm just thinking about the assignment." I lifted my bags and watched Hunter trying to walk up the down escalator. "Christian can't come, and we work well together."

Claude put his hand on my shoulder. "I'll be there, and I won't let any harm come to you, female. And I'll do everything I can to weed out any suspects."

"What makes Viktor think his plan will work?"

"He's very skilled at setting traps, and I'm certain that he's not only worked out the odds but also has a backup plan. Criminals are stupid. They stick to the same routine."

Claude had a point. Criminals were creatures of habit. Even I had developed a routine when I lived on the streets. Recognizing my own habits made trapping my targets that much easier.

When Shepherd and Hunter finally made it off the escalator, Hunter scampered toward us, blue lights blinking on the soles of his new shoes.

"Hey, little monkey." Wyatt entered the scene, tucking a slip of paper into his pocket. "Those are some snappy shoes."

Hunter beamed, oblivious to an older woman walking by who was gawking at him. We'd gotten so used to his facial scar that it wasn't until he garnered public stares that we were reminded of it.

Shepherd mussed Hunter's hair from behind him. "Show them your socks."

Hunter obligingly lifted his pant leg and showed off his pink socks. The horizontal black stripes went all the way up to his knees.

Shepherd lit up a cigarette and tossed the match on the floor. "I think he likes them better than the shoes. Kinda like having a secret under his pants."

Wyatt stretched. "Yup. I know *exactly* what that's like."

Claude frowned, and lines bunched up between his eyebrows. "You shouldn't make innuendos around a child."

"That kid has no idea what we're talking about," Wyatt said dismissively. "Besides, you shouldn't get worked up over a little innuendo considering what we do for a living. You think that's not gonna traumatize him?"

Shepherd exhaled and stared down the long hall. He abruptly waved the smoke away from his face and squinted. "Is that who I think it is?"

I craned my neck to see around a kiosk. Heading in our direction at breakneck speed was Gem on a pogo stick. Her shoulder-length hair bounced up and down like butterfly wings as people cleared the way. Some laughed, and a few others pulled out their phones to take video, but she would be nothing but a blur of movement. The purple pogo stick tilted forward, and the sound of the spring made heads turn. If *that* wasn't enough of a spectacle, a flustered man in a blue work shirt was chasing after her. Gem glanced over her shoulder at him, and the next thing I knew, that stick soared high into the air.

Hunter squealed with delight and clapped his hands.

"I'll meet you outside!" she said, bouncing right over Wyatt as he ducked.

Blue's falcon swooped down from the second floor and plucked the toupee right off the man's head.

Shepherd pivoted on his heel to watch Gem bounce away. He puffed on his cigarette. "This looks like something we'll have to deny later."

Chapter 6

AFTER PLACING MY RUBY NECKLACE inside my jewelry box for safekeeping, I took one final glance at my reflection in the standing mirror. I barely recognized myself. I was Raven 2.0—what I might look like had I gone another way and lived on the fringes of society.

While Christian had provided a list of appropriate attire, clothes weren't the whole package. After applying vanilla-scented lotion to my entire body, I borrowed makeup from Gem. I went heavy with the smoky eye even though I'd be wearing a mask. Deep burgundy lipstick was my favorite, so I used a heavy matte that would make my lips stand out. I didn't own a curling iron, but the club would probably be too hot to worry about hair anyhow, so I tied it up in a sexy knot.

I turned to the side, admiring the zippers on the sides of my leather shorts. The two buckles in front were a nice touch, especially for shorts that weren't low-rise. I needed to ensure the Keystone tattoo on my hip remained covered. Despite the leather corset with buckles up the front, I wasn't exactly pinup material. I didn't have voluptuous curves or a soft body. Instead, you could see lean muscles on my arms and thighs. My hands weren't dainty but made for punching a man's lights out. Perhaps those were the features Christian wanted me to show off. If it weren't for the over-the-knee boots, I'd look naked.

I closed my bedroom door and marched toward Wyatt's World on floor two like a soldier heading to battle. The whole house could probably hear me coming as I tromped down the stairs, ready to toss Christian out the window for making me buy these slutty clothes.

As soon as I reached the room, I bored a hole through the back of Christian's skull as he looked inside Wyatt's vending machine.

I flung papers at his back, and they showered the floor. "I've memorized my alias, you sadistic fanghole. And just to clear the air, I'm not using prostitution as a former job. If anyone asks, I was a thief."

When Shepherd's cigarette fell out of his mouth, he launched from the sofa, patting the lit cherry off his crotch.

Wyatt turned in his chair, and his jaw dropped. "Holy Toledo! You're a *woman*."

Christian half turned, peering at me over his shoulder with a hot look.

Gem poked her head out from the beanbag chair where she was watching an old musical. "Is that for real?" She scrambled out of the chair and skirted around it, her violet eyes saucer-wide. "I don't think I'm mad anymore about not going. No offense, Raven, but you look like a hooker."

No one else was in the room, and I guessed Niko was resting after a long day training me.

I glanced down at my cleavage. "Objects are smaller than they appear. The corset is squeezing the hell out of everything, and I feel more naked without my weapons than I do wearing this outfit."

"No complaints here." Wyatt waggled his eyebrows as he wolfed down his Three Musketeers. "Do me a favor and spin around so we can see everything."

Shepherd swaggered to Wyatt's desk and leaned against it. He gave his partner a hard look. "If you keep on with that mouth, the only thing you'll be seeing is my fist."

"I'm just saying what we're all thinking."

"Button it up, Spooky."

That was the first time Shepherd had ever defended my honor, and it made me squirm.

Wyatt tossed the candy wrapper into the trash. "We need to leave soon. I've got everyone's hotel booked. Raven, you're coming with me, and Shepherd's dropping Claude off a block away. I booked him at a hotel near his salon to make his life easy."

Christian leaned against the vending machine, arms folded. "Those boots weren't on my approved list."

I shifted my stance. "You didn't specify anything about shoes. I had to improvise."

"Take them off."

I folded my arms. "Make me."

Clutching her quartz pendant, Gem backed away as if someone had lit a stick of dynamite.

Christian stalked toward me and knelt at my feet. Before I knew it, he yanked down the zipper on one of the boots. Then he flung it across the room. I would have smacked him, but my brain went on hold when he ran his hand up my leg and slowly lifted his gaze. "Your legs are your best asset."

Shepherd and Wyatt turned away, grimacing at each other and hunching their shoulders.

"And you expect me to walk around in my socks?"

He reached beneath Wyatt's desk and pulled out a brown box. Shepherd scooted aside as Christian popped off the lid and tossed the white tissue paper aside.

I sucked in a sharp breath when I saw the boots.

Expensive Christian Louboutin boots.

I reached inside and touched the red bottom of one. "Hello, darling."

Christian set the box down and put the sexy ankle boots on my feet. They fit like a glove.

I lifted one leg to look at the bottom. "Are the heels stunners?"

Wyatt snorted. "Leave it to Raven to ask a question like that."

Christian let his fingers trail up my thigh as he stood up. "I'm afraid I didn't have time to customize your footwear, but I wager they'll hurt all the same when planted firmly in an eye socket."

I smiled at him. "Good thinking."

Wyatt cracked open a can of root beer. "I put a tracker inside one of them, so be like Dorothy and don't take them off."

I looked them over, not seeing anything out of the ordinary. "How?"

He wiggled his fingers. "Magic. I know a guy who makes microchips. Just do me a favor and don't get them wet."

Blue hustled into the room, her face beaming with excitement. "Wait'll you see *this*," she said quietly.

Christian and I parted like the Red Sea and faced the doorway. A few seconds later, Claude appeared in nothing but combat boots and skintight shorts.

Shiny. Gold. Shorts.

His look soured when he was greeted by wolf whistles and stunned looks.

Claude's skin had a soft golden hue, but now it shimmered as if someone had dipped him in a vat of gold. I swiped my finger across his bicep and looked at the creamy residue that left flecks of glitter on my hands when I tried to wipe it off. Claude had curly hair but not tight curls. His lustrous blond locks were large and messy—like those Greek statues I'd seen in books.

"*Jesus fuck,*" Shepherd muttered. "You're not riding in my car with that shit all over you. I'll be picking it out of my seats for the next century."

Claude's eyebrows sloped down as he gave Christian a thorny look. "Blame the Vamp. Body glitter was on his list. Or was this a joke?"

"It's not a joke," I said, drawing his attention to my outfit.

Claude glowered. "At least you have a shirt on."

Wyatt spun his chair back around to look at his computer screen. "Since when do you wear a shirt around here? I've seen more of your nipples than I've seen from my dates."

"He's got you there." Blue's jaunty smile belied the black mood I'd found her in earlier. "I wouldn't worry about standing out. You'll blend in with everyone else. Just another piece of meat."

Christian snapped his fingers. "That reminds me." He reached for a small bag beneath his desk and handed it to Claude. "Since you couldn't find any at the mall, I bought these at the costume shop."

Inside the bag was a handful of masks that would cover our eyes. Some were fabric and a few were embroidered lace. The cloth ones reminded me of the Zorro mask that Hunter sometimes wore.

Wyatt typed on his keyboard. "I think Claude should just paint his on. That would look awesome—like a superhero or something. Captain Glitter."

"He looks like a unicorn pissed on him," Shepherd remarked.

Blue plopped down on the sofa. "I don't know. I think he resembles a prestigious award."

Claude heaved a sigh before exiting the room. We all stared at his buns in those tight shorts, and they were something to behold. With broad shoulders, nice legs, and a V-shaped torso, Claude was the whole package.

Yep. This was going to be a memorable assignment.

Wyatt turned the steering wheel with one hand and grabbed a handful of fries out of a paper sack with the other. Between bites, he would shift gears, leaving granules of salt all over the place. I couldn't get used to sitting on what was supposed to be the driver's side. Wyatt's red 1971 Austin Mini Cooper looked like a toy with its bucket seats, manual windows, loud engine, and one blue door.

I cracked my window. "Did we really need to stop at McDonald's? Now I smell like you."

Steering the car with his knee, he rolled up the sack and tossed it in the back seat. "They should bottle this stuff and make it into perfume. Food is the only way to attract men. Do you have your alias memorized?"

"Yep."

Wyatt gave me a dubious look. "Run it by me."

"I'm Robin White. It sounds like a talk show host."

"It'll be easy to remember since it's the opposite color. Where are you from, Robin?"

"Right here in Cognito. What if they try to look me up?"

When he turned a sharp corner, I gripped the door. "The

number one rule about pulling off a false identity is making it as close to the truth as possible. Let's pretend you lied about being from New York. Then the guy says, 'Hey, me too. I grew up on Arthur Avenue. Whereabouts are you from? What school did you go to?' That's a rookie mistake. Always keep it close to the truth. The only thing you're changing up is the story about your maker and background."

"So that's why Christian made me a runaway?"

"Nobody will ask what high school you went to, buttercup, and without your given name, they can't find anything. Just stick to the story, because it's not that far from the truth. You're a runaway who's been living on the streets. Your Creator made you and dumped you, so you've been fending for yourself. You don't know who he is, and you don't care. Don't go into details."

I looked out the window. "Believe me, I won't."

"Good. Liars give unnecessary details. Christian knows what he's doing, so just answer questions the way you normally would. When we first met, if I had asked about your Creator or what your gifts were, what would you have said?"

"Fuck off."

"Exactly. Stick with your gut reaction. A runaway living on the streets is a good background, one nobody can trace. But just in case someone decides to do a little poking around, Viktor submitted a fake file to the Mageri. What they don't know won't hurt 'em."

I rolled my window back up as streetlights sliced through the dark car. "Why the Mageri? Criminals can't access their records, can they?"

"We don't know who we're dealing with or what kind of connections they have. Better safe than sorry."

The car shook when we hit a pothole.

"Son of a ghost! Aren't city taxes supposed to fix these blasted roads? I've already had two flats this year. One of these days, the whole damn axle's going to fall off. Might as well go back to horse-drawn wagons."

He weaved to the curb and hit the brakes with enough force

that I threw my hands out to keep from hitting the dash. It was a wonder he hadn't killed anyone with his safety hazard of a car.

I glanced around but saw no sign of the club.

"Can't drop you off at the front door," he said, noticing my wandering gaze. "You're on your own from here. The club's a block up to the right." Wyatt glanced down at my legs. "You should have brought a purse. When you go to the hotel later, the guy at the desk will give you a card key."

"These better be comfortable shoes," I grumbled as I climbed out of the car and crossed in front until I reached the sidewalk.

Wyatt leaned out the window. "See ya later, Robin." After a wink, he hit the gas. His tires squealed as he did a U-turn in the middle of the street and sped off.

As I ventured up the sidewalk, I fell back into familiar habits and concealed my light. People with downcast eyes were easy targets, so I held my head high and made direct eye contact with everyone. Nothing went unnoticed. Fire escape ladders, buildings with easy access points, discarded items in alleyways I could improvise as weapons—funny how you never let go of things like that. Viktor had warned me this assignment could go on for weeks or months, so I needed to learn my surroundings.

At least I didn't have to work two jobs like Claude.

When I reached the White Owl, I cased the outside of the club. There wasn't a sign with the club name anywhere in sight, only a neon owl in a red circle. The painted logo on the door had a Breed mark below it, but those were the only two indicators that I was at the right place. I gazed up at the three-story building and wondered if the windows were fake. No light came from them. Maybe they were painted over.

The crowd lined up outside the metal door appeared human. Not that humans had any physical difference that made them identifiable, but they possessed certain temperamental characteristics that most Breed didn't. These people had no idea what kind of club this was, only that they needed to check it out.

The doorman's muscular physique and blank expression came

off as intimidating. When I cut the line and reached the door, he held out his arm to block me.

"I'm Robin White."

He slid his mirrored sunglasses down his nose and looked me over. When he flared, I flared back. After a quick appraisal, he slid his sunglasses back in place. "Be sure you get stamped," he said, opening the door.

I entered a dark hall lit with sconces. The next door was heavy, and when I pulled it open, music flooded into the hall. It wasn't uncomfortably loud, but they had excellent soundproofing in this place. Shepherd had used a blueprint that Wyatt dug up and compared it to the actual layout. After returning from the club, he'd sat down and gave me a walk-through.

But nothing prepared me for the Saint Andrew's cross. The man strapped to it wore shorts smaller than mine, and I guessed he was just décor since nobody was paying any attention to him.

My nervous energy was pinging off the walls, so I took a deep breath and reminded myself that this was just a job. I'd grown used to our regular haunts during the past year, but now I was alone and out of my element. Being half-naked and unarmed didn't help.

"Wanna play?" A shirtless Chitah gave me a toothy grin. Displaying fangs, regardless of Breed, was rude if not a form of aggression. But clearly the rules didn't apply here.

I slinked through the crowd, taking it all in. This place wasn't filthy at all. I'd imagined people having sex on tables, and while sexuality was on full display, nothing lewd was happening. Some were scantily clad in provocative attire, while others wore jeans, suits, and even fedoras. The spacious room had passages that led to other areas. Opulent chandeliers hung in the lounge to my right, showering a frosty glow onto the low tables and lush red and gold furniture. In the center of the room, a red strip of light ran beneath an oval-shaped bar. While I couldn't see the other side, I presumed there were barstools there as well. An accent piece hung from a gold-paneled ceiling, and the bottles in the center were sparkling like Christmas ornaments on a tree. Meanwhile, dancers were seducing the crowd from platforms or gilded cages. Performers and customers alike didn't fall under any category of specific beauty. Two tall brunettes were orbiting a slender man, who was short in stature, vying for his attention. A large woman in lace entertained a Chitah who knelt at her chair and kissed her fingers.

I approached the bar and flagged one of the two bartenders.

A stunning woman in a sparkly black bra and leather skirt looked in my direction while pouring a drink. Her jaw set, and I turned around to see what had caught her attention.

A redhead stood slack-jawed with a leash in her hand. The other end was attached to a collar worn by a rawboned man in leather pants. His mask was similar to mine, and though I couldn't see his eyes very well, I noticed his flushed neck and balled-up fists as he raised his voice to a seated man who, evident by his salacious smile, had done something to offend him. The instigator laughed haughtily, and with that, the leashed man pounced and flipped the table over. The redhead lost control of her submissive and the situation as a whole.

With lightning speed, the bartender hopped over the bar and into the fray. The man on bottom snarled like a wild animal, and people stepped back as if a lion might thrash through his skin.

The bartender grabbed the leash and yanked the man off. "Bad boy. Bad!"

Then she knelt down and straddled the other man, her hands flat on his chest. A red glow pulsed beneath her palms, and a few seconds later, he shifted into a whimpering brown wolf.

The redhead rushed to the flustered man and collected his leash before leading him away. Chairs and tables were righted by men in black attire, and after the spilled drinks were cleaned up, one of them carried the wolf away.

Cool and collected, the bartender strutted toward me, not a hair out of place on her short Mohawk. When she turned and nodded at someone, I admired the shaved designs on the side of her scalp. She tipped her head to the side with a half smile, a look of "Same shit, different night" on her face.

"You're new here," she said, flipping up the counter and crossing into the bar.

"How can you tell?"

She winked. "You get to know the regulars. What's your poison?"

"Tequila. But I probably shouldn't drink on the job. I'm the new bartender."

She gave me a long appraisal before filling a shot glass with tequila. "Since this is your first night, I'll allow it. Want any sensory magic?"

"What?"

She slid the glass in front of me and ran her finger around the rim. "Do you want me to spike your drink to boost your confidence or get rid of those nerves?"

I shook my head.

She poured herself a glass of club soda and then rested an elbow on the bar. Our glasses clinked together, and I downed my shot.

"I'm Simone."

I grinned. "I used that name once."

When I caught my flub, I wanted to bang my head against the wall.

Her head jerked back. "What do you mean by that?"

I laughed and set down my glass. "When I was eighteen, I got a fake ID to get in all the cool clubs. I'm Robin."

Simone had full, beautiful lips and cunning brown eyes. She looked at me as if I were a puzzle. "What's your Breed? I have to know who's got my back." She spoke purposefully, like a serpent moving through the grass.

"Mage."

She set down her glass. "Great. Just what we need, another Mage."

"Why do you say it like that?"

"They come. They go. Sensors are better for a job like this. We don't just serve beer. You have to be on your toes, and if you're scared to get physical, this isn't the job for you."

"What did you do to that guy? I didn't think Sensors could make someone shift."

She set our glasses beneath the bar. "It's a little trick I learned.

Gave him a taste of his own medicine. We have a rule around here: you don't touch *anyone* on a leash. Only their handlers are allowed to touch them. He broke that rule. I saw him pat the man's ass when he walked by, and that gets him a swift kick out the door. He'll be lucky if the owner lets him return."

The man who had thrown out the wolf leaned over the bar, tattoos all up and down his arms. "Simone, do you really have to put a fright in them? He pissed all over my leg." The man's British accent caught my attention.

Simone threw back her head and laughed as she made her way down the bar to fill orders.

"Women are wicked little creatures." He scooted onto the stool. "I should have never broken her heart."

"You didn't break my heart, Flynn," she said loudly. "Just my bank account."

Flynn nonchalantly turned toward me. "A bit of advice, love? Never shag someone you have to work with. When a relationship ends, there should be a law that you never see them again."

I shifted my stance to face him. "Maybe you shouldn't have been a dickhead."

Flynn had crazy brown hair, like a man who had never seen a hairbrush. He stroked his short beard and looked me over. He seemed more interested in my legs than anything else. "Did you come to play? I'm suddenly feeling a bit randy."

"Leave her alone, Flynn. That's Robin."

"The new girl?" Flynn gave a mischievous smile. "You don't say?"

Without warning, he grabbed my wrist and smacked my arm with his other palm.

I reflexively punched him in the throat, put his head in a lock, and then threw him to the ground.

Simone leaned over the bar to look at him and then gave me a nod. "You'll do."

A glow caught my attention, and I looked down. The light on my upper arm was in the distinct shape of an owl.

"It's your stamp," Simone said matter-of-factly as she popped the lid off a beer bottle and handed it to a topless woman. "It only lasts a week, so you'll need him to give you a new one every seven days. If you're still here, that is."

I rubbed at the mark. Instead of ink, it was as if someone had tattooed electricity onto my arm. "What's wrong with using a stamp?"

"Regular ink doesn't show up well in these dim rooms. On a white girl like you, maybe. But we need our crew to stand out at all times. These glow, so there's no confusion as to who works here. Nobody can sneak in as a worker because they can't replicate our stamp. Just be sure you cover it up when you leave the club."

We continued ignoring Flynn, who was still gasping for breath on the floor.

"How the hell did he do it?" I asked.

She wiped off the bar with a clean rag. "Flynn is a Mage of many unique talents. He uses a special ink with liquid fire."

My eyes widened in horror. "Wait a minute. You said this comes off in a week."

"It does."

"Liquid fire is permanent."

Flynn pulled himself to his feet while rubbing his throat.

"I warned you to stop doing that." Simone clucked her tongue at him. "You think every woman is graced by your touch."

He coughed while taking a seat on the stool, not irritated at all by my throat punch. "Liquid fire seals injuries to your skin. When you get a tattoo, the needle penetrates. I don't."

Simone chuckled but said nothing.

Flynn opened his right hand to show me an owl tattoo. "When I draw an image on my hand with special ink, I can transfer my light through the liquid fire. It binds my light to your flesh, creating an exact replica of the pattern. Temporarily, of course."

"Nifty. So you draw that thing on your hand every night?"

"What else have I got to do? Watch reruns of *Fantasy Island*?"

Simone had the same mark on her inside forearm. I hadn't noticed before, but she moved around a lot and there were too many distractions.

"Flynn, give her the tour. When you're done, bring her straight down. We're about to get busy in the next hour."

He plucked a pair of orange glasses with round lenses from his shirt collar and made sure they weren't broken before putting them on. "Whatever you say, my queen."

Chapter 7

Flynn escorted me through the first floor to show me all the sections. The caged dancers were part of the show but not the main attraction. The White Owl gave people absolute freedom to express themselves without judgment. Some were engaged in intimate conversations while others role-played under the watchful eyes of onlookers.

Flynn gestured toward a door. "That's the loo."

The symbol on the door was a man and woman holding hands.

"It's for everyone," he explained. "If you want privacy, I suggest using the staff room in the back."

"What's the big deal?"

"These don't have stalls. It's all very… voyeuristic."

"That's the worst first date I could possibly imagine."

He barked out a laugh. "Nobody comes here to find true love. They come to play and to watch. To fantasize. For some blokes, peeping in the loo is a fantasy." We passed a long row of black doors with sliding peepholes. "They come to escape. Have a look."

I leaned forward and slid open the cover.

"The window is mirrored on their side, so they never know when someone's watching them," he explained, leaning against the door.

A woman in nothing but candy-red heels was choosing an outfit from a clothes rack. She held a gold dress up and looked at herself in the corner mirror. A red love seat faced the door, and I wondered if this was her fantasy or one she might be playing out for someone else.

"On *this* floor, we have strict rules. One person per room. Otherwise, it's hard to keep an eye on them all and things can get messy."

I slid the latch closed. "What do *you* do around here?"

He pushed away from the door and led me to the stairs. "I'm part of the cleanup crew."

I wrinkled my nose.

"Don't get the wrong idea," he said, smiling at me over his shoulder. "I pick up broken chairs, clean spilled drinks, toss out rule breakers, put people on the naughty list, and keep the place spotless and copasetic. So that means I've got my eye on everyone, making sure they follow the rules. The owner doesn't want his fantasy club turning into a cheap brothel."

"How the hell do you police that in a place like this?"

We reached the top of the wide, carpeted stairs, and he stopped at the door. "The bartenders keep the peace. They handle the fights on the floor, and my blokes keep everything else in order. We enforce the rules, and most people follow them. The consequences mean getting blacklisted, and to be honest, there aren't any other clubs like this one. They've gone downhill by attracting the wrong sort. People are shagging in the open and all kinds of sordid things. Customers don't come here for that." He glanced down at my feet. "Hope those are comfy. You'll be standing for a long time."

The red-and-gold theme carried throughout the club, and while each level was more explicit than the last, I didn't see anyone engaging in any sex acts. Simulated? Yes. Touching? Yes. And a whole lot of sexual role-playing I'd never seen before. There were chairs and other adult equipment, panthers on leashes, sensory exchange for either fun or profit, and some corners were set aside for the hard-core stuff—like whipping and masochism. The private rooms weren't private. Anyone could walk in or watch through the viewing windows. Each level had a bar, and I gathered that most of the bartenders were Sensors by the way they were spiking the drinks. As we walked, men and women approached me, asking if I wanted to play in whatever fantasy they were engaged in. But once they noticed the owl on my arm, they backed off.

When we returned to the first floor, Flynn nudged me. "What do you think?"

"I don't see any Vamps in here."

"We have a policy about the famously fanged. Our customers don't want to be near anyone who might snitch. Vamps are notorious charmers who blackmail for a living. Aristocrats snub places like these, but I've seen many a Councilman sneak through the doors with a mask on their face. Aside from all that, the only way to control Vampires is impalement wood, and that's not in the budget. A peckish one might bleed someone dry. And that's not the worst of it. They can do serious damage, and not just to the walls and furniture. I've got twenty-four ribs in my chest, and I aim to keep them. The younglings don't know their own strength." Flynn continued our walk. "So, are you up for it?"

"As long as nobody touches me, I'll be fine."

Flynn jumped in front of me. "If anyone touches you without consent, let me know who the scamp is, and I'll take care of it. It's not just the leashed we protect. We have rules about staff, and anyone who disobeys those rules gets blacklisted. Got it?"

I folded my arms and tilted my tattooed arm toward him. "Including you?"

Flynn sighed and gave me a little eye roll. "That was different."

"Grab me again and you'll find one of my heels in your eye socket."

"Duly noted." He tipped his orange glasses down his nose while looking behind me. "We part from here."

Flynn danced off toward a group of people in latex. They were lounging on large plush sofas, ignoring the panther that was knocking glasses off a low table.

Flynn literally had the worst job in this place from what I could tell.

When I reached the bar, I lifted the counter to make my way behind it. "Where do you want me?"

"Everywhere," Simone said. "Beer coolers are down below, but ask if they want tap."

I glanced down at the coolers. "Are you kidding me? There's only one brand."

"Of course there is. We only sell Breed beer from one distributor."

"Is there any difference?"

Simone patted her hand on the bar. "The difference is the money doesn't go to humans. It goes to a local brewery run by Shifters, and Shifters are the ones who order it most. Hard liquor is on the wall behind you."

"Breed alcohol?"

She smiled and pinched my chin. "You're catching on. We have red and white wine but no varieties. And we only accept cash," she said, pointing to a sign. "If anyone wants to open a tab, use their alias ID to enter into the system. You won't have to do that often since almost everyone pays in cash. People don't come here to drink all night long, but they like a little to loosen up."

Simone gave me a quick demonstration of how to use the computer, which looked cut and dry.

"Keep the bar clean. Spilled magic is messy, and it'll hurt our reputation. If someone orders a Sensor special, fix the drink and hand it to me. If I'm not available, grab Rena on the other side." Simone pointed to a row of sinks. "That's your cleaning station. Make sure you rinse all the magic off the glasses and toss the dirty rags. We have an endless supply under that cabinet."

"Got it."

Simone took a clean rag and wiped a wet spot on the wood bar. "That's what they all say."

"Why do you think Sensors are better for a job like this?"

"The owner wants more like you, but I do just fine. Also, a Mage is pretty useless at spiking drinks."

Simone cracked open a beer bottle and handed it to an older man in an expensive suit. "It's always a pleasure seeing you, Mr. Crawford. Let me know if you need anything else." The gentleman tipped his head and carried his beer across the room.

"He didn't pay you," I said. "Why didn't you open a tab?"

"That's Mr. Crawford. You don't *ever* ask him to pay." She pointed to a laminated menu on the bar. "Memorize the prices."

A woman sidled up. "I'll have the same."

I popped off the lid and set her beer on a napkin. "Why doesn't he pay?" I asked Simone, returning to our conversation.

"The owner has a short list of VIP customers. I'll keep an eye out and show you who they are. The *why* is none of our business. Good luck, and wear something cooler. It gets hot back here."

Cooler? Was she kidding? I was practically naked in these nothing shorts and corset.

A burly man slid a few bills across the bar. "Vodka neat."

After serving him, I put the money in the till and realized I had no pockets for tips. "Simone?" I waved a few bills.

Many human bars divided the tips, so I wasn't sure of the protocol. Simone gestured under the bar, where I found two black boxes. One had a decorative *S* by the slot, so I put my money in the one beside it that had no name or letter.

When I stood up, I nearly howled with laughter.

Claude set a serving tray on the bar and dazzled me with his shimmering torso. "One screwdriver and a pint."

I leaned across the bar and admired his gold shorts. "Where do you keep *your* tips?"

Placing his hands on the bar, he gave me a curt look. "The red box with my initials."

When I glanced underneath the bar, I spotted five boxes on a different shelf—each a different color and labeled with monograms.

"Can I get an Angel's Kiss?" A bald man with crisp blue eyes gave me an impatient look.

"What the hell's that?" I murmured to Claude.

Simone appeared and filled a glass with a red liquid before swirling her finger inside. After serving the man, she pointed to a row of colorful bottles on a lower shelf behind us. Each had a label with an unusual name. "Most people order the standard drinks, but if you get something you haven't heard of, find the bottle behind you and fill a glass. Then give it to me. I'll give it back to you, and we split the tip since I did half the work."

"Are you kidding me?"

She shrugged and walked away. "That's why we have a high turnaround with your kind."

"That's bullshit," I muttered.

Claude frowned, and the cloth tied around his eyes did nothing to conceal his disapproval. "Do you really care?"

"We need to pretend we don't know each other."

Claude took the drinks with a reluctant sigh and swaggered across the room to a sectional. Two men wanted to slip money into his shorts, but Claude collected his tips and walked off. He had the same light tattoo as me, only his was on his lower back. Probably so customers could admire his body without the distraction.

At least he wasn't one of the dancers.

Eight hours into my shift, I wanted to rip off my corset and dive into a swimming pool. Did the air vents even work? I hadn't noticed. When the club got busier, I was constantly on the move. As it turned out, most people ordered Sensor-spiked drinks. The majority of the bottles behind me were vodka. Nothing special, someone had just added color to brighten them up. Selling spiked bottles was illegal, so that meant handing over every single glass to either Simone or Rena. It cut my tips in half—not that I should have cared since this wasn't my real job, but it was the principle of the thing.

Clearly there was a hierarchy among workers, which placed bartenders at the top of the food chain and Flynn's crew at the bottom. I hadn't met the manager yet—apparently she kept busy on the upper floors. And I was still trying to get used to handlers leading customers around by a leash as if they were pets. That turned out to be pretty popular—at one point there was a scramble when new people came in and couldn't find a handler. Some of the handlers ended up walking three submissives at once.

Another girl came in to take Rena's place on the second shift. Simone worked both shifts, and I remembered her remark to

Flynn about money. She was probably trying to recoup whatever he'd pilfered from her.

I spotted Shepherd skulking about, striking up conversations with customers and reading emotional imprints.

When we finally hit a lull, Simone held one of those little electric fans in front of her face. "Did Flynn show you the staff room? That's where we take our breaks."

"Yep."

"It's clean, so you can eat in there. Just don't leave behind a mess. Keep your street clothes in a locker and change before you leave."

"How do I know which lockers are available?"

"The ones that don't have a padlock. If you don't want someone stealing your valuables, bring a lock. I keep a close eye on the tips, but we've had a few things go missing from people who didn't secure their lockers." She returned the fan to a lower shelf. "Do me a favor and watch the tip boxes. I'm taking a break." Simone slinked around me and then gripped my arm. "And if I ever catch you stealing my money, I'll cut you into a million pieces."

After she sauntered off, I headed to the far end of the bar and worked my way around.

"Give me a Tickler."

"You'll have to wait," I informed the man with the Viking beard. "How about a pint to tide you over?"

"I asked for a fucking Tickler. Are you new around here? Because I'm not, and this isn't how you treat customers."

Irritated, I grabbed the green vodka and filled a glass. I wanted to keep my eye on the tip boxes, and that meant not abandoning my station. "Hey, can you tickle this?" I asked the blond bartender on the opposite side of the bar. I could see her through the gaps in the center shelves. "Sorry, I don't know your name."

"Busy," she said tersely.

Yep. She was giving me the cold shoulder.

"Just put your fucking finger in the glass. Pretty please."

"You mean this finger?" She gave me the middle finger before serving a large order.

I grumbled and headed back to deliver my virgin drink to the Viking.

"Whiskey on the rocks!" someone called out.

I poured drinks, moved fast, and collected my tips like a robot.

"Hey, are you trying to screw me over?" the Viking asked. "This isn't spiked."

"I said you'll have to wait," I fired back.

"You can't just serve me a virgin drink and expect to get away with it."

As he looked for another bartender, I noticed the leather collar on his neck. Viktor *did* say I needed to stand out. I put my hands on the counter and glowered. "You'll take whatever the hell I give you."

He furrowed his brow. "Do you think I'm gonna pay for it?"

I leaned in and locked eyes with him. "Oh, you're gonna pay for it. And when you finish that glass like a good boy, you're going to order another. If you've got a problem with taking orders, you can lick my boots."

His lips parted, and he slowly downed his drink.

"That goes for anyone else," I said, speaking to the onlookers who weren't used to seeing the bartender lose their shit. "Until Simone gets back, you'll take whatever the hell I give you. I'm in charge here. If anyone decides to stiff me on a tip, I'll hurt you so bad that you'll scream like a newborn."

People surrounded the bar, and a line formed.

"I'll have a beer," the next man said.

I filled a glass and set it on a napkin.

"I wanted a bottle," he said meekly, his pupils dilated.

I lifted his glass and gulped it down. "When you learn how to behave, I'll give you a refill. Next!"

He left bills on the bar before hurrying off to a nearby table. The next man approached and wanted a whiskey sour. Instead, I grabbed whiskey, ice, bitters, lemon, and a sugar cube.

"That's not a sour," he said glumly.

I set the old-fashioned on a napkin. "That drink isn't you. *This* is you. Understood?"

With a salacious glint in his eyes, he left me a stack of bills and trotted off with his drink.

Before I knew it, handlers were standing in line with leashed customers. I was attracting a certain type of crowd, and they tipped whatever I asked them to tip.

After some time, Flynn stopped by and rested his inked arms on the bar. "You've got a knack for this. Simone won't like you stealing all the good tips."

"I doubt I'm the first who's ever done this," I said while cleaning a glass.

"Most people here like their job, and they follow the rules so they won't get fired. That usually means not yelling at the customers." He wagged his finger at me. "You're a rebel."

"So I've been told."

My eyes widened when a panther sprinted across the room and pounced on a man. "Watch the bar!"

I flung up the countertop and flashed across the room. A female worker in all leather ran over and tried to grab the leash on the panther, but she couldn't get close enough. The man waved a chair like a lion tamer.

I sharpened my light as I moved in. Shifters made my pulse jump. Gathering my courage, I gripped the panther's collar and gave it a hard yank.

"Down!" I ordered him. "*Get down.*" I held out my left hand, ready to blast him if he so much as turned in my direction.

The panther growled fiercely and then retreated.

"Thanks." The walker collected his leash and wrapped it once around her wrist. "He's not usually like this, but that man wouldn't stop pestering him."

I raised my eyebrows. "Did he touch him?"

She nodded. "They can't pet Shifters. It's not allowed."

"I'll deal with it."

After she led the feline away, I yanked the chair out of the man's hands. "You broke the rules. You're out."

He tucked his shirt back in. "Misunderstanding."

"The misunderstanding was you not paying attention to the rules. *Out.*"

He held up his hands. "Won't do it again. No need to get your panties in a twist."

Based on the fact he hadn't fought the panther, I guessed he wasn't a Mage. So I gripped his forearm and yanked him forward. Before he could resist, I blasted him with my other hand. He recoiled and threatened me with his red, glowing palms.

Damn Sensors.

Sharpening my light, I widened my stance. "I'm only gonna ask once."

"Touch me and I'll touch you back." He grinned at the challenge and wiggled his fingers.

I hurled a chair at him. Before it hit the ground, I flashed behind him and kicked the back of his knee with my heel. When his knees buckled, I grappled his shoulders and slammed enough volts in him to make my point crystal clear without killing him. As he fell to the ground, the man seized my hands, and an unbearable pain engulfed me like an inferno.

I shrieked and wrenched my hands away. My mind knew that nothing was happening to me, but every nerve ending in my body convinced me I was burning alive, and I desperately slapped my arms as if putting out flames. When that proved a waste of time, I grimaced and found the courage to fight through the agony long enough to knock him unconscious with another blast of energy.

Then I kicked him once for good measure.

As my skin cooled, it was as if someone had tossed ice water onto my raw, burned flesh. The magic wasn't wearing off fast enough, so I stalked to the bar, stole a drink from someone's hand, and downed it.

Sweat beaded on my brow. When I noticed the line of customers watching me, I waved them off. "Find another bartender. I'm taking a break."

Once behind the bar, I poured a double shot of tequila.

Flynn clucked his tongue. "You have to watch out for Sensors. The manager thinks they make good bouncers, but people like us are the only ones who can control a situation."

"Us?" I returned the tequila bottle to its home. "I didn't see *you* doing anything to help."

He shrugged. "Not in my pay grade. If they give me a raise, I might pitch in. But I don't earn tips, and my shit wages aren't enough to risk my neck." Flynn glanced over his shoulder and sighed as he pushed away from the bar. "Do me a favor and don't break so many chairs next time. I have to crawl around and look for the small bits of wood." He trudged off toward the mess and then dragged the Sensor out of the building.

An elderly man in a fine suit took the barstool across from me. "That was an impressive show."

I recognized Mr. Crawford, Simone's VIP. "Would you like a drink? Beer, right?"

He laced his fingers together and smiled, so I served him a cold beer.

After sipping his drink, he set the bottle on the napkin and gave me a congenial grin. "I'm John Crawford."

"R-Robin White," I said, almost slipping and saying my real name.

"What did he give you?"

Uncertain of what Crawford meant, I frowned.

"The Sensor," he clarified. "What did he make you feel?"

A regular signaled for two more beers, so I quickly served him. "Fire."

"Yowzer." Mr. Crawford rested his chin against his fist. "You seem like a tough broad. I've heard a firebrand can sting for hours."

"So can my energy punch."

He chuckled as he scooted off the barstool. "I just wanted to introduce myself since you're new. I hope to see you again, Miss White."

As I watched him walk away, I considered how careful I needed to be when fighting Sensors. I'd spent so much time training with Niko and Christian that it hadn't occurred to me to ask Shepherd for pointers. I'd never considered Sensors a threat.

Until now.

Chapter 8

When I reached my hotel, I collected my card key from the manager and took the elevator up to my room. *Man, what a night.* Someone was supposed to have left a bag in my room with all my approved clothing and personal items.

I could have worked until dawn, but Simone made me go home after hearing what had happened with the Sensor. She probably wanted me to take off early so she could collect more tips. This was starting to feel like my real life and not an undercover job. I could actually envision myself bartending for a living.

Once inside the room, I flipped the light switch by the door and jumped with surprise when I saw a man sitting by the windows. My heart ricocheted in my chest for a brief moment before I recognized him.

Christian stood up. "Didn't mean to put a fright in you."

I tossed my money-stuffed bag that Flynn had lent me on the bed. "Are you supposed to be here?"

He strode toward me and touched my cardigan. "What's this?"

"A loaner. I have to cover myself up walking home."

Christian smiled and traced his finger between my breasts. "They don't arrest anyone for prostitution on this side of town."

"That's not the reason." I shucked off the sweater and let it drop to the floor.

Christian seized my arm and rubbed his thumb over the tattoo. "What the feck is this?"

"My permanent tattoo. I thought about getting a butterfly, but it would clash with my reputation. Like it?"

"Don't be telling me fibs."

"It stays on for about a week, and then he has to reapply it. It's club policy."

"How is it lit up like a fecking Christmas tree?"

"Mage magic, I guess. Some guy slapped it on me when I wasn't paying attention."

Christian gave me a black look. "What shitebag put his hands on you? I want his name."

"Calm down, lover. If it makes you feel any better, Claude has one too, and it's not on his arm." I sat on the bed and stared at his fit body beneath that tight charcoal-grey shirt. After seeing so much skin during the past evening, I had developed a newfound appreciation for modesty. "These boots were comfy."

He knelt in front of me and took them off. "I put those gelatinous inserts inside."

"I don't think that's what they're called, but thanks for looking after my soles."

When Christian rubbed my calf, I winced. His gaze sharpened. "What happened?"

"I got in a tussle with a Sensor. He threw some dirty magic into me. Fire."

Christian let go and turned the onyx ring on his finger. "Do you want me to draw a bath?"

I shuddered at the thought. "No, I'll shower tomorrow. My skin's too sensitive."

Stroking his beard, Christian stood and then rummaged through my bag.

"Don't bother getting out my sleep clothes," I said, stripping off my corset. "I'm sleeping naked tonight. I don't want anything touching my skin."

He leaned against the dresser. "Even me?"

After removing my shorts, I crawled up to the pillows. "Think you can stay away from me for one night?"

Christian's sultry black eyes lingered on my bare breasts before sliding down to my panties. "I miss you already."

"I didn't see your Honda outside."

"Do you think I'm that careless? I parked my motorbike up the street. Viktor had me bring your bags, so I charmed the man downstairs to lend me a spare key. I'm not allowed to stay here on this assignment. Viktor doesn't want to chance it." Christian approached the bed like a panther and sat down. "You've been drinking."

"It was a rough night. I needed something extra before the walk home."

"You should take out your contact lens. You might scratch up your eyeball if you sleep with it in."

I reached up and pulled off the mask. "Why did you hang out at fantasy clubs?"

He brushed a tress away from my face. "Immortals get bored easily."

"Am I boring?"

He bent over until his lips touched mine. "Far from it."

I turned my head away. "I'm not in the mood. I've never been so turned off from sex."

"Something I said?"

"No. I just don't get the whole domination thing."

An enigmatic look crossed his expression.

When the room began to spin, I reached between the two beds and switched off the lamp. My tattoo illuminated the dark like a night-light, allowing me to see Christian perfectly.

"This comforter sure is soft," I said after a wide yawn. "Not like most hotels."

"I had them unwrap a new one from the supply room."

I chuckled softly. "Why?"

"I have exceptional vision. I could see stains on that bedding that would make you shudder. I'll not have you sleeping on filth."

"Since when are you a germophobe? I seem to recall you having sex with a random woman on top of a table in a bar."

He straightened his back. "Now that was entirely different."

"How so?"

"Well, for one, you can wipe down wood. It's not like these linens that have been collecting waste for years. Secondly, in case you haven't noticed, I prefer to stand."

That was true.

"Too bad you can't stay with me on this mission," I said.

"And why's that?"

"Just look at that big picture window over there. We could open the curtains all the way, even flip on the lights. Imagine all the eyes watching us. My breasts smashed against the glass as you pound me from behind."

He put his hand over my mouth. "That'll be enough of that."

I smiled and rested my hand on his lap. "I'm good at this job. I think I found my calling."

He furrowed his brow. "As a dominatrix?"

"No. I meant working as a bartender. I grew up in a bar; it's like second nature."

Christian tilted his head. "And dominating men isn't?"

I squeezed his thigh until I heard a light gasp. "Men and women were lined up at my station, and they *liked* me ordering them around."

"Are you trying to get yourself fired from an undercover job?"

"You didn't see the way they were talking to me. Sometimes you gotta stand your ground. I know Viktor wants me to play a role, but I'll never be a doormat for any amount of money. My father used to always call me an alpha cat as a joke. He didn't like the word *bossy*. Said it was one of those negative labels that people put on strong women. My attitude doesn't get me in trouble in the club. I got more tips in that short amount of time than I did the entire night."

"'Tis a shame I missed it."

I slid my hand farther up his thigh. "If you're good, I'll let you watch me."

"You're a naughty girl, Miss Black."

"But that's what you like, isn't it?"

"Aye."

"Good. Are you sure you're ready for this?"

He licked his bottom lip. "Aye."

I squeezed his thigh and rolled away from him. I needed to get some shut-eye and shake the Sensor-induced fever. "Good night, Poe."

His lips were suddenly next to my ear. "Good night, Precious. I'll be watching."

Christian waited until Raven fell asleep before slipping out. He watched the rhythmic pattern of her breathing, listened to the soft beat of her fierce heart, and fantasized about killing every man who touched her. He couldn't help the compulsive thoughts. They festered. Christian had spent decades learning patience through his job as a guard. He had mastered control and exercised ruthless behavior only when warranted. But with Raven, that old side of him was reemerging. The one that predated his years as a guard, back when he served Lenore.

Viktor had forbidden him from staying with Raven. On undercover assignments, one couldn't be too careful, and his constant presence would pose a security threat. But Viktor didn't mention anything about guarding Raven on her walk home. While Christian couldn't go into the club, he could at least see that she got home safely. As long as he kept his distance and didn't interfere, he didn't see the harm.

Christian fired up his Ducati and rode home in the early light of day. He delighted in the sharp turns, the speed, and the wind in his hair. It was more thrilling at night on a dark road with the headlamps off. Now that dawn had broken, he was trying to get home as quickly as possible before his retinas burned out of his skull.

Once he reached Keystone, he parked his bike in the underground garage and walked toward the mansion. He thought about the disdain in Raven's voice when she mentioned domination. The games they played in the bedroom were tame compared to what she must have witnessed in the club. Whether she realized it or not, her difficulty understanding the pleasure people got from it stemmed from her time with Fletcher. Christian didn't dare bring it up with her, but he'd witnessed what abuse could do to a person. Fletcher had beaten and chained her, performed repulsive sexual acts in front of her as a way to assert his dominance. He'd stolen her light, which was a kind word for energy rape. And to have endured such atrocities from her own Creator? The one who was supposed to mentor and protect her? The one whose light coursed throughout her body?

Christian touched the onyx ring on his middle finger. Raven would always be tormented by those memories, and there wasn't a damn thing he could do about it. As tempting as it was to scrub her mind of the whole affair, it was better that she remembered. Hate was Raven's accelerant. It lit a fire within her soul and made her the woman she was. Fire was what forged Christian into a better Vampire and gave him a tenacious grip on life.

Before reaching the door, he stripped off his dirty shirt. While filling Raven's thermos prior to leaving her hotel, he'd spilled coffee on himself. The drink would probably be cold by the time she woke up, but it mattered little. Christian didn't have much experience wooing a woman, but that was his way of showing his affection for her.

Raven was supposed to work the early evening—same shift as the murdered women. The White Owl opened at roughly five in the afternoon and didn't close until the next morning. Fantasy clubs rarely opened their doors in the daytime. The expense of staying open all hours wasn't worth it, and the limited availability attracted more people. Not to mention, most people didn't want to walk the streets in their leather thong during noontime hours.

With his sunglasses still on, Christian strode into the house. The moment he shut the door behind him, a familiar laugh emanated from the dining room.

"Fecking hell," he muttered, not caring that Lenore could hear him.

Christian entered the short hall, passing a few rooms on the left before reaching the entryway on the right. The booths were empty, and through the windows in the gathering room, he glimpsed dappled sunlight in the courtyard.

"Christian, come say hello to our guest." Viktor invited him over to the long wooden table.

He didn't like that Lenore was sitting in Raven's chair. Reluctantly, he drifted toward them but chose to linger at the kitchen entrance. The breakfast plates still had a few bites of scrambled eggs and toast left behind.

"I was just dropping off my dirty laundry." Christian squeezed the ball of fabric in his hand.

"Let Kira take that when she comes back. She is making *banitsa*. Have you had this pastry? Sit! You must try." Viktor was certainly in good spirits.

Christian draped his shirt over the back of Wyatt's chair and sat down across from Lenore. Her perfume smelled like honeysuckle, and her floral off-the-shoulder dress fit her body like a glove. Lenore had always favored bright colors, and the yellow material complemented her flaxen hair, which was styled in an elaborate braided bun. Her trademark was pulling out wisps of hair to give her a more casual appearance. Lenore never wanted to look overly prim, but these were different times, and nobody gave a shite about rules of etiquette.

Lenore lifted her glass of orange juice and held it close to her lips. "Someone is bright-eyed and bushy-tailed this morning." Her eyes skimmed down to his bare chest and settled on the tattoo. Lenore was a reticent woman, and she still hadn't said anything about his ink. She danced around the topic as if it were a strapping young lad in the center of a ballroom. Instead, she sipped her juice and admired the room décor.

Christian took off his sunglasses. "And to what do we owe the pleasure of your company?"

She set down her crystal glass. "I've heard wonderful things about Mr. Valentine. Not so long ago, your Chitah gave me his business card. I asked around, and he's one of the most sought-after hairstylists in Cognito. Naturally I had to have him. I was afraid he might be booked up until Christmas, so I thought I'd come by and"—she touched Viktor's arm—"see if Mr. Kazan could pull some strings."

Viktor's eyes sparkled as he patted her hand. "Call me Viktor."

"I'm so accustomed to the rigid formalities of the higher authority." She let go and rested her arms on the table. "If only you knew, Christian. So many rules, so many secrets. I had no idea they kept a dossier on everyone."

Christian flicked his eyes up.

"Yes," she said, confirming his bemused look. "Even me. But we're not permitted to look at our own. Technically we're not allowed to look at anyone we're not investigating or prosecuting, but they're flexible when it comes to those you do business with."

Christian shifted in his seat, not only unsettled by the idea that the higher authority kept records on all of them but that Lenore had access.

"Let us not talk about work." Viktor stroked his silver beard. He looked extra dapper this morning. His blue button-up had nary a wrinkle, and the sleeves were neatly rolled to his elbows.

Kira whooshed into the room and presented a round pan with a pastry inside. Then she set down two dessert plates.

"Spasibo, Kira."

Kira wiped her hands on her white apron and returned to the kitchen.

"What a lovely creature," Lenore remarked with the utmost seriousness. "I once wanted to be a redhead."

Viktor cut her a piece of the pastry and set it on a yellow plate. "And what changed your mind?"

"Shifters."

"Ah."

"That isn't the type of attention I invite, even if I'm not a Shifter." Lenore pulled a cloth napkin onto her lap. "Where on earth did you find such good help? I need a servant with her discipline. Someone who knows how to be invisible. Everyone has an agenda these days. Before the higher authority and Mageri, we were allowed to hire humans. They're so obedient—so willing to please. They romanticized the idea of immortality and perhaps hoped we would choose them. Isn't that silly? Aside from that, they don't live very long, so you don't have to worry about someone knowing all your secrets." She winked at Christian. "Now that I'm an official, maybe I should change the laws."

Christian listened while Viktor and Lenore made small talk. He examined her body language and carefully chosen words, but nothing led him to believe she was up to anything nefarious. He'd made her out to be a villain in his mind, but what if she *had* changed? Even he wasn't the same man he once was back in 1921. In any case, he needed to put his pride aside for Viktor's sake. It was always better to be on a person's good side than bad.

"Absolutely decadent." Lenore wiped her mouth and simply beamed. "I don't eat as much as I used to, but how can one resist something so sinful?"

Viktor brushed a few crumbs off his beard. "I will speak to Claude and see what he can do about fitting you in as a personal client. He is currently on an important assignment."

She leaned into him. "Yes, do let me know if there's *anything* you need."

Viktor scooted back his chair, and Christian noticed the man's heart rate had accelerated. He looked uncomfortable. Had Viktor told her about their confidential assignment?

"Please forgive me." His cheeks flushed as he pushed in his chair. "I have much work to do, but I will speak with Claude and see if he can free up his schedule. You let me know a good time. Christian will see you out. It was a pleasure, Miss Parrish." Viktor bowed before leaving the room.

"And then there were two," she said offhandedly. "Sometimes I don't think people have a clue how much they give away in body language. They guard their emotions around Chitahs and Sensors but never Vampires. Why is that? The less people say, the more they reveal."

Christian folded his arms on the table. "Aye. Like the way you haven't mentioned my tattoo."

"Foolish actions are paid in kind. What is there to say?" Lenore took one of those deep, disapproving sighs. "Why would you desire a Mage? They're fragile little things. It's only a matter of time before you break her," she said with derision. "Or perhaps it's something *else* you're addicted to."

He bristled at her accusation. "What you know about our relationship could fill a thimble."

"Oh, Chrissy. I'm only trying to shake some sense into you. We both know that interbreeding never works between Vampires and other races. How long before you two have a heated argument and you crush her skull? And don't say it can't happen. Remember Fernando and his little Shifter companion? He was never the same after her accidental death. I heard he walked into a fire."

Christian drummed his fingers on the table. "I'm glad to hear he finally acquired some common sense. I never did like that fanghole."

"You could do so much better." She lifted her glass of juice and sniffed the contents. "Her eyes are unnerving."

That was Lenore's indirect way of calling Raven a defect for having two different eye colors. In another time, Christian might have lost his temper. But what Lenore didn't know was how strong Raven was, and most especially that she was also half Vampire.

He smiled obliquely at her crass remark, and that seemed to ruffle her prehistoric feathers.

Lenore set her glass back down. "Well, if I can't talk some sense into you, the least I can do is offer you my unwavering support. If you ever need anything, don't hesitate to call. The past is where it belongs, but now that we're both in powerful positions, we can help each other."

"Why don't you help me understand what it is you're doing here at the arse crack of dawn? And don't be telling me fibs about booking an appointment with Claude. There's an invention called a telephone."

"I prefer face-to-face meetings. Besides, I've learned that early morning is the time of day that someone is least likely to be busy with work."

Lenore's skin looked so radiant—so flawless. The gentle blush on her cheeks drew attention to her pink lips. She was never a woman who needed makeup to enhance her beauty. Her delicate features bewitched men, from her stunning black eyes to her sylphlike body. Even in a floral dress, Lenore exuded sensuality. As Christian stared at her sharp chin and slender neck, he wondered how he could have ever been attracted to such an overly feminine woman. While naturally powerful, Lenore had no muscle tone. Her vanilla features were bereft of genuine emotion. And most of all, her eyes were unremarkable and hollow. Christian could spend hours searching Raven's eyes, and he understood her better than she understood herself. She was direct, if not blunt, but he had grown to appreciate her unambiguous personality.

"What I wouldn't do for a drop of your blood," Lenore said quietly.

That was Vampire speak for "penny for your thoughts."

Christian slowly rose from the table, his fingertips pressed against it. "If you don't mind, I need a shower."

Lenore got up and circled the table faster than he could track. When he turned to leave, she captured his wrist. "I want us to be friends again."

"Friends? Is that what you thought of me? A fine thing you did for a *friend*."

"How many times will we have this discussion? If you know what's good for you, you'll move on. Grudges are for the weak."

"When you've spent a decade underground, you can tell me all about moving on." He tried to break her grip, but it was iron.

"You and I are both in key positions," she said quietly. "It would serve Keystone to have me as an ally. I can help you in ways that other higher authority members can't. And why? Because I trust you. I know you would never betray me by telling anyone my secrets, now would you?"

Christian averted his eyes when her gaze intensified. She wanted to know if he'd told anyone about her, and the only two people he might have told were Viktor and Raven.

"And what if I have?"

She tilted her head to the side. "I know you're smarter than that. Do you want to invite turmoil into your life? Do you want to be held accountable for all those senseless deaths?"

His fangs punched out. "Are you threatening me?"

"It's a fact. If you seek to ruin me, you'll only ruin yourself." She cupped his cheek in her hand. "There's no statute of limitations for high crimes against humans. Or Breed for that matter. As far as I'm concerned, you served your time in that coffin. I want to protect you. I taught you to lead with your mind and not with your heart. You *cannot* tell people about your past," she said, putting pressure on his wrist. "You may think you love this woman now, but will it last a hundred years? Five hundred? Will you break her heart so badly that she'll do anything to get back at you, even sink you in your own admissions? Never give anyone ammunition they can use against you, no matter how much you think you can trust them. Men who do that never last in our world." Lenore drew so close that their bodies touched. "I mentored a smarter Vampire than that."

The sound of her pulse filled his ears, and his eyes fixed on the warm blood rushing through the veins just below her skin. It was intoxicating, and she knew it. Lenore stood there as if she were offering heroin to a former addict. His gums ached from the memory.

Distracted by his traitorous thoughts, Christian didn't hear Wyatt bustle in until it was too late.

"My driver should be here any moment." Lenore drew back slowly. "It's always good to see you, old friend."

As she gracefully sauntered out of the room, Wyatt pulled off his loose beanie and stared at her ass. When the front door finally closed in the distance, he turned on his heel and smacked Christian with his hat. "Now that's a twist I didn't see coming. Old friend, huh? My old friends don't glue themselves to me like that."

"It's not what you think." Christian put his hands in his pants pockets.

"I've heard *that* before." Wyatt's eyes rounded when he looked at the breakfast dish. "Say, who made food without telling me?" He circled the table like a vulture and pulled the pan closer. Instead of cutting a piece of the banitsa, he used Lenore's fork to eat straight from the pan. "So *this* is what he serves all the hoity-toity guests," Wyatt said around a mouthful of food.

Christian pushed in his chair. "Shouldn't you be tracking Raven?"

"Unless she's a sleepwalker, I'm on a break. She's not allowed to leave the hotel except to go to work. That way I'll know if something's up. It's the only way I can get some shut-eye, unless you expect me to stare at a screen for sixteen hours straight. In case you haven't noticed, I'm not a Vampire. Though I once stayed up for a record three days."

"Well, isn't that astonishing?"

"Almost went insane." Wyatt licked his fork and stared at Christian. "You two looked… chummy."

"She's an old acquaintance," he replied flatly.

"I'll say." Wyatt gave a sideways smile and took another big bite of pastry before setting the fork down. "Shepherd has a few leads I'm looking into. If any of them look promising, I'll pass that along to Raven."

"What smells good?" Blue strutted into the room in her dark red gown with the bell sleeves. She'd hung the garment by the door the previous night. It was unusual to see her in it during daylight hours, but their schedules were now upside down. "I'm starving."

Wyatt pulled the pan of banitsa closer to him like a dog guarding its bowl. "Just the person I wanted to see. How did the phone work out?"

"No problems. The breakaway design is better than looping something around my neck. You might want to put a rubber case around it."

Wyatt crossed his arms over the back of Raven's chair. "Why's that?"

She rounded the table and yanked the pan toward her. After slicing off a piece, she scooped it up in her hand. "Whenever I shift, it falls on the ground and makes noise. I'm also afraid it'll break." Blue took a huge bite of the pastry, crumbs sprinkling onto the table. "You have no idea how hard it was to restrain my falcon from chasing down rats in the alley. All she wanted to do was hunt. Tonight I'm leaving on a full stomach."

Wyatt cut himself a large piece and held it like a prize against his ratty old T-shirt of a ghost that said: DEJA BOO. The two headed toward the hall. "I'll find a case for your phone. Just be sure to keep it turned off. You don't want it ringing while you're in bird mode."

She patted his shoulder as she walked through the doorway ahead of him. "Thanks, amigo. I'm hitting the sack. This is the most boring assignment I've ever had."

"I'd rather be sitting on a building all night than in my chair," Wyatt grumbled as he followed behind her. "I really need lumbar support."

Christian fell into step beside Wyatt and put his arm around him. "You won't be telling Raven about our visitor, now will you?"

"What do you take me for?"

"A man who likes to stir the pot."

Wyatt put the pastry in his left hand and made a gesture over his chest. "Cross my heart."

"And hope to die?"

"Just don't stick any needles in my eye."

Christian put their heads together as they walked, his voice thick with malice. "Do you? Do you hope to die?"

Chapter 9

A WEEK HAD ZIPPED BY. A week of slinging beer and watching people achieve sexual fulfillment. While I didn't require as much sleep as the average person, I slept for as many hours as I could. The job was tiring, and I needed to stay alert.

Christian left me coffee in a thermos every morning. Even though he wasn't supposed to be there, and even though I never saw him do it, he did it without fail. Usually it was cold by the time I woke up, so I poured it into a cup and tossed it in the microwave. At least this place wasn't a dump. The vending machines in the hall had oodles of good snacks, cheaper than the ones in Wyatt's overpriced machine. They also served a continental breakfast downstairs early each morning. Unable to leave the hotel in the daytime, I usually ordered a pizza around midafternoon, showered, and watched TV. The monotonous routine made me feel human again.

It also made me feel like the living dead.

My internal alarm clock went off, so I got dressed and popped the contact lens into my right eye. The leather shorts had worked out great, but the corset was ridiculously constricting and hot. If it were up to me, I'd just cut an old T-shirt in half. But the White Owl didn't want its workers looking like groupies at a rock concert, so I'd been wearing a leather bra with two spikes where my nipples were. Leather cuff bracelets were my only accessories; anything else would have been overkill. After pulling my hair up, I grabbed a long duster, my purse, and my mask, and headed out the door.

Breed cops patrolled this district. Insiders in every profession kept Breed business under wraps, so at least I didn't have to worry about a cop pulling me over for dressing like a prostitute.

Once I reached the club, I swung by my station and flagged Simone, who was holding a compact mirror and touching up her black lipstick. "I'm here—sorry I'm late. Give me two minutes."

I knew she heard me, but she didn't look up.

On my way to the employee locker room, I bumped into Flynn. He was always easy to spot in those orange-tinted glasses.

"Did you forget your leather pants today?" I quipped.

"The cleaning crew isn't permitted to dress provocatively. I'm afraid black trousers are all we're allowed."

We avoided two men engaged in sensory magic and headed down a short hall.

"Your shirt is five sizes too small," I remarked. "Is that for tips?"

He opened the door for me. "Already told you, love, we don't earn tips."

"I won't tell."

Flynn plopped down on the black loveseat. "The boss doesn't tolerate deceit. Careful who you talk to around here. There are a lot of snitches."

I leaned toward the mirror and applied my eyeliner. "So why not get a job working tables?"

He crossed one leg over his knee. "I've applied, but those positions don't open very often, and the one that just did was filled by a Chitah."

"What about bartending?"

"In case you haven't noticed, they're all women." He gave me a forced smile.

I crossed the room and opened my locker. "Why is that?"

"Bartenders are women, servers are men. That's the way the owner likes it."

After putting up my bag and coat, I sprayed a mist of perfume on myself. "How do you survive on wages alone?"

His eyes traveled down to my long legs. "Everyone has a side hustle. You're trouble, aren't you?"

I tied the mask behind my head and slammed the locker. "What makes you say that?"

"I can always spot trouble with a capital *T*. Nobody gets in a fight on their first night here. People would kill for your position. And you should know that Simone's not pleased with you."

"Why?"

Flynn got up and approached me like a new sheriff who had just rode into town. "When she heard what you did last week, ordering customers around like a dominatrix, she tried it when you weren't here."

"And?"

He made a nosedive movement with his hand. "Crash and burn. With her, the regulars know it's all an act. But you're new, so they don't know what to expect from you." Flynn's eyebrows touched his hairline as he admired my body again. "I wouldn't want to be in your shoes right now. That section is Simone's turf."

"It was a fluke."

"Rubbish. Do you know how many times I've heard someone asking for Mistress White? They won't stop, as I'm sure you know."

Word *had* gotten around, and customers would linger by the bar in hopes that I'd dish out what I'd served that night. I pushed away from the lockers. "I'm not here to cause problems, but she has nothing to complain about. She takes half my tips for spiking the drinks. Maybe they should spike the bottles and make it a level tipping field."

"Can't. It's a liability for the boss. The higher authority would send Regulators in here faster than a jackrabbit, and nothing spooks people more than those redcoats." He strode toward the door and gripped the knob. "Stay on her good side. It's not easy to switch sections around here, so you're stuck with each other. And nobody wants to be on Simone's bad side. I've been there and back and bought a T-shirt." He opened the door. "After you, milady."

People gyrated to the sexual beat of the music. The air-conditioning ran all day, so by the time the club was ready to open, the air was cool and clean. Somewhere past midnight, all that changed, and the heady smell of sweat, stale cologne, spilled booze, arousal, and Chitah markings permeated every corner of the building.

As I approached the bar, I made contact with everyone I passed, putting their faces to memory and nodding at the regulars.

"Busy night?" I asked Simone as I stepped behind the bar.

"Busy is good," she replied. After serving a customer, she collected a dirty glass and tossed the wet napkin into the trash.

A plump man with beady little eyes approached the bar. "Are you Mistress White?"

I rested my hands on the bar. "Yes."

He swallowed hard, the look of anticipation unmistakable. "I want a beer, and I want it now."

He didn't really want a beer. He wanted to be a bad boy and get a scolding. I'd thought this would blow over after a day or two, but they just kept on coming. I stole a glance of Simone getting stiffed on a tip.

Screw it.

I gave him a sharp look. "Mistress White will give you a drink when she's good and ready. Got it? Until then, I want you to ask Simone for the special. And if you tip her good, I'll deal with you later."

To my surprise, he obediently sidled to the left and ordered from Simone. She gave me a quizzical stare before walking over.

"And what exactly is our special?" she asked.

I dipped out of the man's sight. "Whatever you want to give him. He'll tip you really good, and if he doesn't, let me know. Can you only put emotions in the glass or sensory experiences? Like him getting paddled real hard?"

A smile touched her lips. "I've got just the thing."

I peered around her and noticed the man walking off. "Hey! Did I say you could leave? Sit your ass down like a good boy and take what she gives you. Do you want me to come over there? Because I will." That caught the attention of a few interested parties nearby.

Simone arched an eyebrow. "You're good at this. What did you do before you worked here?"

"This is my first real job, but I've spent my life in bars. I've just never been around people who liked me telling them off."

She touched the shaved sides of her head. "It's a different crowd here. Do you know Clyde?"

"Who?"

"The new server. That tall drink of Chitah over by the lounge."

I followed her gaze to Claude. I'd almost forgotten his alias, one they made similar to his name. That way if I messed up saying his name, people would think I just heard it wrong. "I just met him. Why?"

"I saw you two chatting last night. It seemed a little… familiar."

I grinned coyly and bit my bottom lip. "He's cute. I don't normally go for Chitahs, but have you seen his ass in those shorts?"

Simone reached inside her bra and lifted her breasts to make them appear larger. "Careful where you stake your flag. Flynn's got his eye on Clyde."

"You two dated, right? I thought he was straight?"

She reached on the shelf to my left and lifted a purple bottle. "Honey, Flynn dates anyone he thinks has money, and your golden boy over there is raking in the tips. I wouldn't be surprised if Clyde has a sugar mama somewhere. Or a sugar daddy."

"I doubt it. Who would take a job waiting tables when they've got a sugar-whatever at home?"

A grunt settled deep in her throat as she watched him strut across the room in his tight gold shorts. "We don't get boys that pretty in here."

Maybe Viktor had chosen the wrong team member, but who was left? I sure as hell couldn't imagine Shepherd lumbering around in a pair of gold shorts, and Niko would be out of the question. Christian wasn't allowed in the club, which left Wyatt.

Who just so happened to be walking up to the bar.

My throat went dry.

"I better take care of your naughty customer," Simone said.

"What can I get for you?" I asked loud enough that Simone could hear. Then I leaned in closer to Wyatt and lowered my voice. "What the hell are you doing here?"

Wyatt's grin rivaled that of a child walking through the gates of Disneyland.

"I feel way overdressed." He stripped off his T-shirt and tossed it in a heap on the bar. "Ah. That's better. I'll have a draft."

After filling his mug, I set it on a napkin in front of him.

"Good head." He sipped his drink slowly, which gave me time to serve a few customers who were impatiently waiting. One man in a tuxedo opened a tab, so I ran his info through the computer.

"How much do you make a night?" Wyatt asked.

"Not enough to pay for your overpriced donuts," I muttered.

He rapped his knuckles against the bar. "Do you believe in open relationships?"

"What kind of question is that?"

He leaned in and lowered his voice. "A Vampire friend of mine is in a relationship. I *thought* it was exclusive, but I saw something earlier that has me second-guessing."

I polished a glass, my eyes downcast. "Explain?"

"Let's just say that I saw him getting real chummy with another woman. Maybe I got the wrong idea, but then he asked me not to tell his significant other. He made me promise, but I had my fingers crossed. See, here's the deal. I don't follow the guy code, whatever the hell that is. If you're gonna do something behind someone's back, better not do it in front of me. I don't like to see people get screwed over."

I set down the glass. "Who was the other woman?"

"Some hoity-toity rep."

I gritted my teeth and set down the glass. "You mean he was messing around with a higher authority member?"

"They weren't in bed or anything, but they were standing awfully *close*," he said, making air quotes with his fingers.

Lenore would have it no other way. She must have known that I wasn't around and seized the opportunity. Unfortunately, I didn't have the power to keep a woman of her standing away. She and Viktor were now acquaintances, and as much as it peeved me to imagine her slinking around the mansion in my absence and stalking Christian, I trusted him. Not to the point of foolishness, but he'd proven his loyalty to me. I didn't like surprises, and I'd made it clear that if he had an inclination to cheat on me, I'd rather him tell me ahead of time than find out later.

His odds of survival would be greater.

"So... what should I do about my friend?" he prodded, a genuine look of concern on his face. Wyatt wasn't trying to start a war; I could see he had my best interest in mind. "Maybe he needs a pet dog to keep him occupied."

"I think you should let them work it out," I suggested. "Sometimes things aren't always what they seem. You're in a club where they do some seriously kinky stuff, especially upstairs. People might look at you sitting here and draw conclusions." I leaned in close. "If only they knew that your version of Friday-night fun is doing mushrooms while playing *Super Mario*."

He lifted his mug to his lips. "Touché."

A woman sat next to Wyatt, and her leather top covered every inch of her torso except for her breasts. Wyatt almost spit out his beer when he noticed her.

"Are you Mistress White? Someone told me this is where the naughty girls order their drinks."

Wyatt's grin widened, and his olive-green eyes sparkled when he looked up at me. "What about naughty boys?"

Ignoring him, I crooked my finger and leaned toward the woman. "Go see Simone and ask for the special. Come see me later."

She placed a twenty on the bar and fanned her long lashes. "Will do."

A blush covered Wyatt's neck and upper torso as she walked away. "I've been going to the wrong places all these years for a drink."

I wiped down the bar with a clean rag. "Does that mean you'll be staying for another beer?"

"Afraid not, buttercup. I'm here for another reason. My partner is busy doing the rounds but wanted me to relay a message."

He meant Shepherd, and I glanced over at Simone to make sure she wasn't within earshot. It wasn't uncommon to strike up a conversation with customers, but I didn't want to appear overly engaged.

Wyatt guzzled his drink, his Adam's apple bobbing up and down with each gulp. When he finished, he set the empty mug on the wood top instead of the napkin. Annoyed, I put his dirty glass in the sink and wiped down the bar with his T-shirt before tossing it onto his lap.

Wyatt licked the beer foam on his upper lip. "Your *tip* is under the napkin. See ya later, Mistress White."

Wyatt didn't pay for his beer, and I almost called him back until I saw that he'd slipped a piece of paper under his napkin. I discretely tucked it inside my bra and went back to work.

Just after midnight, I sent another customer Simone's way to smooth things over between us, but they always swung back around to get a dose of verbal abuse from yours truly. I'm not sure what bothered me more: the fact that they liked it or that I was a pro at it.

I'd broken up two fights, so a fifteen-minute break was in order. After sneaking a shot of tequila, I went into the staff room and ran a hand towel under the faucet to freshen up. While both male and female workers shared the same space, everyone minded their own business. Wiping the back of my neck, I waited patiently for two male servers to change into their street clothes. Once they left, I pulled the paper Wyatt had left me out of my bra.

Three names were listed, one of them being Mr. John Crawford. This must have been Shepherd's suspect list.

The door opened, startling me. I quickly wadded up the paper in my hand.

"Easy, female." Claude shut the door behind him. His nostrils twitched, something Chitahs did when reading emotional scents.

My heart pounded against my rib cage, but a deep breath slowed it down. I pitched the towel into the laundry basket and sat on the long counter. "How's your night going?"

"Is it empty in here?"

"I checked the bathrooms. It's clear."

He neared the sinks and wet a towel. "Let me add this to my long list of jobs I never want."

"Why?"

"Whenever I walk through a crowd, they grab me from behind. There's a 'no touch' policy, but when you move through a busy room, you can't pinpoint the culprit in a sea of faces. I'm treated like a piece of meat." Claude angrily washed his armpits. "At least you have a bar between you and them."

"Sorry." I furrowed my brow. "What happened to your pit hair?"

He tossed the towel into the open hamper. "Club policy. Servers can't have excessive body hair. Just as well. I thought I'd never get the glitter off that first night. It looked like a glitter bomb exploded in my hotel bathroom. I'm sure the maid is wondering why, a week later, there's still glitter in my sheets and towels."

I lowered my head to conceal my smile.

"Don't bother," he said. "I can scent your amusement."

"The glitter was overkill, but you looked great."

Claude was sans glitter, but he still had a natural glow to his bronze skin.

"Christian has a twisted sense of humor." He sat on the sink to my left, neither of us dressed in more than our underwear. "Any leads?"

"Wyatt gave me this." I handed him the paper. "Suspects. Don't let anyone see it."

After studying the names, he put the small paper into his mouth and ate it. "I'll see if I can get close to any of them. I've met two."

"Same." I leaned against him for support.

"Someone might walk in," he cautioned me.

"Simone thinks I have a crush on you. Just go with it. If you start running off every time someone walks up, they'll get suspicious. There's no rule against dating coworkers."

Claude's voice softened. "What troubles you?"

HEARTLESS

"The possibility of working this job for the next four months."

It wasn't just the separation from Christian, it was this particular assignment. It was seeing people in power play positions. Domination made more sense because of the power and control. But I'd suffered at the hands of a sadist, so I couldn't comprehend why anyone would choose to be a willing victim.

Or, as they called it, submissive.

I leaned away from Claude. "Have you seen what they do in the rooms upstairs?"

"I've heard, but Chitahs are discouraged from venturing up there. While I understand they have safe words and it's all consensual, my instincts will kick in if I see a male degrading or chaining up a female."

"I saw a man tied to a rack while someone whipped him, and they were whipping him hard. Why the hell would anyone want to be abused like that?"

Claude sighed. "You can't judge someone else's lifestyle based on your own experiences. Places like this are about control, whether it's taking or giving it away. It's also about trust in a safe place. I'm not a psychologist, but you're asking a lot about the submissive roles. What about the dominants?"

My legs rubbed against the sink when I slid off.

"People share a lot of personal stuff at the salon," he went on. "For some, it's a fantasy. For others, they have too much control in life and want to give it to someone else. Abuse victims or those in imbalanced relationships go to these clubs to regain power. But you need to do it for the right reasons or else it becomes self-destructive."

"The right reasons?" I turned toward him, arms folded. "I don't see how there's a right reason to beat someone or—"

"Degrade customers at the bar?" Claude stood up and rested his hands on my shoulders.

I shrugged him off. "*They're* the ones lining up for it. I'm not making anyone do anything they don't want."

His golden eyes narrowed. "Yes, but what is it that *you* want?

Are you treating them that way to fulfill their needs or yours? Think about that."

The door opened, and two women bustled in, their loud chatter filling the room.

"I need a drink," I said.

"It was nice officially meeting you, Robin. Don't be a stranger."

He gave the two women a flirtatious smile as he walked in those clunky combat boots toward the private restrooms.

I stalked back to the bar with a fire in my belly. It had only been a week, and this place was already getting under my thick skin. I hadn't dreamed about Fletcher in a long time, and something about this job was giving me nightmares about the monster who made me. He was out there somewhere, probably in a place like this.

When I reached the bar, I cleared the napkins and empty glasses from my station. Across the dimly lit room, over by the red and black furniture, a white-haired man locked eyes with me. My breath caught. It felt as if the entire universe had cracked wide open.

Instead of provocative clothing, he had on faded jeans and a smart grey jacket with the collar up. Though he looked like a man in his early twenties, his regal features and demeanor set him apart. Arms spread over the back of the sofa, he stared at me as if no one else existed.

I spun around and faced the bottles of liquor.

Simone waved her hand in front of my face. "You look like you've just seen a ghost."

I had.

And his name was Houdini.

Chapter 10

WHEN I TURNED BACK AROUND, Houdini had vanished. Had I just imagined him? Had I drunk too much tequila? Maybe the lights were playing tricks on me. Then again, Houdini wasn't a stranger to clubs. We'd first met in a bar, and after a night of heavy drinking and sharing deep thoughts, he gave me his immortal blood.

Right before abandoning me.

Houdini had assured me it was not done maliciously, and as I'd come to know him better in the past year, I believed him. He didn't commit heinous acts against people. Even when I was his captive, he treated me with respect. Fed me, clothed me, and even protected me from harming myself. But it didn't excuse the fact that he made younglings and sold them on the black market. He justified his actions with such genuine belief that it made me wonder if either he was clinically insane, or I resented him so much that I refused to see the truth. It might have been better if he had won the auction instead of Christian. I wouldn't have the necklace, but I'd have his money, and Lenore wouldn't have walked away with a big chunk of Christian's life savings.

I knocked back a shot of tequila and carried on with my duties, but I couldn't stop scanning the room. People stood in puddles of blue and gold, but not every corner was lit. The influx of customers should have been enough to distract me, but I couldn't stop thinking about Houdini. When I turned around, I bumped into Simone and dropped a glass on the floor.

"Dammit. I'm sorry." I grabbed a dustpan, knelt, and swept up the broken pieces.

"That's coming out of your paycheck, not mine." She stepped around me, avoiding the shards. "And if you keep sneaking drinks, you won't have much of a check left."

I dumped the glass into a trash can. "What drinks?"

She tilted her head and arched her eyebrows to show she wasn't playing around. "I do the inventory."

"Fine."

Simone offered me her outstretched hand. "Maybe you should go home."

"And miss out on all the fun?" I took her hand and stood.

Claude approached the bar and rested an arm on it. "I have a table requesting twenty Red Apples."

Simone looked at him in disbelief. "Which table? Are you sure it was twenty and not two?"

Claude gestured behind him. "That group in the corner by the stairs. And they want twenty."

She put her hand around the neck of a red bottle and gave them a long appraisal. "Do they have a tab open?"

Claude nodded. "Under Abernathy."

"What have they ordered so far? Any spiked alcohol?"

"A pitcher of beer."

"What's the head count?"

"Ten."

She tapped her fingernails against the glass. "Flynn!"

A few seconds later, Flynn waltzed up next to Claude and mirrored his position. "Yes, my queen?"

"I'm sending over ten Red Apples to the group at table five. They tried ordering double shots, but I recognize one of them, and he knows better. I want you and Clyde to keep an eye on them. Robin, pull out the shot glasses."

This sounded interesting. I followed her command. "What's a Red Apple?"

"Not a trip to New York." Flynn threw Claude a smoldering look. "Ever been to New York?"

"Once or twice," Claude replied.

I lined up the glasses while Simone poured.

"If a customer ever asks for a Red Apple, come see me first," she said. "Don't have Rena do it. She's not allowed after the last incident." Once Simone finished pouring the drinks, she conjured up Sensor magic until her fingertips glowed red. Then she carefully dipped her finger into each glass for the same length of time. "A Red Apple is named after the Garden of Eden story. It's a highly potent drink that only a few of us can make. It unlocks desires that people have suppressed—sometimes desires they didn't know they had. This is a premium drink. One hundred dollars per shot."

My jaw dropped. "You're kidding me."

"Clyde, as soon as they're done, clear the table and wipe it down. Wash your hands after handling the glasses, and no more drinks. When a customer orders a Red Apple, we close their tab and cut them off. No exceptions. It's risky mixing sensory experiences with Red Apple." She set the glasses on a tray. "Spread the word. Tell the other servers to put their faces to memory. They know the drill. Don't let anyone at that table order a sensory drink on the sly or accept a drink from someone else. I can't see everyone from here, so I won't be able to keep track. They're *your* special project for the rest of the night."

"It's under control, female," Claude assured her. He collected the tray and sauntered off.

Flynn looked over his shoulder and gave Claude a long, admiring glance. "I haven't decided if he looks better coming or going."

"Going," Simone answered while screwing the cap on the bottle.

"What makes you say that?"

She set the bottle back on the shelf and adjusted her breasts in her bra. "Because no man ever looks good coming."

He gave a boisterous laugh and held up an invisible glass. "Cheers."

A phone rang underneath the bar. One of those old-fashioned phones with a curly cord attached to the receiver.

Without missing a beat, Simone answered. "Yes, sir?"

Flynn grimaced and headed toward Claude's table. He stopped by a pillar and stood guard while Claude set the drinks down.

"Right away, sir. Is there anything else?" Simone nodded and then hung up the phone.

I reached for two beer mugs.

"I got this." She took my glasses away. "The boss wants to see you."

"Why?"

Her eyes widened as she filled the glasses. "I don't know, but the last girl who went to his office never came back."

Hopefully that wouldn't be an issue with me since I wasn't technically here to serve beer. "Is he an asshole?"

She set the beer in front of two men and collected their money. "Never met him."

"You've never met the boss?"

"Not the head honcho. All management issues are handled by Karen. You've never had a real job, have you? Do you think the president of a company has time for the little people?" She turned toward me and shook her head as if this was our last exchange. "His office is the red door near the exit. Good luck."

Fucking hell. I don't have time for this.

On my way to the back, I glimpsed my reflection in a mirror. That messy bun had turned into a waterfall of hair, so I shook it all out and turned on my heel. I nearly jumped out of my boots when I noticed two women engaged in oral sex. As I neared, I realized one of them was wearing a strap-on, and it was all simulated.

"Wanna play?" A butch, leather-clad guy puffed out his chest and gave me a lascivious smile. "I'm a Sensor, and I give it away for free. Third floor, room two."

I flashed my tattoo like a badge.

A rolling chuckle settled deep in his throat, and he arched an eyebrow as if he still wanted an answer.

I shoved past him and kept going. When I reached the red door, I rapped my knuckles against it.

"Enter," a muffled voice said.

I stepped into what looked more like a surveillance room than an office. Numerous screens covered the wall behind the desk, each with clear images of different areas of the building. I saw the activities going on upstairs in private rooms, bartenders serving customers, the front door, and even the employee break room, which made my cheeks heat.

The man had his chair turned facing the wall.

"That's an invasion of privacy," I pointed out. "The employee break room isn't part of the show."

"Yes, but I have to know what my people are up to."

The hair on the back of my neck stood on end. When the chair slowly turned, Houdini greeted me with an impish smile.

Once again, destiny screws me over.

He looked the same. Still wore the black ear studs, still whitened his hair and styled it into chunky spikes. The coat I'd just seen him in was hanging on a wall hook, and his light grey shirt with long sleeves fit him like a glove.

Houdini played with one of his studded earlobes as he dragged his eyes up and down the length of my underdressed body. I hadn't felt self-conscious until that moment, and I folded my arms, only to lower them when the spikes on my bra pricked my skin.

"I almost didn't recognize you with the mask around your eyes. Is that a brown contact lens?" He chuckled softly. "Have a seat, Raven. Would you like my jacket? I keep it a bit chilly in here."

I strutted over to the leather chair, sat down, and crossed my legs. "*You're* the owner?"

Houdini kept his hands on his lap. "I do love a good plot twist, don't you?"

"I thought you were busy selling bloodslaves on the black market."

"It was a lucrative business venture, but then Keystone came along, and we all know how that went. You've made a new man of me. I retired from that life and started anew."

"Bullshit."

He leaned forward and laced his fingers together. "You underestimate how persuasive you can be. Anyhow, I never could make another quite like you, so I decided to retire and give this city exactly what it needs."

"Porn?"

He tilted his head to the side. "Do you see anyone having sex? What we do here transcends intercourse. Sensory exchange is allowed. Binding is allowed." His hazel eyes sparkled. "I sometimes wonder what that might be like, but I'm not a Mage. Have you ever done it?"

"That's none of your business." Incensed by the personal questions, I decided to threaten him with the truth. "My boss knows who you are."

"I doubt he knows anything about me. Nobody does."

"Then I'll tell him."

"I think you're smarter than that. Even if he knew, what could he do? I'm an upstanding businessman, and you have no physical evidence against me for any crime. I scrubbed every youngling I ever made so they wouldn't remember me. And they wanted to be with me. They sought a new life and asked for my blood. Just like you did."

"You tricked me. I'm sure you did the same with them, but I guess it doesn't matter."

Houdini stood up and approached a long counter to my right. When he opened up a lower cabinet, a light popped on like in a refrigerator. After pulling out a bottle of milk, he looked over his shoulder at me. "Would you like some?"

"No."

He poured it into a glass, his back to me. "Then perhaps you'd like a cup of coffee to sober up."

"I'm not drunk."

He wandered back to his seat. "I've watched you pilfer my alcohol when you think nobody's looking. Has this job been *that* difficult? It's nothing you haven't seen before." He took a long drink and turned his chair halfway to look at the screen. "You'd think after centuries, people would grow weary of tits and ass. I have a wealthy customer who's over five thousand years old. He could be spending his time anywhere in the world, but there he is in the dungeon, getting whipped by a woman he dresses in a red wig and royal garb. He supplies the clothes himself, and it makes me wonder where they came from. Sometimes I think this place isn't about sexual fulfillment but a house of lost souls. Many come for fun and exploration, but the older ones just want to role-play some long-lost memory from their past."

"If you hate it so much, why did you open up a sex club?"

"Fantasy club," he said before facing me again. "I have particular standards and won't put up with raunchy behavior. Full nudity isn't allowed on the open floors. Waist up is fine, but I have furniture to consider. Private rooms are the only places you can engage in the next level of play. I have some customers who just stop by for the Sensor-spiked drinks and the atmosphere."

"You should have just opened up a bar."

"But then I wouldn't be able to charge a membership fee. When I tire of this place, I'll sell it for a small fortune. Always go where the money is, Raven. If there's anything I can teach you, it's to acquire assets. But… we've been over this before. Someday you'll either thank me or kick yourself, because in the end, wealth is the only thing that'll bring you comfort. People come and go. Societies come and go. Inventions, fashion—all the modern conveniences that have spoiled you will be gone in a hundred years, and you may not be equipped to survive in an unknown future. Don't belong to anyone, because when they're gone, you won't know how to fend for yourself. You'll wind up working in places like this and living in the Bricks," He took another sip of his milk and licked his lips. "Districts like those have a bad reputation, but you misunderstand their purpose. It's not just a place for criminals; it's a refuge for those who are ill-equipped to survive in today's world. They don't understand the technology. They don't agree with the rules of the establishment, and I'm fairly certain that you don't entirely agree with them either. But living in the Bricks will isolate you from living free."

"Don't *you* live in the Bricks?"

He gave me an enigmatic smile and sat back. "I live lots of places, Butterfly."

"Are you behind the missing girls? It wouldn't be the first time that girls go missing when you're around."

His face went rigid, and he reached for his milk. "Do you really think I'd be stupid enough to recruit my own staff in nefarious activities?"

I barked out a laugh. "Since when are you above cage fighting? I bet it's a lucrative investment, and it's probably easier to vet potential candidates in a place where you see them every day."

"You think you have me all figured out, don't you?" He wiped his upper lip. "It's illegal."

"You and I both know that you don't obey the law."

"Neither do you."

I uncrossed my legs and leaned in. "Simone said one of the girls came in here to see you and was never seen again."

Houdini's dark eyebrows slanted over his hazel eyes before he tipped his head back. "Ah. You mean Willow. I caught her sneaking into one of the rooms upstairs and performing sex acts for money. That's against my rules. She was escorted out the back door and banned for life. I don't give second chances."

I glanced up at the moving images. "So if you're not behind it, show me the footage of the night the girls disappeared. Maybe I'll recognize someone they were talking to."

He polished off his milk and stood up. "I would, except that I don't record anything."

"You run all these cameras and don't record?"

He set his glass in the sink. "It's against the law." After a moment of silence, he turned around and rested his hands on the counter behind him. "You might not believe this, but I'd like to run my club without the higher authority sticking its nose into my business. I have no choice but to conform. That's what smart men do. Those who balk about their circumstance will never adapt."

"What's the point of cameras if you don't record?" I threw up my hand. "Never mind. I think I can guess."

Houdini snorted. "I'm sure you can. The cameras are all hidden; not even my staff knows about them. There's no law against running them so long as they aren't recording. They came with the establishment."

I put my foot on his desk and then crossed my other one over it. "I've got a job to do, so any information you can give me would be great."

Houdini approached the desk and leaned against it, next to my feet. "I told the Regulators everything I know. Now *you're* here. What an auspicious sign."

"You didn't specifically ask for us?"

"I asked for them to let me handle it, but the Mageri got involved when they heard about the deaths. You know how difficult they can be, so I agreed to work with the higher authority and hire undercover investigators. Then I heard a Mage with black hair showed up, so I had to come see for myself. Better it was you than one of the others on your team."

When he touched the heel of my boot, I put my feet on the floor.

"What a pity your Irishman couldn't join you," he said. "But I don't allow Vampires."

"Hypocrite."

"No one knows what I am. Not many here even know *who* I am. It keeps them on their toes if they think I might be in the crowd watching."

He rested his palms on the desk and fell silent. Random images from the screens behind him lit up the room. Women dancing, men serving, someone getting paddled in a hallway, a woman strapped in a bizarre swing. As I watched a man with a ball gag crawl down a hallway behind his mistress, I realized how completely tame those rituals were in comparison to what was going on in the private rooms. Why in the world did Houdini watch this stuff? I remembered him once telling me how nudity bored him, and yet here he was, running a fantasy club.

"Do you still have my key?" he asked.

"You shouldn't obsess over something that never belonged to you."

His fingers gripped the edge of the desk until I heard the wood pop. "I only want what's mine."

I stood up and circled behind his chair, briefly glancing up at the screens before staring at the back of Houdini's head. "I'm here to figure out why girls are dropping like flies. I heard some of your staff fled before questioning. Something's going on around here, and I don't see how you *couldn't* know about it."

He swiveled around, and the apathetic look on his face gave little of his thoughts away. "Because I'm rarely here. And what do I care? My only concern is filling the positions and keeping this place profitable. What my employees do in their spare time doesn't interest me."

"Even if it kills them?"

"You have a dangerous job, Raven. You could die. Does that mean your boss is a sadistic monster?" Houdini gave a one-sided smile, the kind that crept up your face when you had a wicked idea. "Maybe I should be concerned and save you. Is that what you want? Someone to rescue you from your decisions?"

"You've made your point." The sincerity in his question made me take a step back. "When Christian finds out you're here, he'll kill you."

"That wouldn't be productive to your investigation. Would you really jeopardize everything? Come on now. The higher authority would arrest your partner and break apart your organization. Poe doesn't strike me as impetuous, but people have been known to surprise me." He put his fingers in the pockets of his jeans and smiled. "I do love surprises. Perhaps I'm being too restrictive on club rules. I don't see any reason we need to keep the Vampire ban in place. Do you?"

I saw where he was going with this, and I wasn't on board with the plan. "I'm not here to change your rules. If you let in Vamps, people will stop coming. It might scare away the person hiring your girls, and we'll never catch him. So unless you want to obstruct our search, I'd suggest you keep the rules as they are."

He tilted his head to the side. "Good point. I sometimes forget how clever you are. Clever, clever." His eyes skated down, and he looked displeased with my attire. "Hurry back, Butterfly. Trouble is brewing."

I put my hands on my hips. "What do you mean?"

Houdini gestured up at a brawl happening on one of the screens. "Another asinine display. You better take care of that before it gets out of control."

"Why don't you hire bouncers so the bartenders can do their job?"

"I have enough employees as it is. The whole point of a business is to profit. If I hire competent bartenders, who needs bouncers? We've had more of these fights lately, and I can't seem to find a Mage who will stay."

"Yeah, maybe you should do something about that."

Houdini swaggered around the desk and kept his eyes locked on mine. "Your pupils are slow to dilate."

I gave him an indignant sigh. "It's past my shift, and I'm tired."

"You're here to track a recruiter, but just remember to follow my rules. I won't have you influencing my people. If anyone asks, you were in here getting a verbal warning for drinking on the job."

I subtly shook my head. "Since when does Chaos like rules?"

Amusement played on his features as he tugged on his ear stud. "I do miss our chats. Most immortals aren't as candid and take offense to everything. I hope someday we can be as close as we were the night we met. Perhaps the fates want us together after all."

I strutted toward the door. As I gripped the knob, I looked over my shoulder. I didn't like keeping secrets from Christian. He didn't hold Houdini in high regard to begin with, but after my maker had kidnapped and sold me back to my Creator, all bets were off. Christian had never made any specific threats, but I knew if given the chance, he'd end Houdini. And frankly, I didn't know how to feel about that.

Houdini turned away to watch the commotion on three cameras. "See you when I see you."

Chapter 11

My adrenaline spiked as I tunneled through the crowd. A ring of onlookers had formed around the lounge area, some standing on their tiptoes to see.

"We should leave," one man said to his companion. "I can't get involved in this." They quickly turned away and fought against the rising tide of spectators.

I elbowed my way to the front and saw the group who'd ordered the Red Apple drinks. Only five were causing a scene.

Flynn and his men pushed the crowd back, trying to get them to leave. One of the Red Apple boys waved a broken beer bottle at a pissed-off shirtless man. After slashing the man's chest, the Lone Musketeer slashed his own chest and laughed maniacally. The shirtless guy looked unfazed, and I couldn't even tell if he was bleeding since his chest was so hairy that a small mouse could have nested in there. His eyes were locked on the brunette pinned beneath another Red Apple boy. By the possessive look on his face, that was *his* woman. Or at least that was the impression she had given him at some point. Had she been screaming or beating her fists against the buffoon on top of her, the furry boyfriend might have exploded into action. It was unclear whether she was drunk on magic, but as the man pounded his hips into hers on the red sofa, she moaned. They weren't simulating sex, and they were both into it. That titillated the onlookers.

Rena crept up behind the Lone Musketeer, who was still wielding the broken bottle, and put her hands on his back. His eyes rounded as the red glow on her palms swelled. He pivoted, but instead of slicing her throat with the shard, he blasted her with Mage energy using his free hand. Rena hurtled backward as if pulled by invisible rope.

Simone fought her way through the crowd until she reached me.

"What the hell happened?" I asked her. "I've only been gone a few minutes."

"There were only *five* at the table. They lied about how many were in their group. That means each one of them had *two* Red Apples. Flynn! Get everyone out."

Flynn pushed at the bevy of onlookers. "Stand back, the lot of you! There's nothing to see. Get your jollies off in another room," he said, trying to maintain order. Some obeyed, but the vast majority wanted to watch.

The hairy guy grimaced when the Lone Musketeer cut his chest again.

"I bet that's her boyfriend," I said to Simone.

"Let's hope he's not a Shifter." She took out her nose ring and put it inside her bra. "See that guy who looks like Sonny Crockett?"

"Sonny who?"

She turned to me matter-of-factly as chaos erupted around us. "Don Johnson played him." Met with my blank stare, she looked at me in disbelief. "Don Johnson? *Miami Vice*? None of that rings a bell?"

"I don't watch a lot of movies."

She gave a contemptuous sigh. "Some days I weep for humanity. He's the one in the blue shirt and grey sports jacket. The one grabbing everyone's wrist."

"What about him?"

"He juiced a man unconscious, and now he's trying to find another Mage. His bald friend over there is doing the same."

"Are they all the same Breed?"

Simone scanned the scene. "I don't know about Romeo on the couch or *him*."

I followed her gaze to a long-haired man who looked like someone from an old rock band. He stripped off his suit jacket and white button-up shirt, his hands drenched in blood and his eyes wild with delight.

"*That* one disemboweled a man. That's how this whole thing started."

"*Holy shit.* Right in the middle of the club?"

Simone took a deep breath, her hands shaking as she wrung them. "Luckily it was a Shifter, and he's mostly healed. But I almost got torn apart carrying him to a private room."

Three puncture marks branded her shoulder, but she didn't seem to know they were there.

"The juicers knocked out two of my people already. They're looking for a female Mage they can bind with and are blasting everyone in the process. The one at nine o'clock holding the beer bottle—blood excites him. The woman on the sofa is willing, so the man fucking her is the least of my concerns. We don't have the authority to kill these men. They'll shut us down."

I could see why they were hesitating. For one, they didn't have anyone qualified to handle this level of violence. Most of the workers were busy trying to lead customers away, and we anxiously waited for them to disperse. The fewer people around, the fewer potential victims.

Simone snapped her fingers at Flynn. "Lock the stairwells. Don't let anyone down until we get this contained."

Flynn relayed the command to three of his crew. I spotted Claude scooping up women like ice cream and heading to the back door.

What kind of fuckery was about to unfold? Five men juiced up on toxic levels of sensory magic, which amplified their desires, whether that was sex, juicing, or violence. And not a single Mage employee in sight to help me out.

"Clyde!" I shouted, relieved I hadn't blurted out his real name in the heat of the moment.

Still in his gold shorts, Claude sliced through the thinning crowd until he reached us.

I looked between him and Simone. "How many Chitahs are on the floor?"

She shook her head. "Workers? Clyde's the only one. We have a few upstairs, but we've had trouble in the past with them flipping their switch."

"Think you can take down a Mage?" I asked him. "No killing."

He let only his top two canines elongate. "I think I can handle it."

I gave him a pointed look. "Don't flip your switch, and don't put more venom in him than two fangs. If you do, it'll shut down this club, and we're all screwed." I glanced at the room. "Take out Sonny Crockett."

He glanced at a man rising from an unconscious body on the floor. "Don Johnson over there in the jacket?"

"See?" Simone said, judging me with her coffee-colored eyes.

"Can you handle the Lone Musketeer with the broken beer bottle?" I asked her.

She looked down to where Rena lay on the floor, still knocked out from the blast of energy. "Why not the humping fool on the couch? Seems like we should take out the easy ones first."

"Because I have a feeling that the furry guy over there wants him more than we do. If you take care of the Lone Musketeer, the furry guy will take care of Romeo. Clyde, after you take down Miami Vice, go for Vin Diesel. I'll take care of Bon Jovi."

Simone blinked. "Who?"

I grinned at her. "You're kidding me, right? 'Living on a Prayer'? *You're* the one who started the celebrity look-alike contest."

Claude's eyes narrowed. "He gutted a man."

I tapped my wrist. "Time's a-ticking." I flashed to the opposite side of the room and stopped behind the deranged rock star look-alike.

Like the angel of death, he indiscriminately selected his next victim, which happened to be a short-haired woman. He swung his fist in a sweeping motion, and a narrow line of blood appeared on her neck. She reached for the bleeding wound and then looked at her bloodstained hands. My heart sank, but then she suddenly grabbed the hands of the man next to her, and blue light flashed between their palms. The bleeding on her neck stopped, and while she could have blasted her attacker, she fled. Not every Mage knew how to fight.

I grinned mercilessly at the realization that Mr. Rockstar wasn't a Mage. Had he been, he would have blasted everyone with energy or flashed after the woman. My fangs ached, but I locked up my Vampire. It was time to handle this situation like a Mage.

He slowly turned until his eyes locked on mine. The short blade of a bloody push dagger protruded between his index and middle fingers.

I sharpened my light. "Why don't you pick on someone your own size?"

A stream of words flew past his lips, but they sounded Latin. It was as if his mind and body had disconnected, and there was nothing coherent in the depths of his soulless eyes.

When he lunged at me, I hopped onto a coffee table and then jumped behind him. Though I could have blasted him with energy, why not make this fun? I grabbed a beer bottle and smashed it over his thick skull. He staggered for a moment before spinning around and headbutting me in the stomach like a bull. The air punched out of my lungs as I toppled over a chair and hit the ground. Staring up at the dark ceiling, I gasped as the worst kind of agony suddenly tore through my body—as if lions were feasting upon me. He forced sensory magic through my hands, and I experienced all the terror and pain of a victim being mauled and eaten by lions. Each time I closed my eyes, gory images that seemed real filled my head.

I wanted to scream. I wanted to run and blast the imaginary lions with energy.

Still muttering in Latin, he backhanded me. When he raised his right arm, the blade shimmered in his hand. I threw up my arms in a crisscross motion seconds before he swiped at my neck. Pain lanced my left forearm.

"Get the hell off me!" I angrily thrust my legs upward and then flipped him onto his back.

I bit his arm, and the blade fell out of his hand and skittered across the floor when he swiped his arm upward to get away from my choppers. Though his long hair curtained his face, I could see his eyes closing as he continued muttering Latin. This guy was in another world. Straddling him to make sure he didn't go anywhere, I turned away from the wall to see what was going on.

Simone had teamed up with the furry customer as they circled the crazy Mage with the broken beer bottle. Gold lights showered them in an open area near a gilded cage. She threw some kick-ass punches, but these men were high on magic and difficult to control or predict.

Across the way, what remained of the crowd scattered like leaves in the wind. From a crouched position by a cluster of chairs, Claude slowly raised his head, his lips dripping with blood. He'd bitten the Mage, who was lying motionless beneath him.

Between Simone and Claude was the red sofa where Romeo was having the sex of his life. They were both nude from the waist down, and he pounded into her as if his life depended on it.

I winced when fire seared the flesh away from my skin. The pain intensified, and when I closed my eyes, I stood on a pyre, flames dancing at my feet and scorching my lungs.

The Sensor, now lucid, pushed dirty magic into me through my upper thighs. I punched him in the face and then seized his wrists, slamming his hands against the floor. When our palms locked, I juiced his energy to dangerously low levels. "How do you like *that*? Huh? I can make your toenails hurt." Once he was weak enough, I blasted him so hard that I smelled burning hair. "Lights out."

His eyelids fluttered and his chest heaved. When he finally lay motionless beneath me, I let go and took a breath. *Holy crap.* His energy was so vile that I doubled over and retched. I still had intermittent pain from the lion attack and torching, and the whole room was vibrating because of it. I scooted back and leaned against a pillar.

Flynn hovered. "Are you all right?"

Just then, Romeo and the woman sang out an orgasmic duet.

"We're going to have to burn that sofa," Flynn muttered.

The furry-chested boyfriend had fled the scene, and we were finally getting the upper hand. Claude pinned the bald Mage down while Simone struggled to get the Lone Musketeer under control as he waved the broken bottle at her. There were lingering spectators, but most had put distance between themselves and the chaos. A few were sitting at the bar, enjoying their drink as if nothing was happening. The music still played, but all the dancers were helping to keep the crowd away. A few people on Flynn's team were cleaning the tables and chairs where dirty magic had spilled.

Ready to end this, I stalked behind Simone's foe, locked my arm around his neck, and swept his feet out from beneath him. He dropped like a stone, and I wrested the makeshift weapon from his hand, cutting my own in the process.

Simone pounced on him like a lion and then slammed her hands against his chest. As an ominous red glow lit beneath her palms, I turned and walked away. I didn't want to hear his screams in one ear and the cries of pleasure in the other. After crossing behind the bar, I reached for the bottle of tequila I'd hidden on a shelf. Bad energy coursed through me—Sensor energy. My arm was still bleeding, my eye swollen, and I couldn't be certain if I'd lost a contact during the scuffle. I wrapped a towel around the cut to stanch the bleeding. The cut on my hand was superficial and had already stopped bleeding, so I wiped it off with a rag while watching Flynn and his men hauling bodies toward the back of the club. The servers righted the chairs while the dancers got back to dancing.

Officially off the clock, I poured myself a double.

"That was some show. I have to admit, half the fun of coming here is watching how well the bartenders handle the disorderly."

I looked up at Mr. Crawford, who was combing his dark grey hair. I used to think guys like him were too sophisticated for clubs like this, but nothing surprised me anymore.

"You want a drink? I'm about to take off."

He licked his bottom lip while sliding me a business card. "If you want to earn extra money, give me a call."

I discreetly took the card and stuck it inside my shorts. "I'm free now. We can talk outside."

A smile curved up his cheek. "Clean yourself up. Get some sleep. Then call me."

Flynn appeared at the bar. "You all right?" He gave Crawford a long look that made me uncomfortable.

Mr. Crawford inclined his head and left.

Flynn watched him sit down by one of the caged dancers. "What did *he* want? Because it wasn't a drink."

"Nothing."

"You should stay away from him."

I wrapped my fingers around my glass. "Why?"

He rested his elbow on the bar and cast a critical gaze at Crawford. "Slander is against the law. Just trust me on this one."

I knocked back my drink. "I've had enough for the night."

"I wish I hadn't been so bloody busy tossing everyone out. I would have loved to see all of it."

While Flynn rambled on about the fight, my body flushed all over. An unstoppable heat pulsed through me, but it was nothing like the fire that burned me earlier. This was different.

Sexual.

Intense.

And it was building.

"You look flushed," he said.

A relentless throbbing ached between my legs. The leather bra was suddenly making my nipples sensitive, and all I could think about were visuals of that couple having sex, of someone touching me, licking me, doing sinful things to my body.

As I moved to set my glass in the sink, my knees buckled, and I dropped to the floor. Being on all fours didn't help either, because all I wanted was for someone to come up and take me from behind.

"*Fuck,*" I whispered. "What's happening to me?"

"Robin!" Flynn darted behind the bar and knelt beside me. "Did you lose too much blood?"

Blood? What blood was he talking about? I no longer felt the gash on my arm, the bruises on my knuckles, or even my swollen eye beneath my mask.

I began rocking back and forth as if an invisible man were penetrating me.

"Uh, Robin?" Flynn took my arm to help me up.

I lowered my head to his hand and smelled his skin. Dark desire consumed me, and I moaned.

"Simone!" Flynn yelled. "Get the bloody hell over here!"

Hearing his panic made me pull myself up. "I need to go," I whispered. But when I took a step, I collapsed in his arms.

And he felt so… damn… good.

I toddled against the bar and knocked over a beer bottle. All I could do was lean over the bar and grip the other side.

"What's wrong with her?" Simone asked.

I tried to look, but it was as if I were watching television and they didn't exist.

Simone rested her hand on my arm, and her eyes widened. "Who touched her?"

Flynn shook his head. "No one. She was talking to me one minute, and the next she's on the floor, begging for it. I get that a lot, by the way."

When Simone touched me again, she hissed and clutched her hand to her chest. "What was she doing before this happened?"

"Talking. Drinking."

"Drinking what?"

He bent over and dipped out of sight. Then he set my empty glass on the bar.

Simone lifted to her nose and sniffed it. She touched the inside, but there was no reaction until she licked her finger. Then she flew toward the sink and rinsed her mouth out.

With my cheek against the bar, I closed my eyes as carnal images filled my head. It was as if I could feel every experience at once. There was no resisting the desire that clutched me in its arms. Shutting it off was an exercise in futility, and my sexual appetite was growing by the second. Behind my flushed chest, my heart raced like a hummingbird.

Simone huffed. "Where did this bottle come from?"

Then I heard the glug-glug sound of liquid going down the drain.

"The whole damn bottle," she said grimly. "And she had a glass? I wouldn't even serve a thimbleful of that swill. Someone's going to get fired for this, and it's not me."

"Are you sure about that?"

"And what's that supposed to mean, Flynn?" She chucked the bottle into the trash.

"The new girl's cutting in on your tips. You didn't like Lizzy either. For that matter, you didn't like Roe."

"If you think I had something to do with their disappearance, you can kiss my ass."

"Maybe Rena's selling on the side."

"It takes a powerful Sensor to put that kind of magic in a whole bottle. Rena's weak; that's why she has fewer customers."

I started making out with the bar. My tongue polished that wood like it was Christian's cock. If there was a tiny voice in my head trying to reason with me, someone had gagged it.

Flynn pulled me off the bar and onto the floor. "We can't let anyone see her like this. How long does it take to wear off?"

"You're asking me something I don't know."

"You're a Sensor. This is your specialty."

"Dark magic isn't my specialty, and I don't know how much she drank."

Standing next to me, Simone looked like a skyscraper, and all I could see were her beautiful, dark legs. I rolled to my side and pressed my lips against her ankle. The urge to taste her blood hit me hard, but I managed to keep my fangs retracted.

How long would that last? I was unraveling with each passing moment.

Claude craned his neck and looked down at me from across the bar. "My nose is burning. What's wrong with that female?"

Simone threw my glass into the trash. "She drank pure sensory magic. Undiluted."

"And a lot of it," Flynn added. "The sex stuff."

"You can't let her walk home in this condition," Claude growled.

Simone stepped away from me and leaned against the bar. "Hey, new guy. Do you know where she lives? Because none of us do."

He mashed his lips together.

"Get back to your tables and let us handle this," she ordered him. "Flynn, pick her up."

"And do what?"

"We'll put her in room twelve until it wears off… or closing time. Whichever comes first."

"Something tells me *she'll* be coming first," he muttered, hoisting me to my feet.

I moaned against the feel of his hard body and clutched him to me.

"Someone's feeling randy." He led me away from the bar. "Stand back," he barked at a man encroaching on our space. "Unless you want vomit on your shoes, clear a path for the sickly woman."

Flynn dragged me through the club and down a hall. My knees wobbled like Jell-O, and all I wanted to do was dry hump his thigh.

Flynn stopped in front of a door with a piece of paper taped to it that said CLOSED. When he flipped the switch, red lights came on. Chains hung from the ceiling and walls, and the only furniture was a table with straps and two X-shaped pieces of equipment with cuffs for the hands and ankles.

"Stay here."

When he turned to leave, I followed him toward the sound of thumping music and the pulse of raw energy.

"Oh no you don't." He pushed me back.

Though my knees were weak, my legs insisted on taking me where the action was.

He shut the door and blocked it. I could see why Simone would have been attracted to Flynn. He was a bit of a swashbuckler with his messy hair—the kind of kinky hair that a woman could tunnel her fingers through while riding him hard. He smelled like cheap cologne and beer, and I wondered what it might be like to kiss those tempting lips. Would he let me drink his blood? Would he let me take it from anywhere?

Flynn gripped my arm and led me to the center of the room. "I've never seen a woman fight like that before. Did you have professional training?" He lifted my arm and cuffed my wrist. "You're not supposed to drink on the clock. Don't you want this job?" He cuffed my other wrist and gazed down into my eyes. "You're trouble." His fingers traced down the length of my raised arms, caressing my middle before resting on my hips.

When the door swung open, Flynn jumped back a foot.

"Simone said you were in here." A flustered young man with a crew cut tilted his head to get a look at me. So did a few passing by the door. "We're having trouble with one of those dickheads. He's trying to get back inside, and it's drawing a crowd of humans."

Flynn walked backward with a devilish grin and inclined his head. "On my way."

When they closed the door and left me alone, I realized Flynn had shackled me to a chain hanging from the ceiling. That also meant I couldn't lie down or touch myself.

I threw my head back, the heat between my legs unbearable. Seconds turned into minutes. First fifteen, then thirty. I didn't have a coherent thought in my head. Lust had overcome me—never had I experienced anything so powerful as to take away all my rational decision-making skills. Instead of finding a way out of the shackles, I crossed my legs at the ankles and squeezed my thigh muscles in a sad attempt to satiate my cravings. The red lighting was entrancing, and I wondered what was going on in the rooms upstairs.

The door opened.

Then closed.

A man approached, and I didn't know him. The only thing I recognized was the lust in his eyes.

Chapter 12

Sensory magic had reduced me to nothing but carnal desire. The chains that bound my wrists were strangely familiar, but no memories were attached to these sensations. Anytime I tried to remember anything about my life, the fever would grip me like the devil's hand. I was no longer a vessel of memories, opinions, and thought.

The man who entered the room wasn't dressed like staff. His bushy black beard was a stark contrast against his shiny bald head. When he reached me, his massive biceps and shoulders eclipsed everything else. A musky scent filled my nose when he stripped off his tank top, and he cupped my breast with his large, beefy hand. Cool air hardened my nipples when he pulled my black bra down, releasing my breasts.

"You've been a bad girl, and I'm gonna punish you." He reached around and smacked my ass. "You like that?"

I did and I didn't. Through the haze of desire, a voice in my head was screaming *no*. Something about feeling pain while shackled. Something about seeing desire in a man's eyes while I was helpless. Yet I couldn't stop the renegade pleasure that had me writhing in anticipation as he circled behind me.

"Take it harder," he said, slapping my ass again.

I cried out, because this time it hurt.

He appeared in front of me and pinched my nipple. Tears hovered at the corners of my eyes. Was it pain or pleasure? The two sensations had merged, and I couldn't tell the difference anymore.

He unzipped the sides of my leather shorts, exposing more

skin. "You're a little slut, aren't you? Daddy's gonna keep spanking you until you promise to be a good girl." His jaw slid forward and his eyes narrowed. "Then I'm going to make you get down on your knees and suck on my dick. After that, I'm going to spank you so hard that you're gonna scream for mercy."

A shadow moved behind him so fast that it was dreamlike. Christian gripped the man by the neck and hauled him away from me.

Christian's fangs punched out. "You first, you insipid shitebag." His black eyes were wrought with fury and violence.

A cold chill ran down my spine.

Instead of biting him, Christian slammed him against the wall. The man bellowed in pain when a bone snapped. Christian stalked toward him, lifted him by the throat, and flung him across the room. The man crashed into the Saint Andrew's cross, breaking it to pieces. While I'd been in a stupor for almost an hour, seeing Christian jogged my memory.

Only the sex bits. I remembered how good his hands felt against my skin and his tongue in my mouth. The taste of his blood and the way he knew my body like no one else. When I looked at him, the only word that filled my mind was *yes*. I gripped the chain above me and watched with delight as he beat the stranger senseless. Blood spattered the walls but barely showed up against the red lighting.

After wiping his bloody knuckles on the man's jeans, Christian finally rose to his feet and approached me with a menacing stride. He reached above my head and broke the chain in two. My muscles ached as I lowered them. Christian snapped off the shackles as if he were breaking open fortune cookies.

When I thought he might barrage me with questions, he took me into his arms and carried me out. He moved down the dark hall with his head down. The back door opened, and I took a breath of fresh air.

Christian set my feet on the ground and adjusted my bra so that it covered my nipples. Then he wrapped his trench coat around me and forced me into the back seat of a car. The door shut, he tapped on the hood, and off I went.

Alone.

With my arms free, I could finally touch myself. And I did. My hands dove between my legs to ease a suffering so destructive that I felt myself coming unhinged. The driver didn't look back at me. Not once. His eyes never watched me in the rearview mirror, and he didn't ask me where I wanted to go. City lights blurred outside the fogged-up windows, and the sound of a loud motorcycle roared past us.

The car eventually came to a stop, and the driver got out. When my door opened, I almost fell into the gutter. The driver caught me and helped me inside the hotel. The next thing I knew, I was in the elevator. He punched a button and turned away while I slumped down to the floor, Christian's coat still wrapped around my shoulders. It was a struggle to keep my eyes open. Closing them intensified the sensory experience, but I was so exhausted. I just wanted it all to end.

When the doors opened, Christian was there. He scooped me into his arms and carried me down the hall.

"I've got you, Precious," he muttered against my hair.

I looked up and wrapped my arms around his neck. When I pulled myself closer so that I could taste his skin, he leaned away. The beep of the card key sounded, and he set me down inside the hotel room.

"Stay here." Christian locked the door and roamed through the dark room toward the windows. After closing the heavy drapes, he switched on the lamp to a low setting. Then he came back and flung my trench coat across the room into the corner chair. Once my boots were off, he led me into the bathroom and stripped off my shorts and panties.

"Finally," I whispered, clutching his shirt.

He took off my leather bra. "There'll be none of that."

Naked and ready, I forced myself against him. Christian gripped my arm and removed the thin towel bandaging my cut. After giving my forearm a thorough inspection, he removed the cloth mask around my eyes and turned my head to examine my bruised face.

"You lost your contact," he said absently. "But there's no damage to your cornea."

I grabbed the back of his neck and tried to pull him to kiss me, but Christian had the will of an oak tree and stood firm.

He stared at my stab wound. "I can't give you my blood when you're like this. You'll have to heal in the morning."

"Blood," I whispered, reaching for his neck again. Memories of his sinful blood filled my mind—that erotic taste to which nothing compared.

Christian led me into the standing shower and turned on the water. I grimaced when the water chilled my skin like ice pellets. Within moments, it went from ice to fire, and steam fogged up the shower door. Christian stepped inside, fully dressed, and washed my bloody arm. Unable to stand another second, I backed up and sat down in the corner seat, my legs spread wide.

He knelt in front of me, the water beating against his back, and lathered soap in his hands. He worked that soap up my calves, behind my knees, across my thighs, and over my hips. The suds turned pink as they washed away the dried blood that painted my body. When his fingers grazed between my legs, I shivered and reached for him.

"Why can't I tempt you?"

He rapidly moved his hands upward and washed every inch of my body. "You smell like the floor of a pub."

Droplets of water clung to his face and beard. I couldn't take my eyes off his wet lips. Christian had such a soft and demanding kiss—a kiss that could make a woman forget all others before him.

I ran my fingers through his wet hair. "Kiss me."

His eyes fell to my breasts. "*Jaysus wept.* You'll be the ruin of me." Christian leaned in and gazed deep into my eyes. It made my heart flutter. After pouring shampoo in his hands, he lathered my hair, starting from the nape. "Raven?"

"*Yes?*" I hissed.

He blinked and shot to his feet. "Never mind. Stand up."

I did as he commanded. It felt as if we were dancing as he turned us until the water struck my back. I reclined my head while he rinsed the shampoo out, but my hands fastidiously worked to unlatch his belt.

It became a race as to who would finish their task first. Christian poured too much conditioner in his hands and quickly ran it through my hair. When I'd gotten the belt free, I shoved my hands inside his pants and felt the blunt head of his hard cock.

A low rumble settled in his chest as he rinsed my hair. He wanted this just as much as I did. When I popped the button open on his trousers, he lifted me up and stepped out of the shower.

Christian toweled me, and I suddenly felt like a car going through a car wash. I was his puppet as he put my arms through the robe sleeves, tied the belt, and dried my hair. When my forearm started bleeding again, he took off his shirt and ripped it into long strips. I should have felt the pain when he wrapped it around my arm and made a knot, but I didn't. Why was he stalling? Didn't he realize how much I craved him?

Then he lifted me straight up as if I weighed nothing and entered the bedroom. When we reached the bed by the windows, he set me down on the comforter.

I locked my fingers behind his neck and pulled him toward me. "I need you."

"What you need is sleep."

"*Please* fuck me, Christian."

His eyes fluttered, and he sat down. "You don't know what you're saying."

I loosened the belt on my robe and exposed myself to show him how serious I was. "*Please.*"

"I'll not do it."

When I saw he was serious, I beat my fists against his chest. "You fanghole! You don't love me—you only love yourself. Why did you even come for me? Why didn't you just leave me there? This is torture. Is that what gets you off? Watching me suffer?"

He tenderly tucked a swath of hair behind my ear. "I'm sorry you're vexed, but I'll not take you in this condition. You're not yourself."

"Get out."

"I'm not leaving you here alone. Of that you can be sure."

Incensed, I shut my eyes. Sexual images flooded my mind, and all my anger floated away in a bubble. I forgot Christian. I forgot the hotel. I forgot everything. All I wanted was to release all this desire. My fingers slid between my legs, between and inside the wet folds. With my eyes closed, sexual images and sensations consumed me, and I experienced each encounter as if it were actually happening to me. I felt the warmth and tingling of a mouth sucking my nipple, and it was so real. In one scene, I was on all fours while a man pounded me from behind. His hands were on my hips, controlling the rhythm. Suddenly I was in another scene where I was a man lying on my back while a woman sucked on the head of my cock. I could have never imagined what that felt like, but now I knew. The throbbing ache, the sensitive nerves, the wet warmth all around. Then I was riding on top of a man made of muscles and chest hair. I could smell his sweat and feel the coarse hair between my fingertips.

As I chased my orgasm, I realized I was never going to get there. No one climaxed in the fantasies; it just kept shuffling from one sex act to the next. Frustrated, I opened my eyes to Christian in the corner chair, watching me. He gripped the armrests, his fangs fully extended and his eyes hooded.

I whimpered. This pain was never going to go away.

"Open your legs," he growled. "*Wider.*"

His textured words moved across my sensitive skin like the tassels of a whip. I bent my knees.

"Pinch your nipples," he said next.

A pulse of desire shot through me like white lightning when I did as he commanded, and I realized it was *his* voice I needed to hear. It was *his* face I needed to see. His smoldering eyes, his sharp cheekbones, and the raven tattoo that spread across his arm and chest like a cloak. My belly dipped at the sight of water glistening on his chest.

"I want my tongue… right there," he growled. "Remember what it feels like, Raven? My tongue inside you, and then the secret bite that makes you scream."

My breath hitched at the memory. The chair creaked beneath his grip as he steadily watched me. Tiny bursts of light shimmered around me, and I surrendered to them as my whole body tensed.

"Don't stop what you're doing," he said, his voice rough and sexy. "Stroke it for me. That's the way. Keep coming, Precious. The things I'll do to you later you can't imagine."

I rode out my orgasm for as long as I could until all the energy melted away to nothing.

And that was only round one.

For the next two hours, Christian sat in the chair, coaching me through dirty talk, one orgasm after another.

Christian sat on the edge of the bed and melted me with his warm eyes. "Do you feel up for coffee?"

I squinted at the light invading through the top of the heavy drapes. "What time is it?"

He crossed the room to the counter and fetched me a cup of coffee. "What happened to your Mage clock?"

"I think it's fried after last night." I propped pillows behind me and sat up. My robe was wide open, so I closed it and tried to comb my hair with my fingers. "How did you know I was awake?"

"I know the sounds your body makes when you sleep." He approached the bed and sat to my left, the coffee cup in his hands. The way he was holding it would have burned anyone else's palms.

I gripped the handle. "Hello, darling."

"I know you like it black."

I breathed in the delicious aroma before slurping it. Not exactly gourmet, but it was exactly what I needed.

"I never really understood the term blue balls until now," he said matter-of-factly.

When I remembered every sordid detail, a blush heated my cheeks. "Why didn't you take care of yourself?"

He shook his head. "Wouldn't have been right."

I set the cup down on the nightstand. "I'm sorry."

He jerked his neck back. "For what?"

"All that ugly stuff I said to you. Hitting you. I didn't mean it."

"Cast your fears aside. I know that wasn't you talking."

"Can you open the drapes? Not all the way—my eyes are sensitive."

Christian stood up and squinted when he pulled back the drapes. A stream of light spilled across the bed, and I reached out to draw healing light through my fingertips.

When the wound on my arm sealed, I touched my eye to make sure the swelling was gone. "Why didn't you give me your blood last night?"

He closed the drapes and returned to the bed. "Had I done that, I wouldn't have been able to control you. Not in that condition. You would have forced yourself on me."

"Would that have been so bad?"

He gave my hand a light squeeze.

I thought back to being chained up in that room. My God, I'd come so close to cheating on Christian. How could he ever trust me again? I covered my face with my hands. "How did you know to come get me?"

"Claude. I tried to get there as fast as I could. He wedged something in the back door so I could get in."

I lowered my arms. "You shouldn't have come for me. It was risky."

"Are you out of your fecking mind? Do you really think that flimsy note on the door would have kept anyone out of that room? I'm sure Chitahs two blocks away could scent your arousal, and a Sensor could easily touch the door and feel your emotions from the other side. I came for you so you wouldn't have to suffer the guilt of taking another."

I averted my gaze. "I almost did."

"Not by choice."

I glared at him. "I *wanted* him to do things to me. I don't think I would have stopped him."

Christian scratched his cheek and then stroked his chin. "Sensory magic isn't just a novelty. Maybe that's all you've seen, but it can be weaponized and completely inhibit your ability to make rational decisions. When it's powerful enough, you can't fight it. How did it happen?"

I reached for my coffee. "Someone spiked my drink."

"Are you daft? That wasn't a spike. Those wear off in a couple of hours. Yours raged on through the night. Whatever you drank was in its purest form, and not many Sensors are powerful enough to do it. Someone infused a shite-ton of magic into your drink. That takes either skill or money."

"Money?"

"Aye. People buy bottles of it on the black market. Whoever did that to you is on my hit list for life."

I sipped my coffee. "So you're not mad? Don't lie to me now and tell me it's nothing if you're going to hold it against me in the future."

He took the cup away and leaned over me to set it on the nightstand. Instead of sitting up, he rested on top of me, his face an inch away from mine. "You're not to blame. Do you understand me? I'll not have you doubting me on this one. That's why I didn't touch you last night. It wouldn't have been right. No matter how I feel about you, Raven, I'll never take advantage when you're under the influence of magic." His voice softened. "That's not to say you didn't drive me mad with desire. How's your fanny this morning?"

"Traumatized."

He kissed me softly on the mouth. "Another time."

"What were you going to say to me last night in the shower?"

His gaze lowered as he searched his memory. "I thought about charming you into submissive behavior. Then you'd be easier to control. But I vowed to never use my powers on you."

My head thumped against the wall. "I'm mortified everyone saw me like that. I was licking people's ankles and dry humping them—people I work with. And the cab driver! I'll never be able to look at the hotel desk clerk after this."

Christian chuckled darkly. "I charmed the cab driver to ignore your condition. And if it gives you peace of mind, I'll do a memory wipe on the staff downstairs."

I rolled away from him and got up. After dressing in sweatpants and a T-shirt, I sat at the foot of the other bed.

"What's wrong?" he asked.

I stared at his reflection in the television. Christian looked like a shirtless model lying diagonal on the bed, his head propped in his hand. How could I express the immense guilt I felt? "I almost betrayed you. I don't think you should brush it off. We need to talk about it."

"Put it out of your mind."

"I can't."

He got up and stood before me. "You will."

My lip quivered. I rested my elbows on my knees and lowered my head so he couldn't see. It suddenly dawned on me what had felt so insidious about last night—my shackled wrists, the vulnerability, and a man abusing his dominance. It was everything I'd tried to forget about Fletcher Black, my Creator. Those months I'd spent in captivity, when he tried to break me, had never left my mind. Nausea slithered in my belly like a snake when I remembered last night. That stranger had struck me while I hung helpless in chains, and I *liked* it.

I bolted from the bed and into the bathroom. As I vomited the coffee that Christian had generously made for me, he pulled my hair away from my face and stroked my back as I silently wept into the bowl. I had a brief out-of-body experience where I saw myself in a pathetic heap, and anger flooded my veins. I heard my father's voice saying, "Get your ass off the floor. You're not a mop."

Eager to put this behind me, I shot to my feet and rinsed out my mouth. When I looked up at my reflection, I smashed the bottle of soap against the mirror. Then I threw everything within reach until little bottles and towels littered the floor.

Christian remained by the door, his hands clasped behind him.

"I hate him," I growled through clenched teeth. "He ruined my fucking life. I can't get him out of my head. No matter how much I try, there he is, staring at me with those demonic blue eyes. Whenever I see a man with a shaved head and a beard, I look twice. He's out there somewhere. Sometimes I wish he'd walk right up to me so I could put a dagger in his eye, and other times I never want to see his face again. He should suffer like I've suffered."

Christian's silence was deafening.

I rested my hands on the sink and sighed. "I thought it would be easy to find out who's running the cage fights, but I don't know if I can keep doing this for the next few weeks, let alone months. And before you say anything, I know how you hate someone dumping their feelings all over your lap, but I don't have anyone to talk to." I reached beneath the sink and set a bottle of tequila on the counter. "Bet you didn't know I had this in here, did you? I'm stuck in this hotel room, dealing with all the bullshit I see at the club. It's not the fighting; it's everything. Worst of all, I can't walk away. Viktor's counting on me, and all I want to do is drink myself into a coma."

When I tried to leave the room, Christian caught me from behind and locked his arms across my chest in a loose grip.

He rested his chin on my shoulder. "It grieves me to see you suffering."

Tears streamed down my cheeks. "I used to hate my father for being an alcoholic. I kept telling him he had a choice. I knew it had to do with the war, but he never talked about all the bad stuff that happened. He didn't even talk about my mother's death. Now I understand. I get it." I reached up and held his arms. "How do I make it stop?"

The next words he spoke sent a chill up my spine.

"You kill yourself. That's how immortals survive. You have to kill the human inside you, Raven. If you think that part of you died in Fletcher's basement, you're mistaken."

"Even if I could, it's too late." I turned around, my back against the door. "Alcohol was something I've always known how to handle. I never got drunk alone. But that changed with this assignment. My father almost drank himself to death, but I can't get liver disease, Christian. Hell, I could do all the drugs in the city and it wouldn't make a dent. But none of it erases the memories or dulls the pain. You know what does? Killing. When I'm beating my fists into someone's face or draining their blood, it goes away. I feel alive and powerful, and that scares the hell out of me. If violence is my true addiction, then will this job make me a better person or a monster?"

He lifted my chin with the crook of his finger. "You're hardly killing nuns."

I lowered my eyes to his bare chest.

"You're not a monster," he insisted. "I spent over a decade buried alive, but my humanity was long gone by then. All the innocents who died by my hand were what did me in. Had I not killed that last good part of my soul, I would have never survived those years underground. I would have gone mad. Every Mage and Vampire has to embrace their wickedness. You can't be an immortal saint. No one's completely pure."

"What about Gem?"

"She was born Breed. She doesn't know what it is to be human. Even Relics are hardwired differently. They make choices and sacrifices that humans would never understand. To be a Mage or a Vampire is to be a killer. It's what we're designed to do best. It's why some of us shed our human names and leave our families behind. It's a death ritual. But the final nail in the coffin is one you have to put in yourself. That will be the day you won't need to drink or talk about it anymore."

"The day I won't have feelings."

"Not the way you think. Niko has feelings, but I doubt he'll be weeping at our funerals." Christian cradled my neck in his strong hands. "When I'm in your presence, I sometimes remember what it's like to feel human. When we have these conversations, when you look into my eyes like I'm not a killer. But then I see you retching on the floor and drinking all hours, and I'm glad that part of me is dead." He stroked my cheek with his thumbs and reeled me in with his hypnotic gaze. "Don't have another thought about last night. You were a victim of magic, and I'll not dwell on anything you might have done. Nor should you. We're better than that."

I lowered my hands until they rested near his V-cut. "You shouldn't be here. It jeopardizes the mission."

He wrapped his arms around me. "It's lonely without you around."

"I've got hours before I have to go to work. Want to fool around?"

"After you put your head in a toilet bowl?"

My hands slid down to his pants. "Then let me take care of *your* needs."

He captured my wrists and lowered my arms. "If there's one thing I have, it's patience. For you, I'll wait an eternity."

I fell into his arms and rested my cheek against his warm chest. "Thanks for looking after me."

"It was either that or let you wander the streets mounting light poles."

"I might have caused another blackout and electrocuted myself."

He gently kissed my head. "I'd have passed out sparklers and vibrators at your funeral."

Christian's heart thumped in a steady rhythm. His embrace was safe, something I'd only ever experienced with my father. "Anything new happening at home?" I asked, curious if he'd tell me about Lenore's visit.

He stroked my hair. "Nothing you need worry about."

Christian was right. We were stronger than that, and this conversation didn't need to devolve into a petty argument about another woman. I had something she wanted, and that was Christian's loyalty. Maybe there were two sides to the story, and I was trying too hard to villainize a woman who might have done what she did to protect herself. Maybe you can only toy with a killer's emotions for so long before they turn that rage on you. Christian was willing to do anything for me, and because of that, I'd kept secrets about Houdini. Not because I wanted to, but it was the only way I could protect Christian from self-destructing.

In any case, Lenore no longer had influence over him. She might have a sweet position with the higher authority, but money or power wasn't enough to sway Christian. His second home was a shack in the woods, and he'd spent all his money to save my father, a man he didn't particularly care for.

"Do you have any suspects?" he asked. "Shepherd has a few in mind."

"None that jump out." I backed up toward the door. "I do have one guy that approached me last night and gave me his business card." I stared at it on the floor where it lay next to my bra. "I'm going to call him and see if it leads anywhere."

"Keep your boots on so Wyatt can track you. And if you leave the club, use the front door so Blue will see you. I had to call her this morning to let her know you were here."

"Do you think she'll tell Viktor?"

"Aye. She's loyal like that. But Viktor will understand why I had no choice but to get involved, and Claude was a witness. We haven't compromised the mission. I was careful moving about the club. I put you in the cab alone and rode separately." He propped his hand on the door and looked down at me.

I reached up and stroked his beard. "Can you do me a favor?"

"And what's that, lass?"

"Order me Chinese food. I have an insatiable appetite."

A crooked grin wound up his cheek. "So do I, Precious. So do I."

Chapter 13

After ordering Raven orange chicken with fried rice and egg rolls, Christian surreptitiously left the hotel through a back door. Without sunglasses, driving his Ducati with the sun in his eyes was pure torture. Since he had ripped up his shirt, all he had was his trench coat, which flapped behind him in the wind.

As he sped down the long and winding rural road, he regretted leaving that man at the club alive. But a dead body would have shut the place down and drawn attention to Raven. Still, if Claude hadn't called him, Raven would be having a different kind of morning. Christian would have never held her accountable for doing anything under the influence of magic. All that guilt she felt was her human side talking—the one she cleaved to. Despite her past experiences, there were many things she didn't yet know about the Breed world. Most of them she would have to learn on her own, like how potent Sensor magic could be. Sometimes telling a person wasn't enough.

Christian throttled the engine at an intersection, impatiently waiting for the light to turn green. Who had given her that drink? After this assignment was over, it would become his mission to find out. Thinking about the ways he'd kill that bastard had distracted him during the painfully long hours he'd spent watching Raven pleasure herself. Last night's visual would stay with him forever, and just the thought of it was making him hard.

Once he entered Keystone's gates, he slowed his bike near the house. Instead of veering toward the underground garage, he drove around the circular driveway and parked next to the Harley-Davidson. He didn't have to guess who was here. After he shut off his bike, a tapping sound from inside was all he could make out.

Christian glided through the front door, flung his coat on a winged statue, and spotted Crush facing the stairwell, one foot on the bottom step and his arms folded. Oil stains covered his jeans and white T-shirt. Those weren't clothes he wore around his house, so he must have come straight from work.

When Crush heard the door shut, he stopped tapping his foot and turned around. "Where's Raven?"

"As always, delightful to see you, Mr. Graves. Can I get you a drink? Perhaps a fire hose to clean your soiled garments?"

"Cut the shit. I want to know where my daughter is."

Christian heard the light footfalls of Gem in sneakers. He'd gotten to know the unique sound of everyone's movements around the mansion. The types of shoes they wore, how quick or slow their gait, how light or heavy their tread.

Gem bounded down the stairs in a teal romper, her shoulder-length hair bouncing with every step. Her whimsical spirit made it impossible to dislike her. "He's not up there. Oh, Christian's here! Maybe he knows. Have you seen Viktor?"

"Did you try calling?" He looked at Crush. "It's a big house. We can't exactly go around yelling for each other."

Gem slowed her pace until she reached the last step. "I'm sorry, Mr. Graves. We can't talk about where Raven is unless Viktor's here, and I can't find him."

Grumbling obscenities under his breath, Crush put his hands on his hips and turned away.

Switch appeared from behind the stairs, Hunter dawdling beside him with a picture book in his hand. The long-haired Shifter stopped at the staircase and rested his arm on the newel. "Hey, old man. What are you doing in this neck of the woods?"

"Looking for Raven. Have you seen her? Seems to be a mystery around here, and it's pissing me off."

"Not my job." Switch pulled an elastic band from his jeans

pocket and tied his hair at the nape. He gave Christian a cursory glance. "Working on your tan?"

Gem giggled and leaned against the railing. "I think he just likes showing off his big ole tattoo."

"Maybe you should get one," Switch suggested, smiling up at her.

"Alas, I've got enough pizzazz. A tattoo would only detract."

Crush approached Christian and lowered his voice. "Where is she?"

"Is this an emergency?"

"She's not answering her phone, and no one here is answering my questions."

"Maybe if you tell us what you're doing here…"

Crush's blue eyes narrowed, and Christian flicked a glance downward to see if the man was holding an impalement stake. He wouldn't put it past him. "Tell me where she is, Vamp."

"Now, there's no need to get hostile."

"Raven!" he bellowed, turning on his heel. Crush moved swiftly past Gem, up the stairs.

Her eyes widened. "He can't go up there. He can't!"

"Worry not," Christian assured her. "I'll take care of the old gobshite."

She gave him an admonishing look. "You shouldn't talk that way about Raven's dad."

"Yeah," Switch agreed, his voice a threatening growl. "You shouldn't say that about—"

"*Jaysus.* One more word and I'll drain you. Stay here and I'll bring him down."

Christian jogged up the stairs and followed the sound of Crush's shouts on the second floor. Wyatt came out of his office, a green beanie on his head and a bag of pretzels in his hand. "What the immortal hell is going on around here?"

"Where's Raven?" Crush sounded like a motorcycle getting fired up.

When Wyatt noticed him heading toward his office, he backed

up, dropped the snacks, and blocked the door with his arms. "You can't come in here. I mean it."

Christian jogged toward them and grabbed the back of Crush's shirt before he plowed right over Wyatt and got an eyeful of sensitive data that was surely on the computer.

Crush turned and threw a hard right, socking Christian in the eye.

Christian didn't flinch. "That'll hurt you more than it does me."

"I've got personal stuff pulled up on the computer," Wyatt said. "If you come in here, Christian will have to scrub you."

Crush's lips peeled back, and he reluctantly turned away.

"Walk with me," Christian said, moving past Crush. He didn't need to look back to know the old man was following.

After ascending a flight of stairs in the back of the mansion, he led Crush to Raven's room and opened the door.

Crush wandered in and drank in his first glimpse of his daughter's room: the red armoire by the door, the scenic painting over the quaint bed, the rustic fireplace to the left, and the arched windows tucked away in an alcove.

Christian leaned against the doorjamb. "This is where she sleeps, but she's not here right now."

Crush rounded the bed and stood before the desk. Christian couldn't see what he was doing but guessed he was wondering about Raven's peculiar keepsakes. After a minute, the sound of "Für Elise" played from the jewelry box. Crush lifted his arm as if wiping his face.

"She has a grand view," Christian pointed out.

The music stopped.

"Does she climb on the roof?"

"Aye. How did you know?"

Crush turned around and sighed. "Because I know my little girl. She used to climb trees and sit on top of the trailer. I had to keep an eye on her when she got older because sometimes we'd go out and she'd wind up on a roof somewhere." His gaze lingered on the fake roses on a nightstand. "It's immaculate. Nothing like how she kept her room as a kid. You set her up real nice here."

"It's everything she desires, which isn't much."

"Does that include you?"

"Perhaps. You want to tell me what's on your mind?"

Crush rubbed his weathered face and then looked at the knuckles on his right hand. "I had a nightmare about her. Can't get it out of my head."

"Dreams aren't real."

Not that Christian had any. He never slept.

Crush drifted toward the windows and looked out. "The week Bonnie died in the fire, I had a nightmare that she was falling into a black pit and screaming for Raven. Then years ago, before they told me Raven was dead, I had the same nightmare. Only Raven was calling out my name."

"And last night?"

Crush faced the room. "I had another dream. Raven was falling down a dark hole, but she was calling *your* name. I'm not ignoring this shit anymore. It cost me the woman I loved, and if I'd listened the second time, maybe Raven wouldn't have wound up in the hands of a sadistic Mage."

Christian noticed Crush's heart beating faster. His breathing also changed as the chemicals in his body reacted to fear. That was an emotion Christian had seen many times in his victims, and the fear in Crush's eyes belied his stoic expression.

"Can we expect your company each time you have a nightmare? What we do is dangerous, and I suspect you'll have nightmares thinking about it. But this is the life your daughter's chosen. You can't save her anymore."

"Can you?"

Christian gestured to the door and invited Crush into the hall. They walked for a spell until they reached the staircase. "I can't ease your fears, but I'll always look after Raven. However, what I can do comes with limitations."

"That's where you and I part. A father's love *has* no limitations. I'd give up everything if she needed me to. Can you say the same?"

"What if it meant her losing this job?"

"I don't give two shits about this job. There's always another job, and a job after that, but you only get one life."

"Do you mind me asking a personal question?"

"What's stopped you before?"

Christian reached the second-floor landing. "Do you ever get the urge to drink booze? Or is the craving gone?"

He clutched the stone railing. "It gets easier with time. But days like this make it hard. Why? Is this about Raven?"

Christian put his hands in his pockets and stared at his feet. "I'm sure you know all about Fletcher. She's not ready to face him."

"How's she gonna face him when he's on the loose?"

"That's not what I mean. Facing what he did and how that changed her. Even if she found him and killed him, that wouldn't put an end to it."

"Really? Because it seems like putting a man six feet under is pretty final to me."

"She's not ready for that. Raven would brood and let those memories control her. 'Tis worse to be haunted by a ghost than a living monster. What'll it take? What made it easy for you to quit drinking that one time and not all the times before?"

Crush stroked his goatee. "Almost dying and losing my daughter. I was drunk one night and swerving all over the damn place. I drove the wrong way on a one-way road and almost hit another car. I served some time, but the judge went easy on me. Sometimes you need a good kick in the ass by the Grim Reaper to figure out what you stand to lose. I couldn't bring myself to make my baby an orphan. Losing her mother was some traumatic shit, and if she lost me, who would have been there to hold her at night when she woke up crying? Nobody, that's who. Raven was my world. Still is. Sometimes you can't talk a man off the ledge. You just gotta let him lean into the wind. I don't know how to help whatever she's going through now, but killing that bastard would be a good start. You out there searching for him? Because maybe she's tired of looking over her shoulder."

Christian marched down the stairs. "She won't have to look

over her shoulder as long as I'm around. You have my word on that."

With every step, Crush's pocket jingled. He was a noisy fella. Sometimes his knee would pop. It seemed absurd to believe this man was ever in a war. Weren't Marines supposed to be stealthy and sneak up on their enemy? Crush sounded like a walking vending machine.

When they reached the first floor, Crush wiped his forehead and blew out a breath. "I can't just go home and sit there. Can't you tell her to call me? At least send a message?"

That posed a problem. Raven didn't have a phone, and Viktor sure as shite wouldn't want anyone knowing her hotel number. Aside from that, she wasn't allowed to make personal calls. No sense in worrying the old man.

"Afraid not," Christian said. "But you have my word that she's alive and well, eating Chinese food."

"And how would you know that?" Viktor interjected.

Christian shut his eyes, afraid to turn around. He didn't make it a habit of tuning in to every sound within the mansion. Had he been listening, he would have heard Viktor approaching from behind the stairs.

Christian pivoted and greeted him with a respectful nod. "I'll fill you in on the details later as it's of a… sensitive nature."

Viktor went to greet Crush and uncharacteristically offered his hand to shake. "Apologies. I did not know you were here, Mr. Graves. Can I offer you a drink?"

Crush gave him a firm handshake. "Just came to check on Raven, but it seems like she's busy."

"Da. Very busy. Perhaps we can arrange a dinner when she returns. I can show you some of my vintage wine."

Crush brushed his hand over his mouth and hid his smile. "I appreciate that, but I don't drink."

"Of course. Cigars?"

"Always loved a good stogie," Crush said with a chuckle. "Don't tell Raven."

"I'd offer you one now, but I'm afraid I have important business matters to attend to."

"That's okay. I need to head back to the shop. If it's possible to get a message to Raven, can you have her call me? I don't need to know what she's doing or where she is, I just want to make sure she's all right."

"Of course. I'll see what I can do."

Crush clapped Christian on the shoulder as he headed to the door. "Put on a shirt. You're not *that* good-looking."

"Don't tumble off your bike and crack your skull, *Dad*."

"Don't call me Dad, peckerhead."

The door slammed.

Viktor shook his head. "You should work on your people skills."

"I'll make a note of it. Were you here all this time? Gem was searching for you."

"I had an appointment. Now what is this about Raven?"

Christian closed the distance between them and lowered his voice. "There was trouble at the club. Someone gave Raven pure sensory magic. Claude had no choice but to call me in. He could have handled it, but it would have raised suspicion. They're on top of this job."

Christian held his breath at the click of high heels in the hall behind the stairwell. When he recognized a light hum, he shook his head at Viktor. "I didn't know you had company, or I wouldn't have said anything about the assignment."

"It is okay."

Lenore appeared from behind the stairs with a light grip on Hunter's hand.

"Did you find the washroom?" Viktor asked. "It can be confusing."

"Yes. I just had to powder my nose," she said with a wink. "This little guy wanted to escort me back." Her slender fingers cupped the back of his head. "I adore children—especially the quiet ones. I could just eat him up."

Christian pressed his lips tightly together.

Lenore let go of Hunter's hand, and Hunter skipped toward the room where Switch usually held lessons. "I would like to include Christian in our meeting if that's okay. I trust him."

Viktor gave Christian a cursory glance before turning away. "As you wish. Follow me."

Christian and Lenore trailed behind Viktor. He passed the office where he often held intimate meetings and headed toward another study at the back of the mansion. The windowless, dark room was suitable for Vampires, but Viktor lit up all the lanterns and candles.

"Have a seat." He gestured to the two wingback chairs before an empty fireplace. The chairs were angled so they faced each other more than the hearth.

Christian sat down on the brown leather and watched Viktor drag over a third chair from a statue of an archer aiming his arrow at Christian's chest.

"I love the Old World charm of your home." Lenore crossed her legs and straightened out one of her wide pant legs. "The courtyard is simply a treasure. I adore greenery, but I can't seem to keep it alive without professional help."

"That sounds about right," Christian muttered.

She sharpened her gaze at him but looked more curious than cross.

Viktor positioned his chair facing them with his back to the fireplace. "Apologies I cannot offer you a drink. I do not have meetings in here often and forgot to replace the wine I finished off last time. If you would like, I can—"

"Please don't trouble yourself," Lenore insisted. "I much prefer tea to wine, and I had a cup earlier." Lenore's lips twitched when she looked at Christian again. "I always seem to catch you without your shirt on. Where on earth would you be at this early hour only half-dressed?"

Christian dramatically crossed his legs but held back from giving her a dirty look. "Getting my chest waxed."

Viktor cleared his throat and shifted to face Lenore. "It is not my habit to include my team in business matters with my clients and contacts. I relay the information to them, and they complete the task."

"And I respect that," Lenore said. "Clearly this is making you uncomfortable, but it's my first time working an assignment like this, and I don't know all the rules."

Christian furrowed his brow. "What do you mean that by that?"

Viktor gestured to Lenore. "Miss Parrish is my secret contact for this mission."

"You don't say?" Christian's stomach turned. *No wonder* she'd popped in the other day, but why would the higher authority give a new person that level of responsibility?

Lenore swept a blond tress away from her face and then studied her pearl ring. "I wanted to preside over execution hearings, but I suppose the powers that be preferred me to start on the bottom rung." She reached over and touched Viktor's hand. "No offense."

"None taken."

She sat back. "I prefer to be involved with seeing justice done. They initially wanted me working on redeveloping district twenty, but I insisted on something more challenging. I despise paperwork."

Viktor clasped his hands together. "I am honored to have you working with us."

Lenore's graceful movements drew attention whenever she did something even as innocuous as admiring her fingernails. "Viktor and I were in a closed meeting unrelated to this case, and he offered to drive me home. I suggested coming here since I enjoyed my last visit."

Viktor swung his gaze to Christian. "Miss Parrish and I were talking in the garage when you were searching for me."

Lenore nodded at him. "I have insider information about the assignment. It would be wise of me to forget I ever heard it, but it's incumbent upon me to share this information despite the risk."

Viktor leaned forward, his congenial expression now riddled with concern.

Lenore uncrossed her legs and fiddled with her slacks as if she weren't used to wearing them. Normally she wore revealing dresses, but trousers somehow made her appear intelligent. "I must warn you that this mission is excessively dangerous, more so than I first thought."

"As all missions are," Viktor replied, assuring her that this wasn't Keystone's first time at bat.

She folded her hands on her lap. "While I know nothing about who might be behind this, a little bird told me that these fights aren't just for the rich. Some powerful clients attend them. Possibly politicians. Nothing would please me more than finding out who. There's a lot of corruption in this city that I'd love to flush out."

Christian frowned. While the rich were often corrupt, and blatantly so, politicians had to be careful. Surely they'd never attend such a public event at the risk of someone recognizing them. "Why don't you make your little bird sing? It would go a lot faster if we had names."

Lenore tilted her neck and lightly traced her finger down her throat. "You have to be careful with birds that sing. Once caged, they'll never fly free again. Where on earth do you think we get half our tips from?"

Viktor eased back in his chair and frowned. "Can your insider be certain that politicians are involved? Did they say if it was the higher authority, Mageri, or other council?"

She lifted her shoulders. "That I don't know, but we have to assume the worst. It's a dreadful predicament that makes this dangerous for everyone involved, including me. People in power will do whatever is necessary to protect themselves, and they have the connections to make it happen. I haven't lived here in many years, and I'm vulnerable. This threat is something I can't express to anyone else on the panel. Without knowing who's involved in the crime ring, I can't chance it getting back to the wrong people. If it weren't for the Regulators who went to the club, I wouldn't have told a single soul about this case. But as it stands, too many people inside our agency know there's an open investigation on locating a fighting ring. I wanted to discuss this in a place where no outsiders could hear. Mr. Kazan—Viktor—do you feel it would be in our best interest to abort the mission?"

He shook his head. "It is too late. As you said, Regulators and Vampires were involved. This is no longer between you and your informant. While I am aware of the confidentiality agreements your employees must abide by, it may not stop this information from leaking to other representatives."

"That's exactly what I'm afraid of," she said. "If the politicians panic, fearing exposure, they might take extreme measures to protect their identity. I'm certain they'll do anything to shut this investigation down."

Christian rose from his chair and circled behind it. "And this is why we have to finish what we've started. If you have a dirty politician, they won't quit their fetish. And if we close the case, they'll make sure that no one will reopen it. Better we expose this operation and shine a light on everyone involved. We're in too deep to turn back now."

Lenore's heart didn't quicken, but she clicked her teeth. "It was my decision to call in your group. Sometimes we work with HALO, but this particular case required a specific set of skills. I feel bad that I dragged you into this."

"Christian is right," Viktor said. "Let's not hasten our decision because of fear. Our work comes with great risk, and forgive my bluntness, but so does yours. I believe this is your first time working with the higher authority. The panel makes life-and-death decisions. They put dangerous criminals behind bars and execute people in front of a crowd. It is not a job without controversy. Surely they briefed you on the risks." Viktor bowed his head. "Forgive me if I speak out of place."

"Honesty is what I value more than anything." She steered her gaze to Christian. "I sincerely hate putting an old friend in danger."

"Christian is not working this assignment," Viktor assured her. "He is not permitted inside the club, so we've sent Raven instead."

Christian searched her face for a reaction, but he didn't get an inkling of what might be going through her mind. Lenore wasn't as transparent as she wanted people to believe, and Christian had a difficult time getting a read on her.

Always had.

"You must feel no guilt for doing your job," Viktor continued, giving her more reassurance than she deserved. "And no responsibility for what might befall us. Keystone does what others will not. I have chosen my people carefully, and they know the sacrifices they must make. They are as committed as you could hope for and eagerly await each new mission. There is nothing too dangerous for us, so do not restrict jobs because you feel responsible for our safety. Safety is an illusion." He rose from his chair. "Do you have a bodyguard? It is commonplace among people of your status. Christian served as a guard for many years."

She took his hand and stood up. "Think I could borrow him until we close this case? If he's available, that is. I don't have time to find a guard on short notice, and to be honest, I don't trust anyone right now. It would give me peace of mind to know that someone as qualified as Christian was protecting me. I can allocate more money for his services. Unless he's working on another project…"

Christian gripped the back of the chair so hard that something ripped.

Viktor squared his shoulders and nodded his head as if mulling the idea over. "I think this is good. Christian needs something to occupy his mind."

For feck's sake, Christian thought. This had to do with him seeing Raven last night. Viktor was probably afraid that Christian wouldn't be able to stay away, but he also didn't have all the facts. Not that it mattered. Once he heard the details, he'd probably find a way to point out all the mistakes and how they could have handled it better—without intervention.

"Splendid." Lenore kissed Viktor on the cheek. "You're an honorable man, and the debt will be repaid."

A blush touched his cheek, and he averted his eyes. "Nonsense. I am only doing what is right."

Christian backed up from the chair. "Viktor, you might need me here."

Lenore touched her pearl ring. "I promise I won't keep Christian all to myself. If there's an emergency, please don't hesitate to call. On that note, if you need anything, I'm available. I want this case to go as smoothly as you do. My life and reputation are on the line, and I think it's in our best interest to work together. I'm sure Christian will agree on that."

As much as he despised siding with Lenore, she was right. "I'll serve as your guard, but no longer than the length of the mission. You'll need at least one guard you can trust going forward. I'll check if my contacts have any openings."

"If I were human, I would say that I'll sleep easier tonight because of you." She turned her attention to Viktor. "I think I'll take you up on that drink. Christian will need time to prepare his things and make any necessary arrangements. Since I'm without my driver, I'll have him take me home." She turned to Christian. "You do have a car, don't you?"

"Will a motorbike do?"

"How absolutely… Neanderthal." She laughed blithely and shook her head.

"Christian makes many jokes," Viktor said, looking between them. "He has a suitable vehicle. If you will excuse me for a moment while I find a vintage wine. Do you prefer red or white?"

Her tongue briefly touched the tip of her canine. "White actually."

Viktor bowed and quickly left the room to dig around in his wine cellar, which was off-limits to everyone.

"Viktor's a good man." Lenore took her seat again. "He's a Shifter, isn't he? I can always tell."

Christian rounded the chair and sat across from her. "What are you scheming?"

She sighed. "Someday you'll realize that I don't have ulterior motives. I need protection, and I trust you like I trust no one else. These are dangerous games we play. Viktor's confidence isn't enough to put me at ease. If people in power are involved in something this nefarious, they'll do whatever it takes to hide their business."

Christian crossed his legs. "Aye. I know all about people who bury their dirty work."

"Still the same unflappable man. Aren't you the least bit concerned about your Mage companion? Why would Viktor choose her over the little one with the purple hair? I find Raven to be a bit of a maverick."

"You almost sound like you care."

"I care about my life, and if she does something foolish to jeopardize this case, it puts all our lives in danger."

"Rest assured, Raven knows what she's doing."

Lenore sighed and crossed her legs. "I heard there was trouble at the club last night. That's another reason I'm here. I hope for your sake she has it under control." Her eyes skated down to Christian's tattoo and lingered. "You seem enthralled by her. I have no say over the Vampire you've become, I only hope you one day realize that love makes you weak. I'm guessing you know that already or you wouldn't have gone to see her when she's undercover. Tell me, why did you agree so quickly to guard me?"

He stroked his beard. "I know you wouldn't do anything to compromise your safety or reputation. Because of your involvement, I can trust you with this mission. That doesn't mean I trust you entirely. I never will. You betrayed me."

Lenore gazed at a lantern on the wall. "One must do whatever necessary to protect oneself. Look at it this way, it made you less trusting. Maybe that's what you needed. You were so young. *So* naive. Everything that happened in your past has led you here. Can you honestly say you regret it?"

"No one was more loyal to you. No one."

She met eyes with him. "Oh, Chrissy. Not a day went by where I didn't wonder if I'd acted hastily. But digging you up would have been far worse. I knew by then you had turned that devotion into hate, and had I let you out, you would have killed me. I thought about sending someone to put you out of your misery, but it was too risky. Tell me, I've heard stories from those who spent years underground. Is there really a point you reach true sleep? Where all the thoughts vanish and you lose sense of consciousness?"

"Pray you never learn firsthand."

Lenore touched her chin and disappeared in her thoughts, her hair just as lovely as ever. Christian remembered how it lit up in the sun as if it were an extension of light.

"I'm inclined to find Viktor a match," she said absently. "He's a powerful man with connections. He needs to work on his grammar, but he is very careful with choosing his words around the right people. Not many are. Handsome, wealthy, polite—all the qualities a woman looks for." She admonished Christian with a glance. "Don't scoff at the idea. You know as well as I do that the only immortals who survive long-term are the ones who either remain single or mate strategically."

"Don't be daft. Viktor can't operate a company like Keystone *and* have a mate."

"You do."

"We're not officially mated, if that's what you're getting at. But even if we were, *both* Raven and I work for Keystone. If Viktor found a wife, he would have to either keep her out of the house and away from our secrets or involve her in them. The latter poses more risks. What woman is willing to risk a memory wipe that spans decades if the marriage goes wrong? *Jaysus*, Mary, and Joseph."

"And if Raven leaves? Does she also get a memory wipe?"

Christian clenched his jaw.

"Are you telling me you two have engaged in a relationship that may one day be doomed to erasure?" Lenore threw back her head and laughed quietly. Then she tapped her chin and regarded him for a minute. "I've underestimated you, old friend. Knowing the risks, you still took them. That's admirable. But things don't always work out as planned. It's just a shame you've marked your body. You'll always carry that reminder if something happens or she leaves you, but you know that already."

"As I said, I'll guard you for as long as Viktor commands, but not a minute longer."

"Do you always do what Viktor asks you to do?"

"Aye."

"Interesting," she replied obliquely.

"Let's just keep this businesslike." He stood from his chair. "One skill I learned in my last job is there's no place for idle chat. When you guard a person, it's not your job to provide entertainment. It's a distraction, and you wouldn't want anything distracting me, now would you?"

She laced her fingers together. "You're absolutely right. Distractions are a weak spot."

Christian headed for the door. "I'll just be packing my bag."

"Christian?"

He gripped the doorknob but didn't look back.

"It's good having you at my side again. I know the feeling isn't mutual, and that's for the best. I have no desire for you to reciprocate those feelings. You wrongfully attached yourself to me, and I think you know now that we would have never been a suitable match. In some ways, I saw you as the progeny I never had. It wouldn't have felt right leading you on."

"Why are you telling me this?"

"I don't want you to get the wrong idea. I never loved you. I never could. And I never will."

That stung far more than it should have. Christian threw her a baleful look over his shoulder. "Are you sure you wouldn't rather borrow a broomstick and fly yourself home?"

She cast him an icy gaze that made his spine straighten. "What a dreadful thing to say."

"That's a keen observation coming from a woman so heartless."

Lenore frowned. "Do you really think a Vampire can keep his heart? You're clinging to the idea that you still need one, but it's futile. You can't be what we are and keep your precious heart. That's what separates us from other immortals. There was a time long ago when makers didn't bother teaching their younglings how to curb their bloodlust. It was a natural part of who we were. But eventually we had no choice but to teach ourselves." She stood up and faced the empty fireplace, her arms folded. "I once loved, when I was young and full of dreams. It almost broke me. Had someone not mentored me through it, I wouldn't be standing here today. Of all the Vampires I've met, you've always been the one with the most potential. I want to see you around in another thousand years. Not everyone has the fortitude to last that long, and it's a lonely journey when friends die or kill themselves. Someday, when you let go of your heart, you'll truly be the Vampire that you were born to be."

"I already let go of it," he said, not sure why she was digging in her heels on a petty argument.

"Yes. But you gave it to someone. When you give your heart away, it always comes back." Lenore turned and lowered her arms. "Sometimes not all in one piece."

Chapter 14

A KNOCK AT THE DOOR MADE me set down my egg roll and tiptoe across the room. Claude bent down to peephole level, and though his face was distorted and he had on a red baseball cap, it was definitely him.

I opened the door.

"What's shakin'?" he asked.

"Do you really think that hat makes all the difference?"

"Clark Kent only needed a pair of glasses." He waltzed in with a plastic bag. "It hides my hair."

"Yeah. That helps," I said, closing the door. "You're not supposed to be here."

He tossed the bag on the bed and frowned. "I don't know your hotel phone number, and I couldn't go to work without making sure you're okay." He tilted my chin up. "You okay?"

When my cheeks heated, I pivoted around. "Take a seat." Once at the table, I munched on my egg roll, unable to meet Claude's direct gaze. "Last night was embarrassing, and I don't want to talk about it. But now I'm worried that somebody saw Christian come in."

Claude pitched his hat onto the bed and took the opposite chair. After raking his fingers through his golden hair, he peered through the slim gap in the heavy drapes. "If our cover is blown, I'll take the heat. I'm the one who called Christian."

I finished the egg roll and wiped my fingers on my sweatpants. "Why didn't you call Viktor instead? Or Blue?"

"Do you think Viktor would have popped in and given you a

ride home? Blue doesn't have clothes, let alone a car. My options were limited. I couldn't leave work, and if I persisted, they might have figured us out. Anyhow, it's not about that. When something goes wrong on our missions, Viktor doesn't want to know. Not unless it's a game changer. He wants us to take care of it. So I took care of it."

"Thanks."

I decided not to tell Claude what had happened in the red room. The door didn't have a lock, and he was probably doing what he thought was right by calling Christian so I wouldn't be left alone for the entire evening.

I sat back and straightened my legs. Though I'd tried to put last night out of my mind, I couldn't stop thinking about what might have happened if Christian hadn't busted in. How could he be so understanding? I'd never been drunk on Sensor magic before, but his reaction really took me aback. Instead of a lecture, I got Chinese food. Instead of suspicious eyes, I got a long kiss to my forehead.

"Have you narrowed down any suspects?" Claude asked, snapping me out of my thoughts.

"One so far. Crawford."

Claude scratched inside his ear. "You mean the older male in the Armani suit?"

"That's the one. Grey-haired and a mole on his left cheek. He gave me his card last night."

Claude stared at the leftovers in my Styrofoam container. "What does he want?"

I shrugged. "I guess I'll find out. He said it has something to do with earning extra money, but he gave the card to me after the ruckus last night. He's a VIP with a lot of money. I've never seen him go into the rooms or upstairs. Have you? He just drinks and watches people."

"I don't recall specifically. Shepherd must have gotten some bad vibes from him if he's on the list."

I glanced at the bed. "What's in the bag?"

Claude sat back and glowered. "My gold panties."

"It must hurt to be that good-looking."

"I'm average."

When I regarded him with a pointed stare, he gave me a winsome smile. Claude had sensual lips, and combined with his beguiling eyes, he could set off a fire alarm.

"Okay. *Above* average," he confessed before standing. While he got plenty of attention in the gold shorts, I could tell that being sexualized was wearing him down.

I noticed my clothes laid out on the bed. Part of me wanted to bail and hide out at my dad's house instead of going back to the club.

Claude looked down at me. "How do you feel? You can take a night off. They'll understand. Viktor will understand."

"We can't afford to. I need to jump on this Crawford lead while it's hot. I don't want him tracing my call back to the hotel, so I have to use the phone at the club. A day off would be great, but it's not the assignment that's getting to me; it's everything else. Dressing in that outfit, people leering, all the stuff that goes on in there. The sooner we close this case, the better."

"Agreed." He sat at the foot of the bed and rubbed his eyes. "It's only been just over a week, but it feels more like a month."

"I don't know why a guy like you signed up with Keystone. You've got the salon, clients—you could totally go out on your own."

Claude lowered his head and clasped his hands together. "I didn't have the salon until Viktor hired me."

I remained quiet, knowing I'd crossed a line by poking into his past. We all respected one another's privacy—most of us wanted to leave the past behind.

"Are you familiar with kindred spirits?" he asked.

I knew a little about it from a diary I'd read on one of our jobs. "A Chitah's mate."

"Not quite. Chitahs have free will to mate anyone we choose, but a kindred spirit is someone we were born to love. It's our soul mate." Claude stared vacantly at a painting on the wall. "Not all of us find our intended. We're often born in different times or countries, but the Prides now have what they call a Gathering. It's held every year locally, and then there are national and international ones."

"Sounds like a giant dating game."

"A male knows his kindred spirit the moment he sees her and draws in her scent. She doesn't. So if we want to court her properly, we must prove ourselves worthy and win her love. I met Josephine in 1965. My parents had passed away by that time. They were old."

"Don't Chitahs live for hundreds or thousands of years?"

"They had my sister and me very late in life—past the age that most females will consider children. Chitahs usually live with their siblings, but my sister was born different, so our parents were protective and kept her home with them."

"Where's your sister now?"

Claude's voice softened. "She died many years before they did. It was a hard adjustment, and I couldn't abandon my parents. I stayed with them until the end. So after they died, I was lost and on my own." He smiled wistfully. "Literally lost. I decided to move from Pennsylvania to Cognito, and I got mixed up. I approached a young woman to ask for directions, and when she turned around, I knew instantly that I'd met my kindred spirit. An empty part of my soul instantly filled up." He held his fist to his chest. "All I wanted to do was mark her and make her mine."

"That might have made it a little awkward in the middle of the road. Do you really do that?" I wrinkled my nose.

"There's no greater honor." He steered his gaze to me. "It's not as vulgar as it sounds. Our chemistry changes, and a unique scent lifts off our skin. It lets every other male know that this female is claimed, and it lets *her* know that she has a serious suitor. One who will die for her." Claude leaned back on his hands. "She backed up a step when she caught it wafting off me. I didn't mark her, but the imprint lifted off my skin as if it were searching for her. Josephine was like no female I'd ever known. She wore patchy bell-bottoms, and two flaxen braids were tied in the back. Her top was so skimpy that I almost took off my own shirt to cover her up."

"People didn't dress like that in your hometown?"

"In Williamsport? No. Even Cognito was a little reserved in those days, so Josie stood out."

"Josie?"

"That was her nickname. I sometimes called her pussycat, after the comics. It was an inside joke." Claude stood up and brewed a pot of coffee. "Humans were protesting the war, fighting for civil rights, and speaking out for women's lib. But it was different for Breed. We had issues of our own, and maybe some of the human protests galvanized people within our own communities to make big changes. Josephine was outspoken against what she called the patriarchy of Breed culture. Almost every organization was run by males. The laws were riddled with holes, and women didn't have all the protection they deserved."

After the coffee brewed, Claude poured two cups and set them on the table. He sat across from me but turned his chair toward the door.

Steam rose from his cup, and he let it sit on the table to cool. "Josie wanted more female leaders. She was part of an activist group that showed up at all the meetings organized by our elders and the Lord. It wasn't just Chitahs, they wanted change everywhere. Especially with the higher authority. Leaders were and still are selected by their peers. It's not a public vote." He sipped his coffee. "Change was more important to her than anything."

"Even you?"

"Especially me."

"Why?"

He released a deep sigh. "I represented something she was fighting against. She equated mating her kindred spirit as a step back. I never pushed her. She was willing to give me her body, just not her heart. Josie wanted to change the world." The light in his eyes dimmed. "She mated another male. He was a Mage, a representative for the higher authority. She thought by publicly mating her natural enemy that it would bring everyone together, but I knew that wasn't the real reason."

I warmed my fingers on my mug. "What was?"

"Josie thought if she could mate with someone in power, she

could be the puppet master who pulled the strings—that she could change the laws from the inside, because their efforts on the outside were failing. Her comrades didn't understand, and their protests escalated to violence. They threw Molotov cocktails into the homes of important men, and when one of those incendiary weapons set fire to a Mageri councilman, everything changed. They became renegades and went underground. The higher authority declared them outlaws and wanted anyone affiliated with them killed."

I furrowed my brow. "They can't do that. Dead or alive is the rule, but they can't order hits."

He lifted his cup. "When eighty percent of the panel was Mage, they could do whatever they wanted. The Mageri formed first, so when the higher authority was conceived, it was hard to get leaders from all the Breeds to join. Nobody wanted to be the bad guy and have a target on his back."

I got up and sat on the edge of the bed to face him. "So what happened?"

"There was an insurgence. When some of the revolutionaries were killed, others joined. The higher authority wanted to snuff them out before they lost control. Many lives were lost on both sides. It lasted several years. They eventually negotiated a peace treaty and allowed the rebels to remain in the Bricks with no fear of retaliation in exchange for adding a few women to leadership. By then everyone wanted peace."

I reached for Claude's baseball hat and held it in my hands. "What happened to Josie? Did she stay with that man?"

The color drained from Claude's face. "Josie was found in the river."

Thunderstruck, I stared at his hat, unsure of what to say. What *can* you say to a blow like that?

He touched the handle of his mug but didn't drink. "I found out on a Monday morning while eating a bagel in a café. I turned the page of the newspaper, and there it was. I still remember the sound of two males laughing, the bell jingling when a female walked in, the jasmine smell of her perfume as she passed my table. Everything in that moment crystallized. My kindred spirit was dead. They said it was suicide, but I didn't believe it. Someone murdered her."

"I'm really sorry."

All four of Claude's canines elongated, but he kept talking as if he wasn't aware. "First I went after her mate to get answers. I smelled lies, went primal, and I killed him. Then I went to question her former acquaintances who were living it up in the Bricks. I smelled lies and killed some of them. I went on a killing spree, and I couldn't stop. I never got answers. I never got the truth."

"How are you still alive?" I shook my head. "Killing a higher authority member is a death sentence."

"True, but I wager they didn't want him there anymore and were glad he was gone. He was a corrupt man, something Josie didn't know when she mated him." Claude stood up, grabbed his bag, and then lingered by the door. "Sometimes you don't get answers, and that's the worst kind of torture there is. To never know how or why your loved one died. To never know what their last words were. And though I probably killed her murderer, I don't know for certain, and I never will. At least they found her body."

I stood up and joined his side. I wanted to say she didn't deserve a guy like Claude, but he would have been offended. His kindred wanted to change the world and thought marrying strategically would help their cause. She was willing to sacrifice her own happiness for a greater good. It was what brave people did. "I'm glad you're here now."

"Viktor rescued me from cage fights, you know. That's where I ended up. I had so much rage. I get why some of these women might do it. They've been held back in life, and they're trying to get what they deserve—money and power. They're easy targets. That's why I took this job. Viktor turned my life around and gave me a chance to help people and not hurt them."

I handed him his hat. "I know what you mean. You didn't have to tell me all that, but I appreciate it. I won't tell anyone else."

He took the hat. "It's not a secret. I'm sure most of my deeds are well documented in the higher authority's files. Viktor fought hard for me, and so I'll fight hard for him. Even if it means wearing gold panties."

I rocked on my heels. "If it's any consolation, you're the hottest guy in the club, even fully dressed."

He leaned down and touched his forehead to mine. "Take care of yourself, female. I worry about you."

"I worry about me too."

Chapter 15

"Pitcher for table nine," Simone called out. Filling pitchers had become my job, and I knew it was because those customers were cheap tippers. But I didn't complain. It gave me a chance to talk to Claude and share information.

"How are the tips, Mistress White?"

I gave Claude a cross look. "Don't call me that. Not unless you have a twenty in your hand."

He licked the tip of his finger and touched my arm before making a sizzling sound. "You're the cat's meow tonight."

The club was abuzz with rumors of the previous night's brawl. Those who had witnessed it firsthand discovered that I wasn't all talk and no action, and that titillated customers. When people began fighting to get in line, I sent them to the other bartenders to even out the work. How the hell had I wound up being so damn good at something I hated? If my father saw what I was doing now, he'd probably lock me in my old bedroom for the rest of my life.

Claude collected the tray and strutted off to the beat of the music. He had a fifty tucked in the back of his shorts and didn't seem to know it, even though it flapped behind him like a tail.

Flynn eased up to the bar and watched Claude hawkishly. He pinched his beard as if contemplating something. "What do you and that lovely man spend so much time talking about?"

I wiped down the bar with a rag. "Give it up. He's out of your league."

"Says the competition." Flynn slid onto the stool and adjusted his orange glasses. "Nobody's out of my league, princess. I just have to figure out how to get on the team. How much do you think he makes a night in tips?"

I sighed. "Is money all you care about?"

"Yes," Simone answered for him while taking care of a woman in red latex.

Flynn tucked his cheek against his fist and leaned to one side. "My Creator was a blacksmith who made the equivalent of a dollar a day. He wanted cheap help, so he made me. I slaved my fingers to the bone, and all I got was a bed and a free meal."

"Why didn't you leave?"

"I was so wrapped up in the whole immortality thing that I didn't care. He said I couldn't leave until he taught me all the magic stuff, and he never did. He kept putting it off so he could keep me around and make more money for himself." Flynn turned his gaze away. "Manky bastard," he muttered under his breath.

"Maybe you should play the lottery."

"I would, but I haven't got any luck. So, Robin White, tell me about yourself. Are you from around here?"

"Born and raised."

He stroked his bottom lip. "Did your Creator teach you all those moves?"

"Nope. Learned them on the streets." I tossed the rag into a bin. "When you meet the right people, you learn what you can."

"Is this what you wanted to be when you grew up? A bartender?"

"Hell no."

"How old are you, if you don't mind my asking?"

"I stopped counting at twenty-five. Does it matter?"

His eyes skated down. "Your breasts are heaving."

"So is that gentleman at table five. Better clean up."

He glanced over his shoulder. "Bollocks."

After Flynn swaggered off, I signaled to Simone that I was taking my break. I wanted to call John Crawford and see what I could shake out of that tree. Men ogled me as I made my way through the room. Some bowed, others leered. The cloth around my head made me look like a superhero, but I sure as hell didn't feel like one. After working my ass off all night, I was having regrets about choosing the leather corset. It felt like my body was in a vise and I might burst free at any moment.

As I reached the door, a handler came out and held it open for me.

"Thanks," I said, taking note of her mask. Maybe she had a day job and working in a club like this would get her in trouble.

When I entered the break room, my reflection in the long mirror above the sinks looked like a stranger. The stools were tucked in beneath the counter, and someone had left behind a tube of lipstick. I passed the lockers on the left and headed toward the bathroom door. Instead of going in, I stopped in the alcove on the right and looked at three empty chairs and a telephone. Then I swung the bathroom door open and went inside. Unlike the customer restroom, we had six private stalls and urinals with dividers. I bent over to make sure I had the place to myself.

When I didn't see any feet beneath the stalls, I ducked into the alcove and plopped into a chair facing the dressing room so I could peer around the privacy wall and keep an eye on the main door. The rotary phone was something I'd seen in old movies, so I had no trouble dialing. It wasn't uncommon for Breed establishments to have rotary phones, jukeboxes, cigarette machines, and other obsolete relics from the past.

"This is Crawford," the man answered.

"Hi. It's Robin. You gave me this number."

"Robin…"

"I tend bar at the White Owl. Black hair, brown eyes, got in a fight last night."

"Ah, yes. Robin. Did you consider my offer?"

"Uh, yeah. But what's the offer for?"

"I don't do business over the phone. When is a good time we can meet?"

"I get off at three."

He chuckled. "Yowzer. I sleep, you know."

"How about noon tomorrow?"

"That works. Why don't we meet at Ruby's Diner. Do you know where that is?"

Panic set in. "In the human district?"

"I like my privacy."

My heart slammed against my rib cage. No way in hell could I walk into Ruby's and risk the staff calling me by my real name. "That place isn't as private as you think. Have you heard of Northern Lights? They're busy at night, but in the daytime, not that many people."

"I know the place. But a man like me wouldn't be seen in a bar like that."

"Do you normally do business in a public place? Seems counterintuitive for a guy who likes his privacy. Anyhow, I don't have a car, so getting over to the human district isn't easy. Not unless I take the train."

"Why don't I just pick you up now so we can talk? I can be there in half an hour." He sounded flustered. "We'll drive around the block, talk it over, and you can go back to work. They do let you have breaks, don't they?"

"Works for me. I'll be out front."

"See you then."

Just as I hung up, someone walked in. Simone wouldn't like me taking two breaks back to back, especially during the evening rush. She'd report me to the manager, and rightly so. I couldn't let my coworkers think I was working undercover—the gossip alone could ruin our mission.

I sprang to my feet and hurried to the door. A woman with Donna Summer hair judged me with her eyes as she bent over the sink and applied pink lipstick.

When I reached Houdini's office, I knocked. What were the chances he was actually there? Probably slim to none, and I had no other way to reach him. But I needed an alibi, and fast.

I stepped back in surprise when the door opened.

Houdini was about Christian's height—just a hair over six feet. Nothing about his style gave away his age. The faded jeans might hint toward a younger man, but I knew he was at least a hundred years old.

At least.

"To what do I owe the honor?"

I pushed past him. "I need to ask a favor."

The door closed, and he turned, looking more stylish than usual in a dark blazer over a grey shirt.

"Why don't you let your employees dress casual?" I asked, looking down at his black dress shoes.

He leaned on the door and propped his foot against it. "This isn't a five-star restaurant."

"I realize that, but bartenders aren't part of the show. You could at least let us wear cut-off T-shirts or something more comfortable."

His hazel eyes settled on me. "You have plenty of options. Have you considered the fishnet tops? I hear they're quite comfortable."

I folded my arms to keep from strangling him. "Simone showed me the dress code. You aren't allowed to wear those with a bra."

A smile touched his broad mouth. "Of all the things you could complain about, it's attire. Is that the favor you wish to ask? If I grant it, you'll stand out."

"No. I need to take an extended break. I'm on a break now, and I don't know how long I'll be gone. Probably less than an hour. Obviously I can work to make up the hours, but that's not the issue."

"Then what is?"

"You have rules, and the employees around here follow them to a tee. In fact, you've got a few snitches on the floor. People are going to start wondering why I'm getting special treatment, and the manager might fire me."

"Don't worry about Karen. She does whatever I ask."

I flicked a glance at all the monitors on the wall behind me.

"Are you feeling better today?"

When I turned back around, Houdini gave me a start as he was only inches in front of me.

"What do you mean?"

He caressed my cheek with his hand. "I told you not to break my rules."

It took me a minute to register what he had just admitted.

"Drinking on the job not only makes you unpredictable, but it puts my customers at risk."

I leaned away from his touch. "Did you spike my drink last night?"

He stared at me as if I'd asked an inane question.

Anger swirled in me like a cyclone, and I shoved his chest. "You asshole! What gives you the right to mess with me like that? Do you realize the danger you put me in?"

He straightened his coat. "A belligerent woman. Is that what Keystone has reduced you to? One of the qualities I most liked about you when we first met was how dispassionate you were. There was little I could do or say that would make you emotional."

"This is different. You sabotaged me. And when it comes to my body, all bets are off."

He wandered over to the row of cabinets against the wall. "I cautioned you not to drink while on duty, and here you are, blaming *me* for something *you* had complete control over. Had you not violated my trust, we wouldn't be having this conversation."

I snorted. "What trust? You left me for dead on day one."

He sighed and unlocked a cabinet. "I won't revisit that conversation anymore. You already know what my intentions were, and your disappearance wasn't something I anticipated." When the cabinet door opened, he pulled out a bottle. "These are my personal collection."

I stared at a row of bottles. The only thing that distinguished one from the next was the color of the screw cap. "Are those bottles spiked? You know that's illegal."

He unscrewed the cap to one and sniffed it. "I'm not a man who likes rules, but we need them to make this place run efficiently. This club is rife with customers who are looking for excitement. That said, I do enjoy a little chaos now and then."

"Your chaos almost got me—"

"'Got you' is the wrong word choice. The magic in that

bottle amplifies your primitive urges, allowing you to relinquish all inhibitions. It's the stripped-down version of you—the most authentic you. Have you ever heard of love potions? They're not a thing of lore. Sensors used to sell them for good money, but things like that have gone out of fashion." He set down the bottle and approached me with an easy stride. "Poe broke the rules and entered my club."

"To save me."

Houdini tilted his head, his features unreadable. "What a hero. I didn't take you for a woman who needed saving, but now I wonder what might have happened with my little experiment had he not interfered. Would you have given in to lust, or would you have fought against it and killed the man? I wonder…"

I stared with blank surprise. "You knew what happened in the red room?"

He jerked his chin at the screens behind me. "I see everything. Did Poe tell you it wasn't your fault? That you were a victim?" Houdini shook his head. "Sensor drinks don't remove free will. Deep down, you always have a choice. You know that, don't you?"

I narrowed my eyes. "Then have a drink and see how much control *you* have."

"They only reveal your deepest desires." He stepped forward into my space. "You're underestimating what I would want. Perhaps we should both have a drink."

"Let's not."

The recessed lighting brought out the white in his hair. "What do you think might happen?"

"Don't try to convince me that I wanted to screw some random guy."

"Would it have been so terrible to give in to your desires with a total stranger?"

"They weren't my desires. They were artificial."

"Did it feel artificial when he spanked you and you moaned for more?"

The blood drained from my head. "You watched the whole thing? And chose to do nothing?"

"Like I said before, I see everything. And what would I have to gain from interfering?"

I slapped him hard. Then I did it again and my palm stung. Despite my sudden violent outburst, I managed to keep a cool and collected tone. "I'm not your experiment anymore. We have to play nice for the sake of this assignment, but if you ever meddle in my life again, so help me, I'll put you in the ground."

"Killing your maker is punishable by death. That will haunt you for the rest of your days."

"I didn't say I'd kill you. I only said I'd bury you."

He arched an eyebrow. "Will you keep my key? Since we're on the topic of meddling."

"Why do you keep turning this back on me?"

Houdini strode to his desk and sat on it. "Because you're desperate to blame me for all your woes. Had you followed my rule about drinking, you wouldn't have put yourself in that predicament. I created an opportunity to expose your weakness. When others see your weaknesses, they use them against you. And if you keep turning to the bottle because you're incapable of suppressing your emotions, you'll make it easy for someone to take advantage of you. You're not a woman who takes orders, so showing you was better than telling."

"You're really good, you know that?"

"What do you mean?"

"Christian warned me, but I didn't want to see it. I still don't want to see it. But there it is. You keep trying to make me believe that everything is my fault and you haven't done anything wrong—that I'm just overreacting or imagining my fears. You think you know what I really wanted last night based on a video, but you weren't inside my head. And because you didn't pour the drink down my throat, you think that absolves you of any responsibility. I've done a lot of bad shit in my life, but I still have a sliver of a conscience. Do you?"

Unperturbed, Houdini reached for the phone and dragged it toward him. "I'll inform the others that you're on a special errand. Be back in two hours." He lifted the receiver. "And don't ever threaten me again. Not unless you mean it."

Chapter 16

"I FIND THE EVENING HOURS DREADFULLY boring." From her wicker chair, Lenore drank white wine in the dark sunroom. "Remember when we had Vampire parties from dusk until dawn? Those truly were the days."

Christian had just finished a security check throughout Lenore's estate. Every window, every door, and every possible way in. He gave her a notepad. "I made a handy list of all your weaknesses."

"I have none," she said with a wink. "Come sit with me."

Christian branched away and began testing the windows—anything to avoid mindless chatter. Lenore had changed into a white nightgown that left nothing to the imagination. Her dark nipples were staring at him through the semisheer fabric like two beady eyes.

"I'm inviting you to join me."

He drifted past her, still checking the windows. "Are you afflicted in some way? This isn't a social affair. I have a job to do. If you want a companion, you should call in your manservant."

"Wilson?" She snorted. "He's loyal, but that old geezer wouldn't know how to hold a conversation any more than he knows how to hold in his farts." She sighed. "Why is there no better word for it? Passing wind seems too refined for such a vulgar act."

"Still pondering life's great mysteries, I see." Christian reached the last window and then admired the lush plants that filled her sunroom. "There's always *toot*."

Lenore snickered and almost spilled her wine. "Do you remember that time we went to Chicago? I think it was 1928. We were trapped in an elevator with that dreadful man who smelled like an outhouse." She wrinkled her nose as she recalled the memory. "I never did like elevators. Not then or now. Are you like that, Chrissy? I find that the more I'm surrounded by innovation, the more I want to escape it."

He backed up against the house wall and looked through the windows that surrounded them. "If you're fearing for your life, you might consider moving to a room with four walls."

"Nonsense. I refuse to alter my lifestyle because of a moron." Her chair faced right, giving him a profile view of her long legs. The slit up her gown revealed every inch of them from toe to thigh.

Lenore studied the tiny bubbles that danced inside her drink. "Lenore isn't my real name, you know. Sometimes the only way to reinvent ourselves is to start over. I wish Vampires had taken on the custom of renaming their younglings. A Mage's immortality begins with their first spark, when they're given a new name. Vampire elders never adopted the same custom. They *want* to know where you came from." She shifted in her chair to look at him. "Do you know why? I do."

"I couldn't care less."

"But you *should* care. The ancients knew the power in knowledge. Most younglings have a family. Parents, siblings, cousins, sometimes a spouse and children. Contrary to what most people believe, a person's true weakness is love. Vampires didn't have the luxury of breaking the rules or fleeing their makers. The elders knew how to locate their family, and that gave makers more control over their progeny. No one wants to put their loved ones in danger. But you see, that same weakness also makes it easy for your enemies to have power over you." She sipped her wine and set the flute on a round glass table. "I find it amusing that you—a trained guard—don't know how to guard your own safety. Anyone you love will always be your weakness."

Christian focused on a moth flitting overhead in hopes that Lenore would drop the subject. She was only verbalizing what he'd always known as truth. He'd seen love ruin men. It made them vulnerable and easy to control. His own misguided feelings for Lenore had been his ruin. Christian didn't live in the land of denial, but his heart and his mind weren't always on the same page.

Lenore rose and strolled to the center of the room. She stopped in a pool of moonlight and stood with her back to him. "I want the best for you. Our friendship deserves a fresh start. We've both evolved, and we're better off as allies than enemies." She turned on her heel, her black eyes sparkling like two dark stars. "You've chosen a worthy match. Raven has the potential to become a powerful Mage—a force to be reckoned with. She's not from the Old World. She'll probably lead the revolution to change our culture." Lenore approached him and arched an eyebrow. "She might even expose us to humans. The new ones are eager to merge the two worlds. They don't know what it was like—how humans banded together to exterminate our kind. Some of the ancients desire war, but if we can't even settle differences amongst ourselves, it's a delusion of grandeur to think we would band together to defeat humans. Mortals haven't evolved." Lenore brushed lint off his shoulder. "They can build all the fancy buildings they want and fly in these tin cans, but learning that *we* exist would flip them back into the Dark Ages. Only *now* we have something to truly fear."

The statement hung in the air, and Christian couldn't resist taking the bait. "And what's that?"

"Nuclear weapons," she replied. "Biochemical warfare. Genetic engineering. They would experiment on us—find a way to genetically change or destroy us. In fact, I think humans would be so envious of our immortality and powers that they would do anything to harness that for themselves. They once wanted to destroy us, but thanks to science, we'll be nothing but lab rats. Take care not to let someone as young as Raven pull you under with wild ideas."

He folded his arms. "What you know about Raven could fill a thimble."

"I never said I didn't like her. I've given her nothing but high praise. She's just not the match I would have chosen for you. I'm still admittedly shocked that you're dating outside your Breed. If memory serves, you were always outspoken about interbreeding."

"You should spend less time worrying about where my cock warms itself at night and more time finding your own fecking suitor."

She lifted her chin. "Oh, but I have."

Christian got a sinking feeling as she sashayed back to her chair and took a seat. "I'll not be joining your side in unholy matrimony. So you can put that infernal thought out of your head, now and forevermore."

Lenore lifted her glass with three fingers and chuckled softly. "I see you haven't lost your sense of humor. No, Chrissy, it's not you I want as my partner."

A weight lifted off his shoulders. He would rather put hornets in his pants for the rest of his life than marry that woman.

She set down her glass. "Viktor continues to impress me."

Christian marched forward and sat in the chair across from her. He tried to remain cordial even though he was having fantasies about tossing her through a window. "Since when do Shifters catch your fancy?"

"They're growing on me." Lenore crossed her legs and gazed out the window. She absently touched the long stem of a fern as if deep in thought. "I think we'd make a splendid match. He's kind but not a pushover. He values secrecy and understands political and social maneuverings. It also doesn't hurt that he has connections all over the world. Aside from that, Viktor's a wolf."

Christian's blood went ice-cold as the horror of it all sank in. "And a wolf does it for you?" he asked coolly. "All that tail wagging and crotch licking. I thought you'd set your sights a little higher, like someone in your organization. We're a wee group who contracts our services for money."

Lenore finished her wine with a smile hidden behind her glass. "Wolves are protective of their mates. I'll never have to worry about someone like Viktor betraying me."

"He's not your type."

She pursed her lips. "And what type is that?"

Christian crossed his legs. "Subservient."

"I prefer an equal."

"I thought you preferred to live alone on a deserted island?"

She smiled wistfully. "It passed the time. For a while. But I missed companionship. Imagine the practicality of it. I could work closely with your team on special projects, and I'd never have to leave the house."

Christian swallowed hard. "Phone messaging is a convenient thing."

"I meant *your* house."

He uncrossed his legs and gave her a thorny look. "Over my rotting corpse."

Lenore drew in a deep breath and moaned as she let it out through her nose. "Would you rather we all live here? If I choose a partner, it only makes sense to combine our fortunes and properties. I wouldn't dream of living across town. Of course, he *would* have to upgrade some of his rooms. They are a bit rustic."

Christian stood and neared the door. "I'll be outside."

"Christian?"

He paused but kept his back to her.

"This isn't about you. Despite the fulfillment that Keystone brings Viktor, he's a lonely man. We make sense together, and I think he's clever enough to know the value of a strategic pairing. We could become a power couple, and I haven't seen too many of those in this city. I have resources at my fingertips. I'll be extremely useful to Keystone."

"You say it as if it's decided."

"You know me, Chrissy. I always get what I want."

Chapter 17

I stood on the curb outside the club, searching the dark streets for Mr. Crawford. Despite the warm weather, I had put on a black blazer to conceal my light tattoo.

Why did Houdini always have to mess with my head? I couldn't stop thinking about our conversation. Had I followed the rules instead of indulging in alcohol to smooth out the edges, I wouldn't have drunk pure Sensor magic. But I didn't deserve what had happened—or what could have happened—and the fact Houdini hadn't intervened only solidified my opinion of him. In any case, that was a wake-up call. I needed to get my shit together before I turned into a wrecking ball and destroyed our plans.

"Hey, what goes on in there?" a young woman asked me from the line.

I ignored her as a black car pulled up in front of me. When the passenger window rolled down, I peered inside and saw Crawford behind the wheel.

"Get in," he said.

"I've only got two hours. Where are we going?"

"Around the block. I know a place."

As I climbed into the leather seat, I looked down at my leather corset and shorts. *Dear God, don't let this man take us to Taco Bell.*

The car made a right, and we drove several blocks with classical music on the radio to fill the awkward silence. I thought about breaking the ice by asking him what he did for a living, but if my hunch was correct, it had something to do with cage fights.

Outside the window, just above the streetlights, I glimpsed a falcon soaring through the shadows.

"So tell me about the side job you're offering," I finally said. "Are you sure that I'm qualified for whatever it is?"

Crawford pulled behind a large department store and drove past the dumpsters and loading dock. The large brick wall gave us complete privacy, and since the store was closed, we wouldn't have to worry about an employee walking up. He shut off the engine but kept the battery on.

Crawford turned off the music. "I'm looking for a special woman. A Mage who's dexterous, strong, and has powerful light. Are you that woman?"

"So I've been told." Since I wasn't supposed to know what he was offering, I had to sell myself without being obvious. "You can't stop a bar fight without having all those qualities. Are you looking for a bodyguard?"

His tongue swiped his bottom lip. "I'm a wealthy man, and I can offer you a chance to make a lot of money. More than the chump change you make at that bar."

"Doing what?"

"I need assurance that I can trust you." Crawford exited the vehicle, slammed the door, and then got into the back seat. "Step into my office and we'll discuss the details. I dislike modern cars. They build a wall between you and the passenger in the front seat." He lowered an LCD screen from the ceiling and typed something on his phone.

I stepped out of the car and climbed into the back, making sure to leave my door open.

Crawford set his phone on the backrest and shifted toward me. "Close the door, please. I don't want a spotlight on us."

I shut the door and noticed a sword mounted on the ceiling. Not a big one, but he'd customized hooks to hold it in place and keep it out of sight.

Crawford twisted toward me and briefly touched the mole on his chin. The smell of his expensive cologne was overwhelming. "I'm looking for a woman who's got fight in her," he began. "Most of the ones I meet play by the rules. You're not that kind of woman, are you?"

"Rules are for sheep."

His lips twitched. "Before I make an offer, I want you to know how serious I am. Each time I call on your services, you'll receive ten thousand."

My breath caught. This was serious money.

He gestured toward the pouch behind the passenger seat. "Reach in there."

When I tucked my fingers inside, I gripped paper and pulled out a yellow envelope. Inside were three stacks of bills.

"Count it if you like," he said. "It's all there. You might want to start carrying a purse."

"I don't get it. You know I can't stay away from work that long. Is this an advance?"

"I want you to see how serious I am about my offer. Money speaks louder than words."

I shoved the cash back into the pouch. "Okay. You're serious, but what's the offer?"

He glanced out the back window. "I want you to juice me."

What the hell? "Is this a test?"

"I like rough play," he said. "I like to resist, and I need a strong woman who can take it from me by force."

I blinked in surprise. "*That's* what this is about? Why all the cloak and dagger? You could ask any woman at the club to do this. I bet there's even a room for it."

My blood pressure skyrocketed, and I shifted in my seat. *What a waste of time.*

"They won't indulge fantasies like mine." When he touched his phone, the LCD in front of us lit up with an image. "I need visual stimulation for this transaction to work."

When I glanced at the screen, my blood chilled. A girl no older than seven was crying. I steered my gaze away when a large hand entered the frame to slap her. That hand wore the same ring as the one on Crawford's middle finger.

My fangs punched out, and blood roared in my ears. Fury stole my reasoning like a thief in the night. John Crawford represented the villains I used to hunt and kill—loathsome men who didn't deserve to breathe the same air as everyone else. Most were human killers, but Crawford was special. He was my white whale.

His eyes rounded when he saw my fangs. "Impossible! I saw you flash. I saw—"

Before he could flee, I lunged and pulled his hand away from the door handle. We tussled for a minute, and I sank my fangs into his neck and drank his noxious blood. Like poison on my tongue, I could taste every wicked thing about him. Something inside me took over—something dark. I wasn't Raven anymore.

I was the Shadow.

My mask fell off as I drank. It didn't take much to weaken this pathetic slug. Before he could even think about fighting me off, I gripped his hands and locked fingers. "You like it rough? Well, you're in luck." I pulled his light so fast that it snapped against my palms.

Crawford bit his bottom lip. What an absolute fucking nightmare. As the video continued, all I heard was the plaintive sound of a sobbing child.

And this evil little toad was getting off on it.

I glared down at him with cutthroat eyes. "Lights out." His energy surged through me like a roaring freight train. An audible snap sounded, followed by a flash of light. Crawford's core light—the light that preserved his immortality—was now mine, leaving him a shell of a man.

He gasped in horror. "You *can't*… You *can't*!"

I tipped my head and grinned foolishly. "But I did." After opening my door, I detached his sword from the interior roof and stepped out. I preferred knives, but the sword felt good in my hands. Like it knew exactly what to do. "Come face your death, mortal."

Anticipating his every move, I coolly walked around to his door and tapped the blade against the glass. There was no escape, and he knew it. I could flash, and he couldn't.

Crawford dove between the seats to drive off, but he wasn't

fast enough. I already had the driver's door open, casually leaning against it as I waited for his next move. No need to make this a gory death. Crawford was a human now, and all it would take was one little poke through the gut.

His car turned on and off using a push button, and I had no idea where the key fob was. All I could do was wait, and my patience was as thin as his grey hair.

Crawford climbed out of the passenger seat and looked at me over the top of the car. "That money is just a drop in the bucket," he said calmly, his composure returned. "I can make you rich. Return my immortality, and we'll work out an exceptional arrangement. You'll never want for anything."

"I just bet." I spat on the ground as his dark blood churned in my stomach like spoiled meat.

"We all have our secrets," he went on, turning his gaze downward. "How many people know about *your* little secret? Does the Mageri know you're a half-breed?"

I slammed the door and rounded the car from the rear. "I don't like veiled threats." When I reached the other side, I set the pointy tip of the sword against the concrete and rested my hands on the pommel. "I'm not here to make deals. You picked the wrong woman. That's a mistake you'll have to live with for the next thirty seconds of your life."

He held out his hands, beads of sweat clinging to his wrinkled forehead. "Wait! If I die, my fortune goes to the Mageri. Wouldn't you rather see it go to the little children? I can make this right. That video isn't what you think. It's old, and she was an actress!"

I gripped the handle with my right hand and drew in a deep breath.

Crawford's last words put the nail in his own coffin. "They had a choice. They *wanted* to do it. And I gave them plenty of money."

I swung my arm. Bright-red blood gushed from his neck. When he tried covering the wound with his hands, blood sprayed outward.

Crawford didn't deserve a quick end. I wanted him to suffer

for years before the sweet release of death. His victims deserved justice.

I tossed the sword to the ground, and the metal clanged against the concrete as Crawford bled out. Ignoring the gurgling and gasping, I reached into the back seat and snatched the envelope filled with cash.

Someone seized my arm, and I spun around and threw energy into him.

Flynn gave me a hard shake and glowered. "What the bloody hell have you done?"

I wrenched away. "Taking out the trash."

He noticed the envelope. "I knew you were trouble."

"How did you know I was here? Did you follow me?"

"*Of course* I followed you. I stepped outside for a smoke when I saw you getting in the car with that deranged cad."

"You warned me to stay away from him."

He snorted. "You suck at taking advice."

I stepped forward and narrowed my eyes. "Did you *know* about his perversions?"

"A few months ago, a lady quit after going off with him. Seems he likes it rough and wanted her to assault him or something along those lines."

I gave Flynn a hard shove and forced him into the back seat. Seconds after viewing the video, he shot out of the car and stumbled backward. When the audio filled his ears, Flynn dove back into the car and pounded his fist against the screen until it broke.

He got out, his breath heavy. "If I'd known about that, I would have done something about that manky bastard myself." Flynn put his hands on his hips and looked down at the body. "We can't leave him here like this."

"Help me lift him," I said. "We'll dump his body in the trash. I can drive the car somewhere and clean it, strip the plates, remove personal items—"

"Have you lost your mind? You want to toss him in the bin? That's exactly the kind of thing that draws attention from the Mageri."

"And what do you know about body disposal?"

"That there's a learning curve." He took out his phone and sent a message. "I know a cleaner who owes me a favor. Did anyone else see you leave together?"

"About thirty humans. What's the doorman's name? He saw me go with Crawford. His name starts with a *G*."

"I'll take care of Gordon."

"What do you mean by 'take care of'?"

Flynn put his phone in his back pocket. "Money takes care of everything. He's a good chap and knows how to keep secrets. Did you think I was going to bury him in cement? I'm not the mafia." He ran his fingers through his windblown hair. It defied gravity and refused to lie flat, as if he'd stuck his finger in a light socket.

Why the hell am I thinking about his hair when I just murdered an elite?

"Why was Crawford considered a VIP?" I asked. "Please don't tell me he works for the higher authority."

"Money makes you important. I don't know what kind of personal connection he has with the owner or if it's just about money, but he's not an official. That much I know."

I sat on the trunk of the car and stared at the wall that stretched all the way down to the end of the shopping center. What would Viktor do if he found out about this? I glanced up at the falcon sitting atop the building.

Great. Blue was the most loyal member of Keystone, and if anyone would report this back to Viktor, it would be her. Maybe it would look better if I got the jump on her and called him myself. Or called the higher authority and reported the incident. Or ran away and joined the circus.

Flynn took the key fob out of Crawford's pocket and tossed it in the driver's seat before shutting off the power. After he closed the doors, he rejoined me.

"Did you see everything?" I asked.

He handed me my mask and folded his arms. "I couldn't see what you were doing. I almost turned around, but I wanted to make sure you were safe. I thought it was just a light exchange. I didn't know all *that* was going on," he said, jerking his chin at the rear window. "When you got out, I couldn't hear what you were saying, but I could tell you weren't up for the task."

"What gave it away? The twenty-three-inch sword?"

Flynn lifted his shirt on the side and scratched several red bumps on his flank. "Bloodsucking mosquitoes," he murmured.

That suddenly reminded me of the fang marks I'd left on Crawford's neck. Maybe the blade had sliced across the puncture marks. Would anyone notice? Would anyone care?

"Do you trust this cleaner guy?" I asked.

"Gal," he said. "She's a professional. Doesn't ask questions."

"How do you know her?"

"I shagged her once."

"I'm surprised you're not the one who owes *her* a favor."

"We all take something from a relationship. Some of us are just more willing to admit what we want. Simone might pretend she hates me, but it's all an act. She knew what I wanted in exchange for a little companionship. And I'm an excellent companion in the sack. When I didn't want more, she resented me for it. That wasn't in the agreement, but women are always changing their minds. I have aspirations for that smashingly handsome Chitah."

I hopped down and decided to take my leave. "If you don't need me here, I'm heading back to work. Thanks for helping me out."

"Just a moment, love. Do you think I hide bodies out of the goodness of my heart?"

I turned on my heel to face him. "I'm not doing you any sexual favors."

Flynn threw back his head and laughed. After wiping his teary eyes, he regained his composure. "That's a first. I'm always the one who performs the favors, but that's not what interests me. In fact, I'm keen on the idea that we met for a reason."

I put on the mask and adjusted it. "Just tell me what the hell you want."

"You didn't drive off with this man for kicks." Flynn nodded at the envelope I was still holding. "How much is in there?"

"Thirty large."

Flynn jerked his head back. "That's all?"

"If you want this money—"

"That's not what I'm getting at. Remember I mentioned earlier about side hustles? I might have just the one for you, but I want a cut. Call it… a finder's fee."

I didn't have the patience for this nonsense. I could still smell Crawford's aftershave. It had transferred to my hair and face during our scuffle in the car. Eager to wash it out, I walked away.

"Have you ever fought professionally?"

I stopped dead in my tracks. *Did he just ask what I think he asked?*

"You see, I have this side business where I get paid for referrals. But few have your obvious talents. I think you'll do very well, and I'd like a small cut of that. Call it payback for tonight. I think that's fair, don't you?"

I slowly turned. "What kind of fighting?"

Flynn closed the distance between us and lowered his voice. "They call it cage fights, but it's more sophisticated than that. It's not against anyone's will. The fighters are handsomely rewarded. I don't even see why it's illegal if everyone is paid."

"How did you get involved in something like that?"

He stuffed his hands in his jean pockets. "I don't exactly have any talents outside of the obvious. Arranged relationships aren't as lucrative as they might seem."

"Aren't you afraid of getting caught? It's illegal."

"I have certain feelings about that. This isn't like the days of slavery when Shifters were thrown into the pits. In fact, I don't recruit Shifters at all. They just happen to have an opening for a female Mage, and I can't think of a better candidate. It's good money, Robin. Enough that you won't even miss my cut."

What was a nice guy like Flynn doing recruiting women for cage fights? Didn't he realize that the higher authority could execute him for his involvement? Then again, money drove people in our world to do the unthinkable. Unless you wanted to work for the rest of your long life, hoarding as much money and property as possible was the only way to secure a good future.

"I don't make this offer to just anyone," he said, dipping his chin. "But the way I see it, you're searching for more money. You've got the skills, and I've got the connections. They have confidentiality rules, but once you're involved, you'll obviously keep them. You're free to come and go as you like. You only fight on the nights you're requested, and I can arrange someone to fill in for you at the club."

"Simone wouldn't raise a stink about it?"

Flynn snorted and leaned against the car. "That's more tips in her pocket. You needn't worry. I've got that woman wrapped around my finger."

"Doesn't look like it to me."

"She's my queen. Simone is the only woman who ever made me think twice about settling down, and she knows it. That's why she didn't take a promotion working at another club for more money. She's sticking around in hopes that I'll straighten out my act. But that's not what a wise man taught me."

"And who was that? Don Juan?"

Flynn winked. "More like Dionysus. So what'll it be, love? Getting into the car with strangers and performing insidious acts in back alleys for a wad of cash, or working a job that utilizes your given talents? You've got moves I've never seen, and you're not afraid of a fight. If you tell me to sod off, I'll respectfully walk away. But keep in mind I need assurance that you won't reveal my secret."

"Meaning you'll have a Vamp scrub my memories."

He winked. "I'll make sure they do it right."

"How much?"

"Six figures to start, and that's after my share. There's a betting pool, so I don't know how they go about figuring everyone's worth, but that's a lot of money for one job."

I twisted my mouth and looked at the ground as if mulling it over. This was no amateur affair. They must have been betting with insane amounts of money in order to offer girls that kind of pay. I kicked a pebble, and it skittered across the concrete. "I can't say no to that kind of money. I'm in."

"Smashing!" He reached out to grip my shoulder and then snapped his hand back. Flynn gave me a wry grin as if to say he remembered my warning about grabbing me. "I'll get in touch with my contact tonight. He'll want to meet with you and go over details." Flynn grew serious and wagged his finger at me. "Do *not* tell anyone. Not a single soul. In fact, don't let anyone at the club know you have a second job. Not unless you want the Regulators sniffing around."

"Don't worry, Flynn. I don't have any urge to spend the rest of my life in jail."

A car rolled up behind me, and the headlights flooded the dark space.

Flynn scratched his tummy. "Did Crawford give you a business card or anything else I should know about?"

"I'll burn it."

He flicked his eyes down to the envelope.

"I'll drop this off at my place before going back to work."

"Get rid of it," he warned me. "That kind of money is cursed." Flynn shuddered before stepping away. "Run along now. I'll take care of the rest."

The cleaner stayed inside her car while I headed off. When I passed an alley about a block away, I set the envelope of money inside the tent of a homeless man.

Chapter 18

Instead of returning to the White Owl, I headed back to the hotel. Now that I had my connection, it left me with mixed feelings. When the bust went down, I would have no choice but to report Flynn. He seemed like a regular guy who just needed the money.

I left a message with the club manager, informing her that the owner had sent me on a special errand that would take the rest of the night. I knew she'd relay it to Houdini, and he could decide if he wanted us in his club anymore. He'd only given me two hours, but Houdini needed a taste of his own medicine. He worried that showing me favoritism would cause his employees to break more rules. It sounded to me like someone needed a little chaos in his rigid structure.

After towel drying my hair and putting on a pair of sweatpants and a tank top, I sat on the bathroom floor. I had thrown up twice, but my stomach had already absorbed most of the blood. Crawford's dark light had a more caustic effect than his blood, however. It tangled with my own and made me sick in ways I couldn't articulate. It felt like insects were crawling beneath my skin and devouring me from the inside out. When the chills came on, I sat against the wall and hugged my knees to my chest. It always took a day or two for another Mage's light to leave my system. The darker the light, the worse the energy hangover. It lived inside every cell of my body and invaded me like a virus.

When a knock sounded at the door, it took every ounce of energy to stand up and answer.

Blue glanced around before she forced her way in and shut the door. "Are you okay?"

I returned to the bathroom and slumped to the floor. "You wouldn't happen to have a bottle of tequila, would you?"

She sat across from me with her back to the sink. I could always tell when Blue had come out of a shift. Her brown hair was long and silken, but even more so when she changed back to human form. No tangles, shiny, and perfectly straight.

Meanwhile, I looked like something the cat spit up. I drew up my knees, the pain bone-deep.

Blue sat cross-legged and studied me. "I saw everything."

I pursed my lips. Not much I could add in my defense to killing a man in cold blood.

Her blue eyes narrowed as she looked away. "I could have stopped you."

"Viktor won't blame you."

"Of course he won't. I'm not telling him what happened."

My jaw slackened. "What?"

She shook her head. "I saw the video. No matter what reasons we give him, he won't support what you did. It's not because he wouldn't have wanted justice, but he has rules that keep our operation running. We only have permission to kill declared outlaws or in self-defense. Now that the car is gone, along with the phone and video, we don't even have evidence to justify your actions. But I know what my animal saw. She has sharp eyesight. It's abhorrent, and I would have done it myself. It's not what he wanted to do with you—it's what he did to those children."

That took me by surprise. Blue was loyal to the core, and keeping this from Viktor jeopardized her standing with Keystone. Especially if that Crawford guy turned out to be important and someone opened an investigation that led back to the group.

"I've got a promising lead," I said, switching topics.

"Is that so?"

"That guy who helped clean up the mess—he made me an offer. Pass the word to Claude. If Flynn gets cold feet, maybe

Claude can get some info out of him. He's got a crush on our boy. Tell Wyatt to keep a closer eye on my tracker from now on."

"I will." She wrung her hands. "After you left the scene, I called the house to tell them it was a false alarm. You sat behind those buildings for a long time, and I was afraid Wyatt would send Shepherd to check it out."

"Thanks."

"Did you learn anything about the fighting ring?"

"It sounds like a legit operation. It's still illegal, but nobody's kidnapping these girls and forcing them to fight. In fact, they're paying them a shitload of money. Life-changing money."

Blue's lip curled, and she sat back with one knee bent. "It doesn't matter if they make it legit. Cage fighting has a bloody and dark history among Shifters. We don't like it. Even if other Breeds are in the ring and they're doing it freely, it's a mockery to what we suffered. This isn't comparable to boxing or any of those human sports. It has deep ties to slavery, and wealthy people are profiting off disadvantaged people in less powerful positions. Don't let them dress it up for you. Just remember that those girls wouldn't be dead if they hadn't gotten involved." Her eyes flicked up. "You be careful."

"What'll happen to Flynn?"

She shrugged. "Who knows and who cares?"

"He's a nice guy."

"Who's committing a crime."

"Like what I did tonight?"

"That's different." She pulled her hair away from her collar. "He's recruiting hapless women to put their bodies and their lives in danger so that others can make money off them. *You* killed a monster."

"But it's still a crime."

"Look, it's not about who's nice and who's not. You have to draw the line somewhere. What if your buddy was stealing children and selling them to loving couples? It's still wrong. I see what you're getting at, but you came from the human world where things were black and white. Our world is grey." She stood up and dusted off her pants. "Don't worry, Raven. I'll cover for you. If there's one crime I won't let you go down for, it's murdering a child abuser. There's a special hell for people who hurt kids."

"Is there a special place in hell for people like us?"

She rested her palms on the sink behind her. "Maybe."

My head thumped against the wall as I reclined it. "I wish Christian was here."

"He's on assignment."

"Doing what?"

Blue bit her thumbnail. "Maybe I should just leave it at that. Viktor wants you focused on the job."

"Is it dangerous?"

She nodded.

I stood up and blocked the doorway. "Tell me."

"He was assigned to guard that woman," Blue said with obvious disdain. "The one who works for the higher authority."

"Lenore?"

"That's her. Anyhow, I guess she's in some kind of danger or else Viktor wouldn't have assigned him to guard her. That's not what we do."

"Is someone trying to kill her?"

"I guess so."

Admittedly, that filled me with relish.

I flipped off the bathroom light and went into the bedroom. After switching on the lamp, I sat on the bed and stared at my reflection in the TV. I didn't like the idea of Christian dying to save that woman, but thinking about it would only distract me from my job. Flynn would be putting me in touch with his contact, and I needed to keep my head in the game.

"I'm going back home." Blue lingered in the entryway. "I'll update Viktor with the offer you got. Anything else you want me to relay?"

I lowered my head, tears stinging my eyes. "This is so fucking hard. The stuff that goes on inside the club gets under your skin."

Blue sat down next to me and bumped shoulders. "I know. Trust me, I know. But you've got to shut it off. The longer assignments will get to you. That's why Viktor bought the Keystone mansion. He wanted to give us a retreat—a place where we could leave all this behind, away from the misery and the stink of the city. That's why he doesn't want televisions all over the house. We see enough murder and corruption as it is; we don't need to invite it into our bedroom." Blue gave my knee a light squeeze. "I know this isn't the real you talking. It's all that blood or whatever you took from him. The real Raven is tough. She wears knives in her boot heels and calls bullshit when she sees it."

I smiled and wiped my eyes.

"I don't like Vamps," she went on. "But you're not half bad."

"Quit while you're ahead."

Blue chuckled softly. "Did I ever tell you about your terrible taste in men?"

"Oh, fuck off."

She clapped me on the shoulder. "There she is." Blue stood up and sighed. "I'll track you as best I can. Try not to get yourself killed."

"Thanks for the pep talk."

"It's the least I can do."

"For what?"

"For killing the Shifter asshole that did this to me." She gently pulled the hood over her head, and it framed her beautiful face. "Get some sleep. You're gonna need it."

Chapter 19

INSTEAD OF FLYING BACK TO the mansion, Blue took a cab. She kept a bag of clothes on the hotel roof, just in case she needed to perform a task on foot. After witnessing last night's murder, she was too wired up to shift, so she sent Wyatt a message to meet her outside and pay the driver. As soon as she entered the mansion, she hung her phone on the winged statue by the door and headed to the gathering room.

She was exhausted—it wasn't easy staying awake all night. Most Shifters black out during their shift, but Blue had the special ability to remain conscious the entire time. Even though her falcon knew to follow Raven, Blue couldn't chance missing out on important details that her animal wouldn't understand.

Like that video. Just thinking about it made her sick to her stomach.

Despite her exhaustion, it took time to wind down after a long night of surveillance. She entered the gathering room and poured herself a generous glass of red wine at the liquor cabinet. It was predawn, and the colorful windows barely captured the light. Her eyes steered up to the floor-to-ceiling bookshelf as she drank her wine. One glass wouldn't be enough to induce sleep, so she gulped down the drink and poured another.

"I saved you a plate of our dinner last night," Niko said.

Blue set the bottle down and then joined him on the leather sofa. It felt good to sit down, but her circadian rhythm was screwed up, and it was difficult to think about sleeping when the sun was on the rise.

Niko clasped his hands in his lap. "Would you like me to heat it up?"

"I think I'm skipping breakfast today, amigo."

"What happened?"

She sipped wine and pushed away thoughts of the vile scene that had unfolded. Niko was a sharp light reader, and he could often detect lies. "It's tough staying up all night and sharing headspace with my falcon. Sometimes she wants to fly off, and I have to fight those urges and keep her still. It's one thing to do it occasionally, but night after night? I feel like I'm losing my mind."

"Wyatt said Raven was active, but you called in a false alarm."

Blue took another sip of wine and then rested the glass on her leg. "I didn't want anyone panicking and busting in on the scene. Raven got an offer that looks promising. She might be going on the job as soon as today. Is Viktor around? I want to talk to him before I go to bed."

"He's in his office. He asked not to be disturbed." Niko stared pensively at the space before him.

What a shame that Niko couldn't see the beautiful window to their left that depicted wolves and humans living in harmony. Did he even know it was there?

"Something troubles you." He shifted in her direction and studied her light. "We're partners, are we not?"

"Sure."

"Christian isn't here. We have privacy if you want to speak freely."

"There's nothing to talk about."

"Is it your scars?"

It wasn't. But in a way it was. Blue had to watch Raven from the sidelines. The Shifter in her wanted to be more involved in this particular case, and if it weren't for her scars, she would have been Raven's backup instead of Claude.

"I wish I had words of comfort, but I don't," he admitted. "I can tell you what I think, but that won't ease your suffering. If it makes you feel better, I haven't noticed them at all."

She chuckled. "Is that so?"

Niko smiled with his eyes. "I would never pry."

Blue swallowed a mouthful of the full-bodied wine and set the glass on the end table. "I know you're looking out for me, but this isn't a subject I want to talk about. I'm just having a bad night."

Niko inclined his head. "Apologies."

"Thank the fates for Viktor. He really changed my life. It's a tough job, but the work I do makes me sleep like a baby."

"Which is more than I can say for our leader. He's been pacing again."

Blue sighed, her thoughts drifting to the long nights between jobs when she'd occasionally hear Viktor playing his violin. Sometimes in the wee hours of the morning, a haunting melody crept through the halls like a distant dream. No one ever mentioned it, so she couldn't be certain if she was the only one who had ever heard him play. She speculated that whatever tormented him reared its ugly head when things got too peaceful.

"He's worried about Raven," she said. "This is her first time on a solo job, and it's a big one."

"If anyone's up for the task, it's Raven. She's young but brave. Fear is our worst enemy."

Blue slouched and closed her eyes. "I just wish my mind would quit spinning."

"The stillness of life makes us dizzy with regrets."

"What makes you think I regret anything?"

Niko sighed. "I know something about quiet moments. When the noise of the world goes away and you're left with your thoughts, they tend to wander in the realm of regret. Things we wish we hadn't done, things we wish we had. Things we wish we could do. That's the noise that keeps us awake. It makes immortality insufferable."

"Maybe we should live a perfect life so we'll have no regrets."

Niko chuckled softly and played with the lace on his shoe. "That's an ambitious goal. Let me know how it works for you."

"Will do."

"Ah, Blue. You're here," Viktor said as he entered the room.

Blue's eyes snapped open. She hopped off the couch to greet

Viktor. "Niko said you were working, or I would have spoken with you right away. I was just having a drink. Can I get you anything?"

"Nyet. I am good." He rounded his favorite chair and took a seat. "Tell me about your evening."

She sat in the chair next to his. "Raven made contact with someone about the fighting rings. It was only an initial offer, but we should know more by this evening."

His eyebrows popped up, deepening the wrinkles in his brow. Viktor was by no means an old man, even in Shifter years. He was what she considered seasoned—a man with years of experience behind his pale winter eyes. She imagined he'd once had coal-black hair, but now it was mostly silver with dark undertones. The lines at the corners of his eyes revealed the laughter and tragedy in his life. His Greek nose gave him character, and his lips only spoke truth—even if she didn't understand a word of Russian. His culture was threaded into his being after hundreds of years living there, and she couldn't fathom how difficult it must have been for him to uproot his life, move to a new country, and learn a new language.

"I filled Claude in," Blue continued. "And Wyatt needs to keep an eye on her tracker."

"This is excellent news." Viktor heaved a sigh, and with that, his spirit seemed lighter. "I may enjoy a celebratory drink after all."

He made a motion to get up, but Blue was already halfway across the room, pouring a small glass of vodka. He worked tirelessly to keep this organization running, so it was the least she could do.

She handed Viktor the glass.

"Spasibo."

Blue returned to her chair and leaned on the armrest. "Wyatt can disregard what he saw last night. That was just a rendezvous point to meet her contact."

While Viktor sipped his drink, Shepherd entered the room with Hunter on his shoulders. His snug white T-shirt had a small red stain on the front. Hunter gobbled down the rest of his strawberry before wiping his fingers on Shepherd's shirt. His pant leg was riding up on one side.

"Nice socks," Blue said, noticing the hot-pink knee-highs.

Hunter smiled proudly as Shepherd lifted him up and set him down on the sofa. His shoes began blinking the moment they made contact with the cushion.

"Isn't it a little early for drinks?" Shepherd asked, noticing the two glasses in the room.

"We're celebrating," Viktor informed him. "Raven made progress on her mission."

Shepherd crossed the room toward the liquor cabinet and opened a drawer where he kept his cigarettes. After striking a match and lighting one up, he ambled toward the divider wall and rested against one of the open archways. "So you don't need me in the club anymore?"

"There is no need," Viktor replied, putting relief on Shepherd's face. "But keep yourself available. I do not know what comes next. I presume Raven will meet with her contact, but she must have enough evidence that we can move in and capture. I want everyone close to home."

Shepherd made a donut ring with his smoke and blew the rest toward the ceiling. "Are you sending in Regulators, or will we do this the old-fashioned way?"

Viktor tapped his fingers against his glass. "We shall see. I need her to identify as many people as she can who are involved. Witnesses will strengthen our case."

"So will video cameras," Blue noted. "How much do you want to bet they film these little events and have private viewings to get new clients interested?"

Viktor sipped his vodka. "That would be even better."

Shepherd gazed up at the windows, the cigarette wedged between his scarred fingers. "I love a good raid."

Hunter got up from the couch and wandered around. His schooling would start after breakfast, so Shepherd liked to spend time with him before then. Things were finally amicable between Shepherd and Switch. At first she'd thought the two might beat the hell out of each other, but they'd worked out a routine. Fathering was a new gig for Shepherd, one he didn't take lightly.

Blue could see him struggling with his affections, and he looked wistful whenever someone else gave Hunter a hug or kiss. But he had no problem calling anyone out who went against his rules or overstepped boundaries. Blue still didn't know if Switch would last as a permanent addition since he was still in a trial period, but she guessed that decision lay with Shepherd. Switch didn't seem like a bad guy. Headstrong, yes, but as a wolf, he'd protect Hunter when they were away, as he'd recently proved during their last mission.

Blue stood up. "I need to get some shut-eye. Did you eat breakfast?" she asked Viktor. "I can make you some scrambled eggs before I go to bed. It won't take but a minute."

He patted his stomach. "I am saving room. Kira will delight us with a casserole fit for kings. Or perhaps *grechka the way my mother used to make.*"

Blue tried not to let her disappointment show. She appreciated how Kira took care of the house, but Blue had always been the one who looked out for Viktor. The others didn't notice or care when he didn't eat enough or rest.

"Don't you miss my eggs?" she said, hoping he'd take the bait. "I can make them just the way you like. A dash of salt, a little butter—"

"Nyet. I want you rested. If Raven moves to a second location and you see people going in, you can identify them. I do not want a sleepy bird on duty. Is this clear?"

"You bet."

"Just don't shit on anyone," Shepherd quipped. "Remember that one time we were tailing that Packmaster and your bird blew our cover?"

She folded her arms, annoyed that they always brought that up for a few chuckles. "That was a fluke."

"Yeah, but it almost got Wyatt killed. It was a good thing that—Hunter!" he boomed.

One second, Shepherd was leaning against the wall. The next, he was sprinting across the room toward the corner ladder. "Get down from there," he snapped.

Hunter scrambled down the ladder and then hid behind it. He

tucked himself into a tiny ball, his arms wrapped around his legs and his head buried from sight.

"Look, I didn't mean to yell, little man, but you have to be careful. Ladders are dangerous. You can't climb them unless someone else is holding on. That's the rule." Shepherd squatted by the ladder and rested his arm on a rung. "You wanna go outside and climb a tree?"

Blue drifted toward the wall and picked up the cigarette that Shepherd had dropped on the floor. She leaned through one of the open archways and stubbed it out in an ashtray on a booth table.

"Don't be mad," Shepherd said, scratching his bristly hair. "Do you wanna hit me?"

"That's not an advisable suggestion," Niko chimed in.

"He's *my* kid." Shepherd stared daggers at Niko from over his shoulder.

Niko turned his head. "What lesson will you teach him? That when he's made to feel small or punished that he should lash out in violence?"

Shepherd rubbed his forehead. His heart was in the right place, but he didn't have any experience with children that Blue knew of. Raising kids was something you learned along the way.

Blue crossed the room and stood by the ladder. "A little bird told me that there's a magical room in this house."

"What are you talking about?" Shepherd stood and gave her a bemused look.

She winked to get him to play along. "It's so magical that only little boys can open the door."

"What's in the room?"

There was a room on the third floor that held musical instruments. Nobody ever went in there since none of them were musically inclined, but it was the sort of thing that a kid Hunter's age would love.

"Magical instruments. There's an old piano that sings when you press the keys. Legend has it that when you sit on the bench, you can fly to faraway places."

Hunter lifted his head and peered at her through his disheveled hair.

She tried to recall what else was in there. "I heard there's a harp named Mr. Brewster and a flute that dances."

Shepherd gave her a "What the fuck are you talking about?" look—he obviously hadn't learned the allure of magic when it came to children. The world wasn't just about lessons in books.

"Anyhow, I was trying to think if I knew any little boys who might be brave enough to open the magic door," she continued while rubbing her chin.

Shepherd folded his arms. "I don't know."

Hunter stood and looked at them from behind the ladder.

Blue maintained eye contact with Shepherd. "Someone put a spell on the door. It's a magical spell that only a father and son can break. They have to be holding hands."

Hunter reached between the rungs for Shepherd's hand.

Shepherd gave her a nod of thanks. The crisis had ended.

She clapped him on the shoulder and lowered her voice. "Third floor, center hall, sixth door on the left. Have fun, and make sure you try out the flying carpet. I hear it goes to Istanbul."

Chapter 20

THE WORST HANGOVER WASN'T A night of heavy drinking. Well, not unless you counted drinking blood. It was the process of waiting for dark core light to leave the body. The blood didn't help matters either. I tried sleeping, but I mostly just remained in the fetal position. Pulling in fresh sunlight helped dilute the energy, but not enough to make a difference. It had to leave on its own.

Instead of returning to work, I called the club and left a message for Karen, the manager. Making that decision killed me. I wanted to check with Flynn to make sure everything went smoothly with the cleaner. Even more important, would Flynn rescind his offer because I took a sick day? Would my absence spook him? No matter how much I wanted to go in, I was in no condition to get out of bed, let alone tend bar. If he saw me with his own eyes, he'd surely change his mind. I needed to be in prime condition when I met his boss—not looking like a haggard mess who can't hold her own. Viktor wouldn't want me to rush this and make mistakes.

So I stayed in bed all day, all that night, and the following day. Christian didn't visit, but I spied Blue on the window ledge the prior evening while gazing at the city lights. I gave her a thumbs-up before closing the drapes.

After two full days of rest, it was time to get back to work.

The corset stayed on the floor, and I put on the spiked bra instead. Same leather shorts and black boots. I kept my tousled hair down, applied makeup, put in my brown contact lens, and grabbed a long duster before heading out.

By the sour look I got from the hotel desk clerk, she thought I was a prostitute. I squinted at the late afternoon sunlight as it pierced through the tall windows in the lobby. As I neared the door, I stopped short.

Flynn waved at me from the outside. His round glasses were pink today.

I moved through the revolving door and approached him. "What are you doing here?"

"Thought I'd see what my investment's up to."

"How did you know I was here?"

"Karen tells me anything when I flirt with her."

The club manager would be the only person who would have my location since it was required on the paperwork.

I casually strolled up the sidewalk, the wind at my back and the sun on my left. "Did you think I skipped town or something?"

"One never knows."

I came up with a quick excuse before he started grilling me. "I was afraid someone busted you while hauling the body, and if so, they'd be looking for me at work. Thought I'd lie low for a day or two."

"You really think I'd snitch?"

"Don't take it personally, but I don't trust anyone. I'm probably fired by now, but better that than going to Breed jail."

"Worry not, love. Everything is copasetic. But if you're having second thoughts about my offer—"

"No, I'm in. The tips at the club are nice, but it would take me decades to get ahead."

He hooked his arm in mine. "Brilliant. Let's take a detour, shall we?"

Instead of going straight, Flynn turned right at the corner. He was surprisingly candid, telling me how he bounced from one convenient relationship to the next. He bragged about the penthouse suites he'd stayed in and cautioned me to avoid Breed apartment living like the plague. Not unless I enjoyed Shifter fights, Vampires complaining about noise, broken doors, and juicers passed out in the halls.

"Where do you live now?" I asked.

"A swanky little place, but I'm running out of time. You see, my last relationship ended in a flood of tears. Hers, not mine. She left but had already paid the lease for six months. It's mine for another five weeks."

"I thought you got paid good money for recruiting?"

"Keep your voice down," he murmured. "And take off that bloody mask. You look like an invitation."

I removed the mask and tucked it in the long pocket of my duster, which had no buttons to cover up my provocative outfit. We walked for twenty minutes. Flynn revealed he didn't have a car or a driver's license, not that he wanted to drive on our crazy American roads. Between relationships, he used public transportation or his two feet. Flynn was quite the chatterbox. I could see why he had no trouble moving from one relationship to the next. He had a gift of making you feel like you'd known him all your life, and that was something he could do with any random stranger.

"Aren't we going to be late to work?" I asked.

The sun had set, but a wonderful early-evening glow filled the world, giving the colors more contrast and depth.

"Never you mind about that. This is far more important. I hope you make a better first impression on my associate than you did with me."

"As long as he doesn't grab my arm."

Flynn chortled. After crossing another street, he began telling me all about his hometown in Manchester.

Just when we reached the curb, my heart accelerated. A scruffy biker strutted toward us, tattoos up and down his arms and a goatee on his chin. When he locked eyes with me, my breath caught. Flynn's voice faded into oblivion, and as I stared at Crush, all I could think of was how this mission was teetering on the brink of disaster.

Looking down at my nonexistent outfit, he practically had flames shooting out of his eyes. Then he gave Flynn a baleful glance.

Oh God, not now.

With every step, I realized my father wasn't going to walk on by. He looked troubled, and maybe it was because I hadn't called him since this mission began.

"Bloody hell!"

I stopped to look at Flynn. His black shirt had a large splatter of bird droppings, more than the average pigeon could deliver. I spied Blue's falcon perched on the ledge.

Flynn held up his arms as if they too were soiled. "Wait for me. I'll be in the loo." He jerked open the glass door to the shop and growled, "Bollocks!"

I stormed past the windows to my father. "What are you doing here?"

"Taking a walk."

"One, you don't exercise. Two, you sure as hell don't hang out in the city."

"Maybe I'm concerned about where my little girl has been." His face was flushed and unusually sweaty, as if he'd been running.

I lowered my voice. "You can't be here. Do you realize the danger you're putting me in?"

He reached inside his pocket and pulled something out. "Put this on. Don't ask questions."

I accepted the onyx-looking pendant and gave him a quizzical stare.

"Hurry up before peabrain comes back."

I quickly slipped it over my head. "What's it for?"

Crush tapped his eye, hinting it was a camera. *What the hell? Had Keystone put my father on assignment?*

I'm going to kill them.

"So it's five blocks *that* way?" he said gruffly, pointing up the road. "Son of a bitch. That's what I get for listening to a fucking tourist with a map."

Flynn eased up to my side. "What's going on here?"

"I'm turned around," Crush grumbled. "That's what's going on. Some asshole with a tow truck impounded my bike for parking bullshit. Do you know where the auto pound is on Foxtrail Avenue? This lady says it's five blocks up the road." Crush pulled a bandana out of his back pocket and wiped his neck. "They close in thirty minutes, and if I don't get my bike back, heads are gonna roll."

If there was one thing that my father excelled at, it was pitching a fit.

"She's right," Flynn agreed. "Go all the way up until you see McDonald's on the right. That's Foxtrail. Take a left and the impound lot is across the street on the right."

"'Preciate it. Son of a—"

Crush went jogging in the direction we steered him, and seeing him run was a sight to behold. My father probably hadn't run faster than a light jog in twenty years. I would have broken out in laughter had it not been for Flynn clutching my arm and leading us on.

"Humans are helpless creatures," he said. "I'm so glad I'm not one of them anymore."

"Did you get everything cleaned off?" I asked, noticing how wet his shirt was.

"Bloody hell. I've never seen so much bird droppings in all my life. If you see that pterodactyl, take cover."

The adrenaline from running into my father was finally wearing off, but now I was paranoid about the necklace. Would Flynn notice?

I turned up the sidewalk. "How did it go with the cleaners?"

Flynn fell into step beside me. "Nothing to fret about."

"I appreciate it."

"Just remember, 'twastn't a favor. Consider it a transaction. I scratch your back and you scratch mine."

When we reached our destination, I turned in a circle. Not to get a look at the park across the street or the bicyclists zooming by, but to provide Wyatt a detailed panorama of my surroundings. The building itself was unremarkable. The first floor didn't have windows, but the second level had arched ones like in an old church. Two buildings flanked it, and there weren't any pedestrians. Flynn led me through the revolving door, and we entered a lobby with marble floors. The paintings and statues gave off a museum vibe, but there weren't any visitors.

Flynn approached the front desk. "I have Robin White for an appointment."

The man sitting at the desk gave him a look of derision, and it was obvious they knew each other. "Keep your mitts off the art this time."

I observed the nameplate on the security desk. Murphy had a stone-cold look like a beat cop with too many years on the streets, now forced to greet visitors and push papers.

Flynn turned on his heel while Murphy made a call. "We're not on speaking terms anymore. Break one statue and it's World War III. Bloody hell, what's the point of putting art on display if you can't touch it?"

"This is a museum?"

"Auction house." He winked.

"Sounds legit."

Five minutes later, a ding sounded by the elevator in the back. Before I saw anyone, I heard a man singing "I Can See Clearly Now" in perfect pitch. When he stepped into view, he didn't look anything like Johnny Nash. His sharp grey suit and black shoes alluded to his wealth, and he must have had them custom made because the man was a dwarf.

The singing diminished to a whistle as he walked briskly toward us. He had a kingly walk, as if he were expecting someone to throw rose petals at his feet. When he flared, my eyebrows popped up. I'd never seen a Mage of his stature. For centuries or longer, men were selected as soldiers. But times had changed, and newer candidates had more to offer, which made me uneasy.

"I've got a new one for you, sir," Flynn announced. "This one is worth her weight in gold."

The man stopped in front of me and forced a smile. "Well? Are you going to introduce us or stand there like a fool?" he said to Flynn, never taking his eyes from mine.

Flynn cleared his throat. "This is Robin White. Robin, this is—"

"Pablo Leonardo Russo." Pablo inclined his head. "You may go, Mr. Washington. I'll escort the lady from here."

HEARTLESS

Flynn rocked on his heels. "And my money?"

Pablo flicked a glance at Flynn and spoke through clenched teeth. "You'll know by tonight what my decision is. Either go to work or buy yourself a decent wardrobe with the money I've already paid you."

Flynn threw up his hands defensively. "I'll just be on my way. Be sure to call me as soon as you decide!"

After Flynn made his exit, Pablo gestured toward the elevator. "Miss White, will you join me?"

Pablo seemed like an affable guy with manners and a code of conduct. Those were usually the ones I didn't trust.

"You don't sound Italian," I said, walking beside him.

"My Creator gave me that name. It means *little lion*. I suppose he thought that would make me sound more formidable, but never judge a book by its cover."

When the elevator doors opened, he let me enter first. I rested my back against the wall and grimaced at my reflection in the doors when they closed. Why the hell did I pick today to wear the spiked bra?

Pablo turned to face me, hands clasped in front of him. "That's the brilliant part about becoming a Mage, don't you agree? A new identity, a second chance at defining who you are and what you're worth to the world." His eyebrows drew together. "How much did Mr. Washington tell you about this job?"

"Flynn? Basically nothing. Only that I'd be fighting for money. I've been doing it for free all my life, so why not get paid?"

"We all excel at something, and it's important to know what those gifts are. People who squander their talents will never know their true potential."

Instead of going up, the elevator went down.

"These aren't the cage fights you've heard about," he said. "We run a classy operation. Our fighters are paid their worth, and our audience is a mixture. Some place bets, others like to watch. It's an exclusive membership, and confidentiality is paramount."

The bell chimed and the doors opened.

"If you please."

I strutted past him into a carpeted hallway and moved left toward a door.

He seized my arm. "We don't go that way."

"What's that way?"

He led me to the right down a slightly longer hall with another door at the end. Once inside, the walls curved as if forming a circle, and the doors were spaced apart. I reached up and made sure my necklace was facing the right way and not tangled up in my hair. Hopefully Wyatt was getting all this.

"What did you do before working at the White Owl?"

I walked a step behind him. "I mostly lived on the streets."

"And how did someone with your lack of experience acquire a job at such a prestigious adult club?"

"I grew up in bars, so I've got the experience. They were looking for a Mage, and I guess I checked off all their boxes."

"It's unfortunate that we don't all have responsible Creators who will guide us through the pitfalls of immortality. Perhaps then we wouldn't have so many like yourself, struggling to make ends meet. You might be surprised to know just how many people have entered this world under false pretenses or even by force." He glanced up at me over his shoulder. "Is that what happened to you?"

I pressed my lips together and nodded.

Pablo reached a narrow staircase against the outer wall and went up two steps before turning to face me. "Is this someone I'm going to have to worry about?"

I opened my mouth but wasn't sure how to answer.

Don't be eager to answer, Raven. Figure out what he wants to hear.

"I have patrons with excessive riches. Is your Creator likely to be one of them?"

I exhaled the breath I'd been holding in. "No. That's not the kind of trouble I thought you were talking about. I'm an independent, and no one has any claim over me. And you can bet your ass that if some rich guy turned me against my will, I would have milked him for every dime before parting ways."

A doleful smile stretched across Pablo's face. "You're candid. I once knew a woman like you, but this world ate her alive." He turned back around, heading upstairs. "Most pretend to be blunt, but they're professional liars."

After a short twist in the stairwell, I followed him to a spacious floor shaped like a donut. Windows circled the center, and when I reached the glass and looked to the other side, I couldn't see my reflection since they were two-way mirrors. Down below, an empty room.

"We used to hold the viewings up here," Pablo said, scooting onto one of many armchairs that faced the glass. "But people wanted more privacy. They were afraid of being blackmailed or found out, so we built them little rooms down below. The renovation took quite some time. We escort them in one at a time through a second entrance to guarantee their anonymity."

Pablo's feet didn't quite touch the ground, but he made no effort to move or stand.

I leaned my shoulder against the glass and looked at the outer walls surrounding us. The sandalwood-brown paint and recessed lighting were classy touches.

"The view is better up here," he said absently.

"What does this job pay?"

"A woman who gets right to the point. I like that." Pablo stood up and stared down at the empty fighting room below. "Two hundred thousand per match. That's the baseline salary, but if you're a proven champion, the sky's the limit."

I joined his side. "How did you get involved in this? You don't look like a guy who's into death matches."

"Death matches?" Pablo tossed back his head and laughed. "Is that what Flynn told you?"

"No. But I just assumed…"

"These are clean fights."

"Seems like there would be more money in death matches."

He looked up at me and arched an eyebrow. "If you don't know how to show mercy, you don't belong here. *This* audience has a very particular taste in watching a Mage fight."

Something about the way he said "this audience" had me wondering if there was another audience, but I didn't want this interview to come off like an interrogation.

"That's a lot of dough," I said on a breath. "I could use that money."

"Splendid. Flynn had nothing but good things to say, but he's made an error in judgment once or twice. I need to see your skills before I commit to hiring you."

I thought about Viktor's instructions. He didn't want me to get as far as fighting—just far enough to get names, faces, and proof, which I didn't have.

"Can I watch one first?" I asked. "That way I know what to expect."

"I'd rather watch *you* fight. That way *I* know what to expect."

I scratched the back of my head. "It's just that I didn't come prepared. Flynn didn't tell me."

He drew in a deep breath through his nose and sighed. "I'm afraid this won't work out."

"Wait, why?"

"One of us has wasted the other's time." He headed toward the door.

"I'll do it."

He stopped in his tracks.

"I'm not afraid of fighting," I assured him. "I've done a lot of bad stuff in my life, so it's not the fighting I'm afraid of."

"Then what is it you *are* afraid of?"

"You."

He turned on his heel. "What, pray tell, could a girl like you have to fear in a man like me?"

"It's always the ones you least expect that are the most dangerous."

That amused him, just the result I wanted.

"If I didn't know better, I'd say you were stroking my ego."

Damn.

"I like you," he added. "Everyone deserves a second chance.

Don't disappoint me, Robin. There's another set of stairs around the corner. Go down to the room below, and we'll begin."

I glanced at the curve. "Um, what are the rules?"

He bowed before walking away. "No killing. That's the only rule."

"Wait!"

Pablo reached the staircase and turned to look at me.

I gave him a dubious smile. "There aren't people in those rooms, are there? I mean, this is just an audition."

He inclined his head. "Impress me, Miss White. If this doesn't work out, we'll scrub your memories of the whole affair. If it does, you'll become a rich woman." Pablo disappeared into the stairwell and said, "Very rich indeed."

Chapter 21

"What the hell am I doing?" I whispered.

I took my time walking toward the stairwell so the camera on my neck could see everything. Were those private rooms empty? Maybe I could accidentally walk into one, then we could nab more than the ringleader.

The stairway Pablo had directed me to curved, and when I reached the bottom, I faced a door. This stairwell didn't give access to the viewing rooms. When I opened the door, I entered the large room where the fights took place. Every small sound was amplified, including my boots tapping against the white floor. As soon as the door behind me closed, it locked. There was another on the opposite side, and twenty-two mirrored windows surrounded me. It didn't seem like that many, which meant they had to be charging these people a fortune. Just thinking about how much *my* pay was boggled the mind, but it must have been a drop in the bucket compared to what Pablo was making.

The white walls were polished like marble, and between each window was a rectangular crack in the wall. I cupped my hands on the glass and tried to peer inside one of the rooms. Couldn't see a damn thing.

When the opposite door opened, my spine went ramrod straight. A woman walked in with confidence in her step. Her blond hair tied back in a tight bun meant business. She was dressed just as skimpily as I was—black shorts, black tank top, and matching boots. Her shoes gave me pause. My father sometimes wore those in his garage to protect his feet. They were steel-toed.

She raked me over with one glance, her arms hanging stiffly at her side.

I approached her, my head high and shoulders squared. "I'm Robin."

"I don't care." She flicked a glance down at my boots and smirked.

I took off my long duster and flung it at the wall. Tying my hair up was a waste of time. I'd been in more scuffles than I could count, and hair got pulled whether you wore it up or down. Our reflections surrounded us like an army. Her physique was more feminine—larger breasts, softer hips, and fuller lips. She was doing her own assessment, looking at the sculpted muscles on my legs and arms. My gaze was colder, my expression stonier, and my determination stronger. At least I hoped it was. Money turned people into jackals, and she looked hungry enough to win this fight even though it was just an audition.

Or was it?

The overhead lights switched off except for a cluster in the middle that shone on us like a spotlight. It drew attention away from the ring of mirrored glass.

"Do we wait for a bell?" I mused.

She flashed across the room. "We fight when they're ready."

"How do we know when they're ready?"

Just then, an intercom clicked on and a British woman began speaking. "The blond fighter is a fourteen-time champion with no losses. The raven-haired woman is an experienced street fighter. This is her first performance. For those interested in placing bets, please do so now. Push the green button when you're ready." Her accent was more refined and polished than Flynn's.

Oh shit. This was the real deal, and I was about to indulge someone's fetish.

When a current of energy rippled through the room, my hair stood on end. It wasn't coming from the woman but the watchers behind the glass.

The blonde flashed to the other side, warming up. I bent over and touched my feet to do a little stretch.

This is ridiculous. I've never warmed up for a street fight in my life. Not unless tequila shots count.

I backed up against a wall while this amateur proceeded to waste her energy prancing around. Maybe it was my impassive stare, or maybe it was the fact I wasn't as hyped up as she was, but the woman slid an apprehensive look my way. This fight was crucial. I had to make sure my fangs didn't accidentally punch out. Were we allowed to use our Mage gifts? Not the basic stuff, but our rare gifts. The only rule Pablo had given me was no killing. That meant everything else was fair game.

With that, a sinister smile crossed my face.

The microphone clicked on. "Ladies, begin."

With lightning speed, Blondie flashed over and punched me in the face.

Holding my eye, I looked up as she flashed off. "So that's how it's gonna be? Hit and run? That's not fighting."

When she came at me a second time, I ducked and threw out my leg to trip her. She smacked into the wall and left a streak of blood where she crumpled to the floor. As I moved toward her, she struck me in the femur with her steel-toed boot.

"Son of a—" I grimaced and looked at my leg to see if a bone was sticking out. Much to my relief, the kick had only broken my skin but nothing else.

Blondie crawled away and then scrambled to her feet.

I loved confined spaces. No escape, no surprises, and…

The wall between two windows opened up like a drawer, and Blondie flashed over and pulled out a dagger.

What was I saying about surprises?

As the rectangular drawer shut, I realized that either the house or the players were in control, and we were nothing but chips on the table.

She gripped the dagger in her left hand and held it above her head.

Amateur.

When Blondie flashed toward me and drove down the knife, I throat-punched her. The blade sank into my shoulder and cut bone, but I was willing to take the hit. She reached for her throat, gasping and coughing. I punched her in the face again and again like a boxer going for the win. Blood sprayed across one of the mirrored windows like raindrops. The knife fell from her grip and skittered across the floor when she accidentally kicked it while stumbling backward.

Blondie fell to all fours, retching and gasping for breath.

I reached down and scooped up the dagger, my palm welcoming the handle like an old friend. "Hello, darling."

As I straightened my back, I glimpsed her in the mirror, moving like a bullet. A punch to the kidney brought me to my knees. The pain radiated through my insides like a sharp sword burying itself deep. The second blow came from her steel-toed boot, and when it hit the same spot, I bellowed in pain.

I rolled to my side and stared at the floor in disbelief. I'd taken a lot of blows in training, but never to the kidney. Nausea swept over me, but I pushed it down and went into survival mode. All the mirrors gave me flashbacks to the days when I fought for my life in bar bathrooms. I had taken all my victims by surprise, but this was no sneak attack, and I finally had an equal who wanted to win just as much as I did.

I caught her movement in the mirrors, and before she could kick me again, I rolled out of reach.

With the knife gripped in my hand—the way you're *supposed* to hold a knife in a fight—I used the wall to steady myself and rose to face her. "Now you've pissed me off," I grumbled.

Her face reddened as she continued coughing, but she wasn't giving up.

In the many reflections, I noticed the stab wound on my back. The dagger wasn't a stunner, so the offering was meant to increase the bloodshed, not win the fight.

Blood trickled down my arm in rivulets as I pointed the dagger at her. "Come and get it."

She spat blood on the floor, her left eye swelling up and those pretty lips split and bleeding. Defeat didn't flicker in her eyes, and she stood like an immovable rock that refused to be broken.

I admired the hell out of her.

We circled each other like predators, each looking for a weakness. Blondie flashed at me, and in a surprise move, bent down and hoisted me off the floor. Airborne for the briefest of seconds, I braced myself for the fall. My back hit the floor with a sickening thud. Before I could wince, we grappled as she tried to disarm me.

I wrenched my hand away, slicing her arm in the process. Stabbing a Mage in the torso wouldn't do much damage, but a leg wound would slow her down. I readjusted the blade and sank it into her thigh. To my delight, Blondie let out a bloodcurdling scream. She then yanked the blade out and aimed it over my chest. With her straddling me and my right arm pinned, I had no escape.

As the blade came down, I knocked her hand with my free arm. She missed, and once again, we fought for the weapon. I threw her off me as I bit her arm and rolled to the side. No Vampire fangs, just good old-fashioned incisors. When her entire body suddenly heated up like a furnace, I roared like a wild animal caught in a trap. Her touch was unbearable, and I scurried backward.

"You Thermal bitch," I growled, my teeth still burning.

Out of breath, she exhaustedly grabbed the knife and remained on one knee, glancing at me over her right shoulder.

"You're tough," she said. "But I'm tougher."

That pissed me off.

I sprang to my feet, and I didn't feel my injuries anymore. Niko's words rang in my head. *When you feel the pain and let it take over, it consumes you with fear and doubt.* Niko said if I learned to separate pain from my conscious mind, I could do anything.

I sprinted toward the wall and ran up it two steps before pushing off and sailing through the air. She didn't have time to process what was happening. I was already on top of her like one of those wrestlers my father used to watch on TV. I body-slammed her, and the knife spiraled out of reach. Blondie crumpled to the ground like a broken tree in a storm, and I was that storm.

Then I twisted around and pinned her head between my thighs, my ankles locked and knees bent like I'd done a hundred times before. As the circulation to her brain ceased, she did what they all had done—tried to pry my legs apart before beating her fists on them. She writhed and struggled to free herself, but I had a tight grip on that bun on her head.

She suddenly switched on her Thermal powers, and it felt like my legs were wrapped around a radiator.

Hold on just one more minute. You can do this. Don't give up. I ignored the intense heat and only thought of survival. This was the end times, we were the last two on earth, and only one of us would walk out alive.

As her struggling decreased, so did the heat. Sweat beaded on my brow and across my chest. My thighs were on fire, and it was everything I could do not to scream.

She finally went limp. This was the part where they lost consciousness for a few brief moments, allowing me to finish the job. I released my hold, my inner thighs bright red from the knees up with two visible handprints on top. I rolled my opponent onto her back and straddled her.

"Light's out," I panted, placing my hands on hers.

Just as the first current of her energy entered my palms, my fangs wanted to punch out. I tasted the power in her light. What would her blood taste like? If she wasn't evil like the others I'd killed, would that blood have the opposite effect, giving me a rush of power?

So many questions.

I reached deep down for her core light. Her eyelids fluttered before her eyes popped open when she realized I was about to steal her immortality. Somehow they could always tell when I went too deep—deeper than any juicer had ever gone.

She feebly shook her head, her eyes welling with tears. "*No,*" she whispered.

Reminded that this was only a game, I severed the connection so fast that the energy snapped against my palms like a stretched rubber band.

I was breathing as if I'd run a mile, and it was the only sound in the room.

Blondie looked away, and with that, she surrendered. I slowly stood, blood dripping from my fingertips, my body blistered and bruised. There was no roar of applause. No referee to raise my arm as the winner. The white room was now freckled with blood spatters, and I saw myself in every direction. This was the real me. Not a scrapper trying to get by. Not a hustler. Not a daughter. Not even a killer.

I was a warrior.

The intercom clicked on. "We have a champion. The raven-haired fighter is the last standing. Congratulations to the winners. Please remain seated until we escort you out. Drinks are available for those waiting. Good evening."

Unimpressed by the announcement, I made my way back to my door and lifted my duster off the ground.

"Well done," Blondie said.

I turned to look at her. She had managed to sit up, but barely. Pablo hadn't suggested that losers were fired, but I guessed that salaries relied heavily on wins. I didn't know this girl or what her story was—why she needed the money so badly to put herself through this—but I inclined my head respectfully before the door opened and I left the room.

My insides still hurt from the kidney assault, enough that I'd probably pee blood for a week, even after healing. My right arm tingled as I walked dizzily up the stairs.

"I must commend you on your fighting techniques. Very impressive," Pablo said, approaching with a towel in hand. "Sit down and let me have a look at you."

I robotically sat in the chair, still feeling that woman's energy coursing through my body.

Pablo took my hand, and before I knew it, he was giving me healing light. Blue light threaded between our palms as energy specific to healing tunneled through me and sealed up my wounds. The red marks on my thighs disappeared along with the blisters, bruises, and cuts.

Pablo wiped the damp towel over my shoulder and cleaned off the blood. "Next time, bring a suitable change of clothing. Casual.

Like something you would wear in a restaurant. The fighters have a private bathroom, and you'll be able to shower in there." He lifted my arm and continued washing me. "It's imperative that we don't make mistakes. You can't walk out of our gallery with blood on you. From now on, you'll enter through the back door."

"Am I hired?"

He looked at me with astonishment. "My dear, you won against our reigning champion."

"Why would you pit me against the best?"

He turned the towel over. "Because we only want the best. I would have hired you if you lasted more than ten minutes in there. No one has lasted more than five." Once my hands were spotless, he stepped back. "Before you leave, someone would like to meet you."

A woman floated toward us from around the bend. Her alabaster skin wasn't without flaws, so I ruled out a Vampire. I always tried to assess people's Breed right off the bat. Her orange hair, which was styled in a finger wave, ruled out Chitah. Candy-apple-red lips turned up in a smile, revealing teeth so white and perfect that she almost didn't seem real. The sequins in her silver gown caught the light and shimmered like diamonds.

Pablo shoved a chair in front of me. Out of breath, he stepped aside to let the lady sit.

She offered me her hand, the emerald ring on her middle finger as deep green as Irish pastures. "Hello, Robin. I'm Audrey." It was the same British announcer from the fight, only now she spoke more softly.

I stared at her hand, wondering if she wanted me to kiss it or something.

"I've never been a fan of all the bowing," she said. "I think that custom began because of people like me."

I took her hand and lightly shook it. "People like you?" Before letting go, I felt what I could only describe as the sensation of running through a meadow of flowers—warm wind in my hair, golden sunshine melting against my skin, and the fragrant smell of lilac and phlox. I retracted my hand. "You're a Sensor."

She crossed her legs. "Breeds have never trusted each other. Beware the stranger. I suppose bowing was one custom we created to avoid a Sensor putting power into another without permission."

"Like you just did?"

She waved her index finger at me while looking at Pablo. "I like her. She has gumption."

I cleared my throat. "I'm sorry, who are you? I got your name, but—"

"I'm the reason you're here. Pablo handles the vetting process, but after tonight's fight, I had to meet you myself."

"I think that woman down there has a lot of gumption. Hope you don't fire her."

Audrey turned her gaze downward to the window as the blonde made her way out of the room. "I never let go of people like her. A fearless woman is a diamond. The word *diamond* comes from a Greek word that means *invincible*. Diamonds are harder than any other mineral, and they're not easy to break. But nothing is unbreakable. You're a Stealer, aren't you?"

"What makes you think that?"

She pinned me with her gaze. "I saw what you almost did in there. Pablo's a Stealer."

"Is that so?"

"Robin, don't hold back on your gifts."

I furrowed my brow. "You don't see the problem? If I stole her core light, she'd be useless to you."

Audrey leaned back in her chair and gestured to the windows. "That's what they pay for. It would certainly put me out, but there are always replacements."

"Do you have any male fighters?"

"Our clients don't want to see men fighting. They've been watching that for centuries. There's a particular audience who relishes in the success of women—seeing their power on full display. They want to feel that power."

"Feel?"

"Before you leave here, I'm going to pull that experience out of you and sell it to the highest bidder. You'll keep the memory but not the sensory information. That's where we make the most money. I implant that memory inside them so it's theirs to keep. They will possess the feel of every blow, every kick, and every rush that you did while dominating your enemy. They *want* you to use your gifts against each other, so long as you both walk out of that room alive."

"You'll run out of fighters."

She laughed brightly and shared a look with Pablo, who gave a mechanical smile. "Now *that's* confidence." After stifling her amusement, she looked me over. "Have you ever killed anyone? Is that why you stopped pulling her light?"

Uncertain what she wanted to hear, I raked my fingers through my hair. I heard Viktor's voice in my head, telling me to get more information. "Who's your audience? It might shock them if they saw what I almost did in there. Making someone mortal is worse than death and strikes fear in a lot of people."

Audrey tapped her bottom lip. "I cannot divulge who pays to play, but you're right. This audience isn't interested in watching a murder. It's about the champion and the battle."

"Are they all men?"

Her brows subtly arched. "What makes you suggest that?"

"Because that's who pays to watch fights like these. Men who get off watching women wrestle each other in skimpy clothes."

She shrugged. "Wear a Mickey Mouse costume for all I care. You can flip on the telly and watch women wrestling for free. That's not why they're here."

"Why don't you hire Vampires or Shifters?"

Audrey uncrossed her legs and leaned against the armrest. "Mage women aren't easy to come by, and ones that can fight? A rarity indeed. I'm quite certain you know your own history. So tell me, have you ever killed anyone? I need to know everything about my fighters before I put them in that room."

I leaned back and folded my arms. I wouldn't be fighting again, so what I chose to say wouldn't matter. I just wanted to keep her talking. "Yes. I've killed a lot of men. Does that make me a liability? Have you had any accidents in there? Is that what you're afraid of?"

I really wanted her to confess to the deaths of the women who were dumped in the alleyways.

Audrey sighed melodically and glanced at Pablo, who kept his eyes downcast. "Robin, would you be satisfied walking away a champion, or do you require the victory of a kill? Be honest with me." She leaned forward and touched my knee.

What fuckery was this? With nowhere to go, I had a Sensor reading me for lies, and that made me all kinds of nervous. Shepherd was gifted, but could this woman read my mind or just my feelings? In any case, I couldn't lie.

"I'm not satisfied unless I kill my opponent. Walking away is like taking a bite of cake and throwing the rest in the trash. It's like a man bringing you to the edge of climax and then leaving the room." I moved my knee away and stood to put distance between us. "But if you have a rule against killing, that's all I need," I said, quickly covering my tracks so she wouldn't have someone scrub my memories before I left the building. "I want this job. I need this money. I can walk away without killing if that's what you need me to do."

When met with silence, I turned away and watched two men in white coveralls mopping the bloody floor in the room below.

"I want to make you a proposition," she began. "This reminds me of that game show with the curtain. What was that one called?"

"*Let's Make a Deal*," Pablo replied.

She laughed blithely. "All those silly humans, dressing up in costumes for a chance at winning a dishwasher. Robin, we'll take care of you as long as you are loyal to us. But if you crave excitement and danger, I can offer you something behind curtain number two. But that would mean walking away from this position, and if you reject my second offer, we'll have no choice but to wipe your memories clean. My assistant is thorough, and you'll lose all memories of everything that's happened between today and Friday. She doesn't pick and choose; it all goes."

"What kind of job?" I asked, still watching the men clean the room.

"If you settle for the current job, we'll provide you with a schedule. If you're curious about my second mystery offer, then reject this position and I'll see you on Friday. I'm afraid you'll have to go in blind. What will it be?"

I turned on my heel. "I guess I'll see you Friday."

"That pleases me more than you know." She rose to her feet and changed the topic to my recent victory.

I glanced down, and horror swept through me. *The necklace!* I clutched my chest and searched the floor.

"What's the matter?" she asked.

"My necklace is gone."

"After today's earnings, you'll have enough to buy a hundred necklaces of your choosing."

"It's sentimental. My father gave it to me."

Pablo neared the glass and looked down. "It's there... by the wall."

"Fetch it, darling." Audrey smiled at him when he gave her a thorny look.

I wanted to smash my fists against the glass. All this juicy information, not to mention Audrey's face, and none of it captured on Wyatt's stupid video camera.

Once Pablo disappeared down the stairwell, Audrey approached the glass. "I don't know why I'm so awful to him. Pablo is the most loyal companion I've ever had. Don't fool yourself, Robin. Money isn't the most valuable thing to an immortal—loyalty is. You can have all the money you like, but you can't buy loyalty. Not truly."

"Why else would he be loyal to someone who talks down to him?"

Her voice fell to a whisper. "Love."

Pablo entered the room below. After retrieving my necklace, he borrowed a clean rag from one of the men and polished it.

"When you find loyalty like that, never let go. That's the only real way to survive. If you have at least one person in this godforsaken world who will fall on a blade for you, then nothing else matters."

I turned to face her.

"Just be sure you never break that loyalty," she said with resolve. "Once you do that, you can never really trust them all the way." Audrey placed her hands on my chest. "Before I leave, I need to collect my winnings. Think about the fight and bring that memory to the top. It makes it easier, dear."

A red glow emanated from her palms, and my body warmed all over. Afraid she might start digging around, I thought about walking into the empty room. As soon as the thought entered my mind, a smile touched her lips, and the memories flipped through my mind like someone thumbing through the pages of a book. Everything rose to the surface—the physical punches and internal pain, the elation I felt when taking control of the fight, the feel of my opponent's body trembling beneath mine as I drank her core light.

"*Mmm*, this one's good," Audrey whispered to herself.

Once she pulled it out, I had a strange feeling of detachment.

After she let go, she wiggled her fingers. "Am I your first?"

I shuddered. "That feels weird to think about it now."

Audrey grinned, revealing perfect teeth behind her red lips. "The memories remain, but the emotions are removed. That's the only way I can get a pure exchange. You'll remember each and every fight, but the emotional highs and lows, the pain—all that's gone now."

As I recalled the fight, it felt more like something I'd watched on television.

"See you on Friday." Audrey gracefully drifted around the bend and disappeared from sight.

I put on the long duster and used it to wipe blood off my thigh. I had so many questions about how she started up a business like this, but too many questions out of the gate would have sealed my doom.

"She's enamored by you."

I looked down at Pablo, who was admiring my necklace. "What makes you say that? I didn't exactly dazzle her with my charm."

"No, but few women impress her. Most are too skittish in her presence—fearful they'll say or do something wrong. They're afraid; you're not. That's what makes you different. It also makes you unpredictable." He let the necklace swing from his fingertips, his eyes trained on the black stone. "This is an odd choice for a father to give a daughter. It's cheaply made."

I snatched it from his hand. "I lied."

Pablo cocked his head to the side. "Do you think it's wise to lie to your future employer?"

I put the necklace over my head. "Rich people like you think everything and everyone's replaceable. It's a cheap necklace on a shitty chain, but it's the only thing I have left of my mother. I don't really like telling people I don't know very well about that part of my life. I shouldn't have worn it tonight."

He clasped his small hands behind his back and strode past me. "How does a savage woman with a sentimental heart have such an astounding number of kills? One behavior seems to contradict the other."

I fell into step beside him as we returned to the stairwell. "If you want to know the truth, that's the question that keeps me up at night."

"An internal battle between good and evil. I wonder which will prevail."

"So do I, Pablo. So do I."

Chapter 22

WITH A SURPLUS OF MAGE energy crackling through my body, I flashed into the subway and snuck aboard a train. Getting past security was too easy in the city of Cognito. Especially for a Mage. I'd never had a reason to hitch a free ride before, but without any cash in my pocket, I had no time to waste.

I navigated through the cars on the train—most empty—until I reached the back. A Vampire watched me with mild interest before getting off at his stop. The train headed east, emerging from the underground tunnel and onto the street. City lights whirred by, and I went over the details of the evening in my head until we reached the next station. As soon as the doors opened, I stepped out and got my bearings. Lenore's mansion wasn't far, and with Christian assigned to her, he couldn't be far.

After a few blocks, I came upon an elite housing division where the aristocratic hotshots lived. It was an older community, and all the homes had been restored to their original glory. Lenore's property looked like a park with all the trees and winding pathways. I didn't feel like ringing the bell and asking permission to speak to my man, so I selected a large oak tree by the house to climb. Christian occasionally talked about his days as a guard, and he had told me he'd either choose a shadowy spot near the house or perch atop a high vantage point. Once my boots were off, I scaled the branches like an acrobat. The bough reached the roof, making it easy to jump over to Lenore's oddly-shaped house. A glass dome in front allowed visitors to be awestruck by unique architecture, chandeliers, gilded furniture, and life-size statues. But all that splendor diminished on a rooftop. From above, it looked as unremarkable as any other house. Only shingles, gutters, chimney pipes, and vents.

I avoided the windows. Lenore might be in one of those rooms, so I quietly climbed the steep roof on the second floor and made my way toward the top. To my surprise, there was a flat space by two chimneys and what appeared to be ventilation pipes. Without moonlight, it was too dark to make anything out beyond a few feet.

I padded toward the wide chimney. Just as I reached it, a shadow blurred around me, and the next thing I knew, I was pinned to the ground. I stared into a pair of black eyes as the sharp prick of a blade touched my jugular.

"It's like when we first met."

Christian cursed under his breath. "*Jaysus wept.* I could have sliced your throat." He set down the knife, his arms still caging me. "What brings you here?"

"I heard you took a new job," I said flatly.

"Not by choice," he replied, still on top of me. "Again, what brings you here? Lenore wouldn't like you snooping around on her roof."

"She has shit security." I smiled insincerely at him.

His gaze shifted, and he placed a sensual kiss on my shoulder. When he lifted his head, I saw him licking his lips. "Why's there blood all over you? And it's not all yours."

"How do you know? I cleaned up."

"Have you ever watched those forensic shows where the killer washes the crime scene with bleach? Then the investigators shine a pretty light in the room, revealing the tiniest blood spatters in places you'd never imagine. I can see them on your eyelids, your shoulder has a long streak of it, and larger clumps are in your hair." His gaze wandered down to my black bra, and I felt him growing erect. "I see them on your breasts, and I wonder if there might be a few drops for me to lick off your nipples."

"You always say things that make my heart go pitter-patter." I attempted to keep up the snark, but damn if he wasn't turning me on with that gruff voice. His body felt good against mine, as if it longed for me.

"I got in a fight," I said, not revealing details in case someone was eavesdropping. "I'm fine."

Christian's eyes skated down, and he cupped my breast in his palm. "I might need to perform an exam and see for myself. Dr. Poe, at your service."

His sincerity sent a tingle between my legs. "Aren't you on duty?"

"She's reading in a private library in the basement. That's why I'm out here, watching for nefarious men."

"Or women?"

"Aye." His hand moved south and unfastened my shorts.

"She might catch us."

He smiled at me wolfishly as he sat back and pulled down my shorts. "When that woman goes to read, she reads the entire book in one sitting." Christian flicked my shorts aside and cocked his head. "Now that's a surprise."

Instead of sexy panties or a thong, I had on boy shorts with a little leg. "Chafing," I explained. "The leather shorts aren't lined, and—"

He used his index finger to pull the panty hem. When he let go, they snapped back in place.

I gave him an impatient look. "You're really taking the sexy out of this moment."

He stroked his beard, a quizzical look on his face. "Is that spandex?"

I drew up my legs and then stood. "Viktor got Crush involved. Can you believe that? I ran into him earlier, and he had something for me. Was that your idea?"

"I give you my word, on my sweet sister's grave, that I don't know a fecking thing about your da getting involved." Christian sat back against the chimney stack. "I thought you trusted me."

Audrey's words resonated, applying to my own situation.

Christian had betrayed me once, and though I felt he'd never do it again, I wasn't as trusting as I thought I was.

"If you tell me you didn't know, I believe you," I said, glancing at the nearby house. "It's what you don't tell me."

"And what's that supposed to mean?"

I met his gaze. "Where do you go at night?" When he gave me a blank stare, I continued. "I've seen you ride off on your motorcycle late at night. Not all the time, but every couple of weeks you go out. Sometimes once a week. I've never asked you about it because I trusted you. But now that you're here, guarding Lenore, I'm beginning to wonder if this is where you've been going."

"Is that what this is? You're worried I'm diddling another woman."

"No, I didn't say that. Vampires don't sleep, and I know firsthand how maddening that can be. So if you ride around the city or go out for a few drinks, that's fine. If you're breaking into zoos or scaling buildings, that would pique my curiosity. You've told me a lot about yourself, but I don't know everything."

"Nor do I, lass. Your skin is still salty with sweat, and the blood on your shoulder tasted like excitement and danger. You wouldn't have left work because of a fight. I can also taste old blood mingling with your own. It's vile, to be sure. Anything you want to share with me?"

"I killed a man the other day."

When Christian spoke again, his tone was sincere. "That's part of the job."

"When it's self-defense or they're an outlaw, but that's…" Remembering I was standing atop Lenore's house, I clamped my mouth shut. "Let's save show-and-tell for another night."

He reached out for my hand and tugged me toward him. "Why don't you show me instead of tell?"

"I came here because I need cab money for a ride home. I didn't collect my tips when I left the club the other night, and if I go back, they'll expect me to work."

"Where has all your money gone?"

"Food. The rest of it I've been giving away."

"Who appointed you Mother Teresa?"

I shrugged. "It's hard to walk home and pass the same homeless people. If I can buy them a meal, a new tent, or maybe some clothes, then I'd rather do that than keep the money. We're gonna get a nice paycheck for this assignment, so I don't need to keep tips. Anyhow, it's too far to walk home, and I need to get home as soon as possible. Claude's at work, and I lost track of Blue. I'd call Viktor, but you know how he doesn't accept calls from public phones to his private cell."

"A resourceful woman such as yourself can't get home? It sounds like you came here to check on me." Still sitting against the chimney stack, Christian reached up and pulled down my stretchy underwear, removing them completely.

The wind cooled my bare ass, which quickly warmed up when his hands cupped my cheeks.

"If an assassin sneaks onto the property, Lenore will have your head on a platter."

"Worry not, lass. I have my hearing turned all the way up for anything beyond ten feet. That's how I heard you coming a mile away in those boots you left by the tree."

"We're *not* having sex on this roof."

His eyes flicked up to mine. "I don't want to penetrate you."

"I don't think anyone's ever said that to me before."

Christian's wanton eyes were dark and all-consuming. Like it or not, he brought out my deepest desires.

His fingers traced around the curve of my hips, and I felt the magic culminating between us. A current of sexual Mage energy raced through me and buzzed between my legs like a vibrator. As if knowing what his touch did to me, Christian ran his tongue up the inside of my thigh.

My breath hitched.

I stepped closer, the wind blowing my hair forward. A moan escaped my lips when his tongue found my clitoris. It wasn't a teasing taste. Christian devoured me, and I gripped the top edge of the chimney stack.

Biting back an anguished moan, I rested my knee on his

shoulder. Christian leaned in and pleasured me. He adored me with his hands, moving them leisurely and intentionally, one thumb pressing against the spike on my bra until it drew blood.

The sight of Christian's blood made me tense as an ancient desire awakened within me. His tongue swirled as he moved his hand up until his thumb was an inch from my mouth.

My Vampire broke loose like a caged animal, and I dipped my head and drew him into my mouth. The moment I tasted his dark mysteries, Christian released a shaky breath. That dark, delicious blood exposed him, revealing his carnal desires, his intentions, and above all, *love*. Damn if he wasn't feeling an emotion so intense that it hypnotized me.

I smoldered as he stroked my sex insistently. The world melted away, and I wondered how one man could hold such power over me. He squeezed my ass when I sucked on his thumb harder. A few drops wasn't enough, and dark thoughts filled my mind of drinking so deep there was nothing left. My hips rocked against him, and I couldn't hold back any longer. All the sensations of sucking, licking, rubbing, and drinking merged into one glorious high.

As my release rushed in, Christian sank his fangs into my groin. The pain and pleasure was exquisite. He pulled hard, drinking in my orgasm as he finished me off with his fingers. I cried out, my release so intense that my heart could have exploded in my chest. I shook again and again, my legs weak as he worked me all the way to the finish line.

Christian licked the bite to seal it. "That's it, Precious. You're mine, you hear?"

My eyes squeezed shut as another pulse made my belly clench. "Stop. I'm gonna pass out if you keep on." I took deep breaths, fighting the dizzy spell as I clutched the chimney stack like I wanted to murder it.

Christian stood up, likely gathering my clothes.

When the blunt head of his cock slid into my wet folds, I gasped with surprise. I glanced back at the house across the way and saw the silhouette of a man on the terrace. The lights in the room behind him illuminated the space. *Holy crap, is he aiming a telescope at us?*

This wasn't like the fantasies we'd played out—someone actually *was* watching us this time.

"Christian." I panted, trying to hold on to the brick as he rocked me against him, his hands on my hips. "There's someone watching."

"*Aye.* Let's give him what he wants."

I surrendered to passion. Christian groaned, and when his fingernails bit into my skin, his hands flew out and propped against the chimney. I watched the brick crumble beneath his grip. His taut muscles were like solid marble as I gripped his arms and held on. Christian tensed, and his fingers turned white as he pulverized Lenore's chimney.

All I could see was that ring—the onyx ring I'd given him.

Christian was in no rush to climax. He slowed down to make it last, and that filled me with insatiable desire. When he gained control, he wrapped his arms around me and drove deep inside. His embrace was an iron shield, protecting me from anyone who would hurt me. With an anguished moan, Christian came.

After a moment, I turned around and folded into his embrace. He kissed the top of my head and did this thing I loved where he would tunnel his fingers into my hair and stroke the back of my neck.

"You don't care that some pervert is watching us hug it out?"

He chuckled. "If he's watching us now, it's not because of the sex. He's blinded."

I leaned back and stared up at him. "What does that mean?"

A gentle look settled in his eyes. "You're a beacon of light in a dim world."

The wind blew, and we stood like two flickering candles.

"Can this beacon of light have her panties back?"

He stroked my cheek with his thumb. "Aye. Let me have a look at you first."

I got butterflies whenever he gazed at me for any length of time. Those tender moments between us were infrequent, but when they happened, it felt as if the entire world just stopped rotating on its axis. As if the past and future had overlapped and we were two souls existing in a timeless space.

After Christian fastened his pants, he gathered up my clothes. I stepped into my underwear and shorts, and he pulled them up.

"Let's do this in private next time," I suggested. "Somewhere… romantic?"

"I have just the place in mind."

"Sounds terrific. How should I dress for cemetery sex?"

"You have a tongue that could clip a hedge."

I brushed grit from my palms and suddenly froze in horror. "Oh… *fuck*."

Christian ran his fingers through his dark hair a few times and straightened his shirt. "What are you on about?"

I held up the chain around my neck, causing the pendant to swing back and forth. "Say hello to Wyatt."

Christian gave me a black look. He reached out for the necklace and bent down to face it. "Hello, you little shitebag. Having a good time, are ya? Tell you what. If I come home to an endless supply of free candy, I won't scrub your memories. If you recorded this or tell anyone, I'll glue your arse cheeks together and force-feed you ten pounds of chili from Raven's favorite diner. You got that, Spooky?" Christian tucked the necklace inside my bra so that Wyatt was now facing my nipple.

I glanced around. "It's dark. Maybe he didn't see anything."

"Is that equipped with audio?"

"I doubt it. While I was on the train, I kept asking him to send a cab to the next station to pick me up. Maybe he's busy trying to make sense of what happened tonight. I don't think Blue has any cash on her, and I didn't want her calling Viktor. He wouldn't risk sending someone to pick me up anyhow, and I need to talk to him in person."

"I might be able to take you in the morning."

"This case goes deep, and I want to find out how deep. I can't do it without Viktor's permission, and I'm afraid after what Wyatt saw tonight, they might move in prematurely."

He opened his wallet and handed me some large bills. "Then you better get going."

I took the money and stuffed it inside my bra. "This transaction feels all wrong."

"I'm sure it'll give the numpty across the way a lot to ponder."

I wrapped my arms around Christian's neck and gave him a long and lingering kiss. When it tapered off, I nibbled his bottom lip. "We'll swap stories when this is all over." My fingers grazed his tattoo. "Just remember who *you* belong to."

Without another word, I sprinted across the roof and catapulted off.

Christian leaned over the edge. "You always need a dramatic exit, don't you? Careful not to fall and crack your skull. I was hoping to prop it on my mantelpiece someday."

I held onto the branch and swung my legs to a lower one so I could descend the tree. Instead of answering him with a sharp reply, I smiled and treaded across the soft grass. Christian had rare moments when he showed his romantic side, but that wasn't what I loved about him. It was the fact that he never changed. I could always count on his boorish remarks, veiled threats, and dark humor. We got each other in a way that no one else could. I didn't want a gentleman; I wanted a loyal man who made me laugh. I wanted an equal who saw me as such. Someone who brought me coffee in the morning and cheered me on during a fight.

When I reached the tree where I'd left my boots, I circled it in search of them.

"Looking for these?" Lenore stepped out of the shadows, holding my boots between two fingers. Her gold gown captured the ambient light from the house like a net, and the pink lilies embroidered on her matching slippers looked like flowers in the grass.

I took the boots and put them on, waiting for the inevitable questions, like what I was doing on her roof and why I was dressed like a tramp.

"Do you like to read?" she asked. "I love reading. Knowledge soothes the soul. There is so much to learn from books. Writers have unfettered imaginations, and they're often the ones who pen ideas before they're ever conceived by the rest of the world. Some of them write about our world, you know. Not because they're a trusted human or have inside knowledge but because deep down, they know we exist. It could be that some of them *do* know about us, but we don't regulate works of fiction." She closed her eyes when the wind swept through her beautiful hair. "I was reading a fascinating story about the cosmos until a peculiar sound coming from the fireplace caught my interest."

"Why do you suddenly need protection?"

She opened her dark eyes and stared at me so intensely that I lowered my gaze. "Anyone in my position of power requires protection."

"That's not his job anymore. Hire a bodyguard."

"It's my understanding that Christian had no assignment, and I trust him. Darling, this is only temporary until the threat passes. In the meantime, I'm reviewing applications. Trusting a stranger with my life is no easy task. Money doesn't always buy loyalty. If I had a dollar for every guard who accepted a bribe to give up secrets, sabotage their employer, or even kill the person they were hired to protect, I'd be a rich woman. Well, a richer woman."

"I need to go."

Lenore captured my wrist. "Dear, oh dear. It's not jealousy that brought you here, is it? You're a strong woman, Raven. Jealousy is a weakness."

"Why are you always giving me unsolicited advice?"

"Because I recognize potential when I see it. When you reach my age, you let go of pettiness. You're still young and don't yet understand how ancients think." Her grip tightened. "But by sneaking onto my property and distracting my guard, you made me vulnerable. I'm certain it wasn't your intent, but this will not do. I don't bite, Raven. If you want to see Christian, you're more than welcome here anytime. Just knock on the door next time so I can make arrangements for any security risks."

I pulled my arm out of her grasp. *Great.* I'm sure Viktor would love nothing more than to find out that Christian put a higher authority member's life in danger by shirking his duties to have sex on the roof. "That wasn't my intention. I'm sorry I busted in like this, but I needed to see Christian for work reasons. He was alert the whole time."

"I'm sure distractions are unwelcome when you're on a dangerous assignment. Am I right? I only ask the same courtesy." She looked toward the road. "Did you park nearby?"

"No. It's a nice night for a stroll." I inclined my head and walked down the long driveway.

"I can have my driver take you wherever you need to go," she called out.

"That's okay," I said quietly, knowing she could hear me just fine. "God gave me these legs for a reason."

Chapter 23

When on guard duty, Christian usually stayed outside all night so he could hear everything. Footfalls in the grass, an approaching car, a racing heart, clothes rustling in the breeze—they were all easy to pick up without the obstructive walls inside a house or building. And because he knew how being inside could interfere with Vampire senses, he was certain Lenore hadn't heard anything—there were enough walls between the basement and the roof.

"Christian, may I see you downstairs in the study?" Lenore asked, her voice distant but loud enough that he knew it must have been carried up through the bathroom pipes.

The pipes.

"For feck's sake." He finished drying off his face with a towel. After shutting off the faucet, he headed to the first floor in no great hurry. Christian had no desire to be anyone's puppy, and yet Lenore still treated him the way she had all those years ago.

Her heartbeat wasn't within range, but clinking noises drew him to the downstairs bathroom. He knocked.

When she didn't answer, Christian slid his jaw to the side and turned the knob. The first thing he saw was Lenore in the bathtub. All four corners of the square monstrosity were alight with candles, but none penetrated through the milk she bathed in. Small silver pins held up her hair as Lenore continued pouring a pale green liquid into a brandy glass.

"Absinthe?" she offered.

His eyes skated over to the glass block window beside the tub. They were old-fashioned and probably original to the house.

"At least close the door behind you."

"As if the draft is bothersome."

"No, but Wilson poured my bath, and he hasn't gone to bed yet. I hear him stirring like a little mouse."

"As if showing off your body to random men is bothersome." Christian closed the door behind him and flattened his back against it.

Lenore placed a sugar cube on a flat absinthe spoon and laid it across the glass rim. The candle beside it flickered when she moved her hand to lift a small glass bottle. It had a spout, and by the looks of the condensation, the water was chilled. It wasn't the traditional fountain enthusiasts used. Lenore slowly poured water over the sugar cube until it dissolved into the crystal glass. Once finished, she lifted the milky alcohol and held it in front of her face. "Beautiful, isn't it? Everything we do in life should have a ritual—a series of planned steps that raises every action to an art form. Not reckless and sloppy, like having sex on a rooftop." Lenore lifted the glass to her lips and drank.

Christian averted his gaze. "I see you're still bathing in milk."

"You're welcome to join me."

"I'm afraid I'm lactose intolerant."

Lenore set the glass aside. "It's not the same as fresh milk from the cow. No one knows where food comes from anymore. It's just cartons on a shelf."

"That's udderly fascinating."

"Perhaps I should purchase a few goats."

"You'll need a lot of teats to fill that tub."

"Puns are for the common folk. Your humor was always your weakest asset."

"If you called me here to reprimand me, save your breath. I'm a grown man, and I'm fully aware of what the parameters of my job are."

"Are you? Before you were spirited away by sexual impulses, your full attention was on keeping me safe."

"I thought she was an intruder."

"Do you seduce all your suspects?"

Christian studied his fingernails. Lenore sounded jealous, and that gave him a measure of amusement.

"If you want to have sex with her, I can arrange something. It'll require my finding a safe place, and we'll have to time it. How does a church sound?" She flicked the milk and sent a few drops in his direction. "It would be trite of me to report such an infraction to Viktor, but if our relationship deepens, I can't make any promises to protect you when mistakes are made."

"You should set your sights a little higher than a man who pays a few misfits to lock up criminals. There are powerful players in this city, Lenore. How many people do you think would respect you shacking up with Viktor Kazan?"

Her eyes danced with amusement, and she stood. White milk cascaded down her pale body, her nipples the darkest feature about her aside from her eyes. It would be impossible for any man not to notice she was shaved smooth between her legs.

Lenore slowly stepped out of the tub and finished her absinthe. She wasn't making sexual advances for a reason. In her mind, every man's weakness boiled down to two things: a beautiful woman and power. She craftily wielded her sexuality, making sure she never gave anyone too much, always leaving them wanting for more.

And they always wanted for more.

But Christian was wise to her tactics. He flicked a tiny washcloth at her. "I've had my share of gorgeous women since we last met. There's nothing you can show me that I haven't seen a hundred times over. Dark, light, tall, large—they're all flowers in a garden, and you're just one of many. Nothing about you impresses me anymore. I don't covet your body, and I sure as shite won't allow you to use it on Viktor."

"You may have walked in the garden, but I'm a flower you haven't plucked." She set down her glass and glided toward him. Droplets of pale milk dripped from her fingertips and left a messy trail on the blue tile. When she reached him, she tipped her head to the side and gazed deep. So deep that Christian redirected his attention on her pointy chin. "I'm curious what entices you these days. Certainly not looks, and it can't be blood. Mage blood is weaker than Vampire blood, so that wouldn't be enough to bond you to her. It's not power, and it certainly isn't money based on her dreadful circumstances. *Oh, Chrissy.* Is this really the life you imagined for yourself?"

"This is the life I made for myself. There's a difference."

Christian could hear all the droplets of milk splashing against the floor, the steady beat of her heart, and even the wet sound of her licking her lips.

"This feels so familiar," she said. "You and I are the same. Leave Keystone, and I will give you power, money, and protection—anything you desire. You won't have to hide in the shadows anymore. Everyone in this city will know who Christian Poe is. What you do for Viktor is respectable, but they're not your family, and he's certainly not raising you to the level that you deserve."

"I have other commitments," Christian pointed out. No job was forever, and he knew better than to get emotionally attached to Keystone. Though he had no intention of accepting her offer, the temptation lingered. Not for her, but for something he'd never had—her approval. Why had he ever allowed himself to love Lenore Parrish? He felt like a dog kicked repeatedly by its master that keeps coming back, hoping for a scratch behind the ear.

Lenore straightened a wrinkle on his shirt. "You'll have to leave her behind as well."

Christian tensed.

"You can't love her, Chrissy. A Vampire's heart is too black and not made for love. We can't feel the way they do, because the ancient blood in our veins forbids it. Love is insidious, and now that you're older, you understand this more." She jerked his wrist when he tried to move back. "Have you ever seen an ancient with a life mate? No, because it can't be done. I can be with you or I can be with Viktor. Either way, I gain a strong alliance. You need to ask yourself how far you want to get ahead in this life. Love held you back the first time—don't let it happen again by making the wrong choice."

Christian didn't even flinch. "Never. Keystone won't always be here, and I'm bright enough to have figured that one out. But I won't sacrifice Raven for anything. Not even your empty promises."

"They're not empty. You know what I'm capable of when I put my mind to it."

He shook his head. "She's the only thing I've got that makes me feel like a man and not a monster. I'll not give her up."

"I wonder if *she* wouldn't give *you* up after I make my advances on Viktor. Think about what might happen if Viktor finds out that you harbor resentment toward his new mate. When he tosses you out, do you think Raven would give up Keystone for you? If you love her, you won't put her in that position."

Lenore reached behind him and retrieved a silk robe hanging from a hook on the door. Even though her naked body had brushed against his, there was no hint of arousal moving through him. Not even a renegade twitch. She was testing him, getting close enough to make any male yearn for her invitation.

The baffled look on her face said it all. She couldn't figure out why his heartbeat ticked at a sedate pace and why his eyes didn't steal glances of her breasts and bald fanny.

If Lenore infiltrated Keystone, Christian's hands were tied. But he couldn't complain to Viktor—not without knowing her true motives. And what would he have to say that wouldn't constitute as slander? Power couples weren't uncommon, and Viktor might find her useful. Christian had just enough information on her past political maneuvers to besmirch her reputation, but she had blackmail on him threefold. Damning her would be damning himself. He'd hoped she would stay busy with her new job and forget about him, but fecking hell, she just kept showing up at the mansion like it was her home. Making enemies with Lenore would be like kicking a hornet's nest.

Lenore slipped on the white robe but left it open in front. "You're much quieter than you used to be. I quite prefer it." She headed back to the bathtub. "You had a tendency to ramble on and on about the latest thing you read. Technology was exploding all around us, and all you could talk about was dinosaurs and whales."

She blew out the candles one at a time. "Remember that time you released all the animals from the zoo?" Lenore stood upright and baited him with a charming laugh that was infectious.

He couldn't help it. He smiled at the memory of a rhino chasing a man on a bicycle in the middle of downtown traffic. They never found all the lions, and one ostrich maimed three men who attempted to catch it with their bare hands. "If those eejits had bothered to read a book, they might have learned that an ostrich can run up to seventy miles per hour. Cornered, they can kick a man to death."

"If you wanted to free exotic animals, you should have purchased them." After wiping off her hands on a towel, she closed the distance between them. "Impulsive behavior never reaps the rewards. You have to meticulously plan and think ahead." She sighed while tying her robe at the waist. "I'm sorry. I've spent years mentoring immortals, and it's difficult not giving advice." Lenore reached up and touched his beard. "I remember how your smile could charm a room. Now it has a peculiar quality… like thorns on a rosebush."

"Don't waste your time on compliments. I don't give a shite about your approval anymore."

Lenore backed up a step. "You and I both know that's a lie. In fact, my approval is more important than ever, given my position. I do wonder what it will take to get yours. You seem… distracted these days. That's not like you. No matter how many years have passed or what hardships you faced, I still see the man who lives to please. That's why you're with Viktor, isn't it? Maybe working on your own as a guard wasn't rewarding enough. Your clients didn't appreciate what you did for them, and you had no one else to tell you how talented you are."

Christian bowed his head and stared at his shoes.

"Every man wants to be seen," she said softly, drawing nearer. "To have his talents, his work, and his trophies admired by all. Or even by just one." Lenore reached down to grip his wrist, and she held it like an iron shackle. Not to show tenderness but to feel the electrical impulses of his heart. To read his emotions with every flutter, with every quickened or skipped beat, and use it to her advantage. "I see you for what you are. I don't wish to ruin you. But this is my time. I'm going to rise to power, and Viktor will be part of it. You're so young and can't see that far ahead, but I've already calculated the moves needed to climb to the top."

"You're already as high as you can go."

"The higher authority fails you because there's no one leader. Decisions are in the hands of the majority, and they don't even have an equal number of representatives from each Breed to make those decisions fair and unbiased. It's a fractious organization in need of an overhaul."

"You're speaking treason."

"Outlining the flaws isn't treason." Lenore's black eyes glittered with secrets. "You'll have all the admiration you've always desired, without strings attached. This isn't an offer; it's a fact. Either you'll rise to the top with me, or you'll languish in fear and weakness. I now realize that money has never meant anything to you, but recognition has. Power has. When Viktor and I become a match, we'll change this world, and those who stand with us will be a part of that change. *Think* about the possibilities. We can create new laws and banish old ones. And I ask nothing of you," she said, her lips nearing his. "If you don't want to accept my offer, I don't hold that against you. I simply wanted to give you a choice. Either way, we'll be working together. You can keep your heart, your soul, and your pride. You can even keep that unsightly beard. All I will ask of you is your loyalty and vision."

His brows furrowed. "Vision?"

"The ability to see ahead. To see *my* vision unclouded. Falling for me all those years ago blinded you. Love is for amusement, but when it clouds your vision, it becomes an obstacle. This city betrayed me. The leaders at the time lied to me and tried to use me like a whore. You didn't see that part." She walked behind him and gripped the doorknob. "Decide which means more to you—catching a butterfly or catching a wave. The wave is coming, Christian. It's an unstoppable force, and there will be a reckoning."

Chapter 24

THE CAB DRIVER DROPPED ME off outside the gate, and it felt good to be home. The iron gates were twenty feet high and impossible to scale, and stone walls bordered our property. Because I didn't have my card key, I pressed a button and Wyatt buzzed me in. The head of a Roman soldier glared solemnly at me as I walked beneath the archway. I flashed up the road until I reached the circular driveway in front. At night, Keystone was easy to miss from the main road. The candles in the hallways were spaced apart, offering just enough light to see but not to illuminate the inside of the mansion. Kira didn't light up all the hallways, just the ones we frequented the most. When I reached the front door, someone had left it unlocked for me.

All homes have a unique smell, and though we lived in a castle, ours was no different. I sometimes caught a whiff of sautéed onions or the lingering goodness of baked bread from the nearby kitchen. But there was also an underlying aroma that I couldn't put my finger on—a complex mixture of scents from the stone floors, the burning candles, and perhaps even the previous tenants. But to me it was the smell of home.

Wyatt was hanging out on the lower steps of the grand staircase. He raised his arm and poured a handful of Raisinets into his mouth.

I approached and rested my hand on the stone newel. "Anything good on TV tonight?"

Still chewing, he said, "I watched a fight that turned into an amateur sex movie."

I gave him a lethal glare.

"Don't worry, buttercup. It was too dark to see anything. I turned it off before I was scarred for life by Christian's woody."

"Woody?" I snorted. "What are you, nine? I thought men looked at each other all the time in bathrooms and locker rooms."

He finished off the last of his candy and left the empty box on the stairs. "There's a difference between hard candy and soft candy."

"It's all candy to me."

"Well, someone needs to keep that candy *wrapped*."

"Enough with the air quotes," Blue said to Wyatt as she joined us from the dining hall. "You're not even using them correctly." She cast a critical gaze my way, and I noticed her bare feet. "Thought I might find you here. When I lost you in the subway, I went to see if Claude knew anything, but he had already left for work."

"Sorry about that," I said. "Something came up. Does anyone know where Viktor is?"

"Reviewing the video," Wyatt answered. "Just the first half," he added with a deliberate wink. "He wants everyone to sit tight and keep our phones on."

"Everyone being you and Shepherd?"

Wyatt adjusted his loose beanie. "Claude's here. When you didn't show up at the club, he went looking, and then Viktor called him home."

Viktor must have been preparing a raid. I needed to get up there and fill him in on the details.

"Hey, wait up. What happened to the other girl? Did they kill her?" Wyatt grilled me as he followed.

"This is private. Stay down here. I mean it, Spooky." When I rounded the stairs and went up to the second floor, I raised my voice. "I'll break into your vending machine and fill it up with kale chips!"

He groaned, and I no longer heard his footfalls. Wyatt responded well to threats, so we had to be creative. If there was one thing I had learned around Keystone, empty threats were unicorns. We delivered on our promises, and we had all been on the giving and receiving end.

When I reached the second floor, my boot kicked a red marble that went skittering across the floor. Hunter's toys were land mines, and I kept waiting for Gem to become the first victim. I reached Wyatt's office and found Viktor sitting in front of the computer, Shepherd hovering over the desk.

"What do you make of that?" Shepherd asked.

"I don't see," Viktor said.

"Let me rewind. There's usually a basement button, but where do the other two below it go?"

When I cleared my throat, the two men turned to look at me. "I need to speak to Viktor. Alone."

Viktor nodded at Shepherd, who obligingly left the room.

I sat down in another computer chair and rolled up to Viktor. "I didn't know they would make me fight. I tried everything to get out of it, but they would have thrown me out and scrubbed my memories."

"You did fine." His grey eyes settled on mine. "Is the woman alive?"

"Yes. They don't allow killing. Apparently that's the only rule." I flicked a nervous gaze at the frozen video, hoping like hell Wyatt had told the truth about not having recorded the sex part.

"There was no audio," Viktor said, confirming my suspicions. "I will need the names and everything discussed."

"Okay, but can I ask you something first?"

"You may ask."

"Why did you send my father to give me the necklace? Why not Blue?"

Viktor scratched his ear. "Wyatt received the special order at the last minute, and we had no time to waste when he tracked your movements. I couldn't risk someone recognizing one of us—especially Shepherd, who had been at the club. The man you were walking with knows Claude, and anyone Breed who might approach you would gain his suspicion."

"So you put my father up to it?"

Viktor chuckled. "He kept calling to check on you, and then he shows up out of nowhere. This was a chance for him to see that you were fine. People never suspect humans to be involved in our affairs, so knowing a trusted human can be of great value."

"He should have left it at the front desk of my hotel."

"The plan was to give it to you on your way to the club, but Wyatt saw you heading a different way. Your father had a microphone in his ear, and Wyatt made him run to meet up with you."

I didn't bother correcting Viktor that people didn't wear microphones in their ear. His English was very good, but it wasn't unusual for him to choose the wrong word.

"Next time send Switch. Nobody knows who he is, and that way you won't have to involve my father."

"That is *not* his job," Viktor informed me. "I cannot involve him when his primary purpose is to look after Shepherd's child. If he involves himself in anything dangerous and men go looking for him, that puts Hunter in danger."

"Sure, but you put my dad in harm's way."

"Let's not be dramatic. Blue would not have allowed any harm to come to your father."

"I'm talking about the heart attack he almost had jogging around the city and then seeing me in this outfit."

Viktor's laugh was a deep chuckle trapped in his chest, one that always made you feel good since he could be such a serious guy. It vanished just as quickly as it came. "You are okay?"

I sat back against the leather. "Pablo Russo is the name of the short man in the auction house. I thought he was the one in charge, but that's not the case. He's the guy who makes sure things run smoothly and does all the work, but there's a woman in charge."

"A woman?"

"Yep. My necklace fell off while fighting, but I met her afterward. She said her clients like seeing women reach their full potential in the ring. They pay six figures. I wasn't sure how they could afford that, but she said the business has multiple streams of income. Members pay to watch, betting is optional, and I have a feeling some pay extra to interfere."

"In what way?"

"Did you see the drawer open up with the knife? There were other gaps in the walls, not just that one. I think maybe there's something going on where they bid on weapons. And then there's sensory exchange."

Viktor's grey eyebrows drew together, and two lines formed between them. "Was the other fighter not a Mage?"

"She was, but Audrey—the woman in charge—is a Sensor. Before I left, she took the emotional experience of the fight and was going to sell it to the highest bidder. Apparently that's where they get a lot of their money from. It's not a single experience, but she implants it."

Viktor slammed his fist against the desk. A cup full of pens rattled, and a little green candy rolled across the surface and then tapped across the floor.

As I watched it roll, movement across the room caught my eye from the sectional.

Hunter shuffled toward us, his hair sticking out in all directions and his eyes half-closed. He dragged a small blanket behind him, his right arm clutching a teddy bear.

I grimaced and lowered my voice. "Sorry, Viktor. I didn't know he was in here."

Viktor rolled his chair back and turned to look at Hunter. "It is time for you to go to bed, little one. Do you know how to find your room?"

"It's dark," I said. "The halls are a little scary."

Viktor scooped him up in his arms. Hunter yawned, and his head lazily fell on Viktor's shoulder. His eyelids drew down like window shades as he fell into a deep slumber. He must have been an adorable toddler.

"Walk with me," Viktor said quietly.

I fell into step beside him, walking on the opposite side from Hunter. "I need to talk to you about the fights. I know Wyatt has more than enough evidence, but something else is going on."

"And what is that?"

"I don't know for sure. The woman's name is Audrey. She's a

Sensor with reddish-orange hair and a British accent. Does that ring any bells?"

"Nyet."

"She seems to have a lot of connections. She made me another offer but wouldn't tell me what it was for. I had to choose between accepting the job or doing something more exciting. I think that's how she put it. Anyhow, I chose the second option. I think we need to see what else they're offering. She wants me back on Friday."

"We have more than enough evidence to move in. Wyatt has run a check on the building owner, and we have the little man's face and name. That would be enough for us to locate the woman if she escapes."

"I know these fights are illegal, but how much time do you really think they'll do? The fighters are there of their own free will, they're compensated, healed afterward, and we still don't have evidence that anyone's watching the fights. All I saw were windows. If we can't prove that anyone was watching, were they committing a crime?"

Viktor stopped in his tracks. After muttering a few words in Russian, he said, "Then we must go deeper."

Shepherd's combat boots tromped loudly as he marched toward us like a man on a mission. His tattoos always stood out when he wore a white tank top. Not just the large phoenix on his right arm but also the compass with Hunter's name. "Sorry. I forgot my kid." Shepherd reached for Hunter and collected him in his arms. "Come on, little man. Time for bed."

"Keep your phone on," Viktor instructed him.

Shepherd looked between us. "Are we going in tonight? I need time to get my weapons together."

"Nyet, but we have plans to make."

"Gotcha. Just let me know whether those plans are to kill or capture."

Shepherd turned away and headed down the hall. The Celtic knot on the back of his neck was partially obscured by Hunter's dark hair.

Viktor drifted to a dim lantern affixed to the wall. "If you do not know what this other offer is, you could be in danger."

"I'm willing to take the risk. If this goes bad, I'll take the heat. What are your thoughts?"

"If you accept the risk, I think we should look into it."

"I'll make sure the necklace stays on this time. Maybe you can keep the van running outside and bust in once you have enough evidence."

"I'll have Wyatt locate blueprints of the building. If there have been any renovations done in secret, we will not have this. Not without time, and I do not know if Friday will be enough for Wyatt to research."

"Then fire his ass. He needs a little motivation." I wrapped the long duster in front of me. "I need this, Viktor. It's my first solo assignment, and I want to do it right. The bodies we found don't line up with what they're saying about the fights. We don't even know if that's *all* the bodies. They might be recruiting from elsewhere. I want to know what happened to those girls. Do you think we have enough time to slap a plan together?"

Viktor pinched his silver beard, one arm folded across his middle. "We will be short one person. Christian cannot leave his current assignment. I will have Shepherd assess the risk. Wyatt will need to provide blueprints in a short time. We go prepared or not at all. Do you know which entrance they escort the patrons in?"

I shifted my weight to my right leg. "Pablo said they come in a different way, but he didn't show me. He mentioned something about privacy."

"Perhaps a tunnel," Viktor murmured. "I want you to go back to the club and pretend nothing is wrong."

"Why bother? We're already in."

"The man who secured this position for you may grow suspicious and report you to this Pablo. The other women did not quit their jobs. You must not do anything… What is the word I seek? A struggling Mage would not walk away from a good job after only one night, and you do not even know what the second offer is."

"How do I get in touch with you? I don't have my phone. Someone will need to tell me the plan."

Viktor reached out and tugged on my necklace chain until the black pendant popped out of my bra. "I will have Blue bring you a shorter chain that is strong. This one slipped off your head too easily. Unacceptable. Do not worry about our plan. The less you know, the better. If they have a Vampire charm you, I do not want them knowing if and when we plan to strike. Or if she touches you. Do not let this woman touch you."

"Got it."

"Do not fight. Try to delay. Get a tour. Visit the facility. Use this necklace to give Wyatt as much information as possible. If they put you in a ring, we will come for you."

I wondered if Viktor wanted to trap as many people as possible.

"I'll do what I can," I promised him. "Just don't leave me hanging. I'll fight to the death if I have to, but I don't want to."

A smile hovered on his lips. "And since when does Raven Black say no to death?"

"I draw the line at having an audience."

Viktor and I turned to the sound of roller skates moving our way. Gem always made an entrance with great panache. She flashed a playful grin, her wavy hair dancing in the air as she seemingly floated toward us.

"Raven! I thought that was your voice I heard." She skidded to a halt and turned in a circle before gripping my shoulders as if she might fall. "What are you doing here? Is the mission over?"

"I had to talk to Viktor. Having fun without me?"

"Alas, I've been poring over a collection of books *riddled* with grammatical errors."

In skates, Gem appeared a lot taller. But I was wearing boots, so she still had to look up at us.

"Am I intruding?" She blinked innocently at Viktor, and he replied to her in Russian.

Meanwhile, my brain was working out scenarios. "Viktor, I think we should have Gem come along."

He shook his head. "That is not her job."

"No, but it used to be. Christian's on assignment, so we're a man down. Gem is powerful and fast. If something happens and you're locked out, Christian won't be there to break down a door."

Gem's eyes widened when she realized I was talking about her ability as a Wielder. "Oh, Viktor, *yes*! I can help. What's this for?"

Despite the curt look he threw me, Viktor was a smart man, albeit a cautious one. This wouldn't be Gem's first time going on a raid. "I will discuss with Shepherd, but right now I must find Wyatt so he can search for blueprints. We must not delay. Raven, go back to working at club. If your plans change, give Blue a message."

Gem hooked her arm in mine as Viktor inclined his head and hastily made his exit. "I normally don't like these outings, but Niko's been giving me advice lately."

"He's good at that." I strolled toward the stairs. "I heard my father came by."

"I just *adore* him," Gem said with a squeeze of my arm. "He loves you so much. What does unconditional love feel like?"

"A pain in the ass sometimes." I chuckled softly. "He's getting older, and I want him to relax and stop leaping into danger."

"Maybe that's how he feels about you. He worries."

"Now I understand why immortals break contact with their family. My job puts him in danger, and he's too stubborn to keep out of my business."

"He seems like a tough guy. No one lives forever, so why not let him do what he wants?" She rolled slowly beside me. "I know how he feels. Viktor's always trying to protect me, but I'm also a Mage. Even though I'm small and don't know how to fight, I can help. That's how your father feels. He knows he's mortal, but he just wants to help. Oh!" She gasped and spun in front of me. "He promised to bring over barbecue from that place we went to. Isn't that divine? We hardly ever have guests, but now that he's a trusted human, we can have him over all the time!"

Perish the thought.

The mere idea of Crush popping in unannounced while I was busy having sex with Christian made me shudder.

"Gem, don't invite him over here without asking me first. I

love him, but we need boundaries. I'm also afraid that he might volunteer himself too much in our business, and Viktor's already recruited him once. You don't know that man like I do. He doesn't just look for trouble, he runs to it headfirst."

She gave me an elfin grin and skated backward. "Sounds like a certain someone I know."

After checking my internal clock, I decided it was time to go. "I need to call a cab before it gets too late." I blew past her toward the end of the hall. "Have you gone swimming lately?"

"No," she said tersely, rolling alongside me. "I've been too busy."

That sounded like a lie.

"Raven?"

I stopped at the stairs and turned. "Yeah?"

"Thanks for believing in me. With Viktor, I mean. I won't let everyone down." She made a motion of crossing her heart.

"You never have."

Chapter 25

Sad to leave Keystone, I called a cab and headed back to the hotel. Viktor wanted me to go straight to work, but Chitahs frequented the club, and wearing *sex-on-a-roof*-scented perfume would attract the wrong sort of customers to my station. After showering, I decided that following club rules wasn't a priority. Now that we'd found our culprits, I just wanted to be comfortable. I took a pair of scissors to a threadbare T-shirt and cut it in half. It wasn't a favorite, just an old concert T-shirt that Crush had bought me a while ago when I was staying with him. After getting ready for work, I headed out.

It was a crisp May night, and the smell of Chinese food hung in the air from a nearby buffet. When I heard a screech from a falcon, I glanced up and was struck in the face by a falling object. A silver chain slid down my nose and into the palm of my hand. At least Viktor hadn't sent Crush this time. While walking, I switched out my onyx pendant to the new chain, which was shorter and much thicker.

Once I reached the White Owl, the bouncer let me through. Most of the outside crowd had dispersed, but inside the club was a different story. I'd put on perfume, something most Chitahs despised. They wrinkled their noses when I passed them to put my coat in the locker room. Now that the pressure was off on sniffing out the ringleader, I decided to enjoy myself and pretend to be like everyone else with a normal job.

"Didn't think you would show," Simone said over the music.

I joined her side at the bar. "Something came up."

"Does he pay you well?" She tossed an empty bottle into a trash bin.

"Who?"

"The boss. For doing these *special* errands." Simone reached around me for a stack of napkins. "I heard all about it from the manager. What's he got you doing?"

I huffed out a sigh and handed a customer a bottle of Breed beer. "Personal stuff, and it's not sex. Trust me, you wouldn't be interested."

"Wouldn't I? Did you know someone stole all my tips during the fight? That's what happens when no one is there to watch them." Simone poured a drink for a woman in a cat mask. Then she leaned her arm on the bar and turned toward me. "Day and night I bust my butt to earn back what that scoundrel took from me."

"Flynn said it was a mutual understanding."

Her eyes rolled. "That boy doesn't even know what a mutual fund is. If you decide that you don't want these special errands, put in a good word for me. I work two jobs, and all I do is serve booze."

"I figured you and Flynn would have schemed up a way to make money on the side. He seems like a good hustler."

"You got that right. And I wouldn't do business with Flynn if my life depended on it. If you're smart, you'll keep it friendly and nothing more."

I wondered if she might have been the one to put Flynn up to all this. "Has he ever offered you anything?"

She chuckled and pulled a glass out. "His great big penis. It wasn't draining my account that made me break it off with him. It was when he asked me to spike alcohol and sell it to a few of his friends. My money wasn't enough, and he'd squandered some of it to purchase a storage unit filled with booze. He planned it all along."

"You could have made a good profit."

Simone shook her head. "A fool and his money will always part. I was a fool once," she said, handing a customer a bottle of beer, "but never again."

"Why didn't you quit the club to get away from him?"

"Because I am the master of my fate, not Flynn. He knows he'll pay me back one way or another. And if I find out he was the one who emptied my tips, I'll spike his drink with erectile dysfunction."

"I thought you still had feelings for him."

Simone laughed. "Is that what he told you? Listen, we're wandering into slander territory, but let's just say that Flynn has a very active imagination." She frowned at my shirt. "Where's your work clothes?"

"I decided that Mistress White can get away with it. I also needed to let the girls out. They don't like being locked up."

Simone reached for an orange bottle behind me and spiked a drink for a customer. As her finger swirled in the glass, I felt bad for assuming she had something to do with all this. She could have been lying, but I was pretty good at spotting a liar. Well, except for Flynn, but maybe he was a professional. On top of that, Simone still had to see him every day. Most humans I knew would have never wanted to see a guy like that again, but who wants to spend their life making more enemies? Plus the tips here were too good to pass up. She busted her ass, working two shifts every night on top of a second day job. When the hell did she have time to sleep or have fun? In the time I'd spent at the White Owl, I hadn't seen anyone pull their weight as much as Simone. Worst of all, I liked Flynn. He was wrapped up in nefarious activities, but underneath all that, he seemed like a nice guy who just took the wrong path.

But I had to put those feelings aside. Being a nice guy didn't justify breaking the law.

The next day came and went, and because Viktor didn't want me wandering outside the hotel, I spent the afternoon idling in my room. After five hours of game shows, courtroom dramas, and talk shows, I was ready to fling myself out the window. I was grateful Viktor hadn't installed electricity in all the rooms, because I didn't feel like myself after watching all that television. As much as I hated the atmosphere at the club, I eagerly looked forward to my shift. At least there would be a fight or two, and not all the patrons wanted my verbal abuse. Some were friendly.

I thought by Friday that Viktor might send me a message, but none came. Flynn invited me to meet him at a Chinese buffet near my hotel that afternoon, and due to the timing, I wondered if he knew about the second offer I received from Audrey.

"More drink?" the pretty server asked.

"Sure."

She smiled at me and topped off my soda.

"Thank you."

After she hustled off to attend to another table, I got up to fill my plate with seconds. I hadn't eaten much in the past few days, and the food here was good. Fresh, hot, and plentiful. Dynasty Star Chicken was a spacious establishment. Nothing fancy, and most of the food was Chinese-American. Greeters stood behind the front register, summoning servers to escort people to their tables. Booths lined the outer walls, and tables filled in the rest of the space. The buffet stations were in the center, sparkling chandeliers glittering over them. Short walls bordered the seating areas, and the recessed lighting did nothing to class up the amusingly bad paintings on the walls. Despite the crowd, I was able to find a quiet corner to enjoy my meal.

I hustled up to the meat station and scooped up more jalapeño chicken and shrimp. When I approached the station with the egg rolls, I bumped into a tall Chitah.

"My apologies, female," he said, his voice as smooth as a blade. His shoulder-length hair obscured some of his formidable features, but I caught a glimpse of his golden eyes.

As I put three egg rolls on my plate, I noticed the Chitah filling his plate with nothing but sugar donuts. He took almost all of them and left only one in the serving pan.

When I returned to my booth by the window, I spied Flynn passing by outside. He had on his all-black work clothes but was also carrying a satchel. When he entered the restaurant, I signaled him over.

"Don't mind if I do." He snatched one of my egg rolls before he sat down. "I'm famished. Haven't eaten all day since I was in the gym lifting weights."

"Impressive," I said flatly.

One bite demolished half his egg roll. "Simone says you took the night off. You should watch yourself. Can't afford to lose a good job. That's your safety net." He glanced over his shoulder suspiciously.

"No Vamps in here," I assured him. "Just a Chitah and some Shifters in the back."

He gobbled up the rest of the egg roll. "How can you tell who the Shifters are?"

After chewing my chicken, I wiped my mouth. "I don't know. Just a feeling, and they're behaving like a pack of coyotes."

"Band."

I furrowed my brow. "Huh?"

"A band of coyotes. That's the official name."

"I don't think you're right."

"Of course I am, love. I memorized it once. A clutch of chickens, a cast of hawks, a flock of geese, a band of coyotes, a horde of gorillas—or is it a band of gorillas and a horde of… what, exactly?"

When Flynn reached for another egg roll, I slammed my hand on top of his. Silverware and plates rattled, drawing a few curious eyes.

"If you're hungry, pay the lady up front," I said. "The buffet is over there, not on my plate."

He sat back and folded his arms. "After all I've done for you."

"You're taking fifty percent of my pay, so I think I'm giving you enough."

I glanced over at the Chitah, who had returned to his table. He extended his arm to the woman across from him, but all I could see of her was the back of her head. When he retracted his arm, I noticed a large bite in a donut he was holding.

Flynn shifted in his seat to have a look and then turned back around. "That's a brave bloke."

"Why do you say that?"

"Chitahs are usually the least likely to interbreed in public. Some classy restaurants will turn them away. Her energy was strong when I walked by the table, so I bet she's a Mage. No wonder they're hiding out in here."

"Why did you want to meet?"

Flynn scratched his short beard, which looked freshly trimmed. It was more like a five-o'clock shadow trying to graduate to the next level. He lifted the satchel and slid it across the table. A warm smile lit up his face. "That's a lot of money."

I pulled the bag onto the bench and peered inside at the stack of bills.

"It's all there."

I flicked a cautious gaze his way. "I'll count it later. You don't exactly have a solid reputation when it comes to money."

He removed his tinted glasses and set them on the table. "Is that where you're going tonight?"

"You don't know?"

He stared at my plate. "They tell me absolutely nothing. I collect the money and distribute it accordingly."

"Wouldn't it be easier to pay fighters directly?"

"If someone discovered women coming out of that building at odd hours with a satchel filled with money, they might use them for information or more money."

I smiled and dipped my egg roll in sweet-and-sour sauce. "Only a crazy person would set them up."

"You got that right. I bloody hell wouldn't want to cross them. And to what gain?" He scoffed. "I'd never be foolish enough."

"How is it you can walk out with all that money?"

"I'm the runner. I take some of it to a banker in the light of day, and the rest goes to the fighters. It gives the boss time to legalize everything, that way if someone questions our transaction, they've got paperwork showing you sold an item in one of their public auctions. There's also a receipt in the bag."

"What if fights were to the death? Would that change your involvement?"

He twirled his glasses on the table and swung his gaze upward. "I don't know. I suppose it depends on if they were both willing. Anyhow, that's not the case. And if it were, I'd want a hell of a lot more money. That said, accidents happen. Take care of yourself."

I got the feeling Flynn didn't know a damn thing about the inner workings of that organization. But accidents might explain what had happened to the victims. I'd almost lost control and killed my opponent, so I could see how an inexperienced Mage without any control might take it too far. Until I found out what the second job offer was, it was all speculation.

"I've got another appointment with them tonight," I admitted. "Are you working? I can fill you in on some of the details—especially if more money is involved." I had no intention of filling him in, but I needed to know Flynn's whereabouts in case Keystone moved in tonight.

"I don't want to know." He put on his orange glasses and smiled. "Well, if they cut you from the program, *that* I want to know."

"You're not even curious what happened the other night? How it went? Who won?"

"It's quite obvious who won, love. When one bag weighs more than the other, I always know."

I sipped my soda and then finished off the egg roll. "Maybe we should do this at your place next time. I don't like public places, and my hotel has too many eyeballs in the lobby. Where do you live?"

"Miss White, are you trying to seduce me?"

"I'd rather seduce a tub of chocolate frosting. No offense. Doing this in a restaurant is amateurish. We're not in a James Bond movie, and if I sit here too long, that Chitah might start to smell a bag full of money and wonder what's going on."

"That's not my concern," he said with a shrug. "Most people exchange money in public so the receiving party can deliver it to their banker. You should get one of those. You'll need help."

I pulled the strap of the bag over my shoulder and stood. "You might change your tune if that Chitah was an off-duty Regulator.

Look, I don't like the idea that someone might cut my throat for what's in this bag. Until I get a banker, I'd rather do this at night in a private location. Where do you live? We'll do the next one at your place, and it might be as early as tonight."

"I'm not at liberty to say."

Perturbed, I turned to leave.

Flynn seized my wrist and gave me a peevish look. "You're not thinking about screwing me over, are you?"

I swallowed hard. "I haven't told a soul about this job."

"That's not what I meant." He tightened his grip. "If I'm out of the picture, you get more money. Am I going to have to sleep with one eye open?"

"Is there a problem?" a man growled.

The hairs on my neck stood on end when I looked over my shoulder at the Chitah, who had left his table to join ours. His eyes locked on Flynn's grip—God only knew what kind of scent we were putting out.

"I'm fine," I assured him. "Do I look like someone who can't take care of herself?"

His nostrils flared as he pulled in my scent, and then his lips twitched. "You remind me of my female. If you need assistance, which I'm certain you don't, I'm at your service." He bowed and returned to his seat.

I wrenched my arm free and gave Flynn a scathing look. "*That's* why we can't do this in public anymore. I'm sure you don't want to be wandering the streets with a bag full of money either."

Flynn held up his hands. "Fine, fine. I'm at 23 Gooseberry Lane."

I chortled. "Is that a real address?"

"Do *not* come over uninvited, and I don't give out my address to anyone else. Karen knows, and probably the club owner, but that's all."

"Are you sure it's not because you don't want all your secret girlfriends running into each other?"

He smiled fiendishly. "We'll do this at my place next time. Say, have you seen that sexy Chitah lately?"

"Which one? We have a lot of Chitahs who visit the club."

"Clyde. Tall bloke with the round arse. Simone says she heard he quit, but I refuse to believe it. Do you happen to know where he resides?"

"No idea. The last time I talked to him, he was complaining about people grabbing him. Maybe he had enough."

Flynn pulled my plate toward him. "Bloody shame," he said, holding up my last egg roll. "I would have liked to see what he had under those shorts."

I clapped his shoulder. "Don't you mean his bank account? See you around."

"You cheeky little devil," he murmured while munching on his egg roll.

As I passed the Chitah, I gave him a nod, hoping he didn't smell my satchel full of money. He probably did, but what could he do? Bust me for being rich? Now I just needed to stay focused on what was about to go down tonight. Danger was on the menu, and while I'd eaten that six-course meal before, I'd always had some kind of preparation. Tonight I had no idea what awaited me.

I just hoped Keystone would be able to find a way in, or I might not be able to find a way out.

Chapter 26

On Friday nights, most people put on their best clothes and enjoyed food, drinks, and flirting. I had no idea what lay in store for me. Without knowing Audrey's intentions, I worried that my evening would be filled with murder and mayhem.

Neither Audrey nor Pablo had specified a preferred arrival time, just that they expected me early evening. Instead of my usual club attire, I put on ripped jeans and a black tank top. Just in case they searched me, I stuffed a pair of fighting clothes into a plastic sack. This wasn't the time to blow my cover. On a mission like this, I would have chosen sneakers, but the boots had the tracking device. If Pablo got the bright idea to shuttle me elsewhere, it would allow Keystone to follow me or change plans.

The back of the auction house had a white door with no knob and a loading dock next to it. There weren't any lights on, so I stood in the shadows, pounding my fist against the door. After a minute or two, I began knocking to the tune of "We Will Rock You" by Queen.

Pablo opened the door and gave me a look of derision. "You need only knock once."

I walked inside. "No one answered."

He glared up at me. "We have motion sensors outside the door that alert me of movement and knocking. This is a large building. If you think I sit in a chair next to the door, you're sadly mistaken. Next time *once*." He held up one finger.

"Fine," I grumbled, knowing there wouldn't be a next time.

"What's in the bag?"

"No one told me if this was just a meeting or something else. I brought a change of clothes." I twirled the plastic bag around.

"Follow me, Miss White."

Instead of escorting me to the elevators in the main room, Pablo turned right and stopped in front of a wide set of doors.

"This is our freight elevator," he said, watching the doors open. "All fighters enter this way, never through the front."

The elevator was longer and taller than any I'd been in before.

"Most of our items are small," he continued. "Paintings, jewelry, maps, et cetera."

"You really auction stuff? I thought it was your cover."

He pressed the button to close the door. "We have to conduct a legitimate business. If the higher authority looks into our operation, we need proof of buyers and sellers. The storage rooms are upstairs, and every so often we receive large items like sculptures. Once we even acquired a four-poster bed from the fifteenth century."

I snorted. "We have a furniture mart down the road that sells that stuff."

Pablo clasped his hands in front of him, the light reflecting off his gold watch. "This one was carved from tree trunks. It was quite an ordeal to get it inside."

The elevator shook as it moved down. Cognizant of the camera around my neck, I made sure to position myself so Wyatt could see anything relevant. When it stopped and the doors opened, I stepped into the curved hall and recognized it as the lower floor where the viewers watched the fights. From this entrance, I was able to see the doors that led to the observation rooms. Each had a keypad above the doorknob.

Pablo strolled to the right. "I thought the necklace was precious to you?"

"I found a stronger chain. After the last fight, I think it might be my lucky charm." I wanted Pablo to talk, but we needed to change the subject before he started asking too many questions. "How many rooms are there?" I already knew since I'd counted twenty-two windows in the ring, but it seemed like a question anyone would ask.

"Twenty-two. That doesn't include the second level for larger groups, but no one ever uses those anymore. They prefer being ground level even though it can hinder their ability to see everything."

"Who put the dagger in the room during our fight? I didn't know we could bring weapons."

"The only weapons allowed are the ones we provide." Pablo stopped by a door on the outside wall and stood beneath an ominous red button. "We open up bidding for those interested. The winner can choose a weapon or any item at all. We once had a customer with a strange sense of humor who put a feather in there."

"What an asshole. I would have broken the glass."

"I'm afraid that would have been useless," he said, retrieving a key card from his pocket. "The glass won't break, and the doors are steel." He knocked on the door in front of him to make a point. After he swiped his card on a reader, the door slid open.

I stared at the small space, no bigger than a coat closet.

"Ladies first," he said.

I stepped inside. "Is this one of those rooms with a secret wall?"

The door shut, and I howled when the floor dropped. I was free-falling before my legs and back met with a smooth surface. In pitch-black, I shot down a slide, into the unknown. It curved in what felt like a large spiral, but the angle was so steep that my descent continued to accelerate. When I reached to grab something to slow down, I felt nothing. Disoriented, I channeled energy into my fingertips and released healing light so I could see a wide cylinder made from polished black material. My stomach lurched, my lungs held on to a scream, and panic flooded my veins. All I could hear was Christian's voice saying, "What if there's a tank of hungry sharks at the end?"

As the angle leveled out, my descent slowed until the tunnel spit me into a large room. I tumbled across the floor, my joints striking the hard surface. Dizzy, I lay on my back and stared up, darkness hovering over me from a ceiling that wasn't there. Torches mounted to the walls flickered and cast shadows across the room.

When the room stopped spinning, I stood up and drank in every detail. The circular wall was similar to the other fighting ring, only this one was right out of the Middle Ages. I looked at the hole in the stone wall from which I'd emerged. On the opposite side of the room was a door, and ahead of me was a gate with thick, rusty bars. Torches flickered from all directions. I tried to pull one out, but it was connected to the mount.

Wow. They really wanted us to put on a show. Weapons hung everywhere like décor—chains, axes, small knives, and even some instruments I'd never seen. Small spikes protruded from the wall in certain places, some at stomach level and others at chest. I passed by a chopping block and raised my eyebrows at the dark stains across the grooved part where a person's head would rest.

Are those gardening shears next to the whip?

I looked up at dark archways on the second level. "Hello?"

My voice reverberated off the walls as if I were in an old church. The damp air had an earthy smell, and it reminded me of the underground tunnels in the Bricks. Was this an extension of it, and how deep were we?

The door opened, and Pablo stepped into the room. "Impressive, isn't it?" His gaze steered upward.

I snatched my plastic bag off the floor. "I'm guessing you took an elevator? Thanks for the warning."

His inscrutable gaze drifted to the upper level. "Fighters aren't permitted to use the main entrance. Security reasons. At least if someone sneaks in the way you came, they'll be trapped in the ring."

"What about leaving? I can't climb up that slide."

"We have taken every security measure," Audrey said. She had the soothing, refined tone of one of those BBC narrators. "Pablo, you can leave us."

Audrey moved away from the doorway as Pablo made himself scarce. The slit up the front of her black evening gown showcased her creamy-white legs. Like before, her orange hair was styled in the same wavy do, and when she turned, the light glinted off the diamonds on her halo-style emerald earrings.

"Robin, charmed to see you again." She held out her flaccid wrist, and again I stared at it with no idea what she wanted me to do.

I lightly shook it, and she chortled.

"Darling, we'll have to work on your manners. You seem absolutely lost, and we need you fit for polite society."

"I'm fighting. What does it matter?"

"We do have the occasional request from elite clients to have a private meeting with our fighters."

"For free?"

"Everything has a price."

"I don't."

Her slender eyebrows arched. "Then why are you here?"

"To fight. I didn't realize prostitution was part of the deal."

"That's absurd. I would never allow my clients to get that close to my best fighters. They could tamper with the product."

I folded my arms. "Tamper?"

"Bribe. Ask them to make things happen in the fight that would yield that individual more money in the betting pool. I don't play those games. If I catch you or anyone having relations with my clients, you'll have a memory wipe as a parting gift and a one-way trip to Lithuania. All private interactions are supervised. They're not interested in dim-witted women who ask inane questions. The more refined you are, which is in opposition to what they see in the ring, the more intriguing you are, and the more they'll pay for a private introduction. This is not an uncommon practice."

"So they're not afraid I might expose their identity?"

Audrey tilted her head to the side. "Exposing their identity would mean exposing our operation. You wouldn't be foolish enough to do that, would you?"

"No, but someone else might. What assurances do they have?"

Audrey branched away and neared the wall. "If you ever receive such an offer, I'll make you aware of the repercussions."

"These are pretty gruesome weapons," I said, scanning the

room. "Doesn't seem like the fight would last long. Most people surrender when there's an axe against their neck."

"You'd be surprised how long a fight will last when your life is at stake."

I blinked. "Are you talking about death matches?"

She held a long chain between her fingers before letting it clink against the wall. "You're a bright woman. Surely you considered this as a possibility."

"Most of these weapons wouldn't finish the job. The axe is small and would take too many strikes to sever a Mage's head."

What really got me thinking was how none of the victims were beheaded. In fact, none of them were reported to have the type of grisly wounds that these weapons would cause.

She gave me a look of reproach. "Perhaps you're not as bright as I thought."

I dropped my bag and stared at the chopping block. "This isn't a Mage fight, is it?"

"The topside matches are simple to arrange. The worst the higher authority can do is lock me away for life, but I have more money than you can imagine and plenty of inside contacts to keep me safe. Keeping *me* safe keeps *them* safe." Audrey glided along the surrounding walls. "But there are ancients who hunger for more than a fight. They want to see pure domination. They want to witness one Breed rule over another, and that Breed is you, Robin. Shifters once played a crucial role in our rise to power. They worked the fields in both human and animal form, they drove and pulled carriages, they acted as bodyguards, and they contributed to an immortal's fortune. Eventually, they rose up. As bodies of law were created, one country after another capitulated. It was even worse here in North America. The higher authority purchased so much land in the early days, and when Shifters were emancipated, they were given a larger share and first choice. They still are. And their behavior is so entitled. Despite the plastic smiles you see topside, animosity lives beneath the surface. As a Sensor, I can feel it. We all can."

"You don't think they deserve a little more for what they've been through? We're not talking about ancestors. Most of the Shifters who were slaves are still alive. They lost their freedom to make their masters rich."

"We're giving privileges to animals." Audrey paused near a torch. The flames rivaled her hair color. "If you have compassion for them, this will not work out in your favor. I would hate to lose another."

I folded my arms. "So I'll be fighting Shifters?"

"That's exactly what I mean. Shifters and *only* Shifters."

"You know as well as I do that a Mage can knock a Shifter out with a blast, and it wouldn't take long to finish the job. They're tough, but it would take a large animal or a couple of wolves to make it a fair fight. Especially with all these weapons conveniently hanging on the walls that they wouldn't be able to use in animal form."

"Precisely."

In the quiet of the room, all I heard was the crackling fire from the torches. I ruminated over the facts and concluded that people were paying to watch only one outcome, and that was for a Shifter to die. Maybe they took bets on how long it would last or which weapon would do it. The people most likely to watch these fights would be ancients, ones with pockets deeper than this ring. Maybe some of them had once owned Shifters and were bitter about their circumstance.

"What happens if a Mage loses and can't fight anymore?" I asked, thinking how the dead women weren't Shifters.

"Now *that's* a smart question." When she resumed walking along the wall, I turned to watch her. "Rumor has it you're a serious fighter, one who isn't a stranger to death. Only one fighter will walk away from the matches down here. Some of the animals won't kill women, so they leave their maimed bodies on the floor. When a Mage is dominated, we stop the fight. We don't like disappointing our clients, so that Mage will never fight here again."

"When the Shifter doesn't kill them and you can't use them anymore, do you scrub their memories?"

"Believe it or not, scrubbing memories isn't guaranteed.

People have gone on to remember fragments of their life, and I can't afford to have anyone remembering my face or anything that could compromise my business. We have no choice but to put them down."

A cold chill swept over me. "How do you do that?" I asked, staring at the chopping block.

She caught the direction of my gaze. "We're not monsters. After Pablo heals them, he removes their light and kills them humanely. Too many bodies showing up with animal wounds would draw attention, and skilled Sensor detectives might be called in. We had someone cleaning for us, but when we found out where he was dumping them, we decided to find another way. It's not as easy as you might think to get rid of a body. The Shifters are easier to manage because they die in animal form. We can drop them off in the woods and no one would look twice at their remains. I'm telling you this, Robin, because you need to know what's at stake. You can't afford to lose. If you lose, even if you live, you won't leave alive. If you triumph, as I fully expect you to, then you will retire a very wealthy woman. By that point you'll be in so deep that you won't be able to report us without signing your own death warrant."

I looked up at the archways, imagining the faces of a captive audience cheering for blood. Cheering for death. "Where do you get the Shifters from?"

When Audrey circled back to the doorway, she lifted a torch from the inside hall. "Come with me."

I caught up and fell into step beside her. "I didn't notice windows up there or private rooms."

"This is an exclusive fellowship," she replied as she led me through a narrow hall with a low ceiling. "We haven't added new members for the past eighty years."

"Aren't you afraid someone might charm them and accidentally find out about this operation?"

"No. We have safeguards in place." Audrey looked over her shoulder at me. "Most of the girls ask about the money first."

My face flushed. I was treating this like an investigation more than a job offer, so it was time to switch gears. "I just like to know what I'm getting into first. Money makes people do stupid things."

"And you find this offer… stupid?"

"Dangerous? Yes. Stupid? Only to someone who doesn't know how to fight. Stupid would be accepting the job without understanding all the risks. That's why I ask a lot of questions. The fighters aren't the only ones I'm concerned about. I might survive the match, but if you haven't covered all your bases, I could wind up in Breed jail."

"I assure you that will never happen. So long as you meet all the qualifications, we shouldn't have a problem."

"I've gotten into more than one death match with a Shifter. I'm about as qualified as you can get."

"How did you wind up working behind a bar, if I might ask? You would be better suited as a personal guard."

I sighed. "Bad life choices."

"I hope you exceed my expectations," she said. "A good fighter can do this for many years before retiring."

"How many are there?"

"One."

I stopped in my tracks.

Audrey turned around, the flames illuminating her stunning features. "This isn't a competition. There's no other Mage competing for your spot. The longer you last, the greater enjoyment you bring my benefactors. Not all of them show up for every event. We reserve their membership even if they go away for thirty years. The idea is to draw in the largest crowd, and if you please them, you'll be handsomely rewarded."

"How did a woman like you become a pit boss? Sensors can make so much money the legal way. I always thought these fights were run by big men with small penises, not a gorgeous woman who can probably get whatever she wants."

"And this is what I want. I was once married, you know. My husband bought and sold Shifters for profit. When it became illegal, we lost everything. Then one night a group of those Shifters returned to our home with torches. I escaped while my dear husband distracted them. I almost didn't make it out alive. I fought a Shifter with my bare hands, and it brought out something in me I didn't know existed. I suppose that's always stayed with me." She rubbed her arms from the slight chill. "When I met Pablo, he had smart ideas."

Audrey continued her walk down the hall until we reached a narrow gate. When she pulled a lever, the gate lifted. "You aren't permitted to bring any electronic devices such as a phone."

That worried me. Audrey was probably concerned about a fighter recording things. Could cell phones even work down here? If not, where did that leave the video camera around my neck? Was I out of range?

We turned down a wide hall and neared a small gate with a room behind it. Audrey set the torch in an empty mount and said, "Open the door."

A man greeted her with a timid bow, and he wasn't a timid-looking man. His brown shirt was tattered and stained, and his large belly showed at the bottom. The dark bags under his eyes made him appear sickly, and his black mustache covered most of his teeth when he smiled. He unlocked the gate and let us in. Pillars secured the ceiling, and the torches mounted to them did little to brighten up this dungeon.

The hefty man plodded back to a wooden table and lifted an axe. I watched him hack into a large piece of meat and toss the scraps into buckets on the floor.

Ignoring him, Audrey reached for my hand. When she grasped it, I quickly pulled it away.

She gave me a beguiling smile. "Are you worried I'm going to sense your fear?"

"I don't like people touching me without permission."

"Have it your way." She moved ahead of me. "This is where we keep them."

Curious, I looked inside one of the cages to my right. A man with a shackle around his neck stared back at me, and my stomach dropped.

His sunken eyes widened with hope, and he reached for the bars. "Help me get out of here! *Please!*"

Audrey moved past the cell to the next one. "Hurry along, Robin. The beggars are so hard to endure."

As I passed his cell, I pinched my nose. The room had a drain in the center, but no furniture or toilet. Just a bucket.

Audrey snapped her fingers. "Mr. Rafferty, I want you to rinse and mop the cells twice a day. If I come down here again and it's not clean, you'll be replaced."

"Yes, Miss Audrey!" He submissively lowered his head and shuffled over to the man's cell with a bucket of raw meat.

I stood beside her. "He can't eat raw meat."

"When you're hungry, you can eat anything. I don't believe in starvation tactics. There used to be fighting rings that would beat and starve the poor things. It made them more aggressive in the ring."

"Where did you get them?" I asked quietly.

"They're outcasts. You said you lived on the streets, so I'm sure you understand how many Breeds are discarded by their own kind. They have nothing to live for. The longer the fight, the happier the audience. So I feed them well. Most of them eat in animal form, but I don't want any of them shifting to human form during a fight."

"You can't control that."

She crossed one arm over her middle and looked inside the dark cage next to us. "When you keep a man in human form too long, his animal grows restless and combative. It fights to come out, and when it does, it usually stays out for a while."

Blue and Viktor had told me the same thing. They said it was like taking hostage of the physical form. I never imagined it could be used against them like this.

"So that man in there, he's the next to fight?"

She nodded, seemingly pleased I was catching on. "And something else you should know—they're all men."

"Why does their gender matter if they're in animal form?"

"My benefactors have a particular preference in not only triumphing over a Shifter but also a man."

This was the first case I'd seen where the victims were men instead of women or children. Curious, I asked, "Is that because your customers are all women?"

"Don't be absurd. It's a different experience when opposite genders battle. Those upstairs prefer same-sex fights, but down here they want to see a Mage dominate a Shifter. They also want to see a woman dominate a man, because a man shows less mercy than a woman in the ring. He'll fight like the savage he is."

I jerked my thumb at the cage behind me. "And what do *they* get out of it?"

"Survival. The one who beat my strongest warrior is now working for me. They have an opportunity to reinvent their life, and what better way to do that than to fight for it? But only if they kill the Mage. Mercy is a weakness."

"It looks like he changed his mind."

"They don't get to change their mind."

This woman was cutthroat. I wasn't sure I'd ever met anyone so apathetic about torture and death. Some got pleasure out of it, others got a thrill. She just looked at it as a business transaction or a job interview. Then I thought about how unplugged Shepherd was at times. Sensors spent their lives feeling intense emotions in a way that others couldn't comprehend, so they often came across as detached.

Audrey lowered her arms and stepped closer. "Fear is useless to me. Those who watch underground fights have full access to the sensory experience. I don't sell it to the highest bidder. That's part of their membership fee. It's important that the victor doesn't win out of fear and desperation. I'm looking for something special." She brushed her hand across my cheek. "Are *you* that something special?"

"That and so much more."

"*Mmm*, I sense truth." She pulled her hand away.

That was the truth, all right. But Audrey couldn't read minds. She couldn't know I was thinking about how I worked for an organization that busted criminals like her or that I was half Vampire and could drain her in less than thirty seconds.

My fangs were throbbing again. They did that whenever I was itching to kill. Woman or not, she brought out the huntress in me, and that old familiar feeling returned. The one that earned me the Shadow nickname. Or Reaper. Or whatever the hell people called me. I was the bump in the night.

I stepped back when something moved in the dark cell. A black panther emerged into the light and stared at me with predatory eyes.

Audrey reached through the bars and stroked his nose without taking her eyes off me.

"Aren't you afraid of losing your fingers?"

"Animals smell fear. They don't know good from evil, and I'm neither. Nor are you. He doesn't understand why he's in the cell, but he knows which one of us is in the dominant position." She withdrew her hand and led me back to the gate. "I also put a little pinch of sensory magic in my touch to allay their fears. It becomes a drug to them. When anxiety and rage are all we know, we seek refuge in any form of escape."

I remembered my trips to Ruby's Diner, how I looked forward to the kind words from a friendly waitress. Especially since I was invisible to the rest of the world. I understood exactly how these animals felt.

The panther growled when Rafferty opened the cell and tossed the bucket of meat inside. He quickly slammed the door, startling the animal.

Audrey clucked her tongue. "One of these days, that one is going to get himself eaten."

Rafferty jogged over and fumbled in his pocket before pulling out the key and opening the gate.

Audrey collected the torch and strolled out as if we were walking alongside a lake on a moonlit night. "Now that we have the questions out of the way, tell me your thoughts."

"Well, I think only a crazy person would accept a job like this. Screw up and you die. Lose the fight and you die. But win, now that's the part that interests me." I moved my plastic bag to my other hand. "I love the rush of a good fight. And whatever Flynn told you, well, he doesn't know the real me. I'm ruthless, and I don't like losing. How much does it pay?"

"Two million per match," she replied, her voice as detached as someone talking about the price of apples. "Flynn takes his cut from the topside fights, but he doesn't know what goes on down here. Any arrangement you have with him stops now."

"I can't take off work without everyone knowing. He'll get suspicious."

She stopped to face me. "The girls who work down here resigned, and you'll do the same. These fights aren't weekly or every fortnight like the ones upstairs. You'll fight once a month. Pablo will set you up with our banker so we can do the transactions directly through him. I'll arrange for an escort. Pablo will fill you in on where you'll enter the building."

"He already has."

"Splendid. As for attire, wear whatever pleases you. I want you to be comfortable and confident. Is that your change of clothes?" she asked, gesturing to my plastic bag.

"I brought these in case, but what I'm wearing now are my fight clothes. I don't like a lot of skin showing. More to slice up."

"You're so different, Robin White. There's something in those brown eyes that reminds me of my best fighter."

"Can I have a tour of the upstairs area? I'd love to see what the ring looks like from above."

"Next time."

"It'll only take a minute."

"I'm afraid I can't spare a minute."

"Maybe Pablo can walk me around if you're occupied."

When we reached the door again, Audrey opened it. "As I said, maybe on your next visit we'll show you the upstairs viewing area."

I strode into the arena. "Is there another secret passageway?"

"Yes. Pablo will show you the way out." She set the torch back in the holder. "*If* you survive."

Audrey closed the door, shutting me in.

Electricity crackled in the air, and when I looked up, all the dark gaps in the archways filled with spectators.

Chapter 27

WYATT GRIPPED HIS LAPTOP WHEN the van hit another pothole. "Son of a ghost! Slow down before you bust my equipment."

Shep took the cigarette out of his mouth and held it between two fingers. "Maybe you need to buckle up, Spooky. And turn that music off. It's distracting me."

"It's my laptop, and nobody touches my playlist."

"How many songs by Bread exist?" Gem grumped from the back. "You should really try something more upbeat. Like maybe a little Spice Girls or, oh! Do you have the 'Love Shack' song?"

Shortly after Raven left the hotel, Shepherd packed the van with weapons, then loaded everyone up and sped to the subway station to get Blue. Now they were headed to the auction house.

Ignoring Gem, Wyatt searched the network connections. He could have installed a router in the van, but anything can be hacked. For trips like these, he preferred piggybacking off someone else's connection. Technology was another reason he'd chosen a classic Mini Cooper as his mode of transportation. Some modern cars had computer systems and Wi-Fi.

"Not too close," Viktor cautioned Shepherd from the back of the van. "I do not want anyone to see our vehicle."

Shepherd slowed down. "Got it. We'll park here unless Spooky has a problem with that."

Wyatt spotted a vulnerability in his list. "No problem at all."

Shepherd shut off the engine. "Turn down the brightness on that thing. It's like the fucking sun is in here."

Wyatt didn't like dimming his workstation, so he got up and climbed into the back of the van for privacy. Since they were parked on a quiet street, he turned off his music.

Viktor stood up. "Sit here. I will go to front."

Wyatt didn't take his eyes off the laptop as he sat behind the passenger seat. Since there weren't windows in the back, no one could see him. No one except Gem, who was leaning over his shoulder to watch his every click.

"How about a little room, Nosy Nellie?"

She leaned back. "What are you looking at?"

He made sure his connection was encrypted as he logged into the black market portal. "I'm hoping we can get a full blueprint."

Niko spoke up from the seat across from him. "I thought you gave us the blueprint. I memorized everything you detailed."

On short notice, Wyatt had managed to access the full blueprints to the auction house. His contact had even provided him with the layout of the basement, which wasn't public record. Nothing fancy down there he hadn't already seen most of in Raven's video—a fighting ring, private rooms encircling it, a bathroom, an upstairs viewing area, and an elevator. Anyone could have hit the wrong button and wound up in the game room. Well, if they could get past security. Wyatt also had the schematics that showed how the central control room powered everything, including the sliding doors to the private rooms. By the looks of it, only the person in the control room could open and close the doors. Probably a security measure to guarantee privacy to all the perverts. That would make things easy, allowing the team to focus on taking down the ringleaders while Wyatt gathered evidence.

"The blueprint I gave you is all there is," he answered Niko.

Shepherd twisted around in his seat. "Then what's the problem?"

That was just it—there was one colossal problem, and Wyatt didn't like it. There were two mystery doors in the basement that he had no information on. "I was hoping to find a back way in, and I don't just mean the back door. I'm talking about an alternate way into the downstairs level. Even if we break into one of the upstairs windows, the lobby elevator is the only way down. There are two doors below that I don't have the full specs on, so I don't know how to access them."

The first door was located near a stairwell that connected the upper viewing area to the fighting level. The second door caught his eye. It didn't fit the profile of a storage closet even though it was the right size. Wires led to it. Electrical engineering wasn't like reading script, so Wyatt was at a loss. Here they were, at the eleventh hour, and he had nothing. If he couldn't find the missing piece of the puzzle, they might be screwed.

Viktor shifted in the passenger seat. "Why did you not mention this before?"

"You looked stressed."

Shepherd chuckled and pulled in another drag off his cigarette. "This is a clusterfuck."

"Maybe it doesn't matter," Gem offered.

Claude scooted closer to Niko from across the van. "Why don't you tell us what's bothering you, Spooky? I can scent it."

Wyatt reached in his pocket for his breath freshener and then squirted it at Claude. It was bad enough that Niko could read his light, but Claude's nasal powers were an invasion of privacy. After opening up the program connected to Raven's camera, Wyatt adjusted the window so he could see multiple applications. His program back at Keystone was recording everything. Once Viktor reviewed the files, he would destroy them. Keeping video records was illegal, but sometimes the higher authority contact Viktor worked with liked a visual confirmation before the sentencing.

Gem gasped. "She's there! She's knocking on a door. Viktor, we have to leave."

Wyatt swallowed the knot in his throat. Without options, they'd have no choice but to use the elevator. Wyatt was in charge of strategizing the best plans, but if they had to go in through the front, there was no telling what they might be facing. Booby traps? They might have the elevator rigged to explode if anyone unauthorized used it. Those were concerns he didn't want to relay to the group. Not just yet. They would either think he was exaggerating or deem him incompetent, and he didn't need that kind of negativity when he was already under a tremendous amount of stress. Everyone's safety and lives depended on him. "Can you hand me my fries?"

"Are you kidding?" Claude growled. "You do this every time."

"They're on the floor," Shepherd muttered.

After a minute, Viktor turned around with a rolled-up sack. It was still warm, and the smell of french fries wafted from the bag as Wyatt opened it. He functioned better on a full stomach. Everyone had a ritual, and his was snacking.

Wyatt quit chewing when a message pinged on the screen behind the video. He minimized Raven talking with the little man and opened up the message. No one ever gave their real identity on the black market sites, and new members often used a string of numbers, which was the default. Wyatt always used the same nickname so he could establish a rapport with others.

One fry stuck out of his mouth and fell onto the keyboard when he read the message and bit down.

User 24267: Use it wisely.

What the immortal hell is this? Wyatt ran a quick virus scan on the attached file before opening it. When he did, he nearly choked on his food.

"Wyatt's got something," Niko said. "His light looks like an atomic bomb."

Wyatt swallowed his fries while zooming in on the blueprints. "Start up the van."

Without delay, Shepherd fired up the engine. "Auction house?" he asked, his hand on the gearshift.

"No." Wyatt followed the path of the door near the short stairwell. The tunnel led to another building just behind it. After a quick internet search, he identified the building. "We're going to the animal shelter. It's on the street just behind it. Hold on a sec or you'll break my connection."

"I don't want to hurt any puppies," Gem whimpered.

The user who had given him the file disappeared. Wyatt scanned the list of active members but didn't find him. Then he did a search in the member database and found no such user. They'd created an account, dropped off the file, and erased their fingerprints. Who the immortal hell would do that without wanting payment?

Dressed in the change of clothes Gem had brought her, Blue got up and sat to Wyatt's right, forcing him to scoot over. "Why not break into the auction house?"

"They have a steel shutter inside. It'll take longer to get in, and we don't know if they've got any alarms installed on the doors or upstairs windows. There's at least one security guard on duty in the daytime and possibly at night. They expect intruders to bust in through the front or back since those are in the blueprints on file. No staircase leads to the basement, just the elevator. And *only* that one elevator. I bet the animal shelter is how they're leading in the visitors."

"Sounds about right," Shepherd said.

Gem leaned over him. "What's all that other stuff?"

Wyatt flipped through another blueprint and the attached data. The second mystery door had an arrow pointing down and led to a chamber even farther underground. Lots of old structures like that existed, and most were sealed off. "I don't want to get sidetracked. I need everyone to brainstorm a way to keep those dogs from barking."

"They're probably barking right now," Shepherd said. "That's what dogs do. They bark."

Blue tucked her hair back. "Can you find out if the shelter has a security system? I've never seen a shelter or pet store owned by Breed."

Shepherd cursed under his breath while revving the engine. "I don't think our suspects own it. That would look suspicious. It's probably a human who doesn't know what the hell goes on at night. Betcha they don't have anything wired up."

"Hold your ponies." Something on the video caught Wyatt's eye. When he maximized the screen, he saw Raven entering a small room no bigger than a coat closet. She turned to face the small man, and he reached for something by the door. Suddenly everything went black.

Gem gasped. "What happened? Is the video broken?"

Wyatt wished he'd equipped her with an audio device, but those weren't reliable. According to the tracker in her boot, she hadn't gone anywhere, but her signal was moving in peculiar circles.

Yeah, she'd gone somewhere.

Down.

Blast! He looked at the down arrow on the blueprints. That wasn't an elevator; it was a slide. Some immortals created them as a quick escape route to the underground sections of the Bricks. Whatever was happening to Raven was now leading them farther underground.

On his document, he looked at the diagram of an oval-shaped room. A tunnel just outside it wound around to a small room, and walls divided the space. If he had to guess, they were cages or cells. Nothing was labeled. He followed the longest tunnel, which led to an unmarked building. The distance was noted, so he compared it to a city map and located the entry point.

"Change of plans," he announced. "Pay attention. There's an underground chamber below the basement level. The equivalent of maybe fifteen stories. Shep, take us to the Green Door."

Shepherd flicked his cigarette butt out the window. "What the hell for?"

"Raven's not in the basement." He kept his eyes on the blueprint, memorizing the layout and zooming in to see where it all led. "She's way underground. Deeper than the specters like to go. And if you'd prefer to take the same route she did, I might as well write up your obituary now."

He braced his feet when Shepherd hit the gas. Wyatt spun the laptop around so everyone could see. "There's a secret entrance. See this long tunnel? It leads to the Green Door. It looks like someone built it back in the twenties. There was a period when Breed went underground and they built elaborate tunnels and structures. The earth is stable down there. Lots of caverns and streams."

"Enough with the geology," Viktor said. "What is your plan?"

"According to this blueprint, there's a cellar door in the basement of the club. That's your way in. There'll be a lot of steps or staircases, but all you have to do is take the tunnel straight to the end."

"What's at the end?" Niko asked with a look of concern.

"It looks like an arena. The main tunnel branches in a few places, but all those were sealed up years ago. Probably to hide what they've been doing down there. You'll have two doors or gates to get through. Probably heavy and probably locked. But who knows? If there's a fight going on down there, they might have it open for their customers. This might be the main route. Maybe the animal shelter is an emergency exit."

"Any security cameras down there?" Blue asked.

Wyatt shook his head and spun the laptop back around to look at it again. "It's hard to say. They don't usually run electricity that deep since it attracts attention. If they have security cameras, then they might. A couple of you are good at picking locks, so that should get you through the doors."

Gem finished putting her hair up in two tight buns. "Aren't you coming along?"

"Negative. I'm going back to the auction house to hack into any security systems. Now that we know they're not in the basement, it might be easier for me to break in. I need to access their computer files, paper files, and any security footage. And don't try to guilt-trip me. Remember what happened during the Valencia bust?"

Claude groaned and sat back. "They incinerated all the evidence."

"Exactly." Wyatt continued analyzing the image while Shepherd tried to kill them with his sharp turns. "We're not making that mistake again. If we have any runners, they'll use the main tunnel. You guys should be able to contain them."

"Is that the only tunnel?" Blue asked.

"There's another circling the main room, but all of them dead-end at some point. I'll probably die breaking into the auction house, but if I don't, there'll be a lot of rooms to search."

"I'll go with you," Viktor said. "Brief everyone on the layout."

Wyatt blew out a breath. Admittedly, he got a natural high whenever he cracked a code or got his hands on secret information. He'd put out a request on the black market for the complete blueprints, but who was this User 24267? Haggling for fair trade was part of the dance. Viktor even set aside money for just these occasions, but this person hadn't asked for anything. That was a twist he didn't see coming.

He studied the layout closely and then spun the laptop around. "Once you're past the two doors or gates, you'll reach a crossing at a dead end."

Claude squinted at the screen. "Which way do we go?"

"A staircase to the right leads to an open viewing area on the second level. Going left will eventually lead to what looks like a holding room or dungeon. I wouldn't go that way."

"I wonder if anyone else is down there," Shepherd said. "Do you think they're running a fight, or is this just a tour?"

"This is no longer a sneak attack," Wyatt said, making air quotes. "If this is more than a tour, Raven's in the middle of it. You might as well go in assuming the worst-case scenario. The redhead will be somewhere in the crowd. I doubt she's in the room to the left. If there's no electricity, she won't have a view. Go right. The upstairs area circles almost all the way around the arena, so you'll be able to trap them. The only way out is down the stairs and through the tunnel."

The van slowed to a stop, and Shepherd turned it off before shifting in his seat. "Suit up, everyone. I brought an extra bag of weapons. Stunners, stakes, and a few guns."

Gem wrung her hands. "If we trap those people, they'll have to cooperate."

Wyatt found another network connection. "Ever tried to corner a feral cat?"

"I don't want to hear your cat story again," Shepherd bit out. "If there are people down there, we can't let them know how many of us there are. Make them think we got Regulators topside."

Blue got up and joined Niko. "Looks like we've got a lot of

stairs, amigo. You wanna just follow my light trail? Once we're inside, the layout is simple."

Niko drew a black hood over his head. "Hand me three stunners and two stakes."

Blue opened the duffel bag and began passing out weapons like candy. They were all sheathed and attached to harnesses or clips. Since Green Door was a Breed club, weapons were permissible, but everyone still did their best to conceal them beneath their cloaks. Shepherd had an arsenal inside his modified leather jacket.

Wyatt pulled up screenshots of Audrey and Pablo. Then he held up the laptop like a teacher showing his students a picture book. "Take a good look. These are your primary targets. Audrey's a Sensor, so that shouldn't be hard. The short guy's a Mage. If any of you turn into ghosties, don't you *dare* follow my ass home. I don't have time to deal with your afterlife drama."

Shepherd opened his door. "Let's roll."

Everyone piled out of the van except Viktor, who hopped behind the wheel. Wyatt climbed into the passenger seat, and they sped away from the club.

He looked at the video and saw Raven standing in front of a cage. Inside, Wyatt could make out the shape of a man, but the image was grainy and dark. Inventors in the Breed world had made huge advances in technology, allowing Wyatt to get his hands on a video camera that worked virtually anywhere. Now that they had enough evidence, they could take down this organization. All Keystone had to do was capture the ringleaders and stay alive.

Wyatt closed the lid on his laptop to preserve the battery. "They're holding people against their will. Do you realize how long I've been trying to crack this case? I've been hearing rumors about organized death matches for years, but I've never been able to get a scrap of evidence. This is it, Viktor. The big one."

"They shouldn't have left bodies in the open."

"Even so, leaving a few corpses lying around wouldn't guarantee we would have found out about their secret death matches. Pure luck. This stuff is so covert that I've heard about people who went missing after asking too many questions."

Viktor reached in his pocket and handed over his phone. "Call Christian. I want him here. Give him the address to the gallery."

"Isn't he on a job?"

"Not anymore."

Chapter 28

THE MOMENT AUDREY SHUT THE door, locking me in the arena, I knew I was screwed. How would Keystone find me all the way down here? I'd told Wyatt everything about the facility, but neither Pablo nor Audrey had hinted to a secret chamber. I'd thought that slide was taking me straight to hell. And as I stared up at the masked faces looking down at me, I began to wonder if I'd gone there after all.

The spectators stood shoulder to shoulder in black robes. Some of the masks were solid white and looked like a mold of someone's face. Others were silver, gold, and a few shaped like animal faces. It was unclear if this group knew each other, but they definitely wanted to hide their identities from the fighters.

Despite the cool air, sweat trickled down the back of my neck. I noticed things I hadn't earlier, like the blunt end of the club on the wall had bloodstains from those it had bludgeoned. And a white tooth was wedged inside a crack in the floor. The crowd murmured as they got their first look at me. Had they been there all along, hiding in the shadows, and I hadn't noticed? Probably. I remembered how the air felt charged when I first came in, like the pulsing electricity I often felt in Breed clubs. But I had so much adrenaline going through me that I'd dismissed it.

Instead of a grand introduction, the iron gate lifted with a *clang, clang, clang*. I stepped back apprehensively and tossed my bag aside. Once the gate reached the top, two men came into view. Rafferty stood behind the nude man with a knife in one hand and a device in the other. The man I'd just seen in the cell had dirty feet, unkempt hair, and his hands were tied. After Rafferty cut the rope that bound the man's hands, he kicked him inside the ring, and the gate slammed shut.

I approached the stranger as his eyes darted up at our audience. The spectators were high enough to be out of earshot.

"Hey, I'm here to help," I said quietly.

He glared at me with dull blue eyes. "Help what? Kill me? I know what this is."

"I'm not part of this."

"Sure you're not."

Did they expect me to fight the Shifter in human form first? "Choose a weapon," I whispered. "Stall for as long as you can. Trust me."

I let my fingers graze over each weapon I passed. It tantalized the crowd, whose murmurs grew louder when I admired a shiny sickle. By the annoyed look on Rafferty's face, who stood inside the closed gate, I guessed that everyone had expected us to get right to fighting.

I settled on a small club, deciding not to take any chances of hurting the man with a blade. When I approached the center of the ring, he was striding toward me with a pointy spear. I tried to get close to talk out a plan, but he aimed it at me.

"Feet don't fail me now." I flashed out of the way when he lunged, and that garnered weak applause.

The second time, I ducked and swung my club at his spear, almost knocking it from his grip. He stumbled backward and then used his right arm to anchor the wood against his body. The guy wasn't an experienced fighter, but the desperate look in his eyes revealed how this situation could spiral out of control.

The second time he tried to gut me, I grabbed the end of his spear and we grappled for the weapon. My club hit the ground, and it took every muscle I had not to lose my grip.

The crowd hissed, and a few gave us a thumbs-down.

"Stop trying to kill me," I ground out, inching closer. "Let's come up with a plan."

"You're a *liar*. You're *all* liars!"

The Shifter jerked the weapon back and then headbutted me. Seconds before he impaled me, I spun out of reach. My father used to make me watch the *Matrix* movies, and I remembered how much he enjoyed the fight scenes. Everything was in slow motion, and every movement defied gravity.

That was me. I let all my training and instinct take over as the Shifter repeatedly thrust his spear at me. I bent backward and spun out of reach. I flashed across the ring. But it hadn't escaped my attention that the crowd was growing restless, eager to see blood spilled.

A bright flash flickered at the gate, one so blinding that I shielded my eyes. Rafferty held a strobe light up to the bars. It flickered at an erratic rhythm, and it dawned on me that this was one of those rare devices used to trigger a Shifter to transform.

I knocked the man to the ground as if to attack. "Shut your eyes!"

But it was too late. He'd looked. His engorged pupils stared blankly as his body trembled beneath me. I'd never felt anything like it before. Seconds before transformation, it was as if his skin wobbled like jelly. Ebony fur replaced his brown hair, and a mouthful of fangs snapped at me.

I recoiled and stumbled away from the large black wolf. With only seconds to spare, I genuflected and bowed my head to appear as submissive as possible. The wolf approached at alarming speed and skidded to a stop. I held my breath, my body rigid as he growled. I'd never put myself in a more vulnerable position.

What the hell am I doing? Getting myself killed, that's what.

"I don't want to hurt you," I whispered, glimpsing the pink gums that surrounded all those sharp teeth. "I know you're still in there. Tell your wolf I don't mean him any harm. I want to get us both out of here, and I need you to help me. Please tell him before you fade out."

Some Shifters remembered the first few seconds while others held on for several minutes. I had no idea about this guy. While he pondered killing me, I scanned the room. Staying in the ring was suicide. I needed to get to the second level.

Spectators gripped the ledge and watched on. To them, it looked as if we were facing off. My knuckles pressed against the ground, the tension palpable. Even I couldn't guess what would transpire in the next few seconds. I peered over my shoulder to see what weapons were within reach. The only thing that caught my eye was an axe.

My hair stood on end when the wolf snarled, and before I could look back, warm liquid splashed all over me. I quickly flipped my wet hair back. Someone had dumped a bucket of blood on us, and it was dripping off the wolf's snout. Now he had blood in his mouth.

Disastrous.

"Don't do it," I whispered, watching him closely. "*Don't do it.*"

The wolf's long tongue stuck out and lapped up the blood on his snout.

"*Shit.*" I flashed across the room just as he lunged, and the chase was on.

I ran from one side of the room to the next like a metal ball in a pinball machine getting knocked around by the flippers. When he sank his teeth into my arm, I blasted him with energy.

The crowd never cheered. No one chanted for blood or death. Instead, they applauded like civilized people. Was it to conceal their voices, or had they attended these fights so many times that the thrill was gone? I was quickly burning through my energy, searching for a way out. The gate was in a recessed wall, so I couldn't use it to climb. The torches were at a decent height, but they were all blazing with fire. I could throw up a chain, but what would it attach to?

Not a shred of humanity remained inside the wolf. He didn't comprehend the watchers above. We danced like two predators in a battle of survival, only *my* goal was to keep both of us alive. He ripped the bottom of my tank top, trying to get at my belly. I punched him before flashing to the far wall. While he shook his head, I took a second to look around. The chopping block wasn't tall enough to use as a launching pad. Then I spotted the plastic bag with my clothes. The chain on the wall just behind it birthed an idea. Blasting the wolf repeatedly would bring this fight to a grinding halt. My core light was growing weak from all the flashing, so prolonging the fight was not an option.

I flashed to the bag and dumped out the contents. The wolf pivoted, wrinkles deepening on his snout as he snarled at me. With blinding speed, he used his hind legs to propel forward and take off like a bullet.

There was a collective gasp just seconds before he crashed into me. I wrapped the bag over his head, jumped to my feet, and pulled the chain off the wall. The wolf backed up, unable to see with his eyes covered.

I yanked the chain free and looped it around the wolf's neck. When I began to tie a knot, I realized there was no way to secure this thing. No hook or latch. But at least I had time to think.

"Calm down, you mangy little mutt. I don't want to hurt you."

I caught sight of Audrey by the gate. Instead of disappointment, she flashed a heartfelt smile. It dawned on me why. The other fighters would've wanted to win, so the fights probably didn't last long. The audience expected my victory, but drawing it out heightened the anticipation. To them, I was toying with my opponent, which pleased them. It was obvious by the way their energy pulsed and quavered.

Straddling the wolf, I wrapped my arms around the beast, the chains still firmly in my grasp. Remembering what Audrey had said, I sent a sharp current of energy through the chain. The wolf yelped, but I had to let him know who was in charge. *I* was the alpha here, and he needed to know that.

"This is hopeless," I whispered against his fur.

Even if I *could* jump to the upper level, then what? Take on fifty immortals? If any were Vampires, they would tear me limb from limb. On the other hand, maybe that wasn't such a bad way to go. Better than falling down an elevator shaft or getting shanked in an alleyway.

How do I survive with no weapons, no backup, and no escape?

No one was coming for me. The only chance of surviving was to kill an innocent man.

I stared at the hole in the wall and thought about that long slide.

"This wasn't in the brochure." I yanked off my boots, hopped off the wolf, and braced myself for one hell of a climb.

Chapter 29

WYATT PACKED UP HIS LAPTOP while Viktor sped to the auction house. He reached inside the glove compartment and swapped out his loose beanie for a black ski mask that belonged to Shepherd. It had a rectangular opening over the eyes and looked like something a serial killer would wear.

"What is all that?" Viktor asked, gesturing to Wyatt's backpack.

"Laptop, spare battery, external drive, flash drives, lockpicks, a phone, lip balm, peanuts—the usual."

Viktor drove by the building.

"Do a U-turn in front. Go slow." Wyatt put his hands on the dash, the ski mask in his grip. "I need a better look."

Viktor slowly turned the wheel and then backed up. The headlights sprayed the brick wall and revolving door. Wyatt spotted the metal shutter behind it.

"Blast!" He flew back in his seat. "Pull over for a minute. I have an idea."

"What is your plan?"

Wyatt raked back his hair. "They don't usually hook up sensors to windows on the upper floors. I doubt they even have an alarm system with all the illegal activity going on inside."

"And if they do?"

Wyatt looked at the open bag of weapons in the back. He didn't like carrying weapons. The dead could be spiteful, and the last thing a Gravewalker wanted to do was kill someone. Wyatt had enough issues with random specters, but he sure as hellfire didn't need a freshy with a grudge following him around for the rest of his mortal life. If they had money hidden somewhere, they might cut a deal with another Gravewalker and put a hit on him.

"I'll worry about that later." Wyatt pressed his nose to the glass and studied the taller building next door. They were crammed together like sardines. That was how city architects used to construct them in the old days. As he studied the windows, he realized it was an apartment building. A brunette woman with a messy bun on her head waddled down the steps and waited by a tree while her little white dog sniffed at a patch of grass.

Wyatt opened the door and looked back at Viktor. "Take your time following me. Act cool. I've got a plan."

Hopping out of the vehicle, Wyatt reached deep down for that boyish charm that the ladies liked. After putting on his backpack, he stuffed the ski mask into his back pocket and rushed across the street. "Hurry up, Dad! We're gonna be late for your party." He smiled at the lady, who looked embarrassed when he glanced at her blue pajama bottoms covered in white crescent moons. But then she noticed his Pac-Man shirt, and Wyatt had found that people were put at ease by the simplest things.

He bent down and gave her little dog a scratch behind the ear. "My dad's finally retiring from the force. Thirty years."

"Congratulations to him."

It was the best lie Wyatt could come up with considering Viktor was crossing the street with a gun on his hip. "SWAT team commander. His buddies are taking him out for drinks after the formal ceremony. I've got to get him in a suit and make sure he looks decent."

She chuckled and gave Viktor a passing glance. "Isn't that your mom's job?"

"She died five years ago."

"Oh, I'm sorry."

Wyatt stood and scratched behind his own ear. "It hasn't been easy, and he turned into a workaholic. Most nights he doesn't even go home, and when he does, it's after midnight. Sorry—I talk a lot."

"No, that's okay."

Viktor stepped over the curb and kept a straight face. He knew better than to speak and give away his accent until he could assess the situation.

"Come on. We have to hurry." Wyatt tugged at Viktor's sleeve and led them up the steps. "Nice meeting you!" he said over his shoulder.

"Have fun," she replied cordially.

When they reached the door, Wyatt frowned at the key swipe. A lot of apartment buildings these days had access-control cards. He tested the door and glanced at the card swipe again.

"Search your pockets," he murmured. Then louder, he said, "Where's your key? Don't tell me you left it at work. I thought you cleaned out your desk? You can't go in your work clothes. I bought you that suit and everything." Wyatt sighed dramatically and stepped down, gazing across the street and pretending not to notice the woman's curiosity. "We'll miss the ceremony if we go back."

"This outfit is fine," Viktor said in his best American accent.

"You look like you're going on a drug bust. It's not fine. They're taking your picture and everything. Don't you have a spare key somewhere?"

His friend in blue pajama bottoms led her dog toward the steps. "I can let you in."

"Thank you! You're a lifesaver. Thank you *so* much," Wyatt went on. "I think he's just looking for an excuse not to go. He doesn't like attention, so this is his version of a nightmare."

Viktor grumbled and folded his arms, which made the lady giggle.

She opened the door and held it for Wyatt. "I don't like parties, so I know how he feels." When Viktor glided past her, she smiled at him. "Congratulations. Thanks for your service."

Viktor's expression softened, and he nodded at her. Viktor had a remarkable way of carrying on a conversation without saying a word. Wyatt had a way of sticking his foot in his mouth, so his best bet was to avoid getting in the elevator with this woman or else she'd start asking questions he wasn't prepared to answer.

"Wait, do you have your door key?" he asked Viktor. "I'm not about to go all the way up there if you left your keys in the van."

"Just like your mother," Viktor grumbled.

"Well, someone has to be the adult here."

The woman held the elevator. "Are you coming?"

Wyatt waved at her. "I need to get his keys out of the van. Thanks again, lady!" As he jogged toward the doors, he listened for the sound of the elevator doors closing. Then he quietly pivoted, relieved that she hadn't suspected anything.

Viktor pushed the elevator button. "It frightens me sometimes how easy it is for you to lie."

He waltzed up to the doors. "I made a career out of it."

After a short ride to the top floor, they jogged upstairs to the roof. There wasn't much to picking the roof lock, but the real challenge was how they were going to get down to the auction house. They were about two stories higher than they needed to be. Not a huge distance, but it wouldn't take much for Wyatt to crack his melon.

Viktor walked to the back corner. "This is good."

Wyatt approached the edge and was hit by a gust of wind as he bent over and studied a pipe going down the wall. "You call this good? A ladder is good. *That's* the thing of nightmares."

Viktor chuckled. "Is my son afraid?"

Wyatt took off his backpack and shoved it into Viktor's arms. "I want a bonus for this, *Dad*."

"It is not as if you will die."

"Says the man who can heal in three seconds. Remember the time I cracked my skull and we had to call the Relic? That was when you sent Niko and Blue on that trip to Dallas. It took me a week to heal all the way, and I had to wear that stupid helmet."

"Niko is not far."

Wyatt sat on the ledge and imagined his head splitting open like a melon. As far as he was concerned, brave men fell into two categories: stupid and smart. The stupid ones put their lives in peril for nothing. The smart ones lived to see another day. As a Gravewalker, he could live to be a thousand as long as he made smart choices. He healed at an accelerated rate and was harder to kill than a human, but death never took a holiday.

He reached down and felt the pipe. "There's no gap. I can't hold on to it."

"Use your fingertips. We have no time to quarrel. Go!"

Wyatt put the ski mask over his face, and Viktor held his hand as he lowered himself off the roof. When he thought he had his boots anchored against the brick on the adjoining walls, he let go of Viktor's hand and clasped the pipe. Wyatt could already feel his weight pulling him down like an anchor. His boots scrabbled in a futile attempt to slow his descent. When his knuckles began to scrape against the brick, he jumped onto the lower roof and rolled across the asphalt.

Despite his stinging knuckles and sore arm, he sprang to his feet and reached up to catch the bag Viktor tossed. Seconds later, Viktor jumped off the roof like a crazy person. Wyatt was so startled by the leap that the backpack struck him on the head.

Right before landing, Viktor shifted into his wolf. His clothes and gun fell on top of him.

"Show-off," Wyatt muttered, rubbing the knot on his head. "They always make it look easy in the movies. You never see Jason Statham pulling a groin muscle. Tell your wolf the plan. There might be a security guy in the lobby, so I'll need you to take a sniff while I check things out." He gathered up Viktor's clothes and weapon. "Since you're in doggie mode, I'll leave these up here by the door."

Viktor's wolf snatched the gun holster from Wyatt's hand and trotted off.

Some of these old buildings didn't have roof access, but to Wyatt's delight, there was a hatch door made of glass. It was raised like a crypt, and when he grabbed the lower bar, it opened. Hopefully the fall hadn't messed up his finger tattoos, but it was too dark to see anything. After descending the stairs, Wyatt got out his lockpick, put a penlight in his mouth, and went to work on the door. Blue had taught him a few techniques that had come in handy on a few occasions.

Viktor's wolf growled impatiently.

"Got it!"

Once inside the main stairwell, they crept through the second floor. Someone had gutted the place for storage, filling it with large crates, tons of paintings covered in tarps, rugs, statues, a piano, and old weapons. He shined his light on the walls and saw nothing but tapestries. If any secret files were hidden in here, it would take him hours to find them.

"Downstairs," he said to the wolf even though Viktor had probably blinked out of consciousness by now.

Instead of the elevator, they took the stairs. Wyatt couldn't breathe in the ski mask, but the lights were off and it helped him blend into the shadows, so he left it on.

When they reached the first floor, Wyatt gave the grey wolf a long look. "I need to look around. Your job is to protect me. You don't understand anything I'm saying, do you? I bet all you want is a bone."

Based on the blueprints, the first floor didn't have any private offices. But Wyatt still wanted to search the place, and they needed to make sure there wasn't a security guard who might set off the alarm or make calls. He shouldered open the door and peered out. Like upstairs, it was an open space, only this room had the art tastefully displayed. To his relief, the front desk was empty. Viktor's wolf sniffed the chair by the desk and investigated all the smells in the room while Wyatt located the elevator.

He took a deep breath and snapped his fingers, summoning Viktor's wolf over.

"Do you even know why you're carrying that around?" he asked, noticing slobber all over the gun belt in the wolf's mouth.

When the elevator door slid shut, Wyatt hit the button and pressed his body against the panel to hide. All he could imagine was a man with a machine gun waiting for them when the door opened. His heart pounded as the elevator moved like molasses.

Wyatt kept his eyes on the wolf. Viktor's nostrils were twitching, but no growl settled in his throat as the elevator came to a stop.

The doors opened. Viktor's wolf craned his neck and then stepped out of view. Wyatt took a deep breath, hooked his thumbs underneath his backpack shoulder straps, and entered a brightly lit hall. The control room was to the left, but Viktor's wolf had already made it clear he wanted to go right.

"This way," he whispered.

The wolf gave him a sharp look.

"Fine. But just remember it was *your* idea to separate." He opened the heavy door and allowed Viktor's wolf to dash through.

Wyatt quickly jogged back to the other door. Time was ticking.

The carpet met with white flooring, and when he passed an elevator on his left, he skidded to a stop. "That wasn't in the blueprint."

He continued on until he reached another door. This one had a small viewing window, so he peered inside the dark room before going inside. Feeling along the wall, he found a light switch and then looked around. None of the monitors on the right-hand wall were operating. Wyatt sat down at a computer station in the center of the room and sputtered with laughter when the computer came on without a password prompt.

No longer able to breathe, he took off the black mask and flung it across the room. It didn't take long to locate the security camera program, and when he did, the monitors lit up. Most of them were aimed at the white floors of an empty fighting ring, but as he went through the commands, he found cameras in hallways and a public seating area. He spied Viktor's wolf sniffing chairs in what appeared to be the upstairs viewing room. Wyatt took off his backpack and began copying everything to his external hard drive. He couldn't afford to waste time digging through computer files. His sole job was to collect evidence and then get out of Dodge.

After he finished up, he walked over to the wall across from the door to check out the control panel. The large metal square had a lot of switches and buttons, each neatly labeled.

"Hold your ponies. External doors?"

Wyatt hurried back to the computer and looked closer at the surveillance system. He clicked on each camera to bring it up on the big screen.

"Empty hall, another empty hall, lobby…" He froze when he pulled up a camera aimed down at Gem. She stood in front of a steel door, wielding an energy ball. Another view showed the rest of the team standing far back.

The ball grew larger, blue light snapping from the exterior like miniature lightning bolts. When it reached the size of a soccer ball, Gem hurled it at the door and collapsed.

"Holy Toledo!" Wyatt knocked his chair over when he shot out of his seat. He'd never seen anything like that up close, let alone from a safe spot where he wouldn't get burned to a crisp.

After the smoke cleared, the door was nothing but a memory. Claude knelt by Gem. There was no sound, but silent pictures told the story as Claude helped his weakened partner to stand. Wyatt located video of the next door. There was no way in hellfire she'd have enough energy to blast through another one, and they couldn't pick the locks since the external doors were activated by a keypad.

He was looking down at the computer when the control room door suddenly burst open. Wyatt flew backward onto the fallen chair, startled by the loud noise. With his heart racing, he looked up to see Christian and heaved a sigh of relief.

"You scared the crazy out of me!"

Christian gave him a mirthless smile. "Would you happen to know where my partner is?"

"I've got stuff to do."

Christian waltzed in, hoisted Wyatt off the floor, and hauled him out of the room. "That can wait. Viktor asked me to join, but I can't seem to hear anyone else running their mouth but you. If my partner's in danger and I don't get there in time, I'll extract your teeth, one by one, and replace them with nails."

Wyatt blanched. Vampires were strong enough to do it. "Fine. Let me go."

Once Christian released his hold, Wyatt hustled down the hall.

He'd memorized the blueprint, so it wasn't difficult to locate the stairwell that led to the upper floor.

Once they emerged from the stairwell, Viktor's wolf lunged at Christian.

"Jaysus wept! It's me, you furry eejit!"

The wolf hopped back and snorted.

Christian wiped his bloody hand on his black T-shirt. "Careful, Spooky. He's got blood in his mouth now."

"That only matters when they're in the middle of a fight."

Large windows encircled the fighting room down below.

Christian gave Wyatt a menacing stare. "Well? Where is she?"

"I thought you wanted to talk to Viktor about a plan."

"I don't speak dog."

Wyatt pointed around the bend. "She went that way."

Christian marched off.

Wyatt caught up and tugged on Christian's shirt. "I wouldn't advise going the way she did."

"You let me make that decision."

Wyatt didn't bother arguing. At least this would get Christian out of his hair, if not eternally. If Christian wanted to join his lover in a fighting ring or a pit of fire, so be it.

Wyatt stopped in front of a door on the outside wall and looked at the card reader. "That's a problem. I need to go back for my bag."

Christian shoved him toward the wall. "Figure it out, Einstein."

Even with the keypad below the reader, Wyatt didn't know the code. Before cracking it open, he decided to run down a list of the most commonly used passwords. Birthdays were ruled out since he didn't have that information, so he punched in the street number of the building's address.

The door opened.

He chortled in disbelief. "What a bunch of idiots."

Christian stepped inside the small closet. "Is this your idea of a joke? You insipid little—"

The door closed, and Wyatt heard a *whoosh*.

"Hope you don't end up in a pie."

Viktor's wolf barked to get Wyatt's attention. Then he picked up the gun belt in his mouth and trotted into the stairwell. Viktor's wolf wanted to go back up to the lobby, but Wyatt had more work to do—like opening the second exterior door to let Keystone through.

"Are you sure you don't want to stay down here and guard me?"

The wolf pounced into the elevator and turned in a circle. Wyatt pushed the button for the lobby and then hauled ass toward the control room. Keystone was still a ways from their destination, and if he didn't hurry and get to that control panel…

Just when he passed the secret elevator, it chimed, and the doors opened.

Chapter 30

AFTER QUICKLY ASSESSING MY PREDICAMENT in the ring, I decided that even if I had wings, I wouldn't have flown to the upper viewing area. Going alone would be suicide, and I liked my life too much to waste it on these trolls. Now that I was barefoot, I might have a fighting chance at climbing up the slide. Or at least far enough to be out of reach. Then I'd have to wait it out.

I bolted toward the dark hole. When I'd nearly reached it, Christian came flying out with his legs spread open. He scissored my neck, and I fell flat on my back. The crowd gasped, but I was beyond caring about their tepid reactions with Christian's crotch in my face.

I shoved him off me and coughed. "What the hell are you doing here?"

Christian got on all fours. "*Jaysus wept.* I think I just relived my birth." He looked up at me with a twinkle in his eye. "Is this a bloodbath in here?"

I tucked my bloody hair behind my ears. "Now isn't the time for your puns. I'm not going to ask why you came down that way, but I sure as hell hope that the rest of the team isn't behind you. That wolf is about to break out of his chains, and this crowd is thirsty for blood. Now we're *both* going to die."

He stood up and dusted off his pants. "First of all, the odds of my survival are better than yours. Worry not, lass. I'll be sure he doesn't devour all your remains."

I glanced at the gate, but Audrey wasn't there.

"Catch me up to speed," Christian said, nearing my side. "I'm a wee bit confused as to why all these shitebags are dressed up for Halloween."

"Welcome to fight club, starring us. I thought you were busy guarding Lenore the Whore?"

"I pulled out early."

"Sounds about right."

Christian swaggered over to the wall and hefted a spiked club. Then he moved toward the wolf, who still had the bag over his head.

"Don't hurt him." I gave Christian a scolding look.

"Are you afflicted in some way? The chains won't hold him for long." Christian hurled the club into the crowd, and it struck someone in the head. They fell backward, yet no one ran screaming. Some even applauded. "We need to get up there."

"Armed with what?"

Christian tossed an axe at me, and I caught it before it accidentally severed my arm. "Gird your loins, lass. We're storming the gates."

"How?"

He erased the distance between us. "Do you trust me?"

"I'm going to regret saying yes, aren't I?"

Christian winked and stood next to me. I looked down as he slid his hand between my legs from behind and gripped my sex nice and tight. His other hand flattened on my chest, and the next thing I knew, he was hurling me into the stands.

A shriek escaped my lips as I soared through the air with an axe in my hand. When I realized I was going to fall short of the ledge, I let go of the axe and grabbed the wall for dear life. Before my weight pulled me down, I threw my leg over and climbed up.

"Your aim sucks!" I yelled at him without looking back.

Masked faces retreated, and someone said, "This isn't allowed."

Banking on the assumption that these were prissy little aristocrats who couldn't throw a punch, I sharpened my light and kept my cool. When I spotted the victim of Christian's club toss, I pulled the spiked weapon from her skull, and her mask fell away.

Chestnut hair spilled across her face, and I felt guilty for just the slightest of moments before I remembered who these lunatics were.

I twirled the club and threw a coldhearted gaze at my audience. "Sorry to crash your party, but this is a sting operation. You're all under arrest. I want everyone to sit down with your hands on your head."

Someone threw their glass at my face and flashed off. Another ripped off her mask and rushed me. I swung the club and struck her arm. Blood sprayed the onlookers to my left. The club fell from my grip and into the ring as two people shoved me toward the ledge.

So much for an orderly arrest.

I spotted Christian in the ring. "I could use some help up here!"

"Working on it!" He charged the gate and bounced off like a quarter against a mattress.

Teetering over the edge of the balcony, I turned my head and chomped someone's arm. When they let go, I elbowed the other person who had ahold of my hair. One look at my fangs and they recoiled. I kicked the person in the stomach, and her mask fell off. Pandemonium ensued as the crowd turned into a mob and surged toward me. I braced for my imminent death, but they ran on by.

"What the hell?" I turned to watch the mayhem.

One of them hurtled over the wall. On the opposite side, others were leaping into the pit.

"Everyone down!" Shepherd's strident voice made me flinch as he fired his gun into the air.

Dust and pebbles showered over Gem, and she shook her head. "Watch where you aim that thing."

Gem curled her fingers rhythmically as a sphere of light rolled in her palm. Her energy ball was throwing the crowd in a panic.

I joined them. "Glad you made it. What's the plan?"

Shepherd frowned at the unconscious woman on the ground. "Where's the boss lady? Viktor wants her in custody before we do anything else."

Striding up to us, Christian tucked a lollipop inside his cheek and rested his arm on Shepherd's shoulder. "Couldn't help but overhear your dilemma. Why don't we throw everyone in the pit before they get it in their wee minds to flee or fight?"

"You busted the gate," I pointed out.

He pulled out the red lollipop and kissed the end of it. "Blue let me in. The gate's closed. Anyone up for a tossing game? Whoever gets the most in the ring takes a cut of everyone's pay."

Shepherd glowered. "Nobody's got time for that. Did you see the redhead or the little man?"

I glanced behind me at the masked crowd. Gem was keeping them at bay with her electric ball, static ripping through the air like needles. "Pablo was down here earlier, and he didn't use the slide. There has to be an elevator somewhere."

Gem's power ball suddenly fizzled out. "Oopsie."

A bystander made a wild lunge at Gem, who didn't see it coming. The person thrust their palm into her face and made a run for it. Shepherd fired his gun, and they fell like a stone. The mask came off, revealing a man who looked twenty.

When the bystanders saw we weren't killing them, they stopped cowering. With the lollipop stick poking out of his mouth, Christian grabbed a woman by the throat and flung her into the ring.

I flashed down the stairwell. Claude was guarding a tunnel entrance, his eyes feral and all four fangs extended. A woman lay at his feet. She was lucky she had only two puncture marks in her neck instead of four, but I couldn't imagine Claude intentionally killing a woman with his venom, even in primal mode. These people didn't know that though, so I couldn't think of a better person to guard the exit than a Mage's mortal enemy.

I took off in search of Audrey. As I passed the gate to the ring, I noticed a woman reaching for the long lever so she could free those inside.

"Oh no you don't." I yanked her away by her black robe.

The woman scowled at me and drew closer. Suddenly I felt an uncontrollable attraction to her—those lovely green eyes, those full lips, that deliciously sexy vein in her slender neck. My Vampire side sounded the alarm bells.

"*Charmer,*" I hissed before biting her neck.

She struggled but eventually weakened in my grip. Her blood revolted me, the vile flavor like bug spray or old chemicals. Everyone had their own unique flavor, but mostly I just tasted their sins.

Instead of pulling her light, which was usually how I finished off my victims, I had to refrain from the urge to kill so I could get a lock on Audrey.

"Let us out of here!" a woman begged, her fingers wrapped around the bars. "I can make you so rich that you'll never have to work again."

I neared the bars and sized her up: diamond-studded earrings, metallic eyeshadow, nude lipstick, blond curls spilling down her black robe. Her nails were bejeweled, and mine were caked in blood. Her perfume filled my nostrils as I leaned in. "Better get used to these," I said, tapping my fingers against the bars. "You'll be seeing them for a long time."

I strutted off and approached a naked man lying on the ground. It looked like Christian had secured the chain around his wolf's neck by bending the metal and looping the other end around a torch holder. The chain was loose, so I took it off and knelt. He was barely lucid.

"Hey, you're gonna be okay. What's your name?"

"Tom," he croaked.

"Tom, do you think you can stay here? It's too dangerous to run around. Can you sit tight for a little while?"

He nodded.

"Don't worry, you'll be fine. We'll take care of you."

He shook his head. "I thought you were lying."

"It doesn't matter. Just sit tight, okay?"

My heart clenched. How bad was this guy's life that death matches were a viable solution? Audrey must have targeted men at rock bottom, but no matter what they initially agreed to, they certainly weren't here of their own free will. Not if they were caged.

"Don't open that gate," I warned him. "Those are the people who wanted to watch you die tonight. Anything they promise you is a lie."

His eyes closed. Tom's condition had nothing to do with injuries sustained in the ring, as I'd done my best to go easy on him. He probably hadn't slept in days, dreading his certain death.

I followed the dark tunnel and approached a gate. After pulling the lever, I jogged down the tunnel until I reached Rafferty's prison. Without a key, I couldn't get inside. "Rafferty, open the door! I promise not to kill you if you cooperate."

I scanned the room and didn't see any plump shadows hiding behind one of the pillars. The only sound I heard was the low growling of a vicious panther. "Audrey? Are you in there?"

"Do you really think she'll answer?" Christian asked darkly.

I turned to face him. "Don't sneak up on me. That's a good way to get yourself killed."

He took the lollipop out of his mouth and let it rest on his bottom lip. "And how will you manage to strike me down without a weapon? Or did you plan to give me a coronary by flashing those blood-soaked knockers? Go on. Give us a peek."

"Open the gate."

With a bored look, he reached over and gave the locking mechanism a hard squeeze until it shattered. "No one's in there but a sniveling man with an atrocious flatulence problem."

I rounded the butcher's block and caught sight of Rafferty cowering on the floor. Grabbing a long knife, I squatted in front of him and pressed the tip to his fleshy gullet. "Where is she?"

His eyes rounded. "I don't know."

Rafferty gasped when I pushed the tip of the blade in deep enough to draw blood. "If you don't tell me where she is, I'm going to pour that bucket of chum all over you and lock you in the cage with the panther. How does that sound? I bet he starts with your intestines first. That's a slow death, you know."

The man whimpered. I didn't sense he was Breed, so he must have been a human servant.

Christian's chuckle was low but audible.

Rafferty pointed at the opposite door. "That way," he breathed. "That way."

I tapped his nose with the blade. "If you're smart, you'll stay right here. You have no idea what's going on out there."

He probably did. If he'd seen Audrey flying through here, it must have tipped him off that something had gone wrong.

I hurried toward the far door and looked back at Christian. "Is anyone upstairs in the auction house? You should call them and let them know Audrey might be taking the elevator."

Christian snorted. "I don't have my phone on me. I'm afraid our fate is in the hands of Spooky McGravewalker."

The door swung outward. "You should still—"

Air whooshed out of my lungs when the ground disappeared. I gasped—my tank top had wrapped around my neck, and it felt like someone was pulling my hair. I flailed my arms to grab something—anything. Christian seized my hand, and I hung suspended for a moment, assessing the fact that my boobs were out.

When he lifted me up and set me down, I stared up at Christian in shock.

His eyes skimmed down to my chest. "Ah, *there* they are. I think I might just have that coronary after all."

I pulled my tank top down. One of the straps was broken, but not as broken as I would have been if I'd fallen into that pit. We both leaned over and looked inside.

"Metal spikes. Nice touch," he said. "Hasn't anyone ever taught you not to run headlong through a dungeon door?"

"Lesson learned. I guess it's safe to assume this isn't the only booby trap?"

He winked. "Nice word choice."

I scowled at Rafferty. "You could have warned us."

The human looked equally amused and terrified. "I didn't know. I *swear* I didn't—"

"One more word and I'll drain you," Christian ground out, his eyes still locked on mine. When Rafferty piped down, Christian lifted my chin with the crook of his finger. "Do you trust me?"

"Hell no."

Without further discussion, I backed up a few paces and then jumped over the pit. I landed on one foot and stumbled a little before turning around.

Christian followed close behind and landed on both feet. "That little gobshite is lucky I don't throw his arse down there along with the jaguar."

Without light, I fell back a step and gripped Christian's arm so he could lead me. "It's a panther."

"Aye. But a panther is just a blanket term for a black cat of any *Panthera* species."

"You have a disturbing knowledge base about animals."

"Remind me to tell you about the mating ritual of honeybees." Christian crunched on his candy. "Isn't this romantic? All that shite about flowers, dinner, and a night on the town is overrated. All a man needs is a woman with supple breasts, a bucket of blood, a dark tunnel, and a slim chance of survival."

"Be still my beating heart."

"Don't ever say that to a Vampire." After two more steps, he yanked me to the ground. "Duck."

Something whooshed over our heads, and the hair on the back of my neck stood up.

"What was that?" I whispered.

"A free haircut. Will you stop distracting me? I missed the trip wire."

Annoyed, I crawled ahead of him.

"Mmm, nice view," he growled. His voice sounded higher up, and before I had the chance to ask if it was safe to stand, he made an *oomph*.

"You okay?"

Wood snapped, and the air whistled overhead. It sounded as if a body hit the ground a short distance away.

"Aye," he grunted. "Just dandy. Get on your feet, lass."

I stood and waited for him to offer me his arm. "This is like an Indiana Jones movie," I mused. "If they unleash spiders, I'm running the other way. Just so you know."

"*Jaysus*. Did you have to say that aloud?"

"Since when is the man who has spiders for roommates scared of spiders?"

"'Tis one thing to have a few wee spiders scurrying about. 'Tis another to have a cluster of foot-long tarantulas."

I slowed my pace. "I never said anything about tarantulas. Why did you just say that?"

"Keep to the left," he said, amusement in his voice.

"I hate you."

After a short turn, he quickly stopped and broke from my grip. I stared into the darkness, trying to make sense of incoherent sounds like rustling clothes, metal vibrations, and Christian heaving a sigh.

"What is it?" I asked.

"Fecking door is thicker than my cock."

I blindly staggered forward and felt for the knob. "Did you try opening it first?"

"What you know about dungeons could fill a thimble."

When I turned the lever, the door swung open. I grinned wide in the darkness. "After you, Poe."

I swear I could hear his jaw clench.

When Christian whooshed past, I heard his feet stomp in the distance.

"Jump, and I'll catch you."

I imagined a dark pit like the other one. "How long is it?"

"If I had a dime for every time I heard that," he murmured.

"What?"

"Pretend it's the Grand Canyon. Just run, and I'll tell you when to jump."

I backed up and ran full speed. My heart dropped when, after a second, I was certain I'd passed the door. Before my feet could skid to a stop, I crashed into Christian.

He belted out a laugh. "Fell for that one, didn't ya?"

"You fanghole." I shoved him away and moved toward a lit hallway on the right. There was a gold elevator at the end. I came to a stop and cocked my head. "Listen. Can you hear all that screaming? We must be close to the fighting pit."

He neared the wall. "Aye. There's a draft behind this stone. Looks like a secret doorway."

"Keep it shut. I don't want anyone escaping. Let's go."

When we got inside the elevator, I pushed the only button on the panel. "Were there really spiders back there?"

Christian clasped his hands behind his back and whistled a tune as the doors closed.

Chapter 31

Moments earlier.

WYATT HAD NO TIME TO spare as he jogged to the control room. If Keystone didn't get past the second set of doors, they might never capture the ringleader, and they would have failed this mission. What good are documents without the criminals? Just as he passed the mysterious elevator, he heard a *ding*. Backing up a few steps, he watched the doors open.

The dwarf met eyes with him and showed no look of surprise or fear. "When I imagined the demise of this organization, I never envisioned it would be led by a man in a Pac-Man shirt. I am Pablo Leonardo Russo." He stepped into the hall and inclined his head. "Well, aren't you going to administer me my rights?"

Wyatt felt like one of those cartoon characters whose tongue was tied in a knot. Small or not, this man was a Mage, and he had to play his cards right. "Do you see any katanas on me? Am I wearing a red jacket with a coattail? I'm nobody," Wyatt said, taking the target off his back.

"Pity. I've always had a fond appreciation for eccentrics. I'm sorry, am I keeping you from something?" The man walked toward the control room. "Let's just see what Mr. Nobody is up to."

Wyatt followed as the man whistled a familiar tune he couldn't quite place. Maybe the specter following him would help. As a Gravewalker, Wyatt saw specters everywhere he went: gas stations, movie theaters, bagel shops, even walking alongside the road. If he acknowledged their existence, they would harass him, question him, and follow him—attracting other specters desperate for a connection to the living world. They usually hung out in busy places, hoping to run into a Gravewalker. But some attached themselves to living people, and they would follow them like a shadow.

Like the buxom blonde in the white dress who was following the little man around like a lost puppy. Was she an old flame? His sister? A woman he'd murdered?

Wyatt fell into step next to her. "If you help me, I'll help you," he whispered.

She whirled in front of him, her eyes wide. "You can see me?"

He put more distance between them and Pablo. "I need a favor. Tell me what you want in return."

"Revenge. Do you know what he did to my body after I died? *After* he stole my immortality? He ordered his little helper to dump me in an alleyway. They treated me like royalty while I fought for them, but in the end, all I got was a one-way ticket to the crematorium. That's what they do with people who don't come from money. No funeral, no white dress, no eulogy."

Wyatt wanted to roll his eyes. She had on her imaginary funeral dress. The dead had a tendency to linger on funeral customs, most of them feeling they deserved horse-drawn carriages, trumpets, a grandiose display of flowers, and an expensive casket. Only those with families or money received a decent funeral—the higher authority preferred cremation to prevent humans from exhuming their bodies.

Wyatt played along with her request. "How does Breed jail sound?"

"You call that revenge? I want him dead so I can strangle him for eternity."

"Do you really want to see him for the rest of your unnatural life? Trust me, jail is the way to go."

Pablo turned his head. "I'm sorry, did you say something?"

Wyatt caught up. "Just trying to figure out where we're going."

"They say brilliant men talk to themselves." Pablo resumed walking, his hands clasped behind his back. "I've never believed it."

When they reached the control room, Pablo noticed Wyatt's gear. "I see you've been busy."

Wyatt stared at the empty space behind Pablo. "Your mother is here. She wants you to be a good boy."

Pablo blushed and shifted uncomfortably. Then he studied Wyatt and followed the direction of his gaze. "You're not a very good liar."

"Your real name was Oswald." He smiled at the imaginary figure behind Pablo. "You're deathly afraid of inchworms. Just between you and me, I'm not a fan of butterflies."

Pablo narrowed his eyes, his cool façade crumbling. "You keep looking over my shoulder, but my mother was almost six feet tall. A beast of a woman. I never did understand what Father saw in her. She lacked moral character." Pablo rested his arm on the table. "Now I'm genuinely curious how you knew that information."

Wyatt shot the blonde a baleful look.

The woman shrugged. "He never mentioned how big his mother was. I just assumed."

Pablo marched toward Wyatt. "*Who* are you speaking to, Gravewalker? *If* that's in fact what you are."

Wyatt eyeballed his equipment and thought about bailing. The cool and collected ones made him nervous, but surely he could outrun this guy. Could a little person flash faster than he could run? Wyatt pondered the thought.

"A smart man would stay right where he is," Pablo cautioned him.

Wyatt swung his gaze up to the monitors. Gem was trying to wield another energy ball, but the spark kept dying in her hands.

"Especially when someone is about to give him the keys to his kingdom." Pablo walked over to the control panel and opened the second door, allowing Keystone in.

Wyatt didn't know what this guy's angle was, but he didn't trust him. What if he'd just invited the Keystone team into a trap? Viktor had given Wyatt a backup number to call if things got out of hand. Did this qualify?

Pablo returned to the computer and made a few keystrokes. "Tell me you're not the best of your kind."

Ignoring his instinct to flee, Wyatt waltzed over to the computer and looked at an encrypted folder that Pablo had pulled up. "I was interrupted."

Pablo arched his brow, unconvinced. "Huh. Did you also miss *these* files?"

"I copied everything to a drive. I didn't have time for the tour."

"Well, you'll have a lot to look at later on then, won't you?" Pablo reached underneath the desk and something ripped, like tape peeling off a hard surface. He handed Wyatt a flash drive. "A word of advice: never leave a room without searching it thoroughly. Some of us actually know how to use technology, and we also hide things in plain sight."

Wyatt took the flash drive and put it in his pocket.

After a few more keystrokes, Pablo pulled up several camera angles on the monitor.

Wyatt watched people in black robes racing around an enclosed pit. Some were climbing into a hole in the wall, and others were attempting to bust through a heavy gate. A different camera showed Claude fending off three women. On another screen, Blue was swinging her axe at a bevy of women. Niko held a warrior's stance with both swords, and no one dared to pass him.

"I could only bring up the outside doors. Didn't think you had any power running down there."

"Aside from the cameras, we don't. Your friends won't be able to hold them off for long." Pablo held a grim look as he stared at the monitors.

Wyatt backed up. "What's your angle, Dr. Evil?"

"Did you ever stop to wonder who your informant was? I lost all hope until your friend came along. That's quite an interesting necklace she wears. A hollow onyx with a camera inside. You should talk to your jeweler. That's a ubiquitous design when it comes to spy cams."

"And I'm supposed to believe you? I'll take bullshit for five hundred, Alex."

Pablo glanced up at the screens. "*Jeopardy* was always a favorite of hers. You see, Audrey is a woman consumed with games. It's her life. It's how she makes money, how she amuses herself, how she treats others. Never love a woman who plays games with your heart—who strings you along, making you sink further into a pit of reprehensible behavior in order to lift her higher." His gaze lowered. "I was promised immunity for this information. I was supposed to have enough advance warning to escape, but it seems I've been played a fool once again by a beautiful woman. I deserve to be locked up for my stupidity. I guess the fates have decided."

"You're not going to fight or try to escape?"

"To what avail? You've already seen my face, and I am not a killer."

Wyatt unplugged his external hard drive. "This says otherwise."

"I stage the events, but I do not partake."

Wyatt flicked a glance at the screen. His team wouldn't be able to control the crowd much longer. Wyatt sent a text message to their emergency backup, giving them the club location and entrance point. Once they got control of those masked buffoons, they could call in the Regulators. Maybe Pablo was distracting him so his redheaded cohort could sneak up and sever Wyatt's head. Wyatt stroked his throat.

"You look pale, my friend. I assure you this isn't a ruse. I haven't been myself lately. Perhaps my evil deeds are catching up with my conscience."

"Whatever you say." Wyatt zipped up his backpack.

"I *am* curious about one thing: how did you know my given name? If my mother isn't the one you're talking to, then who is?"

Wyatt flicked a glance at the blonde, who was giving Pablo a scathing look from her seat on the table. He swiped up his ski mask and shoved it in his back pocket. "Her name is Tiffany. Ring any bells?"

Pablo clasped his hands behind his back and inclined his head. "Ah, now it all makes sense. Tell me, Gravewalker, is it true that the dead can put thoughts in your head?"

"Sometimes. It depends on the person and the circumstance."

"The timing of her death and my guilty conscience is more than a coincidence. I've been having all sorts of dreams, and I wonder if

Tiffany had something to do with that. She wasn't involved in the death matches, but Tiffany was surprisingly competitive. Audrey convinces the girls that if they choose to leave, a Vampire will scrub their memories. That's a lie to make them feel safe. Audrey would never risk anyone leaving our organization with all that knowledge, so the quitters and losers became my responsibility. Taking care of her problems was the hardest part of my job. I never received any specific orders about sexual relations with the fighters, so perhaps it never occurred to Audrey that a woman could be attracted to a dwarf. Tiffany was"— Pablo made the shape of an hourglass with his hands—"but I guess you can see that for yourself."

"She's all yours, buddy. In this life and in the next."

Pablo followed Wyatt's gaze. "Tiffany, you deserved better, and for that I'm eternally sorry. I only hope that you were unconscious the entire time and didn't feel any pain. Don't waste your existence following me. Move on to the next life. I'll be spending many, many years in a cell. That's no place for a woman like you."

Wyatt inched toward the door. "She gives her thanks."

"Do me one favor—say it like she said it. In *her* words, not yours."

This guy was a nutball. If there was one thing Wyatt hated, it was acting as an interpreter for the dead. He drew in a deep breath and sighed. "It's okay, Ozzie Pooh. I forgive you, even though a stray cat ate one of my toes."

Pablo grimaced before pulling out a chair. "Have a seat, my lady. There're things I wish to say before I go."

Feeling a bubble of nausea rise in his throat, Wyatt backed up toward the door. "That's a therapy session I ain't got time for."

His job was to collect evidence and keep his ass alive. No sense hanging around if this guy decided to change his mind. Besides, their backup would be here any moment to take care of Pablo and his ghosty gal.

"I'll leave you two lovebirds alone. Don't do anything I wouldn't do." Wyatt turned on his heel and froze when he spotted a drop-dead gorgeous redhead walking their way. "Now that's a twist I didn't see coming."

Chapter 32

THE ELEVATOR MOVED LIKE MOLASSES, but that gave me a chance to get a good look at myself in the reflective wall. "Did you ever see that movie *Carrie?*"

"You and your da spend far too much time watching movies. You should pick up a book sometime."

"*Everything You Wanted to Know about Tarantulas but Were Afraid to Ask?*"

"One of these days, I'm going to take you to the zoo."

"If you're trying to get rid of me, Poe, bars won't keep me away from you." I batted my eyelashes coquettishly.

"You're a peculiar woman." He leaned against the wall, arms folded. "For your information, animals have a lot to teach us about our true instincts—the ones we repress."

"I suppose your instinct is telling you to lick every drop of blood off my body?"

He leaned forward and gave me a wolfish grin. "That's not what I want to lick."

I flushed all over, and for a brief moment, I entertained the idea of having sex with Christian in the elevator. I could tell by the look in his eyes that he was entertaining the thought too. We stared at each other intensely.

Ding went the elevator.

He pulled his collar away from his neck. "That's us. Feel like taking a ride back down?"

"Don't tempt me."

He stepped close and put his lips to my ear. "Tempting you is what I do best." Christian suddenly jerked up, his eyes wide and alert. "Wyatt's in trouble."

"When is he not in trouble?"

Christian stuck his foot in the doors to prevent them from closing. "The woman's here."

I followed Christian as he sprinted to the left. We jogged through a doorway and stopped short of a brightly lit room. Inside, Pablo lay motionless in a pool of his own blood, his head severed. I could hear Wyatt shouting, and as we drew closer, I spotted him in the back of the room, holding a chair like a lion tamer.

"I didn't conspire anything!" Wyatt barked at her. "I didn't even know him. I'm just a guy who works for a guy. I don't know anything."

"What a terrible liar," I murmured.

Wyatt threw the chair at her and started to run toward the door until a sword blocked it. He backed up against the far wall and slumped to the floor, making himself as small as possible. Audrey peered around the doorway at us.

I waved at her. "How's it going?"

She turned her back on Wyatt to face us, a bloody sword in hand. "I should have known the little man would betray me one day, but you?" Despite her elegance and sophistication, it was clear that Audrey knew how to use a sword.

I stood my ground. "Why do you think I didn't kill the wolf? Did you really believe I was putting on a show just for you? If I'd wanted him dead, I could have done it before you recited the alphabet."

"Now there's a braggart," Christian muttered.

Audrey gestured to Pablo. "Did he put you up to this? I would've given you a whole lot more to keep your mouth shut. You didn't play your cards right."

"But I did. I knew the house was dealing a dirty game from the beginning. I'm not some random bartender. You're smarter than that. Well, not that smart. You made a few mistakes that led us here. It's over, Audrey. There's no way out."

"There's *always* a way out." She whirled around and marched up to Wyatt, holding the blade to his throat. "Get up."

With his back to the wall, Wyatt stood with his hands up.

She poked him in the side, and he winced. "Get moving or I'll gut you like a fish."

"What's the plan?" I whispered to Christian.

"Let her walk out of here, or vacuum Wyatt's intestines off the floor later. Dealer's choice."

"Are you immune to Sensors? Maybe you can grab her when they walk by."

"Fecking not. If she has the Salem witch burnings inside her, I don't want to guess what might happen. I once heard of a Sensor killing a Vampire with a powerful death experience."

I had no urge to grab her either, now that I knew how powerful and debilitating sensory experiences really were.

Once Audrey and Wyatt were out of the room, she held the blade to his throat again, making it impossible to knock it away without mortally injuring Wyatt. I briefly entertained the idea, thinking Christian might be able to heal him with his blood, but that would be a shitty thing to do.

When she gripped Wyatt's shoulder with her other hand, his expression went blank as he fell under her influence. She drew nearer, and I noticed blood spatters on her face.

"Audrey, there's no way you can escape. We've got this place surrounded from top to bottom. If you let him go, I'll cut you a deal."

"Lies."

Some people were gullible, so it had been worth a try. "Fine. If you kill him, then we kill you. How's that for odds?"

"I'd rather die fighting than on my knees in front of the higher authority."

"I bet you have enough money to pay them off. A few decades in confinement, and then you're free."

A rivulet of blood trickled down Wyatt's neck, but the vacant look in his green eyes remained. Christian gave me a grim look, and I read his mind. Once Audrey reached the elevator, she'd cut

Wyatt's throat. She knew it would distract us long enough for those elevator doors to close.

Where the hell is Viktor?

Christian and I stood across from each other, our backs to the wall. Audrey's arm trembled, but she kept the blade against Wyatt's neck. Wyatt shuffled forward like a zombie.

"Don't try anything," she warned us.

"For future reference, daggers are a hell of a lot easier to carry around," I said with derision. "Did you hide that steel under your dress?"

Christian chortled. "I'd wager she hid it in her giant fanny. Have you got a pillow in there? Something I can rest my head on while we wait for you to saunter on to the elevator?"

"It's the high heels," I pointed out. "They slow you down."

Christian glanced at my bare feet. "Speaking of dry hooves, where the feck are your shoes?"

"Someone else wanted to walk a mile in them." I smiled as we strategically distracted Audrey, who was now attempting to walk backward.

Christian glowered. "Those were an expensive pair, I'll have you know."

I stepped toward him. "Maybe you should have bought me cheap shoes like hers. Look, one of them is coming apart." I gestured to Audrey's feet.

She flicked a glance at her heels, and with that, I flashed down the hall and yanked her arm before twirling away. Christian moved like a bullet and fell on top of Wyatt to protect him.

Audrey swung the blade and sliced off a lock of Christian's hair. I charged my light and blasted her from behind. She gasped, teetering for a moment with her arms raised. When she lowered her arms, I expected her to go down. But instead, I glimpsed the sword spearing my gut. I think I made a sound, but the only thing that registered in that moment was the searing pain.

Christian's expression blackened. He launched to his feet, but before he could get to her, she withdrew the sword and sliced the air between them. Christian's shirt ripped across the chest, and blood speckled Wyatt's face.

Audrey wielded that sword as if she were born with it in her hand. I clutched my stomach and watched Christian dodge every swing until he knocked the blade with his forearm, breaking the steel in two. Undeterred, Audrey threw down the pieces and pushed her glowing red hands against his chest.

Christian blanched, and witnessing that vulnerability triggered a protective side of me that I'd only felt for my father.

"No!" I leaped forward and held her head between my hands. Before she could wrench free, I channeled a current of energy and blasted her in the skull.

Audrey made a guttural sound before Christian slammed her against the floor. He straddled her, locked his fingers around her throat, and squeezed until her face turned purple and I heard small bones cracking. She was still seizing from my attack, her eyes rolled back and drool sliding down her face.

"Stop!" I yanked on his shirt, still clutching my stomach with the other hand. "Don't kill her."

Wyatt sat up and rubbed his face as he came out of his trance. "Yeah, don't kill her. Not until I get out of here."

Christian whipped his head around and threw me an icy stare. His fangs were out, and he was in murder mode. "Anyone who harms you is fertilizer."

Wyatt stood up and swayed. "Viktor wants her alive. But hey, if you want to drag her corpse home and explain yourself, by all means, carry on."

Christian loosened his grip, but I could tell it was killing him to do so. Just as he leaned away, he suddenly descended upon her like a monster and buried his fangs in her neck.

Wyatt catapulted off his ass and knocked my partner off the woman, by far the bravest act I'd seen him perform. Even I wouldn't interrupt Christian in the middle of dinner.

"Get off me, you eejit!"

Wyatt locked his legs around Christian's head. "You can't eat the prisoner! It's not allowed."

Christian slowly shifted his body so that he was facing Wyatt's family jewels. Wyatt's eyes rounded at the sight of Christian's fangs, and he scrambled away.

I slumped to the floor, afraid to look down and see my intestines hanging out. I kept a firm grip over the wound to stanch the bleeding.

Christian held out his hand to Wyatt. "Give me your shirt."

"This is my lucky shirt."

"You'll be lucky to live if you don't give it to me."

Wyatt peeled it off and flung it at Christian's head. Christian flipped Audrey onto her stomach and then used the fabric to bind her hands together. Then he stood and forced Wyatt to sit on her back. "Stay there."

When the elevator chimed, we all turned our heads. Niko slowly emerged, his swords stained in blood as he looked right and then left. He took a moment to assess the situation, though I couldn't imagine how he could tell what was going on by looking at energy alone.

"Are there any steps?" he called out.

Christian moved my hands away and examined my wound. "It's a straight walk."

Niko set his swords on the floor and knelt beside me. "Is she all right?"

I smiled reluctantly. "'Tis but a flesh wound."

"You're a terrible liar."

I flicked a glance at the sword and shuddered. "How many did you kill?"

"None," he said on a breath. "But they'll be hurting for a while until someone heals them. I presume there's a lot of blood on my sword."

"Yep." I grimaced when Christian lifted my shirt to get a better look. "You should clean them."

"I will. Is the building safe?"

I nodded even though he couldn't see. "We got the woman. Pablo's dead, and Viktor's upstairs. How's everything down below?"

"It was pandemonium for a short while, but we had help rounding them into the pit."

"What about the Shifters? Is someone looking after them?"

He put his hand on my shoulder. "Rest easy, Raven. Your work here is done."

I'd lost track of the time since capturing Audrey, but it had been at least twenty minutes. Niko and Christian briefly argued over who would heal me, but I insisted that Niko's nonaddictive Healer magic was a far better choice under the circumstances. Christian's blood came with too many distractions. Since the cut on Wyatt's neck was superficial, Niko didn't bother healing him. Wyatt didn't mind. It would only provide him another tall tale to tell at the dinner table. While Niko went on an errand and Christian guarded Audrey, I followed Wyatt into the room where we'd first found him.

From my seat on the table, I watched him typing on the computer. "What are you doing?"

"Erasing everything."

"What?"

"Viktor's orders. I couldn't risk it earlier because of the little guy. Usually we turn over evidence, but there's a lot of sensitive stuff in here that we can't trust with the Regulators. I copied everything, and that's what we'll show our contact before destroying it. They've got more than enough witnesses down below, and I'm sure plenty of them will sing for leniency."

I swung my gaze up to the monitors on the wall and watched Keystone and a few unfamiliar faces secure the prisoners.

Wyatt cleared his throat. "There's a shower on this floor, just so you know."

I stood up on the table. "What's the matter, Gravewalker? Scared of a little blood?" I jumped down. "It's too bad we don't have video of you cowering in the corner."

"I wasn't cowering. I had a chair, and she had a sword."

I frowned at Pablo's headless corpse. "Why did she kill him?"

"Seems the little guy was in on the whole thing. He's a snitch."

I jerked my head back. "Pablo?"

Wyatt scooted back and locked his fingers behind his head. "Oswald. That's the name his ghost girlfriend gave me."

I warily looked around. "Is he still here?"

"Nope. He went into the light or wherever they go. Took the blonde with him."

"Is the light heaven?"

"How should I know? I don't see that part. When they go, they just go. I've heard about a light, and sometimes they talk to someone I can't see. I'm not supposed to see it, and I don't want to see it."

"Why not?"

He looked down at his hard nipples and frowned, probably thinking about his favorite Pac-Man shirt. "What I'd really like to know is who sent me the blueprints to this place at the last minute. It couldn't have been the headless horseman. He was too busy with you at the time."

"Why hasn't Viktor come down from the lobby?"

"Christian busted the steel shutters, so Viktor's guarding the entrance until the Regulators show up. See?" Wyatt switched on a camera in the main room. Viktor's wolf was sitting very still, facing front. "I hope Niko finds Viktor's clothes before everyone shows up. Otherwise that'll be an awkward introduction when he shifts back."

Chatter drew my attention to the hall. Two formidable men swaggered toward Christian. One had a shaved head, broad shoulders, and piercing blue eyes. The other was a tall Chitah with reddish-blond hair. Both had what looked like gold wedding bands on their fingers, which wasn't something you saw in the Breed world.

"Everything under control?" Blue Eyes asked.

Christian stood with his hands clasped. "Aye."

The two men looked at us and then at Pablo's corpse.

"Who are they?" I asked quietly.

Wyatt unhooked a cable from the two computers. "That's

HALO. They were our emergency backup. You can always tell by the rings they wear."

"Since when are we asking other organizations for help?"

"Viktor doesn't make it a habit, but we all have an understanding in case there's an emergency on a high-profile case. We're not exactly competing for the same jobs, so they're not our enemies. I think a raid against a group of hostile women qualifies as an emergency."

"Not all of them were women."

"According to the files, the majority are. What went on down there before we showed up?"

I inched toward the door. "Mage against Shifter, but they wanted the Mage to win. Women against men."

While Wyatt rambled on about reverse sexism, I stood in the doorway, trying to eavesdrop on what the men were discussing. Given the history of women in the Breed world, an underground racket like this wasn't a real surprise. It made me wonder if, in another life, I might have willingly taken a job like this. I would be doing what I loved for money. Wasn't that what I was doing now?

Christian stayed quiet, his arms folded and posture rigid. The Chitah did most of the talking, and I caught a few things here and there about the raid. The tough guy rubbed the tribal tattoo on his bicep, and I felt like I'd seen him before. The Breed world was a small one, and I occasionally ran into the same people in different bars and clubs. After another minute, the Chitah threw Audrey over his shoulder and headed toward the main elevator. The blue-eyed man clapped Christian's shoulder before joining his companion.

I strolled into the hall and watched them disappear past the far door.

Christian turned and gazed at me earnestly. "It looks like someone's getting a bonus. Good work."

"I didn't do this alone."

"Take credit where it's due." He cupped the back of my neck and rested the pads of his thumbs by my ears.

When he leaned in, I tilted back. "I'm not kissing you with another woman's blood on your lips."

He gave me a crooked smile. "You're complaining about a few drops on my lips when you're drenched in blood?"

"That's different. I didn't suck on this person."

Christian tossed back his head and laughed. When he regained his composure, he wiped a tear from his eye with the heel of his hand. "I would have passed my condolences to the unlucky lad."

I rested my head against his chest and slipped my fingertips inside the tear in his shirt. *Thank God* this job was over. Hopefully I'd never have to see another sex club again. At least we'd freed the captive Shifters. That satisfied me more than capturing Audrey and all her little cohorts.

"The Shifters downstairs are victims," I said. "Make sure nobody hurts them."

"Aye, but our work isn't done."

I tilted back. "What do you mean?"

"We—or the Regulators—still have to round up everyone else who knew about the fights, including the fighters."

"Flynn." I sighed and turned my gaze upward. "He's a paid scout who works at the club. Just when I thought I could have a little reprieve."

"No rest for the wicked."

"I know where he lives and what time he gets off work. Let me take a quick shower before we leave. I can't go out like this or I'll get arrested. Feel like coming along?"

Christian practically purred as he pulled me in close. "I could use a shower."

"I meant to Flynn's house."

He lightly squeezed my ass before lifting me up. "I can do that too. Can I tear away your clothes?"

"No. I need something to wear."

"I'm afraid Tide won't take out those stains."

"There's a bag down below. Someone can bring it up."

"Ah, then I *can* tear away your clothes," he said, walking toward the shower room.

"If you insist."

"Aye, Precious. I insist."

Chapter 33

CHRISTIAN PARKED HIS OLD DUCATI in front of a small house. After dismounting, I rubbed my cold arms to get the blood circulating. The only clothes I'd stuffed in that plastic bag were a white tank top and black shorts. Christian had retrieved my boots, so at least my feet weren't frozen from the bike ride.

Christian shut off the bike and stared at the house. A streetlamp cast light on a holly tree, which was in full bloom. "Are you sure he's here?"

"It'll be sunrise soon. According to his schedule, he gets off at 2:00 a.m. That was over an hour ago, so he's had plenty of time to make it home."

"What's his Breed?"

I shivered. "Mage."

After striding up to the porch, Christian gripped the knob and shouldered the door open. The wood splintered as the frame broke.

He glared at me. "I suppose you're going to rabbit on about trying the knob."

I stepped over the threshold. "No, I was only going to suggest using the doorbell. People are less likely to run." After switching on a lamp, I looked inside the tiny house. "Flynn? It's me, Robin." The back door in the kitchen was visible over the pony wall that divided it from the living room on the right.

Christian headed that way.

I went behind a partition wall on the left and searched the bedrooms. The first one was empty and only contained workout equipment. The second bedroom was also empty, so I checked the bathroom. Whiskers covered the sink, towels were on the floor—still damp—and yet I saw no toothbrush or shaver. I returned to the larger bedroom and flipped on the light. A few clothes were askew on the closet floor, but all the hangers were bare.

I sat down on the bed just as Christian appeared in the doorway.

"The garage is empty," he informed me. "The backyard is clear—no storage shed or place to hide. We should turn off the lights."

"What for?"

"If he drives up and sees them on, he'll know something's wrong."

"Flynn doesn't have a car. Anyhow, he'll know something's wrong if he sees the door busted apart. I have a feeling he won't be coming back."

Christian furrowed his brow. "And how do you figure?"

"At first I thought he was a pig who doesn't know how to clean up after himself. But look at that," I said, pointing at the closet. "No shoes, hardly any clothes, and not a single jacket. There's no travel bag, and what immortal or even human doesn't have luggage?" I leaned back on my hands. "He split."

Christian leaned against the doorjamb and folded his arms. "Viktor should have sent someone to the club."

"It doesn't matter. He won't get far without a vehicle. Even if he did manage to get out of the city, we can check clubs and tattoo parlors since he has a special gift for imprinting light. If he took a bus, Wyatt can look into that. He mentioned coming from Manchester." I shook my head. "Why did he cut and run? Even if he dumped a few of the bodies, he wasn't the one who murdered them. Flynn's a hustler, not a killer."

"He's just as culpable as everyone else involved. Your friend made his choice to become a declared outlaw. That means he'll never have his life back. Bounty hunters will consider him an easy target."

I tossed a sock on the floor. "I need to wrap up a few things at the club. There's a bartender who might have information on Flynn's whereabouts."

"Need a lift?"

"No. I can flash there in less than three minutes."

He shook his head and lowered his arms. "Why must time to a Mage always be relative to how fast you can run?"

I stood and shook out my tousled hair. "I can tell by your excitement that you don't want to tag along. I need to check out of the hotel anyhow and grab my stuff. Meet you back at Keystone?"

"After I search the house. The little shitebag might have left behind a scrap of paper with an address."

"Wouldn't that be nice? Too bad Flynn's smarter than that."

I stood on my tiptoes and kissed his soft lips.

Christian returned the featherlight kiss. "You make me feel things," he said softly.

I got tingly just thinking about all the places his mouth had kissed me during our recent shower, but mentally exhausted, all I really wanted to do was finish my errand so I could curl up in a warm bed and sleep. After a drink.

Or two.

My hotel stay was on Viktor's card, so I decided to swing by the front desk and let them know I was checking out. Once I made it to my room, I changed out of my boots and into a comfy pair of sneakers. The boots were too sexy to be flashing all over the city in. I had loads of money in the satchel I'd hidden in the closet, so maybe a cab ride was in order.

After collecting my things, I headed up the street toward the White Owl. The tops of the buildings were gilded in sunlight. Living in the country, I'd forgotten how beautiful the city was at dawn. The brisk walk got my blood circulating, making me forget the temperature was in the fifties. When I reached the club, most of the staff had left, and they were closing for the day.

"Simone!" I waved and caught her attention on her way from the staff room.

"Well, well. Look who decided to grace us with her presence." She gave me a curt smile.

"I almost didn't recognize you," I said, looking at her oversized hoodie with the New England Patriots logo. "I guess you're finally rid of me. I came by to clean out my locker."

She arched her eyebrows. "You're quitting?"

"Yeah, I guess this just isn't the job for me. Maybe I'm better suited as a bodyguard or something."

She tilted her head to the side and gave me a sly smile. "I can see that."

"Have you seen Flynn?"

"He left hours ago."

"I need to speak to him."

"Did you try calling?"

I shifted the bags to my other hand. "I stopped by his house. It looks like he split town. He has something of mine."

"That sounds about right. If he has something of yours, you'll never see it again."

"Do you know where he might have gone? Does he have any other homes?"

Simone chuckled and adjusted her purse strap. "Flynn travels a lot. I think he lived in San Francisco for a while… or was it Santa Barbara? Maybe it was San Antonio. He never shared a lot of details about his past, and if he did, I wouldn't believe it. Not after all the lies. Give me your number. If I hear from him, I'll call you."

I couldn't give out my phone number to just anyone. "That's okay. It's a small world. I'll run into him again eventually."

She got a twinkle in her eye. "Did you put in my name for the boss's special errands?"

I scratched my head. "Tips pay more. It's not worth your time."

She shrugged. "Well, Robin White, I'm late for my second job. Stop by the Red Door sometime and I'll give you a free drink. Though it seems you had plenty here," she said with a pointed look. "Later."

As Simone sauntered off, I headed toward the bar. The colorful accent lights were shut off, and even with the overhead spotlights, the place seemed dark and lifeless. Napkins, cherry stems, cigarette butts, and whip tassels littered the floor. The cleaning crew did a phenomenal job, because each night when I started my shift, the place was spotless.

I dipped behind the bar and squatted in front of the tip shelf. I found the big black box with the large *S* and opened it up. Then I neatly stacked one hundred grand in Simone's box. People cleared their tips each night, so no one would look in there before she did. That money wasn't Viktor's anyhow. Not really. I'd earned it for the fight, and while he would have let me keep it, Simone deserved it more. She made a mistake with Flynn, but who doesn't screw up? Does that mean we didn't deserve second chances? I sure as hell had one, and it changed my life. Maybe this little boost would get her wherever she was going.

When I stood up, Houdini startled me. He sat at the bar, accent lights playing off his bleached hair, which was almost white. I knew it wasn't his natural color because the roots were dark.

Houdini's hazel eyes checked mine as he folded his arms. "How about a drink before you go? You know what I like."

I popped the cap off a beer bottle and set the drink in front of him. "This is my last night here. We closed the case, so you won't be seeing my face anymore."

"What a shame." He sipped his beer and never took his eyes from mine.

It was easy to forget that Houdini was a Vampire, so when I felt the weight of his gaze, I made sure to look away.

"I saw what you put in her box."

"How?" I looked up at a glass ball in the ceiling that likely had a hidden camera behind it. "Never mind."

"If that's a large amount of money, she might quit. Simone is one of my best, and I can't afford to lose her."

"I thought you liked a little chaos?"

"Touché. So… what are your plans from here?"

I heaved a sigh and tossed Flynn's empty satchel into the trash.

"Sleep. Eat. The usual. Then on to the next case. What about you? Planning to open up a strip joint?"

"Until I find a more lucrative venture, I'll stay here. Unless you'd prefer me to start selling on the black market again."

I shrugged. "Go for it. Maybe you'll wind up on our hit list."

Looking as aloof as ever, he took another swig.

"If you see Flynn, turn him in. He's now a declared outlaw. Turns out he was the one recruiting girls from your club and who knows where else."

"I do tire of asinine behavior. Do you see what I have to put up with to earn my keep in this world? He could have put my entire business in jeopardy."

I rested my arms on the bar. "Sure you didn't know anything about it?"

"If I see him, I won't bother turning him in. I'll do what one must do with any dog when it's gone mad."

"Don't. He's not the worst criminal I've ever met. He just made a lot of dumb choices for money, and he didn't know about the death matches."

Houdini tilted his head to the side. "Why the empathy for a criminal and yet none for me? There's nothing that separates us except that I make smarter choices."

"Yep. Dumping me in a morgue was brilliant."

An enigmatic smile crossed his expression. "It was the smartest move I ever made, wouldn't you agree?"

I knew where he was leading this conversation, so I let it go. "You can keep whatever money you owe me. I'm outta here."

After grabbing my bag, I lifted the countertop to head out.

Houdini swiveled on his stool and then rested his elbows on the bar behind him. "Did you fight?"

Without turning around, I stopped. "Yes."

"I'm curious, how did it feel? Powerful? Inconsequential? Savage? Tell me the truth."

I pondered the question before facing him. "People don't choose that life because they want it. They do it because they don't have other options. They want to feel like their life has meaning, and people like you take advantage of that."

He chuckled softly. "You wanted to become a Vampire. You accepted the offer, just as the other women did. Don't play victim. Now I pay people to work in a fantasy club, and they do so willingly. Obviously a few of them received a better offer, but unfortunately for them, it didn't end well. Take responsibility for the choices you make."

"Accountability means nothing to you."

"On the contrary, I'm quite pleased with the woman you've become. Resilient, witty, but not quite independent. Tell me, do you still question whether you're good or evil?"

Houdini would never perceive his actions as evil. Especially if they wound up having a good outcome. What bothered me was that each time we revisited this conversation, he made sense. Why did I come across as the irrational one, ungrateful for the life I had?

I pushed my anger down and walked away.

"I'm always charmed we keep meeting this way. See you when I see you, Butterfly."

I didn't give Houdini the satisfaction of a head turn—I just kept strutting toward the door, hoping it really *would* be the last time we ran into each other. I wanted to leave my past behind, and he was a constant reminder of where it all went wrong.

Once outside, I drew in a deep breath of crisp morning air. The train station wasn't far, and that would get me halfway home. If only I had parked my truck in an indoor parking lot. I hadn't been thinking ahead about what would happen after the assignment was over.

I dashed across the busy street and headed north.

"Donuts," I whispered, my mouth watering as I passed a pastry shop. A beefy-looking Chitah stepped out with a stack of boxes in his arms and made his way to a parked car. The coffee smelled tempting, but I kept thinking about my warm bed. Food and drink could come later.

"Raven!"

I looked ahead and recognized the blonde poking her head

from the back-seat window of a white Rolls-Royce. I stepped up to the curb and admired the antique automobile. "This looks like something the Queen would drive around in."

Lenore smiled. "Good morning! Come have a seat and we'll chat. I'd like to discuss that favor you still owe me."

I circled the car to the other door, which opened opposite than regular car doors. The back seat was roomy and stylish.

"It's a 1948," she said. "I've had it in storage for years, but I also had to pay someone to keep it in mint condition. The newer cars have all the creature comforts, but I have a newfound appreciation for the classics. They're sophisticated and detailed. Just look at the workmanship."

The leather bench in the back was more like a couch. I leaned forward to shut the door. There was an abundance of legroom and no middle hump, and I'd never been in a car quite like it. I set my stuff on the floor next to a black bag.

"Wood paneling," she continued, bragging about all the features. "And these fold down." She lowered a tray attached to the front seat and then showed me a small cabinet in the center. It contained two small glasses and a bottle of alcohol. "Aren't they wonderful?"

"Fancy."

"Let me give you a ride. Where are you heading?"

"Don't bother. I'm going home. It's too far out."

Her blond eyebrows drew together. "Were you planning to walk?"

"I was going to take the train as far as it would go and walk the rest of the way. Or call a cab."

"Nonsense." Lenore snapped her fingers. "Charles, take us to the park with the clock tower—the one by the train station." She sat back and fiddled with her grey sleeves. "I need to start learning all the street names again. It's been so long, and so much has changed. Did you know this street was once filled with brothels? Whores as far as the eye could see."

I bit my tongue. "So what are you doing up at this hour?"

"I was on my way to work when I heard the good news."

I arched an eyebrow. "What good news?"

"The cat's out of the bag, darling. I'm Viktor's primary contact for your assignment. I'm beyond thrilled that we captured so many. I only have the preliminary report, but would you believe that at least *twenty* serve the higher authority?" She shook her head in disgust. "Five right here in Cognito, and the rest are in cities throughout the country. It looks like another power shift is on the horizon."

"Is that why Christian was guarding you?"

She folded her hands on her lap. "Do you find his insolence tiresome? A woman like yourself would be better matched with a man in power. Many power couples are still together. If you ever find yourself single, I have *just* the person in mind. I used to play matchmaker in my time, and I'm quite good at it."

"I'm sure."

"Gracious. Is that blood in your hair?"

I picked at the top of my head and felt a clump. While I'd taken a shower at the auction house, Christian and I were too preoccupied in there to bother with things like shampoo and soap.

"I have something for you." Lenore reached down into her bag. Before she sat up again, she swung back her arm and stabbed me in the chest.

Chapter 34

IT TOOK A SECOND TO register that Lenore had driven a dagger just inches away from my heart. The pain was indescribable, and it had happened so fast that I still had my hands above my head, picking a clump of blood from my hair. The blade split my rib and pierced my lung.

"I do hate getting blood on my seats," she said while sitting back. "Driver, you know where to go."

I yanked the blade out and coughed up a lungful of blood. When I gave her a bloodcurdling look, she sat frozen, eyes wide with disbelief. That bitch had stabbed me with a stunner.

I reached for the window and pulled in healing sunlight. The wound on my chest instantly healed, leaving my white tank top stained with blood. "I bet you're wondering why I'm not paralyzed."

She might have assumed I was a Blocker with special abilities, but I suppose it was my fangs that gave me away.

Lenore flew at me. I swiped the blade at whatever I could, and when it sliced her jaw, I turned my head away from the dripping blood. While her blood could give me strength, Christian had warned me about the unpredictable power of Vampire blood. Lenore had used it to control him for many years, and though rejecting it could be my demise, drinking it would most certainly be my downfall.

Lenore disarmed me, splintered the wooden footrest with one blow, and drove a piece of that wood into my chest. When I smiled, her jaw slackened. I used my free hand to punch her, but it was like smashing my fist against marble. Her cheek split but healed immediately, just as the cut on her jaw had. Lenore yanked out the wood, and the pain was enough to make me stiffen.

Then she leaned in close and reeled me in. "Follow my gaze, Raven. Look nowhere else. The pain is too much, isn't it? You want nothing more than to feel relief and peace. Lie still. Your muscles are useless. You can't speak and you can't move. Not until you're surrounded in darkness will the spell be broken. Now then, we can have a conversation."

When Lenore sat back, I stared at the ceiling, unable to move. A strange euphoria came over me as all the pain melted away along with the sensation in my body. I couldn't feel the temperature or even the seat beneath me. But I could see, and I could hear.

Lenore sighed. "I suppose Christian knows about this. No *wonder*." She reached over and tucked my bag behind my head so I could see her. "I don't like it when things get messy. I plan meticulously, but I couldn't have prepared myself for a half-breed. Immortals like you are an abomination. Immune to both stunners *and* impalement wood? That's an impressive gift. There's so much I'd love to ask you. Like why you don't have physical power or black eyes. Or are those supposed to be the top half of Chitah fangs?" Lenore brushed at the bloodstains on her blouse. "While I could call it fortuitous that we ran into each other, I'm more inclined to think it's serendipitous. The fates gave you to me. You're an important figure, and I'm sorry that I didn't recognize that earlier. You won me a victory in more ways than one, and now I can be rid of you."

Be rid of me? Who the hell did this woman think she was?

"Before you're blinded by jealousy, it's not Christian's love that interests me. I want his loyalty, and I'll never have that as long as you're in the picture. I'm sure you know that he's loyal to a fault, and that's worth more than gold. You have too much influence over him, and if I were to make you leave Keystone, he would follow."

What the hell was she talking about? How could she make me leave Keystone? Unless working for the higher authority gave her a lot of power over how Viktor ran his organization, but he had never given me that impression.

"You make Christian weak," she continued. "He gave you his heart, and as long as you have it, you'll be the one who rules over him. Don't take it personally. I don't hate you, darling. In fact, I admire your potential. In another life, I might have mentored you. But as it stands, you're a liability. I could charm you to find out how much Christian has divulged about our past, but it doesn't matter." She smiled obliquely and leaned in. "I bet you don't even realize that I've charmed you before. Remember when I asked what your passion was, and you answered, 'killing men'? I'm so good at what I do that you can't even feel it. Both you and Christian are equally valuable to me, and I see potential in each of you. This wasn't an easy decision to make."

I tried to move my pinky, but I couldn't feel my body. Not my arms, my legs, not even the sun on my face. All I could do was blink and breathe.

Lenore gazed out the window as the buildings blurred by. "I have ambitious plans, and I won't make the same mistakes twice. Raven, I want you to consider what's happening to you very carefully. You still owe me a large favor for the money, and we return favors in our world. It's never what we desire, but it's the only thing that keeps order—the only currency we can count on. And those who don't pay up will live to regret it. I want to give you peace of mind that you're clearing your debt with me. No matter how you feel about what's happening to you, just know that when it's all over, we'll be even."

The more she talked, the more fearful I became. Was she making me her indentured servant? Or was I about to go on the chopping block? The latter put a chill up my spine. Just the thought of lying in a guillotine, unable to move because of this stupid spell, made me sick to my stomach. Even worse was the level of trust that Lenore had been building between us. She kept trying to twist my relationship with Christian around, and though I'd never doubted him, I'd felt empathy for Lenore because there were always two sides to a story. I had fallen for it.

Now I just wanted to watch her burn on a pyre.

The buildings disappeared from view, replaced by the occasional tree. The car slowed and then stuttered across a rocky surface. I'd busted my ass to catch the perpetrators behind a fighting ring, and I'd rescued Shifters held captive. I'd also had a hand in capturing all the nefarious players who'd paid to play, thanks to Keystone's quick thinking. I'd survived two fights—one of them a death match—and *this* was how I was going out?

The car came to a stop, and the driver exited the vehicle. When my door opened, my head flew back.

"Don't leave behind any evidence," she said, getting out on the other side. "I want you to clean the back seat when we get home and put this car into the garage and out of view. Replace the interior if you have to, but be discreet." Her voice fell out of range.

The driver dragged me out of the car, and my head flopped forward so my hair curtained my view. He immediately lifted me into his arms and carried me a short way. I smelled freshly cut grass as it hissed beneath his shoes, and I could see the blue sky through my hair.

"Dump her bag before we get home. I don't want her things in my possession," Lenore continued.

My bag! My boots were in there—the boots with the tracking device. Why did I have to go and change into my sneakers? Because I planned on walking home, not getting carried to my death. How would Keystone ever find my body? Tears welled in my eyes when I thought of the last time I'd seen my father. I couldn't bear to think of him going through this all over again. Never having closure.

"Be sure you pay the caretaker extra for his cooperation."

Extra. Despite Lenore rambling on about coincidence, this hadn't been a chance meeting. She had planned this. Perhaps she had Christian watch over her to keep us apart. But what if she'd made him an offer? One he couldn't refuse?

The driver placed me in something soft and padded, and it took a minute to realize I was in a coffin.

Lenore hovered over me, the sunlight in her hair. "It took me a little time to learn about you, Raven Black. Or should I say, Raven Graves? Your poor mother was so young. I thought it was only fitting that you two were buried together, so imagine my surprise when I found your headstone next to hers. We paid the caretaker to exhume the coffin—it's amazing what humans are willing to do for money. I'm curious about the burned remains inside. I removed it, of course. I'm not a monster. You really went out of your way to fake your death, didn't you? What a grim irony that this is where you ended up after all." She locked eyes with me. "Speak, Raven. You can't move, but you can speak."

A growl escaped my throat. I wanted to tell her exactly where she could go and what I was going to do to her when I got out, but at this point my only chance might be reasoning with the wench. "You gave me all that advice. Don't you want to mentor me? I thought your purpose was to empower women."

"Not you, Raven. You're the last person I want with power. All those women and men you arrested today were bad apples—unfit for leadership. Oligarchs run this city, and their time is coming to an end. There are stronger women who will assume their roles, and I'll see to that. In another life, you could have been one of those women. But right now you're the only thing that stands between me and what I want."

"Christian? You called him weak."

"And he is. But I know how to manipulate him. You don't. You squander that power, and that simply will not do."

"Why not kill me? You could send Keystone the body. Otherwise, they'll be looking for me."

A smile touched her pink lips. "This is so much more suspenseful, don't you think? I don't like blood on my hands. Never did. That's why I didn't kill Christian. You won't die either, Raven. Well, probably not. I've never buried a Mage before. I've heard even bones can regenerate, but maybe that's just an urban legend. As long as you still draw breath, there's still hope. A Mage doesn't have to breathe. It won't be comfortable, but that's not something I can help. My burying Christian made him who he is today. You don't deserve to die, and someday you'll thank me for this. You'll see that the only way we truly grow is to suffer."

It made me wonder when she had suffered last.

"Don't do this. I'm not your enemy. But if you put me in the ground, you better spend the rest of your life looking over your shoulder, because someday I'm going to claw my way out of here."

"That I don't doubt. But all that hostility you have will fade, darling. Otherwise, Christian would have tried killing me. But he hasn't, because he knows I gave him a gift. And he also gained enough perspective to realize that emotions are a weakness. This is something you'll have a lot of time to reflect on." Lenore tidied a loose lock of her hair before reeling me in with her gaze. "Set your internal clock, Mage. In thirty minutes, you'll have forgotten our conversation. You won't remember seeing me in the car, speaking to me, any of the things we talked about, or my driver carrying you to the grave. Your last memory will be stepping outside the White Owl and crossing the street to the donut shop. Goodbye, Raven."

"Don't do this! You can't just leave me here!"

"Coffins are more luxurious than they used to be. You have a nice pillow and lots of padding. Poor Christian. He had none of these luxuries."

The casket closed, and I heard something turn and click on the side.

Oh God, the casket key.

Immersed in darkness, I felt my limbs tingling, and the feeling returned. My heart pounded against my rib cage as the coffin lowered. I immediately thrust my hands upward at the lid and pushed with all my might. I cursed and cried as I punched against the coffin lid. Despite the padding, I was certain I'd bloodied my knuckles. The heavy sound of dirt thumped against the lid of the coffin, and reality began to sink in.

"Do you hear me?" I shouted, my voice trapped inside the small space. "I'm going to make you regret that you didn't kill me."

I could almost imagine her laughing, because it was Lenore who would have the last laugh. She'd scrubbed my memories of the entire affair, and the clock was ticking. It was only a matter of time before I'd be trapped in the dark with no memory of how I got here.

Fear evaporates when you're fighting for your life. But when you strip away the element of danger, you're confronted with that fear. I was going to suffocate in this coffin, and it would be a slow and agonizing ordeal. As my life flashed before my eyes, I went completely still and slowed my breathing.

Conserve your air.

Even if I had consumed Lenore's blood, she would've still charmed me. And I had doubts that I could break out of the heavy weight of earth above. This wasn't a movie. How exactly did all those undead zombies punch through their coffins and climb through two tons of dirt?

Stupid filmmakers. Think, Raven, think.

How long would it take before Keystone realized I was missing? Christian might wait until dusk before worrying. He knew how I liked to go off and do my own thing.

I shut my eyes. *Oh shit.* Eventually Christian would go searching. And his first stop would be the White Owl. Then he'd run into Houdini and realize that I'd kept that a secret from him. Lenore would continue to work him over like putty until he didn't know up from down. He'd give up looking, thinking I'd deceived him somehow. All the possibilities made me cover my face.

Worst of all, my mother was only a few feet over. I'd visited her grave many times, and there was always comfort looking at her name on the headstone while I told her about my life. But down here, in the dark, my mind went elsewhere. I thought about that fateful night of the fire when she plunged through the weak floor and into the flames. I imagined what a painful death that was and how the last horrific thoughts that went through her mind were that she'd failed at saving me from the same fate. I had so few memories of her, and I clung to them. I heard stories about how soldiers dying on battlefields cried out for their mothers, and I always thought that it would be Crush's name on my lips. But as I lay there in the dark, all I wanted was my mother. I wanted to feel her embrace one last time and hear her soothing words telling me that she loved me and everything would be okay. Maybe it should have been my life taken that night instead of hers.

"I'm sorry, Mom. I tried my best to make something of myself. I know it's not the life you imagined, and I guess in the end, I got what I deserved." I gasped, overcome with grief, and then blew out a calming breath.

It wouldn't be long before I forgot everything, and then I'd have to go through this panic all over again. How many hours of oxygen did I have? Sometimes Wyatt struck up morbid conversations, and I tuned them out, but it seemed like I remembered him saying a few hours. Maybe five? Could I still scream when the air ran out?

Vampires used to be staked and buried, and the only people who could locate them were Gravewalkers. But I was more than a Vampire—I was a Mage. Maybe flaring would attract a nearby Mage.

But in a human cemetery?

How many days would it take?

How many years?

Would I wither away like a dried-up flower? If found, would I even want them to resuscitate me? I couldn't even end my own life—not without a match or a long blade. Then I thought about Christian and the full decade he'd spent underground. With the impalement wood in his chest, he couldn't move. All he could do was lie still and slowly go insane with his own thoughts.

No wonder he had such a short temper.

And now I was about to embark on the same dark journey. I would finally know what he had experienced—not knowing if I'd ever be found, not knowing how long I could endure it all. And I'd only been in here less than a few minutes.

I waited. Waited for the tide of panic to drown me once my memories swept away like a current going out to sea. Waited for my lungs to squeeze tightly when the air ran out and I drowned in darkness. Waited to see if I'd pass out, and if so, for how long. Waited to see when the starvation would consume my every thought. Waited for the bargaining to begin of all the things I would do if only the fates would let me out. Waited to see how long it would take to go insane.

I waited to see the real Raven Black unmasked—the one who lived beneath my skin. The dark and primal core of me—a side that most people never got to see within themselves.

If they were lucky.

Chapter 35

CHRISTIAN STOOD AT KEYSTONE'S FRONT window and looked outside. After searching Flynn's apartment and collecting what evidence he could gather, he'd driven home. It didn't come as a surprise when Raven didn't return. Sometimes after a job, she would treat herself at Ruby's Diner or walk around the city. Sometimes she liked to sit atop buildings or visit her old stomping grounds. He respected her privacy and desire for solitude after a stressful assignment. Since she didn't have a phone on her, all he could do was wait. Patience was something he had an abundance of.

Claude attempted in vain to sneak up and lock his arm around Christian's shoulder, but you can't sneak up on a Vampire. "Come drink with us."

"I don't want to be langered before Raven gets here. It's not even dark."

"I'm not asking you to get drunk. Just have a drink. If Raven wanted to celebrate with us, she'd be here. Viktor just cracked open a three-hundred-year-old bottle, and I think I lost feeling in my lips." Claude leaned toward the window and squinted. "Did she call? Is she on her way?"

Christian sidestepped to distance himself and leaned against the wall, arms folded. "She doesn't have her phone with her. I left a message with her da. She might have gone for a visit."

"My sources say no," Claude replied, swaying.

"Your sources are unreliable."

Claude pointed outside. "My source is riding up the road."

Once Christian unsuppressed his hearing, he heard the distinct sound of a motorcycle. He opened the door and stood outside as Crush rolled up. The old man wore a bandana secured around his head, dark shades on his eyes, and a scowl that seemed to be a genetic trait in the family. Crush throttled the bike before shutting off the engine.

Claude hugged Christian from behind. "I'll leave you two alone to kill each other."

The door closed, but Christian kept his eyes locked on Crush.

Raven's dad strutted up to Christian, putting more weight on his right knee than his left. The man was falling apart before his very eyes.

"And what the feck are you doing here?"

"You don't call me asking if I've seen my baby girl. If *you* don't know where the fuck she is, then something isn't right. Now what's going on?"

"Let's go inside. The sun bothers my eyes."

Crush pulled the lining out of his pockets. "I'm all out of fucks to give."

"We finished our assignment. No troubles. Everything was fine, so Raven and I separated to tie up a few loose ends. She seemed weary, and I thought she'd be back by now. That was this morning."

"And she doesn't have a phone on her?"

Christian shook his head. "I can't imagine she would have walked the whole way home. I assumed she had enough money for a cab."

"Get your bike. Let's go."

There was no point arguing. Crush was on a mission, and Christian needed an excuse to leave the house and become an overbearing lover. Viktor had been gushing over Raven's accomplishments all day, and he rarely did that with anyone. Most of them had slept through the morning after getting back home, and following a late lunch, Viktor broke out the wine, and it all went to hell in a handbasket after that. They were merry and drunk, Kira bringing out a continual parade of food. It didn't seem right celebrating without Raven, so after calling the hotel and finding out that she'd checked out early that morning, Christian paced the halls. An hour later, he left a message with Crush. That man must have sped over like a bullet, because he'd forgotten his wallet from the looks of the faded rectangular mark on his empty back pocket.

At least the sun would be down soon. Once Christian fired up the Ducati, he followed Crush down to the gate and then sped in front of him. Crush suddenly appeared to his left and gave him a death scowl before falling back. Christian didn't know all the social rules when it came to the biker lifestyle, and he didn't give a shite. Crush wouldn't know where to look, and Christian's first instinct was to retrace her steps. She'd mentioned going to the White Owl and the hotel.

Raven was probably having a burger and beer, yet worry nestled deep in his spine. Something wasn't right. Somehow Crush felt it too. Perhaps because they shared the same blood.

But so did Christian and Raven. Not in the same way, but her blood still lingered in his veins as his did in hers, and maybe that connection was more powerful than he could have realized.

Or maybe now that he actually cared about someone in this world, all he could think about was the fear of losing her and what life might be like without Raven to keep him grounded.

They pulled up to the club around dusk. Instead of locating a parking lot, Christian jumped the curb and parked his Ducati by the building. A line of people shot him baleful looks, but Christian ignored the humans as he approached the doorman.

Crush parked his Harley on the street and dismounted.

"Your kind isn't allowed." The bouncer reached inside his sports jacket and flashed impalement wood at Christian. Then he flicked a glance at Crush. "Are you two together?"

Christian glowered. "He's not my type. Now if you'll kindly step out of the way, I won't detach your miniature head from your disproportionately large body."

The man slowly shook his head. "Don't start trouble. You don't want trouble."

Christian stood toe to toe, nose to nose. "Aye, I want trouble."

The man's phone vibrated. He answered, eyes still locked on Christian.

"Let them in," Christian heard a voice on the line say.

The man ground his teeth as he hung up and reluctantly opened the door.

Crush fell into step beside Christian in the dark hall. "What did he mean by *your kind*?"

"No Vampires. He couldn't say it in front of an audience. Not all clubs allow my Breed."

"Huh. I thought he meant peckerheads."

The techno bass assailed Christian's ears, so he made a volume adjustment to tone it down.

"What the fuck is this?" Crush stared at a woman tied to a wooden X.

Christian gripped the old man by the collar and yanked him away. "If you'd rather fool around, I can do this alone."

"I've never seen that out in the open."

"Best you stay downstairs then. It's usually raunchier on the higher floors, and we wouldn't want you keeling over from cardiac arrest." Christian stopped and scoped the bar. He needed to figure out where the offices were so he could speak to a manager.

Women and men were gyrating inside human-size birdcages. Others were leading around submissives on leashes. A lady covered entirely in latex gave Christian a seductive wink before unzipping her mouth and licking her lips.

They made their way toward a hallway in the back. A large man, hands clasped in front, took a step to block him. "The old man stays here."

"He's with me."

The guard shook his head. "The owner won't speak to you unless the human remains here."

"Just go," Crush ordered him. "I'll keep the numbskull company."

Christian blew past the guard, attuned to the sounds behind each door. When he heard whistling, he knocked.

"Enter."

Christian stepped inside and closed the door behind him. The first thing that grabbed his attention in the dark room was all the screens displaying images of the club, inside and out.

The chair behind the desk turned. Houdini regarded Christian with a pensive stare. "To what do I owe the pleasure?"

Christian marched up to the desk and pressed his fingers against the wood. "Well, well. If it isn't the devil incarnate."

"Isn't that the pot calling the kettle black? Did you come here to settle a score? Or did Raven not tell you about our conversations, and jealousy is afoot."

"Where is she?"

"I could have let you stand outside, so use my time wisely."

"And I could have knocked out that pinhead and walked right in."

Houdini put his hands on his lap, his demeanor cool. "I would have seen it and bolted the outside door. In case you didn't notice, there aren't windows. My building is Vampire proof."

Christian stood erect. "I find that rather ironic."

"State your business."

"I'm here for Raven."

"You're serious, aren't you?" Houdini rose from his seat and stood at the edge of the desk. He appeared flummoxed. "If she's missing, what makes you think I have anything to do with it?"

"Because you like to meddle. You've meddled in her creation and done an effective job gaslighting her. You kidnapped her once, and I suspect you had something to do with digging up the bodies of three Shifters who attacked us while we were on a job outside the country. I buried those bodies where no one would find them. Raven could have been jailed for that little incident, but you knew I'd take the blame, didn't you?"

Houdini put his hands in his pockets. "All in good fun."

Christian reeled in his contempt for this insipid excuse of a Vampire. "I suppose it's money you want."

Houdini sighed. "I'll shoot straight with you, Poe. I don't know where Raven is. I didn't search for her the first time, and I won't search for her now. If you've lost her, that's quite unfortunate. She was here this morning. We talked briefly, and then she left. Perhaps for good. Maybe she's finally discovered that the best life is lived outside of another's shadow."

"She's not in my shadow."

"No, but she's in Keystone's." Houdini swiveled around and sat in his seat. "If you don't mind, I have to address my staffing crisis and search for replacements. Should you know of anyone who won't screw me over, send them my way."

Christian paced toward the door and gripped the knob. "If I find out you're behind this, they don't have laws written for what I'll do to you. It won't be murder, I can tell you that much. But you'll pray for death."

"Isn't that what we all pray for in the quiet moments? Maybe you should ask yourself why finding Raven is so important to you. Goodbye, Poe."

After exiting the room, Christian stalked through the club, eager to get as far away from Houdini as possible. Crush jogged after him noisily, his boots stomping against the floor and change jingling in his pockets. Distracted by his emotions, Christian let down his guard. The noisy world closed in on him. The clucking of tongues, thighs rubbing together, voices overlapping, whips cracking, the deafening sound of a hundred hearts beating, loud music, and the clinking of glasses.

Once outside, he paced to the corner and anchored his hands on his hips.

"Are you gonna tell me what the fuck happened in there?" Crush caught his breath and leaned on a lamppost. "Is that where Raven was working undercover? You let my little girl dance on those tables?"

"*Jaysus*, will you get your knickers out of a bunch? She was only working the bar. The job's over, but she wanted to go back and talk to someone. They said she left this morning without incident." Christian turned his eyes up at the buildings. "We can visit a few clubs we frequent, but I don't think she would have gone to those places alone."

"What about that diner—Ruby's? I can swing by there and ask around."

"Aye, that's a grand idea. After that, go home, you hear?"

"I'll go where I wanna go."

Christian wanted to get Crush uninvolved. He couldn't possibly know her whereabouts, and Raven wouldn't want him searching the dark corners of the city. "Perhaps she went to buy her da a nice present."

"That's not where she went. Something's wrong."

Christian looked back at him. "And what makes you so certain? Dreams?"

"A gut feeling. And I'm holding you accountable."

"It's hardly my fault."

Crush stepped up to him. "Anytime something bad happens to my daughter, here you are. When her mother died, there you were."

"I saved her life."

"Doesn't change the fact that you were there. Maybe you're a big scoop of bad luck."

"For feck's sake. Get on that infernal contraption of yours and ride off into the sunset, will ya? I have errands to run."

"I'll call you later," he growled, storming off. "And watch what you say about my Harley!"

Two women crossed the street and headed toward a donut shop. Christian tried to imagine where Raven might have gone, but there were a number of possibilities. She could be sitting on a random rooftop, or maybe she had fallen asleep on the train and wound up on the wrong side of the city.

He called Wyatt, and when he answered, there was singing in the background.

"Unless you're a hot chick, Wyatt's busy."

"Is Raven there? Has she called?"

Wyatt laughed, but it wasn't at Christian. Claude was finishing up a joke. "Nope. What's the scoop?"

"She's gone missing."

"Did you call her?"

"She doesn't have a phone, you eejit."

Wyatt flapped his lips together as he sighed. "Fine. I'm on my way upstairs. I'll look at her necklace and tell you if she's banging another man. Sure you're up for that, compadre?"

"She's not wearing the necklace. She left it at the scene."

"You two did the nasty, didn't you? Shame, shame."

"How much have you had to drink? I need your help, and you're busy killing brain cells."

Wyatt snorted. "They'll grow back."

Christian grimaced when a man whistled to get someone's attention. He shut out everything except Wyatt's drunken ramblings. "What about the tracker?"

"Good idea, Watson. Give me *uno momento, por favor.*"

Lights were popping on around the city, splashing color onto the dreary buildings.

After about a minute of Wyatt singing out of breath, he finally came back on. "Got it. Huh. That's really weird."

"What's the address?"

"The tracker shows she hasn't moved in almost ten hours."

Christian turned around to make sure no one had touched his bike. "Will you tell me where the feck she is?"

"Hold your ponies. I'm trying to pull up the street view on the internet. Did you know they pay people to drive around with a camera mounted on the car so they can film every single street? Back in my day, you had to do real work to earn a coin. It's pretty nifty though. I can look at neighborhoods without leaving the house."

"You're a canker sore. You know that?"

"I'm the life of the party. You can't deny it."

"Be that as it may, you have the attention span of a midge."

"Are you comparing me to a bug? You have more in common with a mosquito than I do a gnat."

"I can't fathom why the dead would seek your company."

"You need to lighten up. Eternity is a long time to be miserable.

All right. I'm looking at the street view, and there's nothing there. The picture was taken in February, so unless they built something in the past three months, she's hanging out on the corner of nowhere. The street's called Rustic Pines, just east of Walnut Grove. A field on one side with a bunch of overgrown grass, and… Yep. Same on the other. Maybe she threw out her shoes. Why does Walnut Grove sound familiar?" His fingers snapped. "Oh! What's the name of that old TV show—the one with the little girl running down a hill?"

"Wyatt, listen to me carefully. Raven's missing. It's not like her to disappear."

"Oh really? I seem to remember her skipping off to stay with her dad for all that time. Did you say something to piss her off? Wait, don't answer that. You piss everyone off."

"Keep your phone nearby. I'll call you back."

Christian didn't tarry. He weaved through traffic like a bullet until he reached Rustic Pines. While he hadn't necessarily been down every road in the city, he knew most of the main ones and a few of the alternate routes. Despite the headlamp from his bike lighting the way down the unlit street, he couldn't get his bearings. This area was unfamiliar to him, and when he reached Walnut Grove, he slowed his bike and looked around. The weeds were high, to be sure. If Raven had wandered out of range, it would be time consuming to search the wide stretch of land. What he needed was a tracker.

He called Wyatt. "Get your arse over here immediately. Bring anyone who's sober enough to search, but I want Claude. I need his nose."

"I think his nose is in a wineglass." Wyatt simultaneously hiccupped and burped. "Fine, fine. We're on our way, just as soon as I locate a designated driver."

Christian tried not to crush the phone in his grip. "I'm not playing around. Raven might be in danger."

"Wyatt Blessing to the rescue."

"*Jaysus wept.*"

Chapter 36

Rustic Pines was so rural that traffic was nonexistent. Nary a car in sight for the length of time that Christian had waded through the tall grass. His worst fear? Finding Raven's body. Maybe that was the reason he didn't hear a heartbeat other than his own and a few wild animals. He violently knocked the weeds aside, imagining what he might do if he stumbled upon those boots still on her feet. He'd seen firsthand how immortal love never lasted. When one of them died, it left the survivor bereft of feeling. Their lives often went in a downward spiral. Christian refused to let that happen to him. He would channel that rage into a destructive force that would lay waste to everyone responsible for her death.

A horn blared from the road.

Gem poked her head out of the window of the driver's side of the Keystone van. "Taxi! Someone said you needed a ride. What are we doing in the middle of nowhere?"

Christian rested his arms on the window and peered at Wyatt, who had his laptop open from the passenger seat. "Who's in the back?"

Claude stuck his head between the seats. "Did you find Raven?"

Christian shook his head. "I don't hear anything."

Gem's eyes widened. "Raven's missing? Why doesn't anyone ever tell me anything? You could have said something, Spooky!"

"You're driving, buttercup. I couldn't have you under the influence of panic."

"I'm getting out." Claude disappeared and jumped from the back of the van. He staggered before falling completely on his face.

"I'm out here with the Three Stooges," Christian murmured.

Claude bent his knees and reached out his hand. "I'm the soberest. Everyone else had to stay home. Blue passed out, and Niko said everyone's energy was mixing into one fantastic light show."

Christian jerked Claude to his feet. "And Shepherd?"

Claude snorted. "Do you want a drunken Shepherd on a search and rescue? He would shoot up this town." Claude stretched out his long arms and scanned the area. "Now, what do you want me to do?"

"The tracking device is out here. Find it."

"I still think she tossed out her shoes, and we're out here for nothing," Wyatt said.

Claude reached inside the back of the van and pulled out one of Raven's old shirts. After a deep breath, he threw it back. "It helps when my senses are impaired."

"You're langered. How much did you have to drink? Because I don't think you can walk a straight line, let alone track anyone's scent."

Claude narrowed his golden eyes and poked Christian's nose. "Challenge accepted." He ran at Chitah speed into the grass, but he also stumbled and fell.

Christian had seen the team drunk, but they were so inebriated it was a wonder they were still conscious. He strode back to the front of the van.

Gem reached out and picked grass off Christian's forehead. "I'm sure she'll turn up soon. I bet she's already back at the mansion. Did you have anyone check the roof? It's possible she got home hours ago and fell asleep up there. You know how she gets."

"Aye, I checked. She never made it home."

Worry filled her eyes, but Gem was searching for an explanation. "Maybe she had the same idea as you fellas and drank too much before attempting to walk home."

Christian gestured to Wyatt. "What's on that computer of yours?"

Wyatt opened up a plastic wrapper and admired a chocolate cake with white filling. "The blinking light."

Christian gave him an icy stare.

After chomping into his pastry, Wyatt set it down on the dash and put on his loose beanie. "Look, I'm three sheets to the wind. I smoked a doobie before you called, and maybe I had another drink for the road. If you get me worked up, I'm gonna get paranoid and have a panic attack. Nobody wants to see that."

Gem played with the quartz pendant around her neck. "I haven't heard the word doobie in an awfully long time. Did you know that they're starting to make it legal?"

Wyatt reached for his chocolate pastry. "If only I cared about human laws."

Christian tipped his head to the side. "You're not concerned about brain function?"

Wyatt furrowed his brow. "It's only temporary. It's not like it affects my hippopotamus."

Gem giggled. "You mean *hippocampus*."

"You see? Who needs the internet when you have a word nerd?"

Christian turned around as Claude approached the van.

Winded, Claude took a breath and swayed before tossing a bag at Christian. "Found the boots. Raven's scent is barely on them anymore. There's no scent trail, so it's probably been out here all day. I didn't see any footprints immediately around it, so I think she must have thrown it from the road. Maybe they carried too many bad memories of the club." Claude widened his eyes all of a sudden as if waking himself up. "What was in that bottle Viktor gave us?"

Wyatt licked his fingers. "I don't know, but some things aren't meant to ferment for that long." He pulled another cake from the box and used his teeth to open the plastic. "I still remember when they used to wrap these in foil. Why do you think they call them Ding Dongs?"

Christian pounded the top of the van and made everyone

jump. "What's nearby? Where the feck are we? This isn't the way home, so where was she going?"

Gem gazed through the front windshield. "I bet she got lost. That happened to me once while flashing. I got turned around and wandered outside city limits."

Wyatt nonchalantly wedged half the cake in his mouth and then took out his phone. After a few finger swipes, he set the half-eaten cake on his closed laptop. "Ten-mile radius shows a few farmhouses, a place that sells yard art—"

"Oh, I've always wanted to go to one of those places!" Gem chimed in before giving Christian a solemn look. "After we find Raven, that is."

Wyatt kept swiping, his upper lip coated with brown crumbs and white cream. "Nothing, nothing, a cemetery, a garden center, a gas station—"

"Go back to the cemetery," Christian said, fearing that Houdini had done the unthinkable. "How far?"

"Five minutes that way." Wyatt pointed straight ahead. "*Please* tell me we're not going to a cemetery. I can handle an old one, but this is a human cemetery. That means they've got freshies all over the place."

"Not my problem. Let's go."

Christian and Claude circled to the back and got in. While Gem took directions from Wyatt, Christian buried his face in his hands. Where could she be? After pulling himself together, he reached down and rifled through her bag. Raven must have switched out her shoes, because her sneakers were missing. Maybe she really did toss out the boots. Raven wasn't sentimental about such things, and would she be able to wear them again without associating them with a sex club? Aside from her boots, all he found in the bag were toiletries and clothes.

"Do you think someone took her?" Claude asked. "Maybe it was the man who recruited all the women."

That hadn't occurred to Christian. He'd never met this other fella, and he might want Raven out of the picture since she could identify him.

Claude leaned back. "I wager she's made a lot of enemies. It would be difficult to narrow them down. Do you think her Creator's behind it? That repugnant Mage is still out there somewhere."

"It's not him."

"How can you be so sure?"

"It's not his style."

Claude rubbed his nose. "All the same, I think it would be prudent to narrow down suspects."

Hearing Claude talk about suspects was making this frighteningly real. It was too convenient for there to be a cemetery on this road, and Christian had a gut feeling that Raven was there.

"We're here," Wyatt sang. "Human cemeteries: the thing nightmares are made of. Look, there's a freshy right there."

Gem slapped his arm. "Well, don't *look* at him!"

"I can't help it! I'm seeing double, so I don't know which way *not* to look."

The van came to an abrupt stop. "The gates are locked." Gem turned in her seat and gave Christian a pointed look.

Taking her signal, he hopped out of the van and busted the locks. Gem slowly steered through the open gates, the high beams providing the only light.

Wyatt hopped out, dressed for the occasion in a long-sleeved shirt. Two cartoonish eyes looked to the side with I SEE DEAD PEOPLE written below them. He might as well have been a walking billboard for Gravewalkers.

Wyatt finished his cake and then tucked his thumbs in his jeans pockets. "So what makes you think the love of your life is *here*? From my experience, when someone buries an immortal, they don't do it in a high-traffic cemetery where someone might see them digging around. This is like the dead's version of a mall. People doing sketchy burials go to old graveyards that are full up—ones with stones that are so broken that you can't even tell if it's a rock or a headstone."

Gem's long grey duster appeared translucent in front of the van's headlights. She bent her leg and propped her white Doc

Marten against the fender. "Maybe she's not here. Where else does that road lead?"

Wyatt joined their circle. "Nowhere. It eventually dead-ends. There's this or the local dump."

"My vote is for the cemetery," Claude cut in. "You take the dump."

Wyatt chortled, and Gem put her hands on her ears as if sensing a distasteful joke on the horizon.

Christian snapped his fingers, his patience thinning. "Do your magic, Spooky. Walk the perimeter."

"The perimeter? Do you know how many acres this place has? I can't see in front of my nose, and if I don't kill myself tripping over a headstone, I'll be so distracted by the ghosties that I won't be able to focus."

Christian's fangs punched out, and he gripped Wyatt by the collar. "Then find a way to focus."

"I need to look for a flashlight."

Claude pointed at a large shed. "What's in there?"

Christian didn't hear anything inside, but he broke the locks and opened the door.

Claude poked his head in and drew in a deep breath. "The female isn't here."

Incensed, Christian stalked by Wyatt, who was beating on the end of an inoperable flashlight. "Do your job. I'll start on the far side if that makes it easier."

Once Christian distanced himself from the van headlights, he shadow walked through the cemetery. They all looked the same. A tree here, a tree there, statues, benches, sometimes a mausoleum. He didn't like spending his time in cemeteries, not since his own long-term residency.

After fifteen minutes, he finished checking every grave in the back for fresh sod or upturned soil. In the distance, Gem called for Raven, and hearing her name shouted into the void with no reply splintered his heart.

"I can't pick up anything," Claude huffed before collapsing in a heap by a headstone. "Someone urinated on a statue though."

Gem dawdled toward them, her eyes wide and arms outstretched. "This place gives me the heebie-jeebies. I can't see a thing! Where's Wyatt? I thought he was getting a flashlight."

"He probably passed out in the van," Claude grumbled. "My head is spinning. Everything's spinning."

Before either Claude or Gem heard anything, Christian picked up the sound of an electric vehicle. But the noise was quickly drowned out by keyboard synthesizers that erased the silence.

Claude stood and squinted at the fast-approaching vehicle. "Is he playing 'The Final Countdown' in a cemetery?"

A golf cart weaved around headstones and trampled the plaques on the ground. Wyatt not only had headlights mounted to the vehicle but flashlights taped to the bars that held up the roof.

As soon as the lyrics to the eighties song kicked in, he moved in a snakelike motion toward them. After another reckless minute, he clipped a bench and lost control. Wyatt flew out of the vehicle and rolled across the grass.

"Now that's a bloody shame," Christian said with derision.

The golf cart rolled toward them and slowed to a stop.

Wyatt sprang to his feet and wiped the grass from his pants. "I didn't pick up any vibes in the front. I searched every plot, but they haven't buried anyone recently."

Gem put her hands on her hips. "Wyatt Blessing, are you trying to get us arrested?"

Wyatt swaggered up to the cart. "Music and flashing lights distract the dead. If specters are hanging around a cemetery, it means they like the peace and quiet."

When the chorus kicked in again, Christian approached the vehicle and smashed the radio. "If she's yelling for help, I won't be able to hear a fecking thing, you numpty."

Gem cupped her arms and shivered. "Did you feel that?"

Wyatt leaned against the cart. "It's not cold, buttercup. But I'm more than happy to lend you my body for heat."

She reached behind her head and rubbed the back of her neck. "That's an energy flare. I knew it! But it's far away." Gem turned in a circle. "Maybe that direction? Did anyone check the middle?"

"Hop on the Wyatt express." Wyatt got behind the wheel, and Gem sat next to him. There was a bench on the back that Claude took.

"Don't you want a ride?" Wyatt offered.

"I'd rather walk."

"Suit yourself." With glazed eyes, Wyatt saluted Christian and hit the gas pedal. As soon as he did, Claude flew off the back seat and did a face-plant in the grass.

Christian helped him up. "Let me impart some wisdom on you that'll save you a lot of grief: never entrust your life to a wanker." He clapped Claude's back. "There's a good lad."

The crickets were chirping, but they had nothing on Wyatt singing the lyrics to the eighties song, which no longer played on the broken radio. There was no wind or nearby traffic, no airplanes overhead or people. It was one reason Christian kept his little concrete shack in the woods. He had always appreciated a quiet retreat—one far removed from the noisy pollution of city life.

Wyatt put distance between them, his lights shining on trees, headstones, and a skittish raccoon. As Christian shadow walked behind them, he got a sinking feeling in the pit of his stomach. Wyatt's cart turned right and headed toward a mausoleum.

"No, not that way. *That* way," Gem argued. "Will you let me drive? You're going to get us killed!"

"We're in the right place, buttercup."

When Christian passed the mausoleum, he recognized the structure and realized exactly where they were. This was the cemetery where Raven's mother was buried. All graveyards looked alike to him, and on his previous visit, he'd hidden himself on top of Raven's vehicle, ignoring the route. It had also been in the day, and shadows made everything look different.

He searched for familiar markers, trying to retrace his steps. Wyatt's headlights briefly blinded him before he steered away erratically. After walking in circles, Christian stopped and turned, looking around. It all looked the same. He could read the names on the headstones until he found Raven's mother, but not without going up to each and every one. Had she come here to talk to her mother? He imagined her passed out on top of the grave. It hadn't even occurred to him that she might come here, but he sometimes forgot how young Raven was. It often took many decades for a young immortal to let go of their old life and all the people tied to it.

Gem launched out of the cart while it was still moving and landed on her rear. She angrily dusted off her leggings before Claude helped her up. "I lost it, Christian. I can't feel the flare anymore. Maybe it was someone by the road."

Claude pulled in a deep breath. "I smell freshly turned soil." He hurried forward, Christian and Gem jogging behind him.

Raven's father thought he'd buried her years ago, so Raven had a grave next to her mother. As soon as Christian noticed the fresh sod, he fell to his knees and used his hands to dig. When Claude saw the name on the headstone, he joined in.

"Someone's *definitely* down there." Wyatt parked the cart and stumbled out of the seat. "And judging by *that* guy's face, the residents aren't too thrilled about it."

Christian didn't bother asking Wyatt about whatever apparition he was referring to. He just kept digging.

"This is impossible." Claude sat back, his hands caked in dirt. "It'll take all night."

A blue light showered the ground, and they looked over their shoulder. Gem wielded an energy ball between her fingertips. "Let me help. Please, Christian. If she's running out of air, we don't have time."

"Lass, put that away. Do you want to blow a hole through her mother's coffin?"

"I can do it! A lady's been teaching me how to control my energy. Stand back and let me show you."

The two men slowly got up and backed away. Claude looked as white as any ghost that was probably watching.

"It might blow up her headstone. Is that okay?" Gem asked, her voice as innocent as a child's.

"Aye, that can be replaced. But if your aim isn't true, you might kill her for sure. If you can't control it, don't risk it."

Gem's eyebrows drew together as she focused on the light spinning between her fingers. Instead of growing larger like it normally did, it grew tighter and more compact. Wyatt clutched his hat and dove behind the cart. When a few white sparks flickered from the core, Gem raised her arm and hurled the ball at the ground.

The explosive impact knocked everyone off their feet.

Christian stuck his fingers in his ringing ears as he sat up. A charred stench filled the air. Claude waved away the haze of dirt, the lights on the cart illuminating every particle of debris.

Wyatt hurried over and peered into the crater. "Holy Toledo! She blew a hole to China."

Christian jumped into the pit without looking. Gem had aimed off-center, so the hole wasn't invading Raven's mother's plot. Christian found it easy to sweep the loose dirt aside until he knocked against the coffin.

"Shut your eyes," he said loudly, hoping Raven could hear him.

Christian punched through the wood before shoving his hand inside and breaking off the top half. He flung it out of the hole, and Wyatt cursed before the lid thumped against the ground.

Nothing could have prepared him for that moment. Though twice buried, Christian had never imagined that Raven would endure the same horror. He sat on the bottom half of the casket and waited. Her eyes were still beneath the closed lids, and when someone shined a flashlight into the coffin, Gem gasped.

"Tell me she's not dead," Gem whimpered, shocked by Raven's purple complexion.

Christian looked at the blood on her tank top by a tear no wider than a dagger. There were also small spatters in another area. She must have put up a hell of a fight before healing herself. He reached out and touched her feverish cheek. Her heartbeat was faint, like a distant drip from a bathroom faucet.

He shook her. "*Breathe*, Raven. Wake up! You're not dead."

Her mouth suddenly opened and made a horrific sound as she pulled in oxygen. Christian watched her chest heave and body arch grotesquely, as if she were some undead creature coming to life. The second gasp was smoother than the first, but her reflexes kicked in and she clawed at thin air.

"Tell her she's okay," Gem said between sniffles. "She's okay, isn't she?"

Claude slid into the grave behind Christian. "Pull her out of there."

"Give her a minute," Christian said, his voice as sharp as a razor's edge.

"A minute for what?"

Christian looked over his shoulder at the Chitah. "To wake herself up from death. You can't just jerk a man out of his own coffin."

"He's right," Wyatt said from above. "Boy, does this bring back memories. Doesn't it, Christian?"

Raven's skin coloring slowly returned, but the capillaries had burst, giving her a sunburned appearance. She opened her eyes and gaped up as if she couldn't see the two men crouched on her coffin. Her eyes had hemorrhaged and were bloodshot.

"We're here, Raven," he said calmly. "You're not dead, and you're not permanently blind. It goes away."

Christian made a fist when she touched her face. Her knuckles were bloodied and bruised. She must have spent hours trying to punch a hole through the coffin.

"Get me out of here," Raven croaked. She sat up and reached out blindly until she found Christian's knees. "How long?"

"No more than a day."

"A day?" she asked in disbelief.

He knew that feeling. Once the air ran out, time moved differently.

"Who did this," he asked, his voice low and dangerous.

She shook her head. "I don't know."

Christian helped her to stand and then encased her in his arms as if she might fly away from this world at any moment.

Claude dipped his head into the casket and then stood. "It's been too long, Christian. I can't pick up another scent. All that's left is rage, fear, and sweat."

Christian felt as if a piece of him had returned. "I found you," he whispered, nuzzling against her hair. "I won't let you go."

Chapter 37

CHRISTIAN STARED INTO THE FIREPLACE. The wood was now ashen and brittle, and deep cracks exposed the intense heat within. Though it wasn't winter anymore, the mansion held a chill at night that affected the others. He looked over his shoulder at Raven, still asleep in his bed.

More like passed out.

On the drive home, it had taken her ten or fifteen minutes before she could breathe without hyperventilating. Christian remembered the process of getting acclimated to oxygen after resurfacing from the ground the first time he was buried. The second time was in Martha Cleavy's tomb, but thankfully that one wasn't airtight. There hadn't been much room in the back of the van with Christian's bike inside, so Raven sat in his lap, her face nestled in the crook of his neck as she drank his blood. Nothing was more natural to a Vampire than drinking blood, and Raven had no need to ask. While he had warned her about the dangers of Vampire blood, Christian would always offer his own to ease her suffering.

What came as a surprise was that afterward, Raven snapped out of it and was herself again. Maybe it was Claude constantly asking if she needed anything, but Raven did everything in her power to allay everyone's fears by cracking jokes and asking about their drinking party. Gem's worry faded just as quickly as she told the story about the energy ball. Viktor didn't know about her disappearance or that some of them had left, so she asked them not to mention it when they got home. She wanted to celebrate, and Viktor wouldn't be able to enjoy his victory if he had to learn about this one minor detail of her getting buried alive.

She had no memory of who put her in the ground or what happened just prior, only that she had last spoken to the club owner. She never mentioned Houdini by name, and Christian didn't press the subject. At first he thought she might be protecting her Vampire maker, but the more Christian thought about it, he realized that she was protecting *him*—afraid of what Christian might do.

Once home, Viktor congratulated Raven on the job, invited her for a drink—which she accepted—and apprised her of everything that had transpired since her disappearance. The total number captured, how many worked for the higher authority, details about the data Wyatt confiscated, and some who'd even provided the Shifters. The fights had been going on for decades, and the higher authority even planned to bust those who no longer attended the matches but were in the records. This was officially the largest crime ring in Cognito history, one that spanned decades and international borders. The public wouldn't be that surprised to hear about the secret death matches, but come tomorrow morning, they would be stunned to hear the names of those involved. People they looked up to and trusted, many of whom were women. Blue remarked that it would shake the foundation on which women had struggled to build. Many had fought for their independence and had tough beginnings, so it was a disappointment to see how a handful of bad apples could set them back.

Raven had said "good riddance" as those women weren't ones they wanted in power anyhow. And she was right. Regardless of gender or Breed, there had to be a purge every so often to flush out all the shite.

After Viktor had gone to bed, Wyatt entertained the others with his account of the rescue, which changed by the fifth retelling. Christian couldn't help but notice how Raven listened with a brave face, minimizing the experience as the others would have done. Hell, like any immortal would have done. Death and mayhem were par for the course. Raven continued drinking long after everyone had gone to bed, and Christian sat with her before inviting her upstairs.

Once alone, he had asked her about her peculiar behavior. She replied, "I didn't want Viktor to see me shaken up like I can't handle a bad break. It was bad enough that Wyatt, Claude, and Gem saw the whole thing, but two of them were drunk, so maybe they'll remember it differently in the morning. Gem panics about everything, but she's one of those people who always looks on the bright side of life."

Madness ensued rather quickly during a burial, most of the terror occurring in the first few hours after the oxygen ran out. When he invited Raven to talk about it now that they were alone, she grabbed a bottle of tequila and said, "Don't put me on the therapy couch. Look at Blue. She almost died and has all those scars, but she bounced back and proved how tough she was. If Viktor sees that I'm an emotional tornado, he'll cut me from the team. Everyone's always telling me to bury my emotions before they do me in. If this is what being an immortal is about, then let me deal with it. I don't want to talk about it, Christian. I just want to get over it."

He looked back at the bed again when the covers rustled, and she turned over.

Raven's version of "getting over it" was sex, but when Christian rejected her, she turned to the bottle. He would give her the world, but sex wouldn't make her forget; it would only associate his passion with her trauma. So instead, she drank herself to sleep, and he let her.

There was no handbook on how to get over a burial. When the air runs out, you glimpse your own mortality for all of thirty seconds before your body goes through an upheaval of change. Then you're alone in the dark, forsaken by all. The others would never understand how just one day is like an eternity. They would never know how that experience would make it harder to handle tight spaces or even dark rooms. Raven might never suffer those same phobias that Christian once had, but one thing was certain—the person responsible would pay.

A knock sounded at the door, and he rose from his chair to answer.

"Is she all right?" Switch peered over Christian's shoulder.

Christian swung the door open. "Well, have a gander. Do you feel like more of a man, now that you've seen a drunk woman in her knickers?" He stepped into the hall and shut the door behind him.

Switch folded his arms and did that hand tuck men do to make their biceps look bigger. "I made myself scarce all day, so I don't know what's been going on with the drinking parties. But Crush called, asking about Raven. He wanted to know if she showed up and where you were."

"The man needs to learn how to put a cork in it."

Switch reached in his pocket and handed Christian his phone. "You tell him. He's been calling me for hours, and I don't know what to say. Said he tried calling you, but your phone kept going to voice mail."

Christian muttered a curse as he called up Raven's da. "Sorry to pull you away from that decrepit piece of furniture you call a chair, but I'm giving you a ring to let you know that Raven's fine." Christian gave Switch a foul look as Crush ranted about how a policeman pulled him over, and he didn't have any ID on him. "Aye, she's fine. I'd wake her, but she's fast asleep. Didn't mean to trouble you over nothing. ... Well, feck you too." He handed Switch the phone.

Raven would never tell her father what had happened, and Christian had no desire to tell him that his daughter had been buried alive, right next to her mother. Some things were better left unsaid.

Switch dropped his arms at his sides. "Look, you and I don't get along. That's fine. But I've known Raven since she was a little girl. We weren't close or anything, but she's like a packmate to me. I ask questions because I care about her, and nothing you say or do will ever change that. Raven grew up with Crush, but she has an extended family, whether she realizes it or not. If there's something I can do for her that maybe you don't have time for, I'm here.

Is there anything you want me to bring up? Food? Water? Her favorite ice cream?"

"If you'd stop your tail wagging for just a minute, you'd see that I've got it under control. She's had a rough go with this assignment, that's all."

Switch narrowed his wolfish eyes, the eyebrows sloping down at an angle. He cast a critical look at Christian. Shifters were especially good at it. It was that desire they had to take charge of a situation.

Christian leaned his back against the door and folded his arms. "And where's the wee one?"

Switch squared his shoulders. "Asleep. I'm not here to talk about Hunter. I'm off the clock now, and what I do with my free time is my own business."

"Well, your business landed on my doorstep. And as long as you're under this roof, you're never off the clock. Your responsibility is the lad, not Raven. I know all about you. You tried kissing my woman and doing it while naked."

"I can't help it if I'm naked around her. I'm a Shifter."

"Keep your lips on Viktor's arse and away from Raven. I'll not have you seducing my woman or getting naked in front of her. Raven's not the girl you once knew, and if you can't handle it, then off you go. She doesn't take kindly to hovering, and if you start bringing her trays of food and asking about her feelings, she's liable to spear you in the gut. Why can't you be more like Viktor?"

"You mean apathetic?"

"He looks after us, provides for us, and respects our boundaries. That's the definition of a man in my book. Not a nursemaid."

When Switch tipped his head down, his long hair fell forward and framed his face. "News flash—I'm not old enough to stop caring. That's a trait that comes with time and loss."

"Aye, and you'll be better for it."

"Maybe so, old man, but you should ask yourself what Raven really needs. She's closer to my age than yours, and despite the façade, there's still a vulnerable woman in there who needs a protector. If she had a tough day at work, cook her dinner instead of boozing her up. I saw the empty bottle by the bed. Do you think that's helping?"

"After what she's been through, she deserves a drink."

Switch shook his head and smiled flatly. "You're gonna put a rift between her and her old man. Crush is a former alcoholic, remember? Do you really want him to watch Raven become the drunk he used to be? It would kill him."

"I can't dictate her life any more than you can, *Shifter*. I'm sure your heart's in the right place, but your cock isn't. It's looking for a way in. Raven told me about you harping on her for drinking. How did that go for you? We all make mistakes, and we have to make them. It's essential to become the person you were meant to be. You've made your fair share of mistakes, which got you banned from joining a pack, and that's why you're here. I'll not be having this conversation every time we meet. Give her your friendship, but there are things you don't know about that woman—things you'll never be privy to."

"I just don't wanna see her hurt."

"Then buy yourself a puppy, because people get hurt. You aren't welcome in my chamber. Now if you'll excuse me, I have things to do. I'll tell Raven you were asking about her."

Christian left Switch in the hall and returned to his chair by the fireside. In any other circumstance, he might like a guy like Switch. But when a man has feelings about a woman beneath the guise of friendship, he would always carry that flame.

Christian could sense when Raven was cold by how many times she would toss and turn. He rarely used the bed unless Raven stayed the night, but he usually had a nice pair of silk sheets on the mattress. What she needed was light and space, so his job was to keep the fire going. If she awoke in the night, he wanted her to feel safe instead of confused in the darkness.

While listening to Switch's footfalls growing distant, Christian reached inside his shirt pocket and retrieved a strand of hair. When Raven had stripped off her clothes to shower, he'd found it stuck to the blood on her shirt. After wiping it clean and holding it to the light, there was no doubt who it belonged to. While Houdini's hair was pale, this didn't belong to her maker.

He stretched his hands apart as the firelight glinted off the blond strand. It was straight, long, delicate, and could only belong to one person: Lenore Parrish. To be certain, Christian had tasted the blood on Raven's shirt. Some of it was hers, and some of it wasn't. The ancient flavor teased his tongue with the opulent taste he'd once revered. Lenore had motive, and burying people was definitely her modus operandi. Being privy to their case, she could have known Raven's whereabouts. Only a Vampire could have scrubbed her memory, and though Christian had promised not to keep secrets from Raven, why not let her assume that Houdini did it? Maybe it would sever that unhealthy relationship once and for all.

If he told Raven the truth, she would go after Lenore. Even if she didn't succeed, the mere attempt would be an act of treason, punishable by death.

He stroked his beard and murmured, "I'm not cut out for this."

When it came to Raven, every decision he made was in her best interest. Christian had never been in a serious relationship, and on top of that, he was a Vampire with a murderous past. Did she really expect him to be truthful at all times? Honesty was an arbitrary demand that served no purpose. His heart had sworn allegiance to love and protect Raven, not to see her to ruin.

When Raven stirred in the bed, Christian let go of the hair and blew out a deep breath. The sinewy strand floated toward the hearth and landed just shy of the grate. The end sparked, and the hair curled up before turning to smoke. The foul stench made him get up and cross the room. Christian sat on the edge of the bed, clasped his hands, and made plans.

Chapter 38

"Raven, come and let me have a look at you." Viktor waved me over to the dining table.

I had slept all day and skipped meals. I thought maybe I could sneak into the kitchen for leftovers and avoid everyone, but it looked like Viktor was having a bite.

He rose from his chair like King Arthur and cupped my face in his hands. "You do not look unwell. It seems that there was much exaggeration at the table this morning."

Damn. He knows. "Isn't there always?"

"Who would put you in a coffin?"

"Who wouldn't?"

He wagged his finger at me. "I can always tell your mood when you answer a question with a question. Sit." Viktor resumed eating his oatmeal. "Nothing brings comfort like warm oatmeal. You must try."

"I'll pass. I just wanted to nibble on fruit or something."

"Kira is sweeping floors on the east wing, so if you are hungry, you must make your own. She organizes and cleans brilliantly. I sometimes take these things for granted, but I do not know what I would do without her. She lights and replaces the candles twice a day," he said, gesturing to the candlelit chandelier overhead, "and has begun organizing our storage rooms." He set down his spoon and then wiped his beard with a cloth napkin. "While I do not need to know everything that happens with my team, if one of you is attacked, it is meaningful."

"I was going to tell you eventually. I just didn't want to ruin your celebration."

After cleaning his bowl, he set the spoon inside and pushed it forward. "If you have new enemies, I must know. This affects everyone. Remember what happened with Niko?"

"Viktor, I don't know what happened. If I did, I'd tell you. The last thing I remember is leaving the club to come home, but after that, it's gone. Do you think all that time without oxygen did something to my brain cells?"

He set his napkin on the table. "Perhaps your memory will return."

"Maybe I've told you this before, but I want to tell you again. Thanks for giving me a second chance. That day I met you, I thought you were a prick. No offense, but I didn't trust anyone. Being with Keystone changed everything. I'm learning to trust people again, and I didn't think that would ever be possible. It's nice to know that people are looking out for me. I just want to make sure that I'm pulling my weight around here. That's all."

"The Raven I see before me is not the same woman I met that day. You have matured into a capable investigator and skilled fighter. This last case was very important, and you gave me so much more than I was expecting." Viktor folded his arms on the table and gave me a pensive stare. "You did not deserve what happened last night. You should have been here to celebrate with us, but we assumed that you wanted to be alone. You have always been a loner. The higher authority is not pleased with the upheaval, but many are singing our praises." He smiled warmly. "My contact has sent our money this afternoon, and there is a bonus included just for you—much more than your share. It is no longer a secret that Miss Parrish was my contact, and she is very pleased that we have taken down this crime ring. She negotiated the money for you; I did not ask for it."

While I should have been thrilled to stockpile more money, something about it didn't feel right. I couldn't put my finger on it, but I also hadn't felt like myself. Not just because of the burial, but these past few weeks had taken a toll on me.

"Can I send it back?"

"Nyet. That would be an insult."

"Then send the extra amount to HALO. You don't have to tell Lenore what we did with it. Maybe it won't be enough to split between them, but it seems like they should get something for helping us out."

He reached over and patted my hand. "What a fine gesture. This team is how I imagined it to be. You complete us. Now Wyatt can do his job and Gem hers. Everyone has a place, like puzzle pieces. I sometimes want to do more, because that is the life I once knew, but my first responsibility is to keep myself alive. And my second responsibility is to keep each of you alive. There can be no compromise."

I gave him a crooked smile, thinking about how many Alka-Seltzers he probably drank a night. "I'll try to stay alive, but I've made a lot of enemies."

"Raven, your personal life is complicated, and I cannot fix those problems."

"If I still lived on the streets, no one would care if I disappeared. I know you're not my family, but it feels like it sometimes."

"I understand what you mean. In some ways, this feels like a pack. I cannot help but run the house like I would as a Packmaster, but I have to remind myself that it is possible I will lose some of you. That is why your relationship with Christian concerns me. It is difficult to truly love someone that you might lose. I have lost hundreds of family members—my brothers, their children, and tragedy has befallen everyone I've cared for."

"How did it happen?"

Viktor pinched the bridge of his nose as if holding back tears. "I do not wish to live in the pain of my past. Find those happy moments and hold them in your heart. Like here, with Keystone. Everyone in this house has endured suffering while under my watch. Niko almost died, Gem lost a man she cared for, Blue is scarred beyond comprehension, and you have also suffered tragedy at the hands of your Creator. I did not know if this organization would last with so many different backgrounds and Breeds, but despite the bickering, you take care of each other. This pleases me." Viktor trailed off in Russian before stopping himself. "We do not know our destiny, so we must make a difference today. No matter what happens, it is better to know that we made sacrifices to give others a better life. Keystone will bring you riches and build your reputation, but when you die, you cannot take those things with you."

I stood and pushed in my chair. "Thanks for trusting me with this job. I just hope it's the last assignment we ever have in a sex club."

Viktor rocked with laughter as he rose from his chair and reached for something on the table behind him. "I almost forgot. This came for you today." He handed me a small brown box with twine wrapped around it. "The delivery boy did not say who it was from, but do not be surprised to receive more gifts in the coming days from those who wish to show their appreciation."

Holding the box in one hand, I strode down the dark hallway toward the staircase and jogged up to the second floor. The hours I'd spent in that coffin were probably the most terrified I'd ever felt, even with Fletcher. I'd channeled some of my energy to produce a little light, but somehow that made it worse. After attempting to punch my way out, I'd calmed myself to reserve oxygen and sporadically flared in hopes that a Mage might be nearby. Christian had sat with me all night and most of the day. He brought my usual cup of hot coffee early this morning, and even though I didn't drink it, the fragrant aroma comforted me. I needed space, and he gave it to me. The last thing I wanted was someone giving me a lecture about what I needed to do or eat or drink. I needed to be a mess for a little while before I cleaned myself up.

As I reached a dark window in the hallways overlooking the courtyard pool, I stood there and watched Niko and Gem talking. She had on a short blue nightgown and kimono untied at the waist. The only light came from the pool.

My thoughts drifted back to the coffin. It was hard to get it out of my head. The panic, the rage, the regret—being stuck in there with nothing but my thoughts. When the oxygen had run out, it didn't happen all at once. The air had grown stale, and I was breathing more rapidly as it seemed impossible to catch my breath. Dizzy and feeling as if my heart might explode, I realized it was impossible to tell my body it wasn't dying. I had passed out a number of times before I stopped resisting. Once I accepted my condition, my heart finally slowed down. Without oxygen, it was pointless to breathe, but that pain and urge never went away. All I could do was just lie there, because if I started to think about breathing, I'd panic all over again.

Most of all, it grieved me that my father would have spent the rest of his life searching for me, and each time he visited my mother's grave, he wouldn't have had any idea that I was down there. After my coffee this morning, I'd borrowed Christian's phone to call Crush. I was surprised to learn that he had gone searching for me last night, so I let him know that there was nothing to worry about and I was out celebrating. Telling him a lie was far easier than causing him unnecessary pain with the truth. I told him I loved him and decided never to leave our last conversation on an argument. Someday it *would* be the last, and what would be the last thing I'd want him to remember me saying to him?

"What are they doing down there?" Switch asked.

I gasped and shoved him back.

He held up his hands. "Whoa, it's just me."

I exhaled and shook my head. "Sorry. Reflexes."

He stepped closer. "I haven't seen you all day. You okay?"

"I had a lot of sleep to catch up on," I said, turning on my heel to face the window again.

Gem let her kimono drop to the ground and looked at the pool apprehensively. When she stepped into the water, she froze as if she might leap out. Niko extended his arm, and she gripped his hand. I realized he was going to walk in with her, so it was a good thing he wasn't wearing shoes. Just his usual late-night attire of baggy pants.

"I haven't seen her swim in eons," I remarked. "Someone drowned her in there, you know."

"I remember. Sometimes you just gotta get back on the horse." Switch joined my side and put his hands in his pockets.

His comment was meant for me. Even though he didn't know the details of my job or what I'd gone through these past weeks, he must have sensed it the way Shifters often did. Maybe that intuition was why he was so good with kids.

He nudged me with his elbow. "Feel like playing a game of darts?"

"Not tonight. Maybe you should go out with your friends more often."

He stepped up to the edge of the window. "I'm not looking for entertainment. I was just trying to make you feel better. You can't talk about your job, but maybe I can help you forget it."

I wanted to say *thanks*, but I had a feeling he already knew I appreciated his thoughtfulness. Switch wanted to look out for me, and I suppose that loyalty went back to my father and how the two of us grew up in the same cluster. Having him around really helped me forget. Switch loved telling stories and making me laugh, but this was something that a game of darts wasn't going to rectify. I didn't want to forget. I needed to remember.

There were so many people who could have buried me, but Houdini was my primary suspect. I'd staked a lot of Vampires in the past whom I presumed dead, and I'd made a lot of enemies since, but maybe Houdini had done it to protect his secrets. He liked fucking with people's minds, and he *was* the last person I remembered seeing. What if Fletcher had done it? It was possible that I'd forgotten from the lack of oxygen and trauma.

In the darkest moment, when the silence in the coffin had been more than I could bear, I'd actually wondered if Christian had done it.

Gem waded deeper into the water with Niko beside her. They were waist deep, the blue-green lights illuminating Gem's frightened expression as she turned around. An owl hooted outside as if he had something to say about it.

"I've got some good news," Switch said, his voice merrier. "The trial period is over. Viktor made me an official offer to work for him. He said I've proven myself more than once, and Hunter is responding well to his education."

"That sounds like Viktor. Congratulations."

"I've never worked with just one child, but Hunter has a lot of issues. I had to consult a specialist to be sure I wasn't fucking him up even more with a rigid schedule, but it's what he needs. I think once he learns how to write properly, we can figure out if he wants to do sign language or learn how to talk. It might be too late for verbal communication. He's got a lot of trauma, and I think he was punished for making noise. That's not something you can easily undo."

"It sounds like he's got a good teacher. I don't think Shepherd could have done it alone."

"Yeah, sometimes love isn't enough to fix what's broken." Switch leaned his shoulder against the wall by the window and gave me a look I couldn't discern with those wolfish brown eyes. "I know Hunter's my job, but you're my friend. It's not easy sitting at home, wondering if you're hurt. Seeing the others go looking for you and not being able to help."

"Your job isn't to look after me, Switch."

"It sure as hell is." He folded his arms, his dark eyebrows slanting down. "It's my job as your friend. We're still friends, aren't we?"

"Just don't go relaying stuff to my father. I tell him what he needs to know, but that's it. He's human, Switch. Don't forget that. You might feel loyalty to him because your father is friends with him, but look how much he's aged because of stress and worry. I contributed to some of that. He already knows my job is dangerous, but I don't want him involved. I just want to give him everything he needs to be happy."

"All he needs is you."

"I know he came around here looking for me. If I find out that you two have a pact—"

"We don't have a pact. He showed up on his own. Your old man has visions or some shit. I heard rumors years ago that he had a dream around the time you went missing. Or maybe it was before." Switch heaved a sigh. "But I know where you're coming from. Crush is a tough son of a bitch, but you're right. He doesn't need to worry around the clock. That's why I had Christian call him last night and let him know that you were okay." Switch stepped closer and let his arms fall to his sides. "You have my word. In fact, secrecy is part of my contract. You should have seen what Viktor made me sign. It looked like the Declaration of fucking Independence. I signed it, he signed it, an alpha from the local council signed it, Christian signed it."

"Why Christian?"

"They needed a witness. Viktor wanted to let the Shifter authorities know about the agreement, but Christian will be the one who scrubs my memories if I bail early."

"I didn't have to sign anything."

"No, you probably signed something in blood."

"Actually…" Then I cut myself off, deciding not to tell Switch about our blood ceremony and tattoos. Viktor probably wanted something more official for Switch since he was also helping to rebuild his reputation among the local packs.

I steered my gaze outside and reached up for the heart-shaped ruby around my neck. Christian had put it on while I slept, and it gave me reassurance to wake up with it, making me feel like myself again. I thought about the Shifters we freed and hoped they were having a nice big meal tonight.

"How do you know if you can really trust someone?" I asked.

As Gem floated on her back, Niko stood nearby, holding her hand.

"I don't know. I guess you just feel it in your gut."

My brain told me that Houdini was behind my burial, but my gut wasn't so sure.

"I was wrong about Christian." Switch took a step behind me so that I couldn't see his face anymore. "He really does love you."

As he walked off, I watched Niko and Gem for a short while, expecting him to let go of her hand, but he never did. Deciding that he'd probably noticed my light in the window and might find it intrusive, I walked up to the third floor and headed to my room.

"I thought you were going to eat something." Christian fell into step beside me.

"I changed my mind. I just needed to talk to Viktor and smooth things over." After a pregnant pause, I asked a question I'd been avoiding. "Do you know who buried me?"

"I'm surprised you haven't asked if it was me." When I didn't answer, he stepped in front of me and held a serious look. "Ask me."

"I know it wasn't you."

He almost looked offended as he quirked an eyebrow. "And how can you be so sure?"

I tugged his beard. "Because then you'd be stuck with that colossal tattoo. Plus you'd have my father to deal with."

"Jaysus."

"How did you find me? I'm not sure what to believe since Wyatt's story kept changing."

"By late afternoon, I didn't have a good feeling about your absence. We traced your boots to an open field. You could have tossed the bag yourself, but Wyatt pulled up a map of the area, and if someone had it in for you, the last stop would be the cemetery. Wyatt fancies himself a hero, but Gem was the one who blasted the hole."

I blanched at the mental image. "And my mother?"

"Worry not, lass. Her grave is intact. I'll stop there tomorrow night to be sure your grave was filled and headstone replaced. I wouldn't want your da having a coronary at the sight of your open casket."

I shuddered and continued my walk. "Were there any clues?"

Christian caught up. "Claude didn't smell anything. Don't trouble yourself thinking about it. We'll find out who did it. Secrets never stay in the dark for long."

I rubbed my forehead, wishing I could find a way to stop thinking about it.

"Do you want to take a drive? I know a diner with the most atrocious chili."

I smiled as I opened my bedroom door. "That sounds good. I need to get out of here for a little while. Can we invite Switch?"

"If that's what you desire."

I crossed the room toward my desk. "He invited me to hang out a minute ago, and I said no. I think he gets lonely around here."

Christian sighed as he followed behind me. "Perhaps the man needs a turtle."

I chortled. "A turtle?"

"Aye. They make excellent companions and outlive most pets."

I sat down at my desk with my package.

"What's in the box?"

"I'm about to find out."

Christian lit a candle and stood close as I cut the twine with a push dagger and peeled off the cardboard paper. I pulled open the flap and stared at a carefully packaged bottle inside. Thick crinkle paper protected it from all sides.

"Is that alcohol?" Christian set down the candle and peered inside the box.

I pulled out the pink bottle and noticed a black label on the front. "Love potion."

"And here all this time I thought you just took a shine to my devilishly good looks."

The box didn't have a note or card, but it didn't require much sleuthing to guess who had sent it. Houdini had briefly mentioned something about love potions during our conversation and suggested they were popular at one time.

"Who sent you that?" Christian asked, playing with a piece of the packaging.

I stood up and wrapped my arms around him. "Someone with a twisted sense of humor."

"I don't think it comes more twisted than mine," he said against my lips.

We fell into a deep kiss that made me push up on my tiptoes. Maybe we could postpone dinner and eat in.

He rubbed his nose against mine. "You're going to keep the potion?"

"I might need it if you ever work for Lenore again."

"What's in that bottle is filled with nothing but shite magic that fades."

"Doesn't all love fade?"

He swept me off my feet and looked deep into my eyes. I felt myself drowning in those tranquil pools of midnight, and butterflies tickled my stomach. "Worry not, lass. What I feel for you will never fade. You can't bottle the magic between us. Now let me buy you an awful bowl of chili."

"Only if you promise to treat me to apple pie à la mode afterward."

He carried me to the door and stopped by the mirror. I caught our reflection, and for a moment, I entertained the idea of him as a groom, carrying me over a threshold. It put a smile on my face.

"What are you thinking about, lass?"

"I was just thinking how good I look in your arms."

"Aye, we make a handsome couple, don't we, Precious?"

"What are *you* thinking?"

He admired our reflection in the mirror. "I was just wondering if your da will ever take a shine to me."

"Maybe when pigs fly."

He opened the door and strolled down the hall. "Did you know that a zebra combined with any other equine is called a zebroid? And a lion crossbreeding with a tiger is called a liger."

"Why are you smiling like that and telling me about zebras?"

"It won't be long before they cross a pig with an eagle. There's hope for me after all."

Printed in Great Britain
by Amazon